THE BOATYARD

Joel Hames is a Lancashire-based writer of crime fiction, and the editor of multi-million-selling books across multiple genres. Joel's own works include the Dead North series featuring lawyer Sam Williams, and the psychological thriller *The Lies I Tell*. Most recently, he has co-written the hugely successful Cumbria Crime series with titan of crime fiction Rachel McLean.

You can follow Joel, and subscribe to his mailing list for news direct to your inbox, on his website at: https://www.joel hamesbooks.com/.

ALSO BY JOEL HAMES (WITH RACHEL MCLEAN)

Cumbria Crime series

The Harbour
The Mine
The Cairn
The Barn
The Lake
The Wood
The Port
The Marsh

JOEL HAMES

WHALEY & GASKILL BOOK 1

THE BOATYARD

A CUMBRIA CRIME NOVEL

FFS Books

Printed and bound in the UK by CPI Group (Uk) Ltd, Croydon CR0 4YY

DAY ONE

CHAPTER ONE

Chris Markham was bored.

He'd been up since five and at the boatyard in Waterhead since half past. He'd spent an hour scrubbing down and trying to work out what that god-awful smell was, and then he'd sparked up a joint, his second of the day, after the one he'd had on the short walk over.

He was bored and tired, and he probably wouldn't see another person until nearly nine, when his boss Dave was due in. It wasn't like he was even getting paid for this. Work experience, they called it.

More like bloody slavery.

At least it wasn't raining. When it rained, he could take shelter in the shed, but every time he took a step towards it the smell got even worse. Like someone had been cleaning something foul and given up before they'd got finished. Dave would be in eventually, and there was more than enough scrubbing and checking things over for Chris to do outside till then.

Dave was the one getting paid. Dave could check out the

shed. Chris had a key to the padlock on the shed door in his pocket, and the key could stay right there until Dave showed up.

He was leaning against one of the hulls he'd just scrubbed, smoking that second joint, when he heard a car pulling up outside and checked his watch.

Seven. Early, for Dave. He'd still be snoring off his hang-over at seven, wouldn't he?

Chris stepped away from the hull, took a long look at his joint, and waited.

He heard the sound of a car door closing, then voices, two of them, one male, the other female.

Footsteps, coming his way.

"Fuck's sake," he said, dropped the joint, and ground it out under a boot, closing his eyes with an acute sense of loss. It wasn't like he had much to look forward to. That joint was supposed to get him through the morning.

"Hello!" shouted a man, and he looked up from the sad remains of his joint to see them looking at him.

Cops.

Shit.

"Hello," he replied, throwing on a smile that he hoped didn't look as goofy as it felt. "Can I help you, officers?"

"Can I help you, officers?" repeated the man, in a high-pitched voice.

The woman sniggered.

"I mean," said Chris, wiping the smile off his face and trying to stand a little taller. "What's up?"

"I'm PC Will Henniker," said the man. "This is PC Ellen O'Donnell. I know you, don't I?"

I bloody hope not, thought Chris.

"Don't think so," he replied. "Is there a problem, then?"

"Had a report. Disturbance here. Someone screaming."

Chris shook his head. He felt suddenly cold, and alone, and younger than his seventeen years. He wished Dave was here.

Dave was a useless arsehole at the best of times. But it would have been nice to have him around.

"No," he said. "Been here an hour and a half. No one here except me, and no screams."

The woman shook her head.

"We're not talking about this morning, Bob Marley," she said, and Chris realised the joint was still smouldering beside his right boot. No point covering it up now. "Someone called it in last night," she continued.

"Why didn't you come then?" asked Chris, and the woman frowned at him.

Idiot, he told himself. You don't challenge the cops. Not when you've got a joint burning by your feet.

"Dunno," said the man. "Not seen anything unusual, then?"

Chris shrugged.

"Nothing," he said.

"OK," said the man, and turned to walk away, and for a moment, Chris thought that was it. If they went now, he might even be in time to rescue the joint. And it was true. He hadn't seen anything unusual.

Hadn't *seen* anything unusual.

They were going. He watched as they walked back around the corner, listened as their footsteps grew fainter, and it wasn't until he heard the sound of a car door opening that he shouted, "Hang on!"

They were back five seconds later, PC Henniker looking expectant, PC O'Donnell looking bored and impatient.

"The smell," he said.

PC Henniker nodded.

"You mean it doesn't usually smell like this?" asked PC O'Donnell.

Chris shook his head.

The officers exchanged a look he couldn't quite understand.

"Wait here," said Henniker, and he watched as they descended the steps, approached the shed, and tried the ancient door with the padlock on it.

"It'll be locked," said Chris, reaching into his pocket for the key, but the door opened. The padlock just hung there, the chain not connected to anything, and that was even weirder than the smell.

The shed was always locked. Dave insisted.

Wait here, Henniker had said, but there was no way that was happening, even though the smell was suddenly ten times stronger now the door was open. He followed the officers, noticing only now the metal links on the ground where the chain had been cut.

Maybe he'd have spotted that sooner if he hadn't been half-stoned. Maybe not.

He closed his eyes before he stepped inside so they'd adjust to the darkness more quickly.

"Christ," said Henniker, and Chris opened his eyes.

The usual half-full buckets and bits of broken boat littered the space. They called it a shed, but it was more like a massive, permanently flooded garage, the half of the derelict Waterhead Marine site that had been restored by the people Dave worked for. It was bigger than Chris's house.

"God in heaven," said O'Donnell.

Chris turned in the direction she was looking and saw what they were talking about.

There was a wooden chair in the dry area at the far end of the room, tied to one of the struts that kept the whole thing from collapsing into the lake. Chris couldn't remember if he'd seen that chair in here before, because it was entirely unremarkable, except for the fact that there was a man tied to it, head lolling to one side.

Chris took a step closer, so he was standing right by the two police officers, and looked at the man's face. There was a mass of blood where a mouth would normally be. Above it, the hair was slick with something that might have been water, might have been something else.

"Look at his fucking fingers, Will," said O'Donnell.

Chris found himself drawn to them, to the blackened stumps at the end of the man's hands.

"Christ," said Henniker, again, and then he turned and vomited into a bucket sitting conveniently by his feet.

CHAPTER TWO

"Sit down," said Detective Inspector Whaley.

Denise took the seat on the other side of the desk, in the fourth floor office her boss occupied in the Cumbria Police building in Durranhill, Carlisle.

"Everything OK, boss?"

"I was going to ask you the same thing," he said, and she paused in the act of sitting and looked at him carefully.

Does he know?

"All fine with me," she said.

Detective Sergeant Denise Gaskill had been back full time in the Professional Standards Division for more than six months now, following the bomb that had put her in a coma and nearly killed her. She'd been bored in hospital, and then she'd been bored at home, and the pain she felt almost every moment of every day was nothing compared to the boredom.

The boss knew all about the boredom. She'd called every two or three days back then, asking to come back to work, and when he hadn't moved fast enough she'd called his boss, DCI Branthwaite, and finally got her way. The DI and the DCI were careful around her, made sure to ask how she was feeling, 'conscious of her recovery', as they put it.

But they didn't know about the pain.

"Good," he said. "I thought since it's been quiet lately, we could take a minute to go through our longer-term projects."

She nodded and tried to hide her smile of relief.

He still didn't know. He didn't know about the pain, or the painkillers, or the less-than-conventional way she was acquiring them. She had a friendly pharmacist, or at least, a pharmacist who'd started out friendly. He'd been sharper the last couple of times Denise had spoken to him. Maybe she'd been pushing that friendship too far.

"Before we do that," Denise said, "there's an anonymous note in from someone who knew to go straight to our team inbox."

"This one?"

He turned his screen to face her, and she saw the same message she'd read first thing.

"That's the one."

"What are your thoughts?" asked DI Whaley.

It was good to start with something easy.

"Well, he claims he has vital information about police corruption, but he won't tell us his name, and insists we travel to meet him before he says anything more. It might be useful, but chances are it's a waste of time."

"And we don't know where he is," said DI Whaley, turning his screen around again. "So we don't know how much time we risk wasting."

Denise smiled. It was a rare treat, knowing something the boss didn't.

"Actually," she said, "we do. Roughly, at least. I got Phil in IT to check his IP address."

DI Whaley looked up from his screen.

"And?"

"He'd tried to disguise the location, but Phil's pretty sure it's somewhere in the southern hemisphere."

"Waste of time, then," said the DI.

"Waste of time," agreed Denise. "But I'll keep it on file. Just in case. In the meantime, there's this potential vigilante attack."

She paused, expecting him to rule it out. The boss had a way of doing that, looking over something and either dismissing it immediately or putting it aside for further investigation, the decision made so quickly it looked almost like magic. She'd learned, over the last couple of years, that what she'd thought was an instinct for distinguishing corruption from coincidence was really just the benefit of experience.

"Go on," he said.

"You've seen the summary?"

"Yes, but run through it anyway."

"Local police pulled in Clifford Gilbert. Looking into potential sexual offences."

"They thought he might be a flasher, right?" said the DI.

"Yes. Someone exposed himself to a young woman on one of the local walking routes. Gilbert looked like a possibility, so he was invited to come in and have a chat."

"Not arrested?"

"Not enough grounds. And it turns out he had no case to answer. Strong alibi. But while he was at the station, someone set his house on fire. And no one outside the police knew who he was. Even the victim didn't know his name."

"So it's a coincidence?" suggested the boss.

"How many people get their house randomly set on fire in Cumbria?" Denise countered. "And then, there's this guy."

She passed him her phone, open on a screenshot from a Facebook profile.

"Who's Dwayne Zimmerman?" asked DI Whaley.

"Not a real person, for a start. But whoever he is, he's local, and he often leaks the names of people accused of sex crimes. Usually paedophiles, but also—"

"Leaks?"

"More like finds out, I suppose. Spreads rumours. It's not like he has access to confidential information. Until now."

"He mentioned Clifford Gilbert by name?"

"No. But at the same time as the attack, he posted a well-known meme on his profile."

She scrolled to the next image on her phone. It showed a young girl looking knowingly at the camera while a house burnt in the background.

"I've seen this," said the boss.

"It's quite famous," she replied. "It's called *Disaster Girl*. And yes, it's all very vague and deniable, and we don't even know who Dwayne Zimmerman is, but I don't like it, boss. It feels like whoever set Clifford Gilbert's house on fire knew something they shouldn't have known."

She waited, and after a moment, he nodded.

"We'll keep an eye out," he said. "It might be nothing. But I agree. It looks worrying. What else have you got for me?"

"I've been looking into the Assistant Chief Constable's office," she told him, and spent a few minutes running through a handful of names. Her job, the job of everyone in PSD, was to track down corrupt officers and civilian workers, and try to work out which of their colleagues were secretly helping the criminals they were supposed to be working against.

Denise found herself watching DI Whaley closely, at the same time as she was briefing him. He'd had it bad himself, lately. His long-term partner, DI Finch, had left him, moving all the way down to Dorset. Denise didn't know the details of the breakup, but she knew it hadn't been easy.

The boss looked tired these days. He sighed a lot, and he was less patient than he had been.

Maybe he was just getting older.

"Hope I'm not interrupting anything."

Denise turned to see DCI Branthwaite pushing open the door.

Douglas Branthwaite had hardly changed in the years Denise had worked under him. Medium height, sandy hair, glasses, and a collection of almost identical grey suits. He'd filled out lately. And he'd stopped swearing since the birth of his first grandson, which had led to some surprising alternative expressions of annoyance and disgust.

"Sir," Denise and DI Whaley said at the same time.

"Don't stand," said DCI Branthwaite, and DI Whaley and Denise exchanged a look. Neither of them had made a move to stand. "I just wanted to remind you of our little arrangement."

"We're keeping it in mind, sir," DI Whaley said. "As soon as we have a suitable investigation, we'll be putting it into action."

"Good, good," said Branthwaite. "Just try to get things moving, if you can."

That, thought Denise, would be tricky. DCI Branthwaite's 'little arrangement' meant that for the first time, PSD would be allowed to run significant investigations on their own, rather than having to play second fiddle to Major Crimes teams like the one run by her friend DI Aaron Keyes in the Cumbria Police Hub. They'd need specialist help, but if there was a murder – and it was usually a murder – along with the possibility of police involvement, then DI Whaley would be calling the shots.

Denise was looking forward to it. But you couldn't just create a major crime, and a corrupt officer to investigate alongside it. It might take a while for the right sort of crime to come along.

"We are keeping an eye out, sir," she said, and Branthwaite nodded.

"Good," he said again. "I had to go all the way to the top to get this approved, and I'd like the chance to flex my muscles before they get too flabby. A lot of people aren't particularly happy with the arrangement. If we give them enough time, they'll come up with a reason to stop it. So let's not give them the pigging time."

He'd turned and walked out of the room before either of them had the chance to say anything else.

CHAPTER THREE

"He'd been tied to a chair," said Detective Constable Lynn Hedley. "Looks like his fingers were burned and his teeth removed, presumably to prevent identification. And his head was wet. My guess is he was drowned. There were a load of buckets in the room."

She was standing in the small team room in Langdale Police Station, briefing DI Jasmine Woolley and DS Isaac Bateman on the boatyard crime scene. DI Woolley stood, listening and nodding occasionally. DS Bateman sat in his chair, slumped over his desk, his head in his hands. Lynn wasn't sure he was even awake.

"The smell was something else, though, Ma'am," she continued.

"Dead people tend not to worry about how they smell," said DI Woolley, drily.

"It wasn't that," continued Lynn. "There was... Well, PC Henniker had been sick into a bucket. But there was bleach there too, or something like that. I'm wondering if it might have been used to clean up the scene, Ma'am. Remove evidence, maybe."

"Maybe you can leave that sort of thing to the experts," DI Woolley told her, and not for the first time that morning, Lynn found herself wondering why they were even involved in this. Yes, they were technically a Major Crimes team, but there were other teams, teams far more qualified. Last time DI Woolley had tried to run a murder investigation, Aaron Keyes had been forced to come in from the Hub and take over, and a good thing, too. DI Woolley hadn't run a murder case since before Lynn had joined the force. And the less said about Isaac Bateman, the better.

"I don't like it, Guv," said DS Bateman, surprising Lynn, who'd decided that he was almost certainly asleep after all.

Bateman had been looking rough the last day or two. The usual stink of booze, the usual awkward shamble, the way the man somehow took up even more space than his outsized frame demanded. But his eyes were even less focussed than Lynn was used to, his speech slower.

"None of us *like* it, Isaac," said DI Woolley. "It's a murder. You're not supposed to *like* it."

"No, Guv. I mean, I don't think it should be us."

DI Woolley blinked.

Without meaning to, Lynn took a step back, towards the door.

"What do you mean?" DI Woolley asked icily.

"I mean..." Bateman shook his head and shrugged.

"Go on," prompted the DI.

"I mean, we're not really equipped for this kind of thing, are we? Last time we—"

"Don't talk to me about *last time*, Isaac," said DI Woolley. "I'd rather not be reminded about Aaron bloody Keyes. But yes, last time they made a fool of us."

"I don't think—" said Lynn, who'd been the only one of the three of them to come out of that debacle well.

"I didn't ask for your opinion, Detective Constable," said the DI, without bothering to turn and look at her. "The fact is, we can run a murder investigation without help from that lot. Now, we've already got media interest."

"We have?" asked Lynn, surprised. They'd only caught the case themselves a couple of hours earlier.

"Yes. The local paper."

Lynn nodded. The *Ambleside Gazette* would have people on the ground. People who'd hear things in passing. And now that they'd merged with the *Whitehaven Chronicle*, they were looking to tackle bigger, more important stories.

It didn't get much bigger than murder.

"And," continued DI Woolley, "the pair of you haven't got the faintest idea how to manage a press conference, so I suppose I'll have to do that."

"I reckon we might be out of our depth here—" began DS Bateman, but the boss was already shaking her head and walking away. Bateman sat there for a moment, his mouth silently opening and closing like a goldfish, before returning to the position he'd occupied earlier.

Slumped over his desk, his head in his hands, half-hidden in the lightweight denim jacket that, Lynn realised, seemed suddenly too big for him.

Seeing Isaac Bateman in that sort of state was no big surprise. Lynn had got used to it over the years. That, the blustering stupidity, and the incompetence.

But it wasn't like Isaac to recognise the incompetence. It

wasn't like him to challenge the DI, to suggest someone else should be handling the big cases. It wasn't like him to do anything as useful as that.

Maybe, just maybe, Isaac Bateman was learning how to be a half-decent police officer.

DAY THREE

CHAPTER FOUR

Over the last two days, DS Isaac Bateman had continued to surprise Lynn.

He still shambled about the place reeking of booze and failing to offer anything useful when it came to the actual work of finding out who'd murdered the Waterhead victim, but that was what she expected.

He still looked half-asleep for half the day, which was something she was getting used to. The other half, it was like he'd just woken from a fever dream, starting at every noise, asking, "What was that?" when no one had said anything, looking up whenever someone entered the room with an expression on his face that said he knew they were coming for him.

He was wrong about that, the same way he was wrong about everything else. No one was coming for Isaac Bateman. Hardly anyone knew who Isaac Bateman was.

If she'd had to guess, Lynn would have said Bateman was stressed. It wasn't an emotion she'd associated with him, until now. But people could surprise you.

The oddest, most surprising thing of all was for Lynn to turn up at eight and see Bateman at his desk already, wearing clothes he hadn't been wearing the day before.

"This is a fucking joke," he grumbled when she walked in. She didn't have to ask what he meant.

"I know. I wish we had some help."

"We need more than help."

She couldn't disagree. It wasn't just the killer who remained unidentified. They hadn't got any closer to finding out who the dead man was. The DI's press conference hadn't resulted in any useful calls, just the usual assortment of time-wasters. It probably hadn't helped that the DI had lost her temper and walked out of the room when asked whether they had any leads at all.

Lynn might almost have sympathised with her, but DI Woolley didn't deserve anyone's sympathy, and it wasn't just the DI who was stuck in a labyrinth of dead ends. CSI hadn't found anything on the victim's personal effects, and nothing had jumped out in mispers when Lynn had entered the basic information they did have.

Height: one hundred and eighty centimetres; weight: seventy-three point five kilograms; eye colour: brown; the pathologist's best guess on age: somewhere between thirty-five and fifty. There had been talk of a tattoo, but the details weren't clear. When the full post-mortem report came through, maybe she'd know more.

It was pointless, but maybe if someone other than Jasmine Woolley had been running it, they'd have found more. As well as the press, the DI had managed to alienate Stella Berry, the crime scene manager, and Keisha Middleton, who worked for Stella and had about as much respect for rank as Lynn did for Isaac Bateman.

"Reckon we should make a call, Sarge?" she asked.

DS Bateman sighed.

"Call who?"

"I don't know." She waited, hoping he'd say it first, but that wasn't really likely. Bateman and Aaron Keyes had never been friends. "Maybe DI Keyes?" she suggested after a short silence, and braced herself for whatever form Bateman's anger would show itself in.

Instead, he turned to her, his eyes wide, and she saw how tired he looked, how red those eyes were.

"You OK, Sarge?" she said.

"Aaron Keyes," he said, quietly. "Yes."

"Yes, we should call him?"

Bateman frowned at her, as if he didn't understand the words.

"Keyes," he said again. "He'll do."

Before Lynn could ask him what he meant, he was up and out of the room, grabbing his jacket as he went, and moving faster than she'd thought him capable of.

Lynn waited. If there were raised voices in the DI's office, she'd be able to hear them from here.

Nothing.

She fired up her computer. There was a message from Dr Chris Robertson, the pathologist in Whitehaven, asking why no one had bothered showing up for the post-mortem.

Probably because he'd made the mistake of telling DI Woolley about it, and she'd not bothered telling anyone else. There was a saying, that sometimes bad cops made decent managers, but Lynn had been working under Jasmine Woolley for long enough to know that wasn't always the case.

She was just typing out a polite reply to Dr Robertson when the DI herself marched into the room and stood there, hands on hips, as if she'd just been insulted and was waiting for a fulsome apology.

"Well?" said DI Woolley, after a moment.

"Well what, Ma'am?"

"Well what the fuck is going on with DS Bateman, Lynn?"

"I don't know—"

"You don't know much, do you? Isaac's just been in to tell me he's sick and he can't work on this case any more."

Lynn frowned and ran back through the last few minutes. Bateman hadn't seemed well, but he rarely did these days. And he hadn't said anything about being ill.

She hoped it was nothing serious. But on the other hand, there was an opportunity here.

"Doesn't this leave us too short-handed to run the case, Ma'am?" she asked.

"I beg your pardon?"

"I mean, if it's just the two of us, maybe we should look at getting some help from—"

"Detective Constable Hedley," said the DI, stepping closer, her voice low but all the more menacing for it. "If the rest of that sentence includes the words 'Aaron Keyes', I'd strongly suggest you end it now."

Lynn nodded, fast.

"It doesn't have to be Aar... him, Ma'am. Just another station. Just to get some more bodies in. As things stand—"

"As things stand, you've had three days and found out bugger all, DC Hedley," snapped the DI. "Now get back to fucking work."

And with that, she turned on her heel, and walked out of the room.

CHAPTER FIVE

DC Harriett Barnes sat in the newly established team room, fighting to keep her eyes open as row after row of numbers passed across her screen.

PSD hadn't had a team room before. DS Gaskill, who'd been used to her own office and wasn't the sort of person who particularly liked being around other people, hadn't taken kindly to the change. But Harriett was pleased.

She'd been part of a team when she'd been working undercover at the Hub, and she'd enjoyed it, even if she had spent most of her working day lying about who she was and what she was really doing. The DCI had decided that, with Harriett back in Carlisle and the team growing, it made sense to sit them together. Not DI Whaley, obviously. He still had his own office, where he seemed to spend half the day sitting in silence with the door closed. And not the DCI himself.

Just Harriett, DS Gaskill, and the new guy, who was supposed to be here already, but hadn't shown up yet.

Not a brilliant start.

DCI Branthwaite had been in again yesterday,

reminding them about his *little arrangement*. The DCI seemed increasingly agitated about their inability to find a suitable case, which meant he was increasingly grumpy, and had even come close to slipping up and swearing out loud. Which was why Harriett had been in since six, sifting through routine data in the hope of finding something that might warrant a closer look.

It was what she'd been trained to do: finding patterns, from unusual clusters of arrests to surprising concentrations of drug overdoses. But she'd spent much of the last two years thinking on her feet, working on instinct rather than data, and it was taking some getting used to.

Hence the fight to keep her eyes open. That, and the five o'clock alarm, which had so infuriated her partner, DC Tom Willis, that he'd almost refused to talk to her that morning.

He'd changed his mind and made her a coffee while she was in the shower. You could always count on Tom. She took a sip now, from its poor-quality vending-machine equivalent, blinked at her screen, and clicked to pause the flow of data.

What was this?

She tapped on the screen, and dragged it backwards.

These new computers were something else.

The vigilante arson attack. She'd discussed that already with DS Gaskill, who'd raised it with the boss. The incident had moved up and beyond Harriett's pay grade. She tapped the window shut, and carried on through the data.

The boatyard killing. She'd read about it, of course; it wasn't like John Does got themselves murdered every day in Cumbria. But she hadn't thought of it as the kind of case that might involve PSD.

Now, as she scanned through the data, she wasn't quite so sure.

She tapped on a timestamp and read a summary, then tapped again and found what she was looking for. The 999 call, the shout from the dispatcher, the conversations between the officers. Transcripts of some, summaries of others.

Harriett grabbed a pen and began to note down the basics.

A member of the public had reported a disturbance.

The dispatcher had alerted the nearest patrol car.

The two PCs in the patrol car had decided to go somewhere else instead, leaving the boatyard to be followed up by colleagues the following morning.

Nothing unusual there; it hadn't been a priority call, after all. No reason to believe a man was being drowned. She read a few paragraphs on-screen, blinking, and decided she needed more coffee.

Even bad coffee was better than nothing.

She returned to the room five minutes later, carrying two plastic cups, because she'd decided that one coffee wouldn't be enough, and pushed the door open with her elbow.

There were two men in the room.

"Harriett," said DCI Branthwaite. "I'd like you to meet DC Marcus Hosgood."

The man who was standing beside Branthwaite turned and favoured her with a broad smile. He was young – mid-twenties, she thought, probably younger than her – with a clean-shaven face and a pair of glasses with those thick plastic frames that were so trendy these days.

He stepped towards her, hand outstretched. Both her hands were still full of coffee.

"Harriett Barnes," she said, nodding towards her hands.

"Team assistant, right?" he replied, taking one of the coffees. "I like mine black, no sugar."

Harriett stared at him.

He stared back, apparently bemused by her expression, and there was a long silence, broken finally by Branthwaite.

"You pigging idiot, Hosgood. Harriett's a DC on the team. Pigging good one, too. Lots of proper experience. You'll spend the next six months apologising if you know what's good for you, lad."

"Shit," said Marcus Hosgood quietly, his eyes now wide, one hand going to his mouth, the other jerking and spilling coffee on his own foot. "Shit!" he said again, louder this time.

"It's OK," said Harriett. "No need to apologise."

"I don't... I don't know why I said that. I'm not... You must think... I'm so sorry," he said, now gently hopping.

"I said, no need to apologise."

"That's very generous of—"

"But six months of you getting me coffee will probably make up for it," she continued. "I need another now you've spilled that one."

Marcus Hosgood carried on staring at her.

"I like mine with milk and one sugar," she added, turning away and taking a seat at her desk.

CHAPTER SIX

"YOU'RE TAKING THE PISS," said DI Aaron Keyes, as DS Nina Kapoor walked into the team room, draped in something that looked horribly familiar.

"You like it?" she asked.

Beside Aaron, DC Tom Willis made a retching noise that wasn't entirely faked.

"I thought I'd cut that thing in half."

Nina unfolded the antimacassar and displayed it proudly to the room. It was white, with a green-and-blue embroidered design of a bird swooping down to the sea to catch a fish.

You couldn't tell what type of bird it was, or what type of fish. The only reason Aaron knew they were a bird and a fish was that he'd seen them before.

Or something very like them.

"Hang on," said Tom. "That's different."

"My mum heard the last one had come to an unhappy end," Nina replied. "So she made me a new one."

Aaron closed his eyes and shook his head. That thing, or its predecessor, had haunted the Major Crimes team room in the Cumbria Police Hub for nearly three years. No one had really liked it, but over time it had become the focus of team bets. The loser had it draped over their chair until the next bet came along. Aaron had taken advantage of a draw in the most recent bet, cutting the thing in half and celebrating its demise.

He should have known better.

"I'm sorry," said a voice from the corner of the room. "But what the hell even *is* that thing?"

DC Harmony Jones was staring at the thing in horror as Nina draped it over her chair. Harmony had only been in the team for three days. So far, she'd been exposed to Nina's Elvis impersonations, the lower half of Jefferson from IT as he wriggled around attaching cables under her desk, and not much else. She'd had it easy until now.

Aaron had the feeling things were about to change. He felt his phone buzz, and checked the display to see an unfamiliar number.

"I'll leave the explaining to you," he said, and walked out of the room, answering as he stepped into the corridor.

"DI Keyes," he said.

"Aaron," said a male voice.

He knew that voice. He couldn't place it for a moment, but as soon as he heard it, he felt tense.

"Yes?" he said.

"It's Isaac Bateman. From Langdale."

Of course. Bateman. They'd known each other since childhood, growing up in the same village, joining the police, moving through the ranks, Aaron more quickly than Isaac.

They'd never been friends.

"What can I do for you, Isaac?" he asked, stepping into

the room that was now his office and closing the door behind him.

"It's a bit delicate," said Bateman.

Aaron was momentarily taken aback. Bateman and 'delicate' didn't go naturally together. He was surprised the man even knew the word.

"How so?" he asked, sitting behind DI Finch's desk.

No. DI Finch was four hundred miles away, in Dorset. He was behind *his own* desk.

"Look, you're close with people in PSD, right?"

Aaron felt the tension ratchet up a notch.

"Yes," he said. He'd worked closely with Harriett Barnes. He'd sat in interview rooms with Carl Whaley. And he and Denise Gaskill were good friends, if Denise had such things as friends.

"Good. Look, it's delicate, this," said Bateman, and gave a tiny, high-pitched laugh.

"You've already said," replied Aaron. "What precisely is it?"

There was a long pause. "I don't know about this," said Bateman, finally. There was a slight slur to his words.

Was Bateman drunk? He'd been drunk during working hours before. He was probably drunk during working hours more often than not. But there'd been that funny little laugh he'd given, when...

There it was again. A little squeal, almost. A burst of something nervous, or frightened.

Or maybe just drunk. It wasn't like Aaron knew Bateman well enough to be sure that wasn't his usual drunken laugh.

"Just tell me what you want, Isaac," he said, finally.

"There's stuff I need to talk about. It's a local matter. It's delicate. I don't know."

"Look, do you want—?"

"Can we meet?"

Aaron was floored, briefly. Bateman wanted to meet him? The two of them had never got on. He'd assumed the man was after a name and a phone number, maybe. But to actually meet...

"Please, Aaron," said Bateman.

"Fine. I can't do anything today, mind."

"OK," said Bateman. "How about tomorrow?"

Aaron tapped open the calendar on his phone and scanned down the list of appointments. It was solid all day. He'd known things would get busy once he'd taken up the DI role. But he hadn't expected it to be *this* busy.

"How about the next day?" he replied. He checked through his calendar again. "It'll have to be evening, mind."

"Suits me," said Bateman. "Wainwrights' OK for you?"

"You want me to come all the way over to Chapel Stile? Can't we just—?"

"Please, Aaron," said Bateman, and Aaron heard something like desperation in his voice.

"Fine," he said. "Wainwrights'. Friday at seven. I'll see you then."

"Thanks, Aaron," said Bateman. "I owe you one."

More than one, thought Aaron. But it wasn't all bad. He could drop in on his parents while he was in town. And Wainwrights' was a great pub.

CHAPTER SEVEN

"You REALLY THINK you've got something?" asked the DCI.

Harriett nodded, gave a slight frown, and nodded again. Carl knew she'd been through worse than this. A lot more dangerous, too. But the pressure of Douglas Branthwaite's *little arrangement* couldn't be comfortable.

"I'm not sure, sir," she said. "It's this boatyard murder."

They were in the team room. Denise and the new DC, Marcus, were sitting. Carl was standing beside DCI Branthwaite, who he'd gone to find as soon as Harriett had briefed him.

And Harriett stood in the centre of it all, four sets of eyes on her.

"Go on," said Branthwaite.

"Two shift officers. PCs. Stephen Grange and Niamh Hanson."

"Anyone know them?" asked Branthwaite, and Carl watched each head shake. He'd have shaken his own, only it was pounding, and he didn't want to make it worse.

"Nothing on the system about either of them. No disciplinaries, no complaints. They took the call from dispatch. It was a non-priority—"

"Why?" said Marcus.

It was a good question, and Harriett turned to him. "I'll come to that. They had another non-priority call. Bowness-on-Windermere, a woman who'd reported a disturbance outside her block of flats. They could have stopped at the boatyard on the way, but they decided to go straight to Bowness."

"And what did they find there?" asked Denise. She'd been fidgeting while Harriett spoke, which wasn't like her.

"Bins tipped over," Harriett said. "They reckoned foxes or cats. And the original call, it was from an old guy taking a walk. He said he'd heard screams coming from the boatyard."

Carl and Denise exchanged a look.

"And that wasn't considered a priority?"

Harriett shrugged. "Apparently not. The dispatcher is a Angela Sherman. Nothing on the system about her either, apart from a long list of illnesses."

There was a short silence.

"I don't know," said Marcus, after a moment. "Seems a bit thin."

Harriett gave him a look like he'd just tried to poison her cat, but he didn't seem to notice.

"Oh?" said Branthwaite.

"It's just, well, there's nothing on any of these officers. If there were complaints on the system, or connections with known criminals, then maybe—"

"And if we had suitable cases dripping from our various orifices," said Branthwaite, "then I might agree with you. But right now, things are dry as a meeting of Methodist accountants. What do you think, Denise?"

Denise shrugged. "Worth a look, I reckon," she said.

She looked nervous, Carl thought. No, not nervous. Tense. Twitchy.

"Carl?" asked Branthwaite.

"Maybe not enough to take over the investigation," he said. "But I agree with Denise. We could just start looking into their actions after the event. The fact that they didn't respond. Take it gently and see if anything comes up."

Branthwaite nodded.

"What are you lot waiting for?" he asked. "You heard what the man said. It's worth looking into. So look into it."

CHAPTER EIGHT

THE POST-MORTEM REPORT was much as Lynn had expected.

Time of death was unclear, as usual, but the call from the previous evening and the arrival of the work experience boy, Chris Markham, in the morning set the edges on the window. Cause of death was drowning. The injuries to the man's hands and mouth had been made post-mortem, which was something, at least. If you were going to end up getting murdered, you'd want the nasty business of hiding who you'd been when you were alive to wait until you couldn't feel it any more.

There were other details, too. There had been a tattoo, but it had been inexpertly removed. The pathologist wasn't clear as to when this had taken place, but had sent off skin samples for further analysis. A betting woman would put her money on this being part of the same process as the mess that had been made of the teeth and fingerprints, but Lynn had never really been a betting woman. No point, when there were people out there who could give you answers instead of guesses.

There was still no hit on mispers, no DNA match, nothing that might help identify the victim, not until the final paragraph, when all the work his killers had done to hide that identity began to unravel.

There was a metal plate in the man's back, and its various parts had been extracted and were being subjected to further analysis. Dr Robertson was confident this analysis would reveal where the surgery had taken place, assuming it was within the UK, and hopefully when, too.

Once they knew that, the man's actual identity would be a mere hop away.

She'd tried to get hold of DS Bateman an hour earlier, but his phone was switched off, which was fair enough if he was off sick.

He wasn't sick. There was something wrong with him, that much was obvious. But Lynn didn't think it was illness.

DI Woolley had retreated to her office and kept the door shut for the last two hours. Anyone else, Lynn might have thought she was making sensitive calls in there, but this was Jasmine Woolley. She was probably just sitting at her desk, rubbing her head, wondering why no one appreciated her, and doing sod all to help with the investigation. 'Just the two of us,' Lynn had said earlier, but both of them had known it was really just the one.

She'd just picked up the scene of crime report for a third read-through when her phone rang, and she snatched it up like it held the secret to life itself.

"Lynn?" she heard, a familiar and comforting voice.

"DI Keyes?"

"How's your murder coming along?"

"You don't want to ask," she said. "Don't suppose you could pull some strings, see if you can come and take over like you did last time?"

There was a short, slightly bitter laugh.

"Things have changed," he told her. "It's not Fiona Kendrick in charge any more."

Lynn had heard that. The Detective Superintendent had moved on, or been pushed out; Lynn wasn't sure which. Too far above her pay grade to matter much. And her replacement was...

"Kiki Carnegie isn't particularly fond of me," DI Keyes added. "If I come to her asking for a favour, she'll probably do the opposite. But that isn't why I called. I was wondering if you could tell me about Isaac."

Lynn sat up straighter.

"Isaac?"

"Bateman, yeah. How's he been?"

"Apart from boorish and incompetent, you mean?"

His laugh sounded slightly strained.

"Yes. Anything unusual in his behaviour?"

"Well, yes, as it happens," Lynn said, and explained what had happened that morning. "And it's not just that," she added. "He's been acting strange for a few days now. Arguing with DI Woolley, which was unexpected. He told her we needed help on the case. You can imagine how she took that. And he seemed..."

She paused, trying to remember how she'd described it to herself.

"Stressed," she said. "He seemed on edge. Very different from the usual Isaac Bateman. And now he's disappeared. What's this all about, then?" she asked, hoping the question sounded more casual than it felt.

"I wish I could tell you," he replied. "Listen, give me a call if you hear from him. And, you know, if you want a sounding board."

Lynn thanked him, and ended the call, and found herself wondering which was the bigger mystery: Isaac Bateman, or the dead man in the boatyard.

CHAPTER NINE

Don't piss off your new colleagues.

The words echoed through Marcus's brain as he sat at his new desk in his new team room, and pulled up the contact details for the officers who'd chosen not to check out the boatyard.

It was the one important thing his dad had told him the previous week, when they'd had one of the four meetings they managed each year at one of half a dozen service stations on the M6. He'd handed over Lolly, and all the paraphernalia that came with her, and had to listen while his dad gave him advice he'd have been better off listening to himself, thirty-something years ago.

Don't piss off your new colleagues, though. That one never got old.

He dialled the first number.

"PC Hanson," said the woman, immediately. He was looking at her photo on the internal system, and she sounded younger than he'd expected. Almost girlish.

"This is Detective Constable Marcus Hosgood," he said,

and then he dug his nails into his palm and went straight in. "I'm calling you from Professional Standards, Cumbria Police. I was hoping we could—"

"Professional Standards?" she said.

"Yes."

"Like, PSD?"

She sounded even younger now. Like a child waking from a bad dream, only to find it wasn't a dream after all.

"Yes. There's nothing to worry about," he added, which might have been more convincing if he hadn't just told her who he was. "I was just hoping you might be willing to come in and have a—"

"Do I need a lawyer?" she asked. "Or a Police Federation rep?"

He affected a casual laugh, which sounded more like the sort of laugh a hostage would give if they'd been told to act casual.

"Of course not. I mean, you're welcome to, if you want. But this isn't a criminal matter, or a disciplinary one."

He might have added 'at this stage', but that wouldn't exactly help, would it?

"What is it, then?"

"We're just in the early investigative stages of a process that probably won't come to anything," he said, and then he looked up and saw Harriett Barnes staring at him, and closed his eyes.

Don't piss off your new colleagues.

"What do you need to talk to me for, then?" asked Niamh Hanson, who sounded less girlish and a little more sure of herself now.

It had actually worked. The stupid laugh and the casual front.

"It's just information-gathering," he told her. "I can explain more when you come in. Oh, and if you'd be willing to grant access to your financial and phone records, that would make things easier."

"Easier?" she echoed. She sounded nervous again.

"It would help us get through things faster," he said. It was true, sort of.

In the absence of a criminal investigation, they couldn't look at any of this stuff, and this wasn't a criminal investigation. It wasn't even misconduct. If they wanted phone records, they'd need to make an application under the Regulation of Investigatory Powers Act, and the consent of the person being investigated would help speed that along.

It was all probably a waste of everyone's time, his and Niamh Hanson's included, and if it was, then the sooner they had all the information, the sooner they could all go back to doing a proper job.

If it wasn't, then the information he'd asked for might yield a lead or two.

He arranged a time for Niamh Hanson to come in, and moved on to the next one, PC Stephen Grange.

Grange was younger, but seemed to take it more easily in his stride, after the first faltering repetition of 'Professional Standards'. He didn't even ask about lawyers or Fed reps.

When he'd finished that call, he stood and approached Harriett Barnes.

"Yes," she said, without looking away from her screen.

"Look," he said. "I'm sorry. I feel like an absolute—"

"I told you, no apologies necessary." She turned and smiled at him, and he felt a wave of relief wash through him. "But I wouldn't mind a coffee."

She held his gaze for a moment, just long enough for him

to realise that she wasn't joking, and for that wave of relief to crash onto the hard rocks of reality.

His dad had managed twenty years on the force without pissing off his colleagues, and then he'd pissed them all off, in the space of a few short weeks. If anyone knew what he was talking about, it was Elias Hosgood.

There was no sign of DS Gaskill, so it was just the one coffee. Milk and one sugar. When Marcus returned to the team room five minutes later, Harriett Barnes took the drink from him without a word, but with a slightly softer smile, he thought. Or maybe he just hoped.

"Rashid," said the next one on the list, as he answered the phone.

"This is Detective Constable Marcus Hosgood," he began. "I'm—"

"I hear you've been calling my team," said Sergeant Samir Rashid. "Pissing them off. I don't know what you think you're playing at, but I don't appreciate you upsetting my people."

Marcus ignored the aggression in the man's voice. "I'm calling you from Professional Standards, Cumbria Police. I was hoping you could come in and help us get to the bottom of—"

"Yeah, yeah. Not like I've got much choice, is it?" said Rashid. Still aggressive, but with the resignation of someone who knew that putting PSD off their stride was about as easy as changing the orbit of the moon. You could close your eyes, hide behind the clouds, and convince yourself it wasn't there, but sooner or later, you'd have to look up and see it.

They'd be in the next day. All three of them. That would be three days after the body had been discovered, which meant more than enough time to hide any evidence. But at least two of them had sounded anxious, and the other one might have been hiding it.

Fair enough, when you had PSD calling you up. And they'd all agreed to provide access to finances and phone records. Not something you'd do if you had something to hide.

Harriett Barnes had drunk her coffee and left by the time he'd finished the calls, and the silence in the team room felt almost oppressive with no one else in it. Marcus sat back and closed his eyes, and allowed that silence to fill his head.

He'd done it. He was here, in PSD. Where he was meant to be.

Where he could right some old wrongs.

He opened his eyes and tapped out information requests, one for PC Niamh Hanson, one for PC Stephen Grange, one for PS Samir Rashid. He sat there scanning the lines on the screen, and when the lights went out, he carried on, not even bothering to wave at the motion sensors to reactivate them.

By the time he left three hours later, he knew all there was to know about Hanson, Grange, and Rashid. Nothing had jumped out at him, but that was fine. Because back when his dad had been a cop, before he'd been obsessed with not making mistakes and, above all, not pissing off his colleagues, he'd told Marcus something else.

'Wait until they're sitting in front of you,' he'd said. 'People who look clean on paper can be a right mess in the flesh.'

Maybe tomorrow, Marcus would be seeing some messy flesh.

He certainly hoped so.

CHAPTER TEN

SEVENTEEN, *eighteen, nineteen.*

Denise had counted three times now. Three times she'd run her fingers over the blister pack, and added it to the other pack, and three times she'd got the same number.

Nineteen pills in this pack. Sixty in the other. Seventy-nine pills in total.

The way things were going, that wouldn't last much more than a week. She walked into the kitchen and put the pills back in the drawer, retrieving the bottle of cheap Irish whiskey she'd stashed in the cupboard underneath it, for emergencies.

She wasn't sure this counted as an emergency. Rationing painkillers she was supposed to have weaned herself off months ago.

She poured herself a generous measure and swallowed it down, relishing the sting at the back of her throat. And then she poured herself another, even larger measure, and took it into the living room, where she sat and sipped as she stared at her screen.

More specifically, she stared at a photo of 'Little Joe' Carghillie.

It seemed implausible that someone as senior as the Assistant Chief Constable could be corrupt, but it wasn't out of the question. More likely, it was someone in his office, but his office was a great, sprawling thing, with advisers and deputy advisers and deputy advisers to the deputy advisers. The joke was that the Assistant Chief Constable had more advisers than the Prime Minister. He certainly had more than the Chief.

And one of them, or Little Joe himself, was bent.

She tapped through from the ACC to his Policy Advisor, then to his Chief of Staff, then to his Head of Media.

Any one of them. Or none of them. She'd been staring at the screen for long enough that the words had started to flow into one another, when she heard a tap on the door.

Eileen was standing outside. She could see Eileen through the window, and now Eileen could see her, and was waving at her, so she forced a smile onto her lips and went to the door.

"Just wanted to see how you've been, Denise," said her neighbour.

"Fine, thank you," Denise replied. She'd taken half a step outside, blocking the door, making it as clear as she could without saying the words that she wouldn't be inviting Eileen in. "Just busy, you know."

"Oh, yes. I could see you tap-tapping away on your little computer."

Eileen smiled indulgently at her. She was only sixty, but she looked and acted like a woman two decades older, or like sixty-year-olds had been back when Denise was a child. Her husband had died nearly twenty years earlier, and they'd never had children, something Eileen had lamented so many times Denise could almost recite the complaint herself.

And the bit that always followed. The bit that Denise knew was coming, now.

"Well, thanks for checking on me," she said.

"Well, you know how I feel," Eileen replied.

Here it comes.

"I do," said Denise.

"You're the closest thing I have to a daughter," Eileen told her.

"You've mentioned it before," replied Denise.

"Well." Eileen gave a nervous laugh, and waited in silence.

She couldn't be expecting Denise to reciprocate. Denise had never reciprocated.

"I like to make sure you're OK," Eileen said, eventually. "It's no trouble keeping an eye on you. And you need something to look after, too. Something to come home to."

This was new.

"I do?" asked Denise.

"Yes. Have you considered getting yourself a pet?"

"No," Denise replied, honestly. "But I will give it some thought," she added, and that, she knew, was a lie. She smiled, and hoped the smile didn't look too false. "Good night," she said.

She made herself wait until Eileen had turned and started to walk back to her house before she shut the door. There was cold, and there was rude, and she tried to stay the right side of the line.

But the notion that Denise should get herself a pet wasn't something she'd be giving any serious consideration to.

She'd barely turned back into the house when her phone

rang. She checked the display, and saw to her relief that it was Aaron Keyes.

"What's new?" she asked.

"Same old," he replied. "Got a new DC."

"You and me both. Bet yours is better than mine." He waited while she told him about Marcus, or more specifically, about Marcus's introduction to Harriett Barnes.

"She wouldn't like that," Aaron observed.

"He'll be bringing her coffee for the next six months," Denise told him, heading back to her laptop and the empty glass beside it.

And the half-full bottle beside that.

"But you didn't call to hear me go on about the new guy, did you?" she continued.

"No. Listen, have you heard anything about Langdale?"

She paused, the bottle tilted over the glass.

"Why do you ask?"

"Look, I know you can't tell me if you're investigating anyone there. And that's fine. But I thought you should know. I've had a call from an old... Let's call him an old colleague. I'm meeting him in a couple of days. But I think it's you lot he really wants to talk to."

"Right. You got a name for me?"

There was a long silence.

"Aaron?" she said. "Come on. This is me. If there's something going on, I need to know."

"Isaac Bateman," he said, finally.

"Never heard of him," she replied. Her phone beeped – another call coming through – and she checked the display and decided to ignore it, pouring herself a generous measure instead. "But thanks for letting me know," she added. "I don't—"

"Have you seen Dr Filey yet?" Aaron asked suddenly, and this time it was Denise's turn to fall silent. "Well?" he said. "Have you?"

"You know I have," she replied. "I've been twice already."

"Not exactly regular, that. If you want to get the most out of—"

"I don't want to get the most out of her, Aaron," she said. "I don't want to see her at all. You know that."

"And you know that regular visits to the force psychiatrist are a condition of your return to work. I've been through it myself, Denise. You've got to—"

"I'm seeing her in three days, Aaron. You don't need to lecture me."

This time, the silence threatened to go on indefinitely. She looked down at her whiskey, back up at the screen, then folded down the laptop and raised the glass to her lips.

She knew he was right. She knew that seeing Dr Filey wasn't just a necessary part of her recovery, but quite possibly a helpful one.

But she also knew what psychiatrists were like. They could sniff things out. Secrets and vulnerabilities.

Like a hidden addiction to painkillers arranged through an under-the-counter supply that would cost you your job if it ever came out.

"Fine," said Aaron, finally. "Message received."

She put the glass back down on the table and apologised, and by the time the call ended five minutes later, they were friends again, the bottle was back in its cupboard, and the blister pack remained untouched.

Three glasses of whiskey and no pills. By recent standards, that was a decent night.

DAY FOUR

CHAPTER ELEVEN

William Hall looked like a worried man.

He sat opposite Lynn in the tiny space they used as an interview room in Langdale Police Station, clutching a mug like his life depended on it, his face almost as pale as the milky white tea inside.

"Is everything OK, Mr Hall?" asked Lynn.

"Yes," he said. "It's just... I've never had cause to enter a police station before. You'd think, at my age, it's not the sort of thing that's likely to happen."

William Hall was seventy-five years old.

"You're not in any trouble at all, Mr Hall," Lynn assured him. "I'd just like to run through what you saw, or heard, on Sunday evening. The night you called the police. Do you remember that?"

"It was the only time I've ever dialled 999, young lady. I'm hardly likely to forget."

There was a tiny part of Lynn that wanted to take offence at that 'young lady'. But there was a certain manner of speaking that was acceptable, if you were over a certain age. And the man was being helpful, after all.

"Can you tell me why you called?" she asked.

"Don't you have a recording?" he asked, frowning.

"Yes." There was a recording, and Lynn had listened to it three times now. She'd heard William Hall telling the operator he could hear noises coming from the boatyard, and he thought it sounded like screaming. "I was just wondering if you remembered any more."

He opened his arms in a gesture of helplessness.

"I wish I could, Miss... What did you say your name was?"

"Lynn," she told him. "Lynn Hedley."

No need to insist on titles. Not now.

"Well, Miss Hedley, I was walking by the boatyard and I heard screaming. That's all, really. I dialled 999, and I told them, and that was the last I heard of it, until you got in touch this morning."

The fact that it had taken three days to contact the only potential witness to a murder was yet another reason Lynn was convinced they needed more help, but Jasmine Woolley still wouldn't have it.

"Can you remember any of the words? Can you describe the voice?"

"I'm sorry." That gesture, again, arms open wide. "I didn't know if it was a man or a woman. I wasn't even sure it was human."

"Right." Lynn scanned the sheet of paper in front of her, the transcript of the call. "And then I understand you told the operator it was probably nothing, and not to worry about it."

"That's right," agreed William Hall.

She looked back up at him.

"Why did you say that?"

"Well, I didn't want to waste anyone's time. And these days, well, you hear it everywhere, don't you?"

"Hear what?"

"Screaming, Miss Hedley. I remember when a scream was serious. When it meant something. Nowadays, it could mean someone's excited, or that they're happy, or that they've just bumped into a friend. Perhaps they've had a drink. It's lost all meaning, hasn't it?"

She stared at him for a moment, then nodded, thanked him for his time, and accompanied him out of the building to his car, which was parked on the double yellow lines just outside. She watched him climb in and start the engine, and it wasn't until he'd slid smoothly into the light passing traffic that she turned and walked back inside.

Jasmine Woolley was waiting for her in the team room.

"Well?" said the DI.

"He doesn't know anything, Ma'am," she replied.

"Have you heard from Isaac?"

Lynn shook her head. She'd tried DS Bateman already that morning, but his phone had gone straight through to voicemail. She'd left a message this time, but he hadn't called back.

"And I suppose you've heard about PSD," added the DI, and Lynn frowned.

"No," she said. "What about PSD?"

"They're taking an interest."

"In this case? The boatyard?"

"We're not working on anything else, are we?" the DI replied.

Lynn's frown deepened.

"But why, Ma'am? Why are they looking into this case?"

"I don't have the faintest idea, Lynn," said DI Woolley. "If you happen to find out, be good enough to let me know."

CHAPTER TWELVE

"So, this is where the rats live, is it?"

PS Samir Rashid sat opposite Carl and Harriett, short, fat and round-faced, a slight curl to his lip, chin jutted forward at enough of an angle to make it clear he wasn't happy and didn't care who knew it.

"Rats?" said Carl, and Rashid gestured at the two of them.

"Thing about rats is, if they're hungry enough, they'll eat each other. Turn on their own. Like you lot, harassing decent cops who are just trying to do their jobs."

"You're here voluntarily," Carl reminded him, forcing a smile onto his face. "This is an informal information-gathering interview, and if you want to leave, you're welcome to."

"And," Harriett added, "no one's harassed anyone, as far as I can see."

Rashid turned his attention to her.

"You wanted phone records, bank accounts, all that. If that's not harassment, I don't know what is."

"I understand you provided all that voluntarily, too, and

as far as we can see, there's nothing in your records to warrant further investigation, Sergeant Rashid."

Rashid stared at her for a moment in silence, then turned back to Carl.

"Not sure why you're bothering with all this just for some dead Scouser, anyway."

Carl kept the smile in place. It was starting to hurt a little, but he couldn't afford to let Rashid get to him.

"Just tell us everything you know about the call-out, and this'll be over, Sergeant Rashid. Please."

"Yeah. Well, I don't know much, do I? Wasn't me in the car."

"PCs Grange and Hanson work under you, don't they?" said Harriett.

"Yeah."

"So we were hoping you might be able to provide some insight into—"

"Look," said Rashid, leaning forward. "I don't know what you lot want me to say. There's nothing to look at here. My people, they get a shout, they get told it's not a priority, they go somewhere else instead. If they'd known someone was dying there, that would have changed things. But they didn't, did they?"

Rashid stopped and stared at Carl. The silence went on for nearly thirty seconds before Carl realised it hadn't been a rhetorical question.

"That's what we're trying to find out."

"Fuck's sake," said Rashid, letting a meaty right hand drop heavily onto the table, then wincing at the noise it made. "Bloody hell. Sorry. Hangover. Team drinks last night. Might have overdone it."

That went some way in explaining the attitude.

"If we could just—" Carl began.

"Look, there's no real issue here, is there? You're just making up problems because that's what you lot do. I've heard the shout. Heard the recording. Not a priority. No reason to think there was anything else to it. You think that was wrong, talk to the dispatcher."

Carl and Harriett exchanged a look. For all his bluster, it was possible Rashid had a point.

"And if you've got a problem with Niamh or Stevie, you're barking up the wrong tree. I've spoken to both of them. They didn't know what was going on. Course they didn't."

"Do you have any reason to doubt that?" asked Carl, and Rashid shook his head, then winced again.

"None. Trust them both completely. We done here?"

There was a small part of Carl that wanted to keep Rashid in a little longer, if only to make it clear that he could, if he wanted to. But the man knew nothing, and having him there wasn't improving anyone's mood.

"Yes," he said. "We'll be in touch if—"

"Whatever," said Rashid, standing and striding out of the room with surprising speed for a man of his size. Wherever he was heading, he was clearly in a hurry to get there.

Bathroom, thought Carl. *Almost certainly the bathroom.*

CHAPTER THIRTEEN

PC Stephen Grange was, by anyone's standards, a good-looking lad.

He flashed a grin at Denise, and then at Marcus Hosgood, sitting next to her, as he took his seat opposite them. Stephen Grange was tall and well-muscled, with a mop of thick, dark hair, artfully disarranged. He wasn't far short of beautiful.

And he knew it.

"Thanks for coming in," Marcus said.

"No problem. Just hope I can help you clear all this up."

Marcus returned the man's smile. There was too much friendliness in the room for Denise's liking, but Grange hadn't done anything wrong, as far as anyone knew, so maybe that was Denise's problem. Three glasses of whiskey and no pills might have seemed like a good idea last night, but this morning it had been four pills, straight down, first thing, and she wasn't sure she could feel much effect.

"'You want to bother with that?'" she read.

"I'm sorry?" asked Grange. He was frowning now, but

even the frown looked good, neat parallel lines etched across an otherwise smooth forehead.

"I'm looking at the transcript of your conversation with PC Hanson, just after you'd received the shout about the disturbance at the boatyard. You said, 'You want to bother with that?' and PC Hanson replied, 'Nah, leave it till morning shift.' Does that ring any bells?"

Grange nodded.

"I didn't realise it had been recorded," he said. "I suppose Niamh was still on with the dispatcher. But it sounds about right."

"It's an accurate reflection of your conversation?"

"Yes," agreed Grange. "Niamh's more experienced than I am, so it was her call, really. And it sounded like the right one." He stopped, opened his mouth wide, then closed it again. "I mean, it wasn't, obviously. But we didn't know that at the time."

Denise nodded.

"That sounds fair enough," said Marcus Hosgood. "I really am sorry to have to drag you in here."

Denise wanted to punch him. Wanted to punch both of them. All the pretty boys together, the poor pretty boys, having their fun ruined by the boring, sensible cops who were just wasting everyone's time.

"That's no problem," said Grange, again. "Really. Anything I can do to help."

"In that case," said Marcus, "I was wondering if you'd mind explaining the provenance of the four thousand pounds received into your current account two days prior to the incident."

Grange gaped. Denise's own mouth fell open, too, and hung there for a moment before she realised and shut it.

Well played, Marcus Hosgood.

"What?" said Grange.

"Four thousand pounds. Here." Marcus produced a sheet of paper and slid it across the table to Grange. "You were kind enough to grant access to your financial records, and I took the liberty of looking into them earlier."

Denise had seen Marcus looking through the documents first thing. And then he'd come in here and lulled Grange into a false sense of security, convincing him they were on the same side before going in for the kill.

You clever bastard.

"Well," said Grange, looking down at the paper and frowning that absurd, comic-book frown again. "Well, that's an insurance payout, isn't it?"

"Is it?" said Marcus. "You tell me, PC Grange."

Grange looked up, smiling now, but there was a forced quality to the smile. "Yes. Had a flood, nearly a year ago now, but you know how long these things take."

"Much damage?" asked Denise.

"Carpets and the fireplace," replied Grange, without missing a beat.

"So this payer," said Marcus. "Havering Milton. If we check them out, we'll find they're an insurance company?"

"Go ahead."

Grange looked relaxed again now. Marcus had thrown him, and that was good interview technique, especially if there was a pit full of spikes behind the man you were throwing. But there was no pit, just a nice soft floor to bounce off and get back up again.

An insurance payout. They'd check, of course, but Grange wouldn't be acting like this if the money wasn't above board.

Good interview technique. It was always useful, being able to throw a suspect off balance. But Grange wasn't really a suspect.

And there was no excuse, as far as Denise could see, for not letting her know in advance.

CHAPTER FOURTEEN

Lynn sat at her desk in the otherwise empty team room, sipping vending machine coffee and scanning through the latest updates on the boatyard killing.

That was a joke, of course. It was just a shame there was no one to laugh at it other than her.

The reason it was a joke was that there was no one providing updates other than her, either. DI Woolley sat in her office all day, doing God alone knew what, and stomping through occasionally to make a snide remark or ask if Lynn had heard from Isaac Bateman. As for Isaac Bateman, well, Lynn hadn't heard from him.

He still hadn't returned her call.

She was just typing in a summary of her interview with William Hall and adding it to HOLMES when her system gave a little ping, and a notification appeared on her screen.

An update. An honest-to-goodness update. And it wasn't one she'd put on there herself.

She put down her coffee and tapped to open it. A revised post-mortem report, containing the very latest information.

The search for the identity of the dead man was finally narrowing.

Dr Robertson's confidence hadn't been misplaced. He now knew that the metal plate had ended up in the victim's back as part of a spinal fusion procedure. He knew the surgery had been carried out between ten and fifteen years earlier.

And he was fairly sure it had been done in the Walton Centre, a specialist hospital in Liverpool.

Lynn stopped what she was doing, opened a new window, and filed a request for patient records, which she knew would be frowned at and rejected first time round, and probably the second, but might make it through on its third attempt.

Liverpool featured a second time in the updated report, in a paragraph concerning the dead man's tattoo.

'Inexpertly removed' had been the pathologist's initial assessment. There had been an 'unsightly blemish', and not a lot else. Now there was a little more clarity. The tattoo had been removed, using the same bleach Lynn had smelled at the scene. It would have hurt like buggery – those were the actual words in the pathologist's report – if it weren't for the fact that the man had been dead already, so he wouldn't have cared about the unsightly blemish it had left after all.

It wasn't the blemish that betrayed the inexpert nature of the removal, though. It was the fact that there was still just enough of the tattoo left to give a hint as to what it had originally been. And with the aid of microscopes, tissue analysis, and an AI cellular reconstruction model, the pathologist had got there in the end.

Liverpool Football Club. The dead man's arm had been

adorned with a tattoo of the club crest for Liverpool Football Club.

There were plenty of Liverpool fans who'd never set foot in the city. But the tattoo, sitting alongside the back surgery, pointed Lynn in a very particular direction. She added both new sets of information into the mispers database and waited for something to come back up.

Nothing did.

She sat there swearing quietly at her screen, and didn't realise she wasn't alone until she heard DI Woolley speak from directly behind her.

"Well?" said the DI, who'd apparently moved on from stomping and was now gliding silently about the station like a ghost.

"Just... Just trying to find out who the dead man was, Ma'am," she said.

"Get on with it, then. Oh, and PSD are still interested."

Lynn nodded.

"Will they be wanting to talk to us?" she asked.

"I doubt it. Not like we've got anything to tell them, is there?" the DI replied, and then she barked out a short, high-pitched laugh, and glided silently away again.

"Oh," she said, turning in the doorway. "I don't suppose you've heard from Isaac, have you?"

Lynn shook her head, and the DI disappeared.

CHAPTER FIFTEEN

THAT HAD GONE WELL, Marcus thought.

Grange certainly hadn't seen it coming.

The two of them were walking together down the main ground floor corridor – he'd volunteered to show the PC out. Grange had been quiet as they left the interview room, but within a few seconds he'd turned chatty again. As they entered the reception area, with its battered wooden desk and the automated doors that didn't work, Grange grinned again, and called across the room to a tall woman with curly red hair who was walking slowly towards them, accompanied by Harriett Barnes.

"Alright, Niamh!"

So this was the other PC from that night. Niamh Hanson. She offered an anxious smile, and stopped briefly to exchange greetings with Grange, who then turned to Harriett, still grinning.

"Stephen Grange," he said, holding out his right hand, as if they were at a drinks reception rather than a police station.

Harriett stared at the hand.

"DC Harriett Barnes," she replied, and walked away, casting a glance back towards Hanson, who hurried to keep up. Grange shrugged.

"Got to try, haven't you?" he said, and headed towards the exit.

Marcus didn't like the man, but he was too relaxed to be bent.

Back in the team room, he sat down and waited for DS Gaskill to say something, but she was focused on her screen, frowning and tapping intermittently on her keyboard, and rolling her shoulders occasionally as if she was in pain. After a couple of minutes he coughed, and she turned.

"You're back," she said.

He nodded.

"You did well in there," she continued, and he nodded again, and then froze as she raised a finger. "It was good, your one-man good-cop-bad-cop routine. Did the trick. But if you're interviewing someone with another officer, you don't pull a stunt like that without telling your colleague."

He stared at her, his mouth moving, no words coming out.

"Understand?" she said.

He felt sick, now. He'd been walking on air a minute earlier. Now he was sinking, fast, a weight in his stomach dragging him down.

"I didn't really have—" he began.

"Don't tell me you didn't have time, Marcus. It would have taken twenty seconds to show me the bank statement and tell me what you were planning. We're a team. The 'D' in 'PSD' stands for 'Division', not 'Do It All By Yourself'. OK?"

"OK," he nodded, and turned quickly to his screen so she couldn't see his face.

Don't let them see you cry.

That was another one of his dad's lines. Meant for the schoolyard rather than the office, for the child rather than the adult with the responsible job who couldn't receive a bit of perfectly reasonable criticism without his eyes turning wet.

"I mean it," said Denise, and he nodded, his back still to her. "You did well. Really."

Too little, too late.

"I'm going to interview Niamh Hanson now," she added. "With Harriett."

He'd assumed it would be him. It made sense, didn't it? You interviewed one, you interviewed the other. Easier to sniff out inconsistencies that way.

Maybe Harriett Barnes didn't pull stupid stunts in the middle of interviews without telling the DS. Maybe that was how you got to make something of yourself round here.

He pulled up the details on Grange's current account. Maybe if he found something...

But no. Five minutes later, he'd traced the account Grange's four thousand pounds had come from, found the name, and checked the regulatory authority registers.

Havering Milton Ltd, the company that had made the payment, was a fully licensed, regulated insurance company. Grange was on the level.

He clicked away from the boatyard investigation and spent a few minutes looking up details of old cases, ongoing investigations, long-term projects.

There was Myron Carter, the former leader of the biggest organised crime gang in the area, whose bomb had almost killed DS Gaskill, and who was now serving life for so many offences the local papers hadn't even bothered listing them all.

There was Ralph Streeting, Carter's tame cop and the man his bomb had been meant to kill, who'd helped them bring Carter down in the end, but was still serving his own life sentence for murder.

There was a file named *Skeleton Key*, but when he tapped to open it, his credentials didn't seem to be enough.

Shut out of the files. Shut out of the interview.

Out in the cold.

He closed his eyes and tried to think of something good, something he could hold onto without it brushing him off, and within half a second he was picturing Lolly, running towards him, joy written all over her face.

It didn't take much. A few seconds later, he was smiling.

CHAPTER SIXTEEN

If Samir Rashid had been hungover, Niamh Hanson was whatever the next step after hungover was. She was older than Grange, at twenty-nine, and a year or two more experienced, but she looked like she was ready to fall until the moment she sat down. When Harriett sat opposite her, she found herself looking into a pair of eyes so bloodshot there was more red there than white. The woman's hands were shaking slightly, which might have been nerves, but was more likely to be the alcohol.

"Are you OK?" she asked, once DS Gaskill had walked in and introduced herself.

"Fine." Hanson nodded. "Team drinks last night. Don't suppose I could get some water?"

Harriett went to fetch a cup of water, and returned to a silent room. DS Gaskill, she realised, didn't look in great shape herself. If she'd not known, she'd have been hard put to say which of the two women was being interviewed here.

But then the DS turned to her and gave her one of those sharp Denise Gaskill looks, and Harriett remembered that this was a woman who'd survived a bomb, who'd dragged herself out of hospital and back into work the moment she could, who'd stood up in court and helped bring down Myron Carter.

Even feeling rough, DS Gaskill would manage. She gave Harriett a small nod.

"We'd like to ask a few questions about the other night," Harriett began, and took PC Hanson through the transcript of the conversation with the dispatcher, and her brief subsequent chat with PC Grange.

"Yeah," said Hanson after a minute.

"Yeah?" echoed DS Gaskill.

"I mean, yeah, that sounds about right. We decided not to go. It wasn't a priority. I mean, if we'd known..."

She fell silent, watching them both for a moment.

"It sounds like it was your decision to head to the other callout instead," Harriett reminded her.

"Maybe," said Hanson, and DS Gaskill leaned forward, across the table.

"A man died, PC Hanson. A man was murdered. I'm not sure 'maybe' is good enough."

For a moment, Hanson looked like she was about to cry, and then she looked sheepish, and then...

"I'm sorry," she said, standing suddenly. "Can I use your bathroom?"

Harriett pointed the way, and then spent fifteen long minutes waiting with the DS for Hanson to return. When she did finally come back, she looked only marginally better.

"Really am sorry," she said. "I don't know what to say."

There were several things Harriett might have said, most of them about the wisdom of getting as drunk as Niamh Hanson clearly had done the night before an important interview with PSD, but maybe it was the interview with PSD that had prompted the drinking.

"Back to the night in question," said DS Gaskill, and they went through it all again, Hanson agreeing with everything Harriett and the DS put to her.

"Why didn't you stop at the boatyard first?" Harriett asked, a slight variation on the same question she'd already asked three times.

Hanson shrugged. "Like I said. It wasn't a priority. I knew morning shift would be in the area. The other one – Bowness, wasn't it?"

"You're the one who went there," said Denise, drily. "But yes. Bowness."

"Little further out of area. Couldn't be sure they'd get to it. I mean, I don't remember the actual reasoning that went through my head, but that was probably it."

She blinked, reached for her water, and drank the whole thing in the space of ten seconds.

"Feeling better?" asked Harriett.

"Yeah. Thanks. Probably drank too much last night."

She clearly had, and so had Rashid. But from the brief glimpse she'd caught of Stephen Grange, Harriett hadn't seen anything similar.

"Your colleague," she said. "PC Grange. He didn't seem to be struggling like this."

"Doesn't drink," replied Hanson. "We get the hangovers, he gets to be designated driver. Last night I'm laughing my head off at him. Today, I'm thinking maybe he's got the right idea."

"We've been looking through your finances," said DS Gaskill, holding a sheet of paper, and Hanson looked briefly shocked at the sudden change of subject. "I can see a number of payments from your colleague, PS Rashid, last night."

Hanson glanced over the numbers and nodded.

"Sarge told us it was his shout, but his card wasn't working. I paid, and he transferred the cash."

"And this item here?"

Harriett watched as Hanson screwed up her eyes, frowning, the frown deepening as she stared at the line DS Gaskill was indicating.

They waited.

"I don't know," Hanson said, after nearly a minute.

"This is a payment of two hundred and fifty pounds, made yesterday, into your bank account, from an account in the name of Winterburn. The reference given is the letter X. And you don't recognise it?"

Hanson looked up at DS Gaskill, then turned to Harriett, an expression of utter bewilderment on her face. It was convincing, thought Harriett.

But bent cops could be good liars.

"PC Hanson?" Harriett prompted.

"I'm sorry," said Hanson. "I just... I don't know. I don't know that account. I don't know anyone called Winterburn. I just... Is that definitely my bank account?"

"It is," said DS Gaskill. "If you don't mind, I'd like to run through your personal life briefly."

"You would?" said Hanson. She looked like a woman who'd been falling for a good few seconds, and had only just realised the ground had disappeared from beneath her feet.

"Yes. Please. Your relationship history."

"Right," said Hanson. "Well, that's easy enough. I'm single."

Harriett nodded. That was what it said on the woman's

file, but people could be lax when it came to updating things. Usually, it just slipped their minds.

But not always.

"And has that been the case since you've been in the job?" asked DS Gaskill.

"I've been single a couple of years, at least," said Hanson.

"That wasn't what I asked," said the DS, and for the first time, Hanson didn't just look sick, or hungover, or tired.

She looked afraid.

"I don't remember. I mean, yeah."

"You mean 'yeah'?" said DS Gaskill.

"Yes. I've been single. Since I've been in the job."

Hanson had recovered now. She was back to looking merely sick.

But there was no doubt in Harriett's mind. That question had put the woman on edge. The payment into her bank account had thrown her, but that last question, that was the one that had Niamh Hanson truly scared.

CHAPTER SEVENTEEN

"PLAY IT," said Carl.

He stood in the team room, daring one of them to add 'Sam', but they were too young. Even Denise was too young.

Had none of these people ever seen *Casablanca*?

Instead, Marcus tapped an icon on his screen, and the voice of William Hall, the man who'd reported the noise in the boatyard, filled the room. They listened in silence as he told the dispatcher what he could hear.

"It's probably nothing," he added, and the dispatcher, Angela Sherman, took down his details and thanked him.

Marcus tapped the pause button.

"Did he really just say that?" he said.

"We all heard it," Harriett replied. "He's an old man. He's trying to be helpful, and then he's worried he's making a fuss about nothing."

"Explains why the dispatcher decided it wasn't a priority, though," Marcus observed.

"No it doesn't," said Carl, and the three of them turned to him. "As Harriett's just pointed out, William Hall is an old man who happens to be walking past the scene. He's a member of the public. His report could be invaluable, but his opinion isn't relevant. It's certainly not something the dispatcher should be taking into account."

Marcus opened his mouth as if to object, then frowned and closed it again, nodding instead.

"The man had just reported hearing what he thought was a scream," Carl continued. "Angela Sherman has questions to answer."

"Call her in?" asked Denise.

"Call her in," agreed Carl. "Information-gathering, again. Nothing formal at this stage. Where are we on the officers who came in today?"

"Grange looks solid," said Marcus.

Carl noticed his eyes flicking towards Denise, and Denise giving a tiny nod.

Good. If Marcus was seeking approval, however subtly, that could only mean he'd been taken down a peg or two. He was a smart lad, no doubt about it, but a cocky one, too.

"Agreed," said Denise. "There's a payment into his current account, but Marcus has looked into that, right?"

"Right. Insurance payout for flooding. Looks legit."

"What about Hanson?" asked Carl, and Denise gave one of those happy little smiles he'd seen her wear just before she delivered a knockout blow in the interview room.

"She's not quite so clear-cut, boss. She's got an unexplained payment."

"Two hundred and fifty pounds," added Harriett.

"Two hundred and fifty pounds," echoed Denise, "so not exactly break-the-bank money, but she can't account for it. But I'm more interested in her personal life."

"Go on," said Carl, and Harriett took up the thread.

"She seemed to freeze up when we asked her about it. Insisted she'd had no relationships over the last couple of years, but when we asked for more information, she looked... Well, she looked scared."

"Rabbit in headlights," added Denise.

"OK. We'll look into that. See what we can find out. I'm not entirely happy about Rashid, the sergeant the two of them report to, either. Obstructive as hell when we spoke to him."

"He was hungover," Harriett pointed out. "As was Hanson. Team drinks last night. Grange was the designated driver, apparently."

"Poor bastard," muttered Marcus.

"A hangover's a convenient excuse for not playing ball, though," Carl said. "And that goes for both of them, Hanson and Rashid. And I know you said Grange looked solid, but he was there in the car. You've got RIPA applications in for the phone data for the three of them, as well as the finances?"

"Yep," said Marcus, then remembered himself, and added, "Sorry. Yes, boss."

"Good. Anything else?"

"Yes," said Denise. "The call Grange and Hanson did attend instead of the boatyard. What do we know about that?"

"Bowness," said Marcus.

"A woman called Claire Saunders," added Harriett. "Twenty-eight years old. Caution for soliciting back in twenty-three, but she's been clean since then."

"I'd like to look into her," said Denise. "And the disturbance she reported. It's always possible that call was deliberately made to divert Hanson and Grange from the boatyard."

Marcus looked sceptical.

"Lot of moving parts there," he pointed out.

"Crimes involving corrupt police officers are rarely straightforward," Carl said. "They're usually complex and well thought-out, and that brings with it lots of moving parts. Of course, we don't know if any officers were involved yet. Chances are they weren't. But the only way to find out is to look into everything. Do it, Denise. Claire Saunders in Bowness, Angela Sherman the dispatcher, and phone records for the three officers involved. Should be enough to keep us busy, right?"

"Right," said the other three, together.

CHAPTER EIGHTEEN

Of all the indignities, thought DC Tom Willis, it was possibly the apron that was the worst.

He sat on the kitchen chair, blindfolded, wearing nothing but an apron that didn't fit. It didn't fit because he'd bought it for Harriett, reckoning she'd look good wearing it, ideally with nothing else, but so far the only person who'd worn it was Tom.

This was what happened when you messed up.

"So, um, is it...?" he began, then stopped, frowning.

"Is it what?" Harriett asked.

"Is it that a tent doesn't have sufficient permanence?"

"Are you asking me or telling me, Detective Constable Willis?"

He waited a moment, trying to picture the book in his mind, all those thousands of black words on white pages.

It was no use. Not like this. All he could do was guess.

"Telling you," he said.

"Correct," Harriett replied. He couldn't see her, but he

could feel her breath on his skin, just below his right ear. He gave a tiny shiver. "Which means?"

"Which means..." He screwed up his face. He could sense her moving in front of him, then just standing there, breathing.

Was she trying to put him off?

"Are you trying to put me off?" he asked.

"Answer the question," she replied, and he squeezed his eyes shut and saw it. The actual page. The actual paragraph. The actual words.

"Which means that it doesn't count as a building in relation to the offence of burglary," he replied, triumphant.

"Very good," said Harriett, her voice further away than he'd expected. He heard the sound of liquid pouring into glass, and then Harriett, drinking.

"Can I have some wine?" he asked.

"Not until you've passed the practice test," she replied. "Now. Jones and Crawford, regulars in their local restaurant, slip out through the toilet window without paying and go home, intending to come back the next day and pay. Are they—?"

"No intention to avoid payment," he said. "No offence under the Theft Act."

"Wrong," Harriett replied.

"What?"

That couldn't be wrong. He'd read the Theft Act. He knew the Theft Act back to front.

"You need to listen to the whole question, DC Willis. Brown, their waitress, runs after them, catches them, and kicks the living shit out of them before they can explain. Jones sustains a broken arm. Crawford has a bleed on the brain. Is there an offence of Grievous or Actual Bodily Harm here? What can we surmise about Brown's intentions, and if Crawford and Jones hadn't drunk six pints each, might they have been able to outrun her?"

Tom laughed.

"Remind me to be careful around Brown," he said, and then he felt her breath, closer, then her mouth on his, and the taste of red wine.

"Delicious," he said.

"I think we'll move this little test to the bedroom," she replied.

"Can I take off the blindfold?" he asked.

"No," she told him, took his hand in hers, and led him away from the chair.

When she'd informed him that they were both going to sit the Sergeant's Exam, he'd objected. He'd never really wanted to progress through the ranks, and he knew the revision would be mind-numbingly dull. Harriett had insisted she had ways of making it more interesting. Tests, forfeits, their own little games.

He hadn't believed her. Not for the first time, he'd been wrong. And, it turned out, losing really wasn't so bad.

But still. He was determined to win their next competition.

It was about time Harriett wore the bloody apron.

DAY FIVE

CHAPTER NINETEEN

If you wanted to create a decent back-story for yourself, Harriett thought, you'd do a better job than Niamh Hanson had.

The last two years of Hanson's life seemed straightforward enough. The usual posts on social media, nights out, holidays, beaches, mountains, short dresses and champagne glasses. And the usual subtleties, the kind of thing you wouldn't notice if you weren't a police officer. Photos cropped in unusual places, names that clearly weren't real, locations obscured.

That was the thing about social media. It turned your life into an open book. And no police officer could tolerate that, not without a few pages ripped out here and there.

But Niamh Hanson had more than a few pages ripped out. Whole chapters were missing, segments of her life from the early twenty-twenties, the later stages of the pandemic and beyond. Months would pass by, followed by a flurry of posts, and then more long absences. Some people were like that; occasional bursts of obsessive posting, followed by long periods of silence and regret. But when that happened, you'd get the comments from friends, 'Good to have you back' or 'Thought you'd closed your account.'

The comments on Niamh Hanson's posts were nothing like that. They were all normal. *Nice top. Wish I could have been there. What a view!*

Which implied that Niamh Hanson had been posting all along, and then deleting, in bulk. The woman had something to hide, and whatever DI Whaley might say about moving parts and complex crimes, this particular bit of hiding hadn't been well thought out at all.

Harriett shut down Hanson's social media and moved on to her bank accounts. Other than the mysterious two hundred and fifty pounds, there was nothing out of place there, but the account that payment had come from, in the name of Winterburn, looked like being a tough nut to crack.

It took an hour, and involved calls to the National Crime Agency, who directed her internally to the National Economic Crime Centre, who told her to call the UK Financial Intelligence Unit downstairs, who referred her back to the Cumbria Police Financial Crime Unit located just twenty miles away in Penrith, before she had her answer, and it was one of those answers that raised a whole gang of fresh questions.

Winterburn wasn't a person.

Winterburn was a company based in the Cayman Islands, which, as well as being a beach paradise, was home to more companies than it had people, the vast majority of them owned outside the country. It attracted one sort of corporate business through its favourable tax regime. It attracted another sort entirely through its rules around secrecy.

Winterburn was a company based in the Cayman Islands, without a UK presence or bank account, and for the time being, that was all she could find out about it. She got back in touch with Paul, her new friend in the Financial Crime Unit, and put in a request for help.

Paul told her he'd get back to her when he had any news. He didn't sound very optimistic about when that might happen, or if it would happen at all.

"Caymans," he said, and sucked in his breath the way she'd seen mechanics do when they were about to tell you your car was on life support. "I'll do what I can."

There was one person who might be able to help, and sooner, and Harriett spent a few minutes pondering the wisdom of making the call before she had a quiet word with herself and just did it.

"Hello?" said Niamh Hanson.

"Niamh? It's Harriett Barnes. From—"

"I remember who you are, DC Barnes. It's not every day I get hauled into PSD."

Probably not. But given the state the woman had been in, Harriett could hardly take her memory for granted.

"I was wondering if you could help me out with a couple of questions."

"For f..." Hanson began, then stopped and gave a long sigh. "OK. What is it?"

"The two hundred and fifty pound payment."

"I told you I didn't know anything about that."

"I was hoping something might have come back to you."

"I didn't know anything then, and I don't know anything now. Is that all?"

"Not quite," said Harriett. "I'd like to ask you again about your private life. Your relationship history. I know you said you'd not been involved over the last two years, but—"

"Is this is disciplinary matter, DC Barnes?" asked Niamh Hanson.

"It's not—"

"Are you instigating a criminal investigation against me?"

Sober and without a hangover, Niamh Hanson was a very different woman from the one Harriett had seen a day earlier.

"We're still just gathering information," Harriett told her.

"In that case, I'd rather not speak to you again," said Niamh Hanson. "And if I do choose to speak to you, I'll ensure I've got either a lawyer or a Police Federation rep with me."

"There's really no need for—" Harriett began, but Hanson had already hung up.

CHAPTER TWENTY

If someone had suggested a few weeks earlier that she might end up missing Isaac Bateman, Lynn wouldn't have known whether to laugh or to cry. She certainly wouldn't have believed them.

But it was weird to be in the team room alone. She was used to being the first one in, to having an hour or two to herself before the DS shambled in and fell into his chair, bringing the reek of stale beer and bacon-flavoured crisps into the team room. And it wasn't like she got much from her interactions with Bateman, who alternated between sullen and smug, not that he had anything to be smug about.

It was lonely being there by herself. And it was hard work trying to work a murder investigation when you were a DC and the only other person involved was DI Woolley.

An updated forensics report had come through overnight, and Lynn had just been through it for the second time, hoping to stumble across something she'd missed, when her phone rang.

"Hello?" she said.

"DC Hedley?"

"Yes, who's this?"

"Stella Berry. Crime Scene Manager."

Lynn sat up. She'd spent plenty of time talking to Keisha and Caroline, the women who made up Stella's team, but she'd never spoken directly with the woman herself.

"Hello," she said. "Erm, how can I help you?"

"Just thought I'd give you a call, see if you've got any questions about the boatyard report."

Lynn glanced at her screen. Six scant pages of text that told her almost nothing, and she wasn't even sure about that.

"Oh," she said.

"Not much to go on, is there?" said Stella, and Lynn breathed a quiet sigh of relief.

"I didn't want to say anything, but—"

"But our report tells you nothing useful at all? I know. That's why I was calling, really. Didn't want you to waste too much time. The problem we've got is the tourists."

"Tourists?" said Lynn.

"Yep. When we find indications of someone's presence, first thing we do is eliminate the obvious. Starting with the police who attended the scene."

"Henniker," said Lynn.

"Exactly. Your man, who vomited in the very bucket the victim probably drowned in. Police, and then the employees, which is six people, all of whom agreed to provide samples. But there are traces from literally dozens more people in the area. It was a busy weekend, the one before the body was found. Lots of people coming in and out, who we don't have contact details for, and whose DNA and prints don't appear on any databases at all. And then you add in the bleach."

"It was used to remove the dead man's tattoo."

"Ouch," said Stella. "I didn't know that. But I've just had a chat with Caroline, and she's convinced it was used to clean up the scene, too. So any traces the killers did leave, chances are they got rid of them, and all we're left with is a bunch of idiots whose idea of fun is falling off a boat on a cold, wet day in the middle of Windermere. I'm assuming they don't know about the sewage."

Lynn shuddered. Surely everyone knew about the sewage?

She thanked Stella for the call, not that it had been much use, but it was nice to have someone to talk to, and it had saved her reading the report a third time.

Someone to talk to.

She dialled DS Bateman's number again. Again, there was no answer, and she left another message.

It was an hour before DI Woolley walked in, asked for news, and enquired as to whether Lynn had heard from Isaac. It must have been depressing, hearing the same negative answers every time, but not as depressing as having to give them.

Lynn missed Isaac Bateman. He was a big, dumb, incompetent sexist, with the sense of humour of a drunk thirteen-year-old and the manners of a feral pig, but somehow, she missed him.

CHAPTER TWENTY-ONE

"Sit down, lad, you're making me uncomfortable."

Carl eased into the seat opposite DCI Branthwaite. More than two years he'd been working for the man, and he'd still not got used to being addressed as 'lad'.

"How's this investigation going, then?" asked the DCI, and Carl outlined what they had so far.

"So," said Branthwaite, when Carl had finished. "What we've got here is a dead man, no actual suspects, and barely a sniff of dirt on the cops involved. Am I right?"

"The PC, sir. Niamh Hanson. There are a couple of holes in her story. A payment that can't be accounted for, and she's playing hardball when we ask her about her personal life. Harriett's convinced she's hiding something."

"And what do you think?"

"I didn't interview her. But Denise did, and she agrees."

Branthwaite nodded.

"She does, does she? Good instincts, that woman. Well, I suppose you'd better keep going, then. But I don't think we're quite ready to assemble the Avengers and go full tilt into the abyss, are we?"

Carl blinked.

"I'm sorry, sir?"

"My little arrangement. Taking over the investigation, running it ourselves. A couple of holes in a PC's story isn't enough for us to do that. Not if it turns out to be nothing more than a judgement call gone wrong. Who's running the murder investigation now, by the way?"

"Jasmine Woolley," Carl said, and watched as a range of expressions crossed the DCI's face in quick succession – incredulity, followed by a mixture of anger and disgust, finally chased away by something like curiosity.

"Jasmine Woolley," echoed the DCI. "There's a woman who couldn't catch a killer if he was standing in front of her with a bloody knife and a signed confession. Maybe we'll end up running this one after all. Big Jo won't want another unsolved murder on her patch. Wouldn't surprise me if she ended up giving us a call."

"The Chief Constable, sir?" asked Carl, and Branthwaite nodded. He'd talked about going to the top to get approval for his 'little arrangement', but Carl hadn't expected Joanne Ainsworth to be personally involved.

No pressure, then.

"She's taken a direct interest," said Branthwaite, as if reading Carl's mind. "Thought it was a good idea, despite others saying otherwise. Jealous little schoolboys, the lot of them. But it means we need a case, sharpish, and we need to solve it. Otherwise the whole thing's going to disappear faster than a lawyer's principles. And we don't want that, do we, Carl?"

"No, sir," said Carl.

"Meanwhile, how've you been bearing up?" asked Branthwaite.

"Fine, sir," he replied.

"That's pigging nonsense, lad," said Branthwaite, and Carl remembered the thing that had always surprised him about the DCI: how perceptive he could be, when the mood took him.

"No, really—"

"Look, Carl, your wife's buggered off to Dorset, and you're on your own moping about the place. Spending too much time by yourself, and probably drinking too much."

"She's not my wife, sir," Carl pointed out.

"Figure of speech, Detective. Now, it's not affecting your work, so I shouldn't really get involved, but you know me, I'm one of those modern, touchy-feely sort of bosses."

Carl stared at the DCI, unsure whether he was joking, and was relieved to see a hint of a smile on his lips.

"Course you are, sir."

"If you want a shoulder to cry on, you can find one somewhere else. But if you want to go t'pub and get yourself drunk with some company, let me know. Any excuse, right?"

"Any excuse," agreed Carl, then thanked the DCI and got up to leave. He'd just put his hand to the door when Branthwaite spoke again.

"I mean it, Carl," he said, and when Carl turned back to him, there was an earnestness to his expression he couldn't remember seeing there before. "You want a drink, you let me know."

"Thank you," said Carl, and walked away.

The DCI was right, of course. He missed Zoe more than he'd have thought he could possibly miss another person.

But a night out drinking with DCI Branthwaite was close to Carl's idea of hell.

CHAPTER TWENTY-TWO

ANGELA SHERMAN STEPPED into the room, eyed the chair opposite Denise and Harriett, and shook her head.

"No," she said. "I don't think so."

"You don't think so?" said Denise.

"This chair. It won't support my back properly. Wouldn't want me injuring myself here, of all places, would you?" said Angela Sherman, and Denise wondered whether that had been a joke, or a threat, or a strange mix of the two. "And anyway, my union rep will need somewhere to sit."

Angela Sherman was a large woman, carrying a large black briefcase, and it wasn't until she stepped forward and to the side that Denise saw the man standing behind her. He was short and slight, barely there at all, nodding at them and then fading into the background again, and if Angela Sherman put Denise in mind of the tank of the same name, her union rep was more like a drone. Silent, almost invisible.

But either could be dangerous.

It took another fifteen minutes to source a suitable chair for Sherman and her briefcase, by which time her rep had introduced himself as Alec, from Unison, and spent fourteen minutes staring silently at his hands. When they finally got started, after a further delay to get Sherman water, 'in a proper glass', Denise wasn't sure why he'd bothered coming at all.

Sherman seemed to have all the answers herself. Most of them before the questions had been asked.

"This is all a bit of a fuss over nothing, isn't it?" she said.

"I'm sorry?" said Harriett.

"Don't be," replied Sherman. "You're just doing your job."

"Can we rewind a little?" Denise suggested. "I'd just like your take on why you categorised William Hall's call as non-priority. I can show you the transcripts if you need to remind yourself of the details."

"That won't be necessary," said Sherman. "I remember it precisely. The man was calling about a noise disturbance. He himself said it was probably nothing."

"He's not really qualified to give that opinion," Harriett observed.

"Well said," agreed Sherman. "That was my call, and yes, it turned out to be wrong, but based on the same information, I'd make the same call again."

"The witness heard screams," Denise pointed out.

"The witness heard something that *might* have been screams," Sherman shot back.

"Either way, weren't you concerned it might have been something more?"

"Was I concerned? Yes, a little. But are you aware of how many incidents take place each night in the area?"

Denise remained silent. She had a feeling she was about to find out.

"There were fifteen calls made within that six-hour period. And only one car available to respond to most of them. As you'll appreciate, that means judgement calls need to be made. I accorded the same priority to this call as the one that the officers chose to attend instead, and I believe that, based on what we knew, I made the right decision, and they made the right decision attending the other call."

"There were no screams reported by Claire Saunders," Harriett pointed out.

"No, but she was a woman on her own. When it came to the boatyard—"

An alarm rang out, and it took Denise a moment to locate its source as the phone sitting on the table in front of Angela Sherman.

"I'm sorry," said Sherman. "I need to take a break every twenty minutes. It's within my reasonable adjustments protocol, you see. Back in five."

She marched out of the room and disappeared, leaving Alec sitting wordlessly in the same space he'd occupied in silence since the interview had begun.

"When it came to the boatyard," she said, five minutes later, sitting down and continuing her sentence as if there hadn't been a break at all, "there was nothing to suggest risk of injury, much less death. If it was anything, I thought it would be minor damage to property."

"Even with the screams?"

"Something that *might* have been screams, yes. You're aware that half the site is still derelict, yes?"

"Yes," agreed Harriett.

"And that half has been in use as a venue for teenage sex, drinking, and drug-taking for as long as I've been in the job.

Meanwhile, I have here a list of callouts in the Ambleside area over the last weck."

She reached into her briefcase and produced a bundle of papers.

"One hundred and thirty-eight incidents. Of these, ninety-four were ultimately characterised as antisocial behaviour. In other words, not a priority. Of those ninety-four, seventy-three involved noise, and of those seventy-three, there were reports of screaming in twenty, and shouting in another thirty-eight."

Harriett seemed about to say something, but Denise could already see it would be pointless. She held up a hand, and Harriett closed her mouth.

"You've made your point, Mrs Sherman," she said. "Thanks for coming in."

Angela Sherman was good-natured enough as she left. Alec remained silent.

"What were you going to say?" asked Denise when they were alone.

"I was just going to probe a bit more. I didn't like her much."

Denise shrugged. She hadn't liked the woman herself, but she'd admired her a little.

"No point. I'm not saying she's clean. I'm just saying she's extremely well-prepared, and if we're going to find anything, we aren't going to find it in this interview, today."

After a moment, Harriett nodded.

It was good, thought Denise, that she still had something to teach the youngsters.

CHAPTER TWENTY-THREE

CLAIRE SAUNDERS HAD a flat in a low-rise block on Quarry Rigg, just a few minutes' stroll from the lake itself. Marcus drove up and down the road a couple of times, noting all the private parking spaces, before giving up and leaving his Citroen on a double yellow line.

He wouldn't be there long.

He'd already checked that she'd be in, so she shouldn't have been surprised at his visit, but he had to wait a minute outside the door to her second-floor flat, and when she finally opened it, she was wearing two towels, one over her hair, the other over everything else.

"Hello," he said, making sure to keep his eyes on her face. "DC Marcus Hosgood. We spoke earlier?"

One hand went to her mouth and then shot quickly out to grab the towel before it fell.

"I'm so sorry," she said. "I forgot. Come through. I'll be with you in a minute."

He followed her through a narrow corridor into a small but well-lit kitchen, and perched on a stool at the counter while she disappeared into what he assumed was the bedroom.

"Make yourself a brew if you fancy," she called out after a minute. "Mine's coffee. Milk, no sugar."

He took the opportunity to look around the room while he boiled the kettle and hunted out cups and coffee, but there wasn't much to see: a decent kitchen in a small but well-maintained flat in a busy corner of the Lake District.

Claire Saunders, the woman who'd been cautioned three years earlier for soliciting, seemed to have done well for herself. According to the limited information Marcus had found, she had a job with a local business now, taking tourists out on the lake in boats, kayaks and paddleboards. No connection with the boatyard, as far as he could see. And it had to be a decent job if she could afford a place like this.

By the time the coffee was done, she was out, dressed in jeans and a white T-shirt, pulling the towel from her head to reveal shoulder-length blonde hair over an oval face with intelligent blue eyes and an apologetic smile.

"You'd think I had the police visiting every day, that I could forget something like that," she said, and he detected a hint of something different in her voice.

"Your accent," he said.

"Geordie. Used to be, at least. Cumbria's been home for more than ten years now. So, this about the cats?"

He passed her a cup.

"Would you like to sit down?" he said, and something in the way he'd said it must have registered as serious, because she took a step back, to a small grey sofa, and almost fell onto it.

"What?" she said. "What's happened?"

"I'm sure it's nothing to worry about," he told her. "But there was an incident."

"Here?" she asked, her eyes wide, and he shook his head.

"In Ambleside. Waterhead, really. In one of the boatyards."

Now she was frowning.

"Read about that in the local paper." She gestured to the counter, where a copy of the *Ambleside Gazette* lay folded by the toaster. "What's that got to do with me?"

"We're just exploring the possibility that the officers who attended your call the other night were being deliberately diverted from the boatyard."

He watched as the frown cleared, and then reappeared, with a hardness to it he hadn't expected on that face.

"Now hang on," she said, the accent suddenly stronger than it had been. "Are you saying I, what? I made it up or something? If you're suggesting—"

"It's nothing like that," he told her. "Please. I know you called because you heard a noise. Can you run through it for me?"

She sat for a moment, staring at him, before her face softened again, and she stood and walked to the large window opposite.

"Here," she said, pointing down towards a fenced-off passageway that ran behind the building. "You see the bins?"

He saw the bins.

"Heard a racket down there. Banging lids. Opening and closing and the like. Thought I could hear laughing, too, but I wasn't sure. Went on so long, I called the police. Thought it might be trouble." She laughed. "Just cats in the end. Or foxes."

"Is it possible there was someone there? What did the officers say when they attended?"

"It was over by then. They just looked around for a minute, helped me pick up a couple of bins, and they were on their way. Like I say, cats or foxes. It's been happening a bit lately. Foxes sound like people sometimes, don't they?"

Marcus nodded. He had no idea what foxes sounded like. He peered to the side, along the passageway and towards the other buildings. This was the sort of place where people might call the police if they heard noises by the bins.

"Hang on," she said. She was sitting on the sofa again, cradling her coffee in her hands, her mouth slightly open. "Are you saying that if those police officers hadn't come here, they might have been able to stop that poor man being killed over in Waterhead?"

He shook his head. "Absolutely not. Almost certainly not. It's just something we have to look into, Ms Saunders."

"Please, do I look like a Ms Saunders? It's Claire."

He returned her smile.

"Claire, then. Is there a security office here, anything like that?"

She nodded.

"They're closed after five. Not usually there anyway, to be honest. Second building on the left, ground floor. You think they might know something?"

"I doubt it, Claire. Look," he said, taking a final sip from his coffee and setting it down on the counter beside the *Ambleside Gazette*. "I hope I haven't alarmed you, and I'm sorry to have wasted your time."

"Never a waste of time having a handsome young man in the flat," she said, and he was glad he was facing away from her, walking towards the door, because he could feel his face turning bright red.

CHAPTER TWENTY-FOUR

"WHAT DID you say your name was?" asked the woman.

"Harriett Barnes."

"And you're calling from where, exactly?"

"Durranhill. Carlisle."

"Right."

There was a long pause, during which Harriett thought she could hear the woman chewing. This was the fifth call she'd made in the last few minutes, and so far, none of them had lasted more than thirty seconds.

"What's in Durranhill, then? And why you asking about Niamh?"

Harriett sighed quietly. The woman she was talking to was Alison Carmichael, a police officer whose record showed her as having worked with Niamh three years earlier, before she'd moved back to her native Essex. The sigh was because she knew what was coming.

"I'm with the Professional Standards Division," she said.

"Fuck off," said Alison Carmichael.

"We just want to—"

"You just want to sniff about, poking your noses in and making life difficult for proper cops who are only trying to get the job done, that's what you want to do. What's Niamh done that's pissed you lot off, then? Farted in church, has she?"

"It's not—"

"I said fuck off," said Alison Carmichael, and ended the call. More than thirty seconds, that one, but only because she hadn't introduced herself as Harriett Barnes *from PSD*. Five former colleagues of Niamh Hanson, and not one of them was willing to speak to Harriett.

Maybe the woman inspired an unusual level of loyalty. More likely, Harriett thought, that PSD was even less popular than she'd assumed.

She looked up to see DI Whaley in the room, watching her.

"No Denise?" he asked.

"She's getting coffee," Harriett told him.

"I caught the end of your call. No luck?"

"No luck with any of them, boss. And when I spoke to Hanson earlier, she—"

"She wasn't playing ball, I know. I read your notes. And the interview with Angela Sherman. That looks like a dead end."

"That's what DS Gaskill thought, boss."

"You don't agree?"

Harriett pursed her lips and tried to think it through. The DS had been right about the interview: whatever else they asked Sherman, she wasn't going to crack.

"I'm not sure, boss. But if we're going to follow up on anyone, I think Hanson's the person to be looking at. And if we are going to follow up on her, we might have to call her in."

There was a brief buzzing noise nearby.

"Formally?" asked the DI.

"Yes, boss. We could bring her in on misconduct and take it from there."

"I'll have a think," said Carl, then stopped and stared at her. "Not going to answer that?" he asked, and Harriett realised the sound she'd heard was the ringing of her own phone. With an embarrassed smile, she picked it up and answered.

"Harriett Barnes?"

"Hello." The voice was male, and vaguely familiar.

"Can I help you?"

The man gave a slight laugh.

"I hope so. Look, I feel a bit of an idiot, calling you. We only met for a few seconds yesterday, but—"

"Stephen Grange," she said, the face finally coming to her, followed an instant later by the name.

It had been quite the face, she remembered.

"Ah, good. You remember me."

"What can I do for you?" she asked.

"Well, I just... I don't know. The people who interviewed me. Your DS, Gaskill, isn't it? And that Marcus bloke. I didn't hit it off with them. And I saw your details on the system, and I thought, maybe I could speak to you."

"Right." She looked up at the DI, who was watching her carefully. "What would you like to speak to me about, PC Grange?"

"Look, do you think I could come in, maybe? I've got some concerns. I'm not sure I... When I was being interviewed, by your colleagues, I think I was a bit thrown. There are other things."

"You're always welcome to come in," she told him.

"But I don't really want to talk to them. I want to talk to you. Would that be OK?"

Harriett tapped on her screen and pulled open her calendar.

"I can do that. How are you set for tomorrow?"

"I was wondering if you might be around today?"

The calendar was empty.

"Today, when?"

"Well, I'm sort of outside your building now, as it happens. If you've got a few minutes..."

"Now," she said. "Hang on."

The DI was nodding. He'd heard it all, or enough to make sense of it.

"Give me ten minutes, and I'll come and find you in reception. OK?"

"I look forward to it, DC Barnes," said Grange, and ended the call.

CHAPTER TWENTY-FIVE

THE SECURITY OFFICE in the second building on the left was closed when Marcus went to investigate, with a note on the door advising residents to ring 999 in the event of an emergency. They'd probably have thought of that for themselves, but it didn't hurt to remind them.

There was another note, saying, 'Back in five minutes', so instead of heading back to Carlisle, he thought he'd spend a few minutes in the passageway with the bins.

Easier said than done. There was a gate leading to it, locked with a combination padlock. He thought about calling Claire again, or popping upstairs to ask her for the code, but decided to hop over the fence instead, using a crossbeam for his foot and resting briefly on top before letting himself down carefully, his sleeves over his hands to prevent splinters.

It was simple enough, but after thirty seconds of looking around, he wasn't sure it had been worth it. There were bins and boxes there, grey for general waste and red for recycling, most of them almost full. In the time since Claire Saunders had called the police, dozens of people might have come through here.

That took thirty seconds. It was another thirty before he realised the gate was still locked, with Marcus on the inside and the padlock on the outside, and there was no crossbeam for his foot on this side. He was pondering whether to call Claire after all, and hoping he wouldn't have to, when he heard a voice.

"Oi!" it said.

He looked up to see a man's head in the nearest window.

"Me?" said Marcus.

"Yeah. I saw you jump the fence. What are you playing at?"

Marcus pulled out his warrant card. The man was too far away to see it properly, but he'd obviously watched enough TV to realise what it was.

"Mind letting me out?" asked Marcus.

The gate was open two minutes later. The man who'd released him was a forty-five-year-old plumber called Gaz, who seemed more than happy to answer questions without asking any of his own.

That made a pleasant change.

"Yeah," said Gaz. "We've had a bit of trouble lately. Dunno if it's foxes or cats. Linda on the top floor says it's feral teenagers, but she's got a thing about feral teenagers. Jealous of anyone under the age of eighty, she is."

"You don't think it's kids, then?"

"If it was kids, they'd have left empty bottles, wouldn't they?"

Marcus examined the ground. There was no sign of any empty bottles. They might have come here and got drunk and thrown them in the recycling, but it wasn't likely. And it wasn't exactly a prime place for a drink, either.

"Good point."

"You want to have a word with Claire. She's already been onto your lot about it."

"I know," said Marcus. "I've been to see her."

He thanked Gaz, and when he returned to the security office, its occupant was unlocking the door.

"Hello," he said, and introduced himself.

Doreen Gulliver was in her late fifties, with dyed red hair and thick glasses that made her look both younger and permanently confused.

"Yeah," she said, after he'd explained why he was there. "They're always complaining about that. Bins being attacked. Who'd attack your bins?"

"Always complaining? How long has this been going on?"

"Few days," she said. "Not sure."

"Do you have a record of the complaints?" he asked, trying to sound more patient than he felt.

"Hang on," she said, trudging sullenly over to a filing cabinet, and producing a ring binder, which she proceeded to consult with such excruciating slowness Marcus wasn't sure the glasses worked at all.

"First complaint was four days ago. About the night before. Then every bloody night since."

"And has this happened before?"

"I dunno," she said. "Only been working here a couple of months."

Doreen Gulliver might have been the fount of all knowledge, but getting it out of her was surely more trouble than it was worth.

But there was one thing she might be able to help with.

"I noticed cameras on the side of the building. Is that your CCTV?" he asked.

"Yeah."

"Is it working?"

"Yeah."

"Where are the screens?"

"Dunno," she said. "We don't watch it live. Gets recorded. For the records."

Marcus felt a throbbing in his temple, and realised he'd been forcing a smile for the last few minutes.

"And do you have access to these recordings?" he asked.

"Yeah."

"Can I have them?"

"They're not here," she said.

It took another fifteen minutes to establish that the recordings went directly to head office 'on the broadband', as Doreen put it, and that she couldn't produce them herself.

"I'll have to put a request in," she said. "I'll need your name and number. Signature. Hang on."

Ten more minutes passed as she located the form, and then watched as he filled it in.

"I'll get this off to head office. They'll get back to you directly," she told him, and he thanked her and left.

He wouldn't hold his breath.

CHAPTER TWENTY-SIX

Denise returned from the canteen to find Harriett and the DI heading out of the team room together.

"What's up?"

"Stephen Grange has come in," said Harriett. "Wants to talk to us."

"Us?"

DI Whaley grinned at her.

"Not you, Denise. Specifically, not you or Marcus. Think he fancies his chances with Harriett here."

"And you're going along to chaperone, are you?" asked Denise.

"Can't leave the youngsters alone together, can we?"

Back in the team room, she pondered that; not the nonsense about Grange fancying his chances with Harriett, but the idea that he'd come in and ask to speak to anyone except the people who'd interviewed him. She ran back through the interview in her mind.

She hadn't played rough, had she? Marcus had started gently and then gone in hard with his questions about the insurance payment, but between them, they'd been reasonable enough. Stephen Grange could have no complaints.

So why didn't he want to talk to her again?

Whatever he had to say, it probably wouldn't take long, so she spent a few minutes running through everything she could find out about Angela Sherman. The dispatcher hadn't seen fit to release her financial or call information, but they hadn't pushed on that, and the fact that she was keeping it to herself didn't mean anything. Not when it came to someone who was so thoroughly aware of her rights.

Looking through the little information Denise did have, she could see that rights were something Angela Sherman was something of an expert on. It was no wonder Alec from Unison hadn't had much to say. If there had been anything, Angela could have said it for him. She was a vocal campaigner for workers' rights, disability rights, and, a little further back, the rights of the victims of police brutality, which said something for the woman, given who she worked for.

She'd given the impression of someone keen to protect herself, but now Denise thought perhaps she'd misjudged her. She was keen to protect everyone, and if it made her an annoying person to interview, that was hardly the worst price you could pay.

Denise closed the file as her system pinged with a fresh notification: the data from the phones was coming through. Grange, Hanson, and Rashid.

In normal circumstances, this would be something she'd have left to Marcus or Harriett, but Marcus and Harriett weren't there. Hanson and Rashid could wait.

But Grange was in the building. If there was anything worth following up in his data, now would be the perfect time to do it, especially when he'd come in of his own accord and wouldn't be expecting anything to come back at him. Denise's head was hurting, but that didn't matter, because her back was hurting more.

She bent over her screen and ran through the information.

Grange had a work phone and a separate personal phone. Nothing unusual there; so did Denise. His work phone was rarely used. His personal phone was more active, and it included messages to and from a bewildering number of people who were referred to in his contacts by short acronyms and nicknames that would have taken years to decipher.

But the content was plain enough, and so innocuous and unsurprising that Denise found herself almost hoping she'd come across something violent or controversial as she waded through it. She didn't. Even the dating apps were vanilla.

Stephen Grange was exactly what he appeared to be: a moderately intelligent, relatively unambitious police constable who was both good-looking and aware of the fact. He enjoyed a night out, but didn't drink, had friends he'd stayed in touch with from school, college and police training, and relationships that lasted a few months at most and ended without acrimony.

If it hadn't been for his face, Denise thought, Stephen Grange would have been one of the most boring people she'd ever met. And it was Harriett and the DI in with him now instead of her.

She smiled to herself as she closed the file and rubbed at her back. If there was one thing worse than going through Grange's data, it would have been sitting in a room with him.

CHAPTER TWENTY-SEVEN

"Ah, right," said Stephen Grange, as he took in the second figure sitting opposite him.

"You weren't expecting the welcoming committee," Carl said.

"No, it's fine," replied Grange, with a smile that didn't quite reach his eyes.

"You said you didn't want to speak to the people who interviewed you yesterday," Harriett reminded him. "DI Whaley here wasn't one of them."

"Yes. Of course."

Carl almost felt sorry for the man. He'd clearly hoped for a few minutes alone with Harriett Barnes.

But this was a live investigation, not a nightclub. What Grange had hoped for didn't matter. And besides, Harriett Barnes wasn't single.

Not that that was any of Carl's business.

"So, Stephen – it's OK if I call you Stephen?"

Grange nodded, and Carl continued.

"You told Harriett you had some concerns. Is that right?"

"Right," agreed Grange, and there was a short silence.

"And?" prompted Harriett.

"Oh, yes. Sorry. It's just... It all seemed natural at the time, but the more I think about it, the more concerned I am that we didn't stop at the boatyard."

"You asked PC Hanson about that, according to the transcript. She said not to bother. You didn't seem to put up much of an argument."

Grange nodded.

"That's right. I didn't. And maybe I should have done. I'm not sure why Niamh said that. I'm not sure, now, why we didn't stop."

"Right." Carl exchanged a brief glance with Harriett. As fresh information went, this was weak.

"There's something else, though," said Grange, sitting forward with the air of someone who knew he'd disappointed them and wanted to make up for it.

"Yes?" asked Carl.

"I should have said yesterday. But I didn't remember."

Come on, man. Get to it.

"Yes?" repeated Carl, his teeth now gritted.

"Niamh took a call on her phone. A few minutes before the boatyard shout."

That *was* new information. There was another glance at Harriett, who gave the tiniest shake of her head, which Carl took to mean that the phone data wasn't in yet.

"Tell us about this call, Stephen," said Carl.

"I don't know who it was. I just remember that it was brief, and Niamh sounded... Well, she sounded pissed off, to be honest. I can say that in here, can't I?"

"You can say whatever you want, Stephen. As long as it's

the truth. Can you remember anything PC Hanson actually said?"

Grange closed his eyes and screwed up his face, tilting his head towards the ceiling, and Carl was relieved to see that in this particular pose, he wasn't so pretty after all.

"Yes. She said, 'Fine. I'll deal with it.'"

"'Fine. I'll deal with it'," repeated Harriett, and Grange nodded again.

"I'm sorry. It didn't last more than a minute or so. She answered. She must have said something else, but I don't remember what. And then she was just listening until she said that, and then she ended the call. Then, a few minutes later, we heard about the boatyard."

"Right. Thank you. We'll look into that," said Carl. "Is there anything else you can tell us?"

Grange thought for a moment, then shook his head.

"I'm sorry," he said.

"Actually," said Harriett, and Carl turned to her, surprised. "While you're here, maybe you could help us learn a little more about PC Hanson."

Clever, thought Carl. The man had already taken the first step in ratting out his partner. If he was going to take a second, now was the perfect moment to give him a little prod. Strike while the iron was hot.

"What do you mean?" asked Grange, a note of wariness entering his voice. "She's a good person, Niamh."

"You've just come in here to report your concerns. You've told us about a mysterious phone call. If you had one hundred per cent faith in her, you wouldn't be here." Carl spoke seriously, then softened his tone as he went on. "And look, chances are, all this is nothing. These are all informal conversations. You know how things work, Stephen. If we had any major issues here, there would be misconduct notices and formal hearings. All we want to do is rule out anything dodgy, and then we can all get on with our lives. But we can't do that until we know everything, so do yourself a favour, listen to what my colleague's asking you, and see if you can help her out."

Grange nodded. "OK," he said.

Harriett smiled. "We're trying to get to grips with Niamh's personal life. Her former relationships, friends, social life, that sort of thing, and between us, she's not been particularly forthcoming. If you could shed any light on that part of her life, particularly going back more than two years, that might be helpful."

Grange shrugged.

"I don't know her that well, I'm afraid. And I didn't really know her at all two years ago. Have you tried talking to her friends? Colleagues from before, maybe?"

"Yes," said Harriett. "The trouble with friends is that they can have a misplaced sense of loyalty."

And the trouble with colleagues, Carl thought, was that they didn't want to tell you a thing the moment they learned you were PSD.

Grange nodded.

"Not all of them," he said.

"I'm sorry?" asked Harriett.

"Loyalty. Not all of them are going to be loyal," Grange said.

Carl frowned, but said nothing.

Harriett waited, and after a minute, Grange went on.

"Millie Tennant," he said. "Speak to Millie Tennant."

CHAPTER TWENTY-EIGHT

AARON KEYES PUSHED OPEN the door of the Wainwrights' Inn, and took a moment, just standing there, breathing it in – the food and the beer and the drinkers – before stepping inside and letting the door fall shut behind him.

If it felt like coming home, that was because it *was* coming home.

It was quiet tonight. Trish Newman sat at a table with a couple of friends Aaron didn't recognise, half a brewery's worth of empties in front of them, laughing loudly at something one of them had said. There were two more tables with people at them Aaron didn't know. Tourists, he thought.

No sign of Bateman.

Eliot was standing behind the bar, drying a glass. He nodded at Aaron, then looked away. Aaron hadn't been in here for months, but that was the kind of place it was. People were friendly, if you wanted them to be. If you wanted to be left to yourself, you could do that, too.

Aaron ordered half a pint of Wainwright Gold and slipped into a corner, half hidden from the rest of the room by slate pillars, but with a clear view of the door. He'd be driving back tonight, so it would be non-alcoholic beers later, but he'd allow himself this one while he waited.

He'd waited twenty minutes before Trish spotted him and called out his name, and he had to go and chat to her, and meet her friends, and spend a few minutes grinning at their drunken jokes and shooting anxious glances at the door, but there was still no sign of Bateman.

The man was late.

He excused himself and stepped outside, into the cold and the light rain, to dial Bateman's number, but it went to voicemail.

Back inside, enveloped in warmth and darkness, he ordered a pint of non-alcoholic beer and returned to the table he'd been sitting at earlier. He gave it twenty more minutes, tried Bateman again, and wondered what he should do next.

The man had always been unreliable. It was possible he'd changed his mind, but it was more likely he'd just forgotten. Or... What was it Lynn Hedley had said? He'd been acting strange. And then he'd disappeared. Gone off sick.

Chances were, the man was just fighting off the mother of all hangovers.

Aaron toyed with the idea of ordering another drink, of sitting at the table with Trish and her friends, ordering another two or three, leaving the car here and walking round to his parents' house and staying there. For a long moment, maybe thirty seconds, he considered it, and then he reminded himself that he was a grown man with a husband and a daughter, a responsible job as a DI with a team working for him, and getting drunk and crashing out at your parents' house on a whim was something he'd left behind a long time ago.

But that was the thing about coming back to the place you'd grown up in. Twenty years could disappear in a heartbeat.

He swallowed down the rest of his non-alcoholic beer, brought the glass back to the bar, nodded at Eliot and said goodbye to Trish on the way out.

Bateman wasn't coming. It was time to go home.

DAY SIX

CHAPTER TWENTY-NINE

TROUGHTON GILL WOULD HAVE BEEN a river, once, but even after months of rain it was little more than a ravine now, a few inches of water burbling listlessly at its bottom as it made it way south from near Rydal Water to the River Brathay between Clappersgate and Skelwith Bridge. It was a walk, or a short drive, from where Lynn had lived most of her life, but she hadn't realised it went as far north as it did, and wasn't sure she'd ever been here.

She hadn't realised a man could drown in just a few inches of water, either. It was barely four in the morning and still dark, but it was already a day when she was learning more than she was comfortable with.

She'd taken the call forty minutes earlier, thrown on clothes, and rushed out of the house, not stopping to think until she'd pulled up by the flashing lights of a patrol car. Only then did she find herself wondering why a detective constable had been woken in the middle of the night to attend what looked like a routine road traffic accident.

Now she knew.

The car was pointing downwards and tilted onto one side, its nose and much of the driver's side lying in those few inches of water. A red MG. She knew that car.

Isaac Bateman's pride and joy.

She scrambled down as far as she could get and shone her torch in through the nearside window. There was a man in there, suspended by his seatbelt, his face turned away from hers, but she could see the jacket, the stupid lightweight denim thing he always wore.

Isaac Bateman.

"He must have lost control on this bend," she heard. It took a moment for the words to take shape and make sense, a moment more for her even to understand who was speaking.

Sergeant Fraser.

She turned to see him shining his torch upwards, away from the ravine.

It wasn't much more than a track, barely noticeable a mile back where it left the tiny winding farm road that led up into the hills from Ambleside. She couldn't see anyone driving fast enough on it to lose control. Maybe he'd just lost focus, his attention wandering for as long as it took to leave the track and plummet into the ravine.

"Who found it?" she asked.

"Farmer. No one uses this track, he said. Blind luck that he happened to be passing. And the car's a little way off it anyway. You could drive past here day or night and you probably wouldn't notice it."

"How come the farmer did?"

"More blind luck. He stopped to light a cigarette, thought he saw something sticking up where the land dips into the ravine. Turned out to be the last inch or so of the car."

She looked back at the car, stared at it for long enough that it seemed to lose all meaning. She didn't know how much time had passed when she felt an arm fall lightly onto her shoulder and turned to see Fraser standing beside her.

"You OK, Lynn?" he asked.

She nodded, but she wasn't sure she was.

"I can't believe it," he continued. "I mean, I know he wasn't everyone's best friend, but he was one of us. We worked with him. You... I'm sorry, Lynn. You sure you're OK?"

She nodded again. She couldn't believe it either.

"He's been off work," she said. "Said he wasn't well. And he was acting weird."

Fraser gave a tiny laugh. "When wasn't he?"

She smiled, remembering Bateman, his bacon crisps and his lunchtime beers, and the way he always revved up before he pulled away from the kerb, and then she felt the smile freeze on her face.

"Seal off the scene, Ben," she said.

"What? Why?"

"Seal it off. I'm calling in forensics."

She turned to see him shaking his head.

"I know it's a shock, Lynn. It's someone we know. But it's an RTC. We don't need to—"

"Isaac was many things," she said. "He was unbearable to work with, and when he bothered to turn up, he wasn't very good at his job—"

"Hang on, Lynn. I know he—"

"But for all his faults, Isaac Bateman was an excellent driver." She pointed at the car. "He drove this thing like it was his worst enemy, forced it to do things it wasn't built to do, like driving it up here, but for all he put it through, there wasn't a scratch on it. In a car, I'd have trusted him with my life," she said. "I might have died from the smell, but we wouldn't have ended up in a ravine. Not without someone helping us get there."

"You sure about this, Lynn?" asked Fraser.

"Seal it off, Ben. Seal the place off."

CHAPTER THIRTY

By the time Denise walked in, Harriett Barnes was already at her desk, leaving a message in a quiet, serious voice.

"Who's Millie Tennant?" asked Denise when Harriett had finished.

The younger woman looked at her blankly.

"The woman you just left a message for," she said.

"Oh, right. Grange said she was a friend of Niamh Hanson's. Someone who might actually be willing to talk to us. I tried her last night, got no answer. Thought I'd leave a message this time."

"Anything else useful from Grange?"

Harriett started to shrug, then stopped, and nodded instead.

"He's having second thoughts about Hanson's decision not to stop at the boatyard."

"Both of their decisions, really," Denise pointed out.

"Sort of. But the way the conversation went, he's asking and she's telling. Yes, he could have argued the point. But it was her point in the first place."

"Right." Denise couldn't help feeling a little disappointed. An old friend of Hanson's, who no doubt had an axe to grind, and some second thoughts. It didn't amount to much. "Anything else?"

"Yes." Harriett grinned. "Hanson took a phone call a few minutes before the shout came through. Grange doesn't know who she was talking to, but she didn't sound happy. Apparently it was brief, and she didn't say much more than 'Fine. I'll deal with it.'"

"'Fine. I'll deal with it,'" repeated Denise.

"Yup."

"Better get checking, then. I've been through Grange's phone data. I'll take Hanson's. You can have Rashid."

The grin didn't shift from Harriett's face, which was impressive, given she'd just been invited to sort through the call and text history of someone who almost certainly had no connection with the case. Denise brought up the Hanson file, and cursed loudly.

The woman liked using the phone, that much was clear. There were hundreds of calls, to and from both her work and personal phones.

"More than you thought?" asked Harriett, and Denise glanced over at the DC's screen.

Barely anything on it.

"I took a quick look first thing," Harriett continued. "Had a feeling you'd want these looked at. Samir Rashid doesn't make many calls, does he?"

No wonder the woman was smiling. Denise took a deep breath, and set to it. Just two pills this morning, and she wasn't feeling too bad.

Five minutes later, Harriett Barnes gave a loud "Oh", and came and stood by Denise's desk.

"What is it?" asked Denise, and Harriett leaned forward, tracing her fingers down the column on the left of Denise's screen, displaying the call times.

"There," she said. "That's got to be it."

It was an incoming call, just four minutes before Angela Sherman had been in touch about the boatyard.

"Times match what Grange said," confirmed Denise, then watched as Harriett's finger slid to the right, along the row, to the data on the caller. She expected to see a number there; there would only be a name if the caller was on the system already, and that was only likely if...

"Oh," she said, echoing Harriett's exclamation of a moment earlier.

There was a name, as well as a number, and the name was Samir Rashid.

"Comes up on his log, too," said Harriett. "Rashid called Hanson just before the boatyard shout came in."

"Bloody hell," said Denise, and then her phone rang. She checked the display, hoping it would be something she could ignore.

Aaron Keyes.

No doubt he wanted to know how she was getting on and give her grief for not spending enough time with the psychiatrist, but just because that had worked for Aaron Keyes, it didn't mean it would work for her. Her finger hovered over the red button to reject the call, and then slipped to the green and tapped.

"Aaron," she said. "Got a lot on here, so yes, I'm fine, yes, I'm seeing Dr Filey soon, and no, I don't need to have a long chat."

"We need to talk," he said.

"I've just told you, I don't—"

"Not about you. You need to get Branthwaite involved. This is..."

He was breathing hard, she realised.

"Are you OK, Aaron?" she asked.

"Yeah. No. I don't know. I've just heard from Lynn Hedley."

She waited a beat for him to explain, but he didn't.

"You're going to have to tell me who Lynn Hedley is, Aaron."

"Sorry. DC at Langdale. Remember, I spoke to you, asked if you'd heard anything about the place. There was an old colleague who wanted to come and talk to you, but he wanted to meet up with me first."

"Yes. Bateman, you said. Isaac Bateman. I'd never heard of him."

"You'll be hearing a lot more of him in the near future," Aaron replied. "His body's just been found in his car. And Lynn's convinced it's not an accident."

CHAPTER THIRTY-ONE

PSD INVESTIGATIONS WERE SLOW, steady things, in the usual course of events. They'd plod their way towards a resolution, and either they'd get there in the end, or everyone would just go back to their jobs and forget about it.

But the pace was different now DCI Branthwaite's 'little arrangement' was in place. Things were moving fast. It was a full team meeting, everyone in the team room, the DCI included, and Aaron Keyes's face looming at them from the big screen that adorned the wall furthest from the door.

Carl had only been in ten minutes. A lot could happen in a short time.

"Everyone here?"

The DCI looked around, meeting eyes, getting nods from the room and from the screen. Behind Aaron, Carl could see Harriet's boyfriend Tom Willis, and Nina Kapoor. There was another face he didn't recognise, but there would be time for introductions later. Phil from IT had already been in to fix a glitch on the big screen, and Jeff, his equivalent at the Hub, had been forced to do the same thing at Aaron's end.

"Here's where we are," said Branthwaite. "And jump in if I get anything wrong. Isaac Bateman, DS at Langdale, called DI Keyes here a couple of days ago to sound him out about coming in to talk to PSD."

"Three days," said Aaron, on the screen.

"Three days. He said it was a local matter, and it was delicate. Right?"

"Right," agreed Aaron.

"Bateman's part of the team investigating the boatyard murder under Jasmine Woolley. He's an old friend of yours, yes?"

"I wouldn't say friend, sir," Aaron replied.

"Potato, potahto. You know the man. So, he's supposed to be looking into the boatyard murder, he wants to see Aaron here about talking to PSD on a delicate local matter. And then he goes off sick and doesn't turn up for work for three days. Aaron arranged to meet him at the Wainwrights' Inn last night, and he didn't show up. Yes?"

"Yes," said Aaron.

"Until this morning when he finally does, upside down in his car in a shallow ravine on the edge of Loughrigg Fell. His DC is on the scene a few hours later. Lynn Begley."

"Hedley, sir," said Aaron.

"Lynn Hedley. She's convinced it's foul play. Gets the scene sealed off, which shouldn't be too difficult given no one's been up there for the last week except Isaac Bateman, a farmer, and a bunch of sheep. Forensics are on the scene. And Aaron tells me their initial view is that Hedley's spot on. Bateman was murdered before being put back in his car, which was then driven into the ravine."

There was a short silence, during which the DCI's eyes ranged the room.

"Everyone still with me?" he asked.

Everyone nodded.

"Given where Bateman worked, I believe it's likely this is connected to our existing investigation. I've spoken to the powers that be, and they're willing to indulge this belief of mine. Which means..." He stopped and clapped his hands, once, loudly. "Which means that we're in business, ladies and gentlemen. I've invoked my new powers, and I'm putting together the investigative team for *both* murders, the boat-yard one, and DS Bateman. Pending clearance from Detective Superintendent Carnegie, Aaron here has agreed to work with us. And I understand you'll be sending young Tom Willis over to help out."

"Hello," said Tom.

Carl saw a smile form on Harriett's face, then disappear as she realised everyone was looking at her.

"We've been granted the use of Langdale Station as required. We've also been granted the assistance of DC Begley—"

"Hedley," said Aaron.

"Hedley, who will remain at Langdale and help us from there. I expect Jasmine Woolley and half of Cumbria Police are going to be up in arms about this, and normally I wouldn't give a sheep's reproductive organs what they think, but we need to make this work or we won't get another chance to do it. You all understand?"

There were murmurs of agreement from the room.

"Do you understand?" said Branthwaite, louder this time, and the response came back stronger.

"Good. You're great cops, all of you, and you've got Aaron here to help you out. No one's put away more killers in this county than his team has in the last two years, so I expect you to hit the ground running, do everything he suggests, and learn fast. And remember, whatever anyone says, however they try to sidetrack you, this *is* a PSD matter. There's police involvement in both murders, whichever way you look at it. You're entitled to be running this case, you will run this case, and you will solve it. Got it?"

"Got it," said Aaron. His response was echoed by the others.

"Good," said Branthwaite. "Now get to work."

CHAPTER THIRTY-TWO

Two women stood at the door to the stone cottage in the heart of Chapel Stile, both of them in white forensic suits, talking together.

"I mean," said one of them, "he was a prick. But I wouldn't have wished him dead."

Marcus stepped up to the one who'd spoken, hand outstretched.

"Lynn Hedley?" he asked.

"That's her." The woman gestured to her companion. "And I'm not gonna shake your bloody hand, am I?" she added, gesturing to her gloves and suit.

"Sorry." Marcus turned to the other woman. "I'm Marcus, DC Hosgood, from PSD."

He saw a smile form behind the second woman's eyes, and decided at once that he liked Lynn Hedley better than the woman he'd just spoken to.

"Don't mind Keisha," she said. "She's like that with everyone. Good to meet you, Marcus."

He felt their eyes on him as he donned his own forensic

suit, and found himself clumsier than usual. He hadn't done this in a while, hadn't expected he'd be doing it at all in PSD. It took nearly five minutes to get kitted out.

"About time," said Keisha. "We nearly died of old age waiting for you, and who'd have searched the house then, eh?"

She hadn't bothered introducing herself, but Marcus knew her by reputation. Keisha Middleton. Only in the CSI team a year or so, but already known across Cumbria as someone you didn't want to get on the wrong side of.

The picture-book impression he'd got from the attractive exterior of the cottage lasted as long as it took him to step into the cramped entrance hall and look around.

The place was a dump. There were letters and fliers piling up by the front door, and smudges of what looked like motor oil on walls that had once been painted white but now seemed unable to decide between grey and brown. Through the open door that led to the living room, between the plastic plates Keisha had set down, he could see a floor littered with pizza boxes and beer cans, and dirty dishes covering most of the surfaces, including a stained two-seater sofa upholstered in an alarming shade of crimson.

There was something foul in the air, something that had Marcus convinced he'd turn and find a rotting corpse at any moment, but if there was one in the room, it was hidden under kebab cartons and empty crisp packets.

"Jesus," he said.

"Not much sign of him here," Keisha shot back.

DS Isaac Bateman's death might have been a mystery, but there was little doubt about the way he'd lived. Squalor, alleviated by fast food and beer. Planting his feet carefully on the plates, Marcus followed the two women through the living room into a kitchen that didn't look like it had been cooked in this side of the millennium.

"Could take a while," said Keisha. "We'll go and see if there's anything obvious upstairs, and then start the boring work."

There was a part of Marcus that felt the need to take charge. No one here outranked him, after all, and the DCI had stressed that this was a PSD case. But he had the sense that an argument with Keisha Middleton wouldn't end well. Not for him, at least.

"OK," he said, and started towards the rear staircase.

"Not you," said Keisha, and he turned. It was a good thing she was wearing a mask, because he couldn't be sure whether that was a sneer she was directing his way, and that meant he could convince himself it wasn't.

"Sorry?"

"Not enough room for all of us here, and I've worked with Lynn before. She knows not to get in my way. Why don't you go and talk to the neighbours or something?"

He opened his mouth to protest, then saw a warning in Lynn's eyes and remembered again what he'd heard about Keisha.

"OK," he said again, and headed outside. At least he could take off his forensic suit without them watching him and judging how long it took.

The neighbours were no use. There were three houses on Bateman's side of the road, with another four in a terrace on the other side, and a quick search told Marcus that there were no doorbell cameras or unregistered CCTV cameras nearby. Of the six neighbours, three weren't in, two didn't know who Isaac Bateman was, despite having lived opposite him for a combined eighteen years, and the other one didn't know him well enough to offer an opinion beyond 'arsehole'.

"Why do you say that?" asked Marcus.

"Did you know him?" said the woman, a black-haired forty-something with a look of infinite weariness on her face.

"No," Marcus acknowledged.

"Well, if you'd woken up first thing every Sunday morning to that prick tinkering with his bloody engine and revving the thing until it shook the slates from Holy Trinity, you might not have liked him much either. Dead then, is he?"

"Erm, yes," Marcus said.

"C'est la vie," said the woman. "Or not, I suppose. Anyway, no, I didn't know him well. Prick kept himself to himself."

"Have you noticed anyone hanging around?"

"Nope." She shook her head. "Not a soul. If anyone was after him, I'd imagine the smell probably kept them away. You could always tell if Bateman had opened his door, because the whole road stank of stale beer and bacon crisps."

That was it. The foul thing he'd sensed in the air in Bateman's house. He'd thought it might be a rotting corpse at first. But no.

Just stale beer and bacon crisps.

CHAPTER THIRTY-THREE

THE PATHOLOGIST WAS ALREADY THERE when Harriett arrived, talking with Caroline Deane from the CSI team, and directing his assistant around the side of the car so they could prepare to remove Bateman's body.

"Ah, good," he called, spotting her approach. "I wanted to talk through a couple of things with you and Caroline before we take this fellow back to Carlisle."

"You're doing the post-mortem at the Cumberland Infirmary?" asked Harriett. For as long as she'd known Dr Robertson, he'd carried them out in Whitehaven.

"I'm flexible," replied the pathologist. "A little like DS Bateman here," he added, gesturing at the car.

Harriett frowned.

"I'm sorry?"

"Rigor mortis. There isn't any. I can't tell you precisely when your colleague died, you'll have to look into his recent movements for that, but I can tell you it was well over twenty-four hours ago. This is Roberta, by the way." He gestured towards his assistant, who was currently hidden by the car.

"Rebecca," said a voice from behind the car.

"Same thing," replied Dr Robertson. "She's kindly volunteered to stand ankle deep in cold running water while we work out what to do with our friend inside."

Harriett had met Dr Robertson before. He made a habit of attending crime scenes, something every other pathologist had stopped doing years earlier. He was a helpful man, unless you were working for him, in which case he made a point of forgetting your name and forcing you to do things like stand in cold running water for hours on end while he chatted to colleagues. It was a wonder that the man hadn't been on the wrong end of a dozen employment tribunals. He had to be extremely good at his job. And maybe he was nicer in private.

"Can you tell me anything at this point?" Harriett asked. If they couldn't, then it had been a waste of time turning up.

"Yes." The pathologist turned to her, his expression suddenly serious. "From what I've seen so far, it's clear this man didn't drown, and didn't die in the crash, either. Even from here, you can see signs that he was smashed over the head with a blunt object, repeatedly, in the same place. Care to take a look?"

"I'll take your word for it," Harriett told him. She'd seen her share of dead bodies. It wasn't that she was squeamish. But unless there was a good reason for it, there was no need for her to stare at another one. And the ravine, shallow as it was, had tiny, barely visible tributaries snaking down to feed it. In the short time she'd been there, Harriet had already managed to soak her shoes. No need to get them even wetter.

"A metal object, I suspect," said Dr Robertson. "But

either way, the pattern of the injuries implies this wasn't the result of an accident."

"So, what, we think he was attacked, killed, then put in his car, which was driven into the river?"

"That's the most plausible explanation," agreed Caroline Deane. "And there's another thing. These injuries. They'd have caused significant spatter."

Harriett nodded. It was an unfortunate word, 'spatter'. For most people, it conjured up images of mishaps with paintbrushes or amusing baking disasters.

For people in her line of work, it had very different connotations.

"And?" she asked.

"And there's not enough blood in the car for it to have happened here. Your colleague who sealed off the scene, Lynn, she did the right thing. We've found what we think is the victim's blood just up there."

She pointed away from the car and a little way along the track, to an area that had already been roped off, with a small white forensic tent protecting the evidence.

"I've found some partial prints on the door of the car," Caroline continued. "Chances are, it's all the victim. But if we're lucky, we might find a match for someone else."

Harriett nodded. She was staring at the car, trying to work out what to do next, trying to ignore the cold seeping through to her feet. Normally she'd arrange for a door-to-door, but there weren't any doors nearby. Unlikely to be any cameras, either, although it might be worth looking into whether there was anything closer to the foot of the track.

She tapped a message into her phone to set that in motion, and had just turned back to the pathologist when it rang in her hand. She didn't know the number.

"Harriett Barnes," she said.

"Yeah, you called me?" said a female voice she didn't recognise.

"Who is this?" Harriett asked.

"Millie Tennant. You left a message."

Harriett gripped her phone tightly and moved away from the others.

"Yes," she said. "I'm with Cumbria Police."

"You said. What do you want?"

"I'd like to talk to you, if you don't mind. About a friend of yours."

The woman laughed.

"Niamh Hanson, is it?"

"How did you know?"

"She's the only copper I've ever been friends with. OK. I can meet later today, if that works for you."

Harriett glanced back at the car, the little knot of people standing around it. This was a double murder investigation now, and the chances were, it had nothing whatsoever to do with Niamh Hanson.

But the DCI had been clear. This was a PSD case, with police involvement in *both* murders.

"Yes," she said. "That would be very helpful."

CHAPTER THIRTY-FOUR

"No sign of either?" Denise asked.

"Not a sausage," replied Keisha Middleton, and Denise sighed in frustration.

Keisha was calling from Bateman's house, where Denise had left a message asking her to look out for Bateman's phones. He had two – a work phone and a personal one – and neither had been found on his body or in his car. Even if they'd found them, it might have been hard work unlocking them, but that would have been preferable to what she was about to do now.

Not really her job. And in different circumstances, the Police Telecom Unit would have done this for her. But not content with the enemies he'd made all over Cumbria Police, it seemed DCI Branthwaite had managed to piss them off, too, and the work was back with PSD.

Harriett was still at the scene, Marcus was on his way back from Bateman's house, and Tom Willis wasn't due to move over from the Hub until tomorrow.

Lucky for Tom. Lucky for all of them.

"Hello," she said, when she finally got through to the man she'd been told she needed to speak to. "This is DS Denise Gaskill from Cumbria Police. We're investigating a double murder, and one of the victims was a client of yours. We have a RIPA application in, but in the meantime, we'd like you to provide all his data as a matter of urgency."

"That's a lot of words for saying you'd like to invade someone's privacy, DS Gaskill," said the man, Nikolas Costas.

"Dead men don't tend to worry about their privacy," she replied.

"Good thing they've got us here to do it for them," said Costas, and Denise felt the tension rising through her body, and with it, the pain.

Maybe two pills hadn't been enough.

She spent fifteen minutes arguing with Nikolas Costas, and in the end he agreed to progress her request. She'd dealt with people like Costas before. They usually gave you what you were after. But they always made you wait.

Without a time of death or any helpful neighbours, Bateman's phones would be the best way to trace his movements. It wasn't an idle request. They needed this data.

Of course, it might not have been necessary if Bateman had died somewhere civilised, with cameras, or possibly even people, but no. He'd been killed in the middle of nowhere, and now Harriett was telling them his death wasn't even particularly recent.

Denise pulled up the register of CCTV and traffic cameras, just on the off chance, but of course there was nothing. Nothing at the scene, nothing anywhere along the road itself, and judging by the satellite images, no sign of any houses that might have doorbell cameras pointing at the road, either. She slammed her arms on the desk in frustration, felt the shock of the contact travel along them to her spine and her neck, and gave a short yelp of pain.

That had been stupid.

Her phone rang, and she snapped it up and answered without checking the display.

"Is that Denise Gaskill?" said a female voice.

"Speaking," she replied.

"This is Jasmine Woolley. Detective Inspector Jasmine Woolley," added the woman, emphasising her rank, as if Denise didn't know who she was.

"I'm sorry for your loss," said Denise.

"What?" asked DI Woolley.

"Isaac Bateman. He worked for you, didn't he?"

"Oh. Yes. I suppose he did. That's what I'm calling about, actually. I've just heard that you've taken over the boatyard investigation from my team, and that you're taking charge of looking into Isaac's death, too."

Just heard? Lynn Hedley had been out at the scene, then back, then over at Bateman's house helping to look for evidence already. Did Jasmine Woolley have no idea what was going on in her own area?

"Yes," said Denise. "We'll be wanting to talk to you about—"

"I'll save you the trouble. I didn't know Isaac well, and I hadn't heard from him in days. But frankly, what the hell is going on there?"

"I'm sorry?" asked Denise.

"Last I heard, PSD don't investigate murders, and now suddenly you've taken on two. One of them's mine, and the other one should be."

There was a lot Denise might have said to that. She'd

have started with Jasmine Woolley's clear inability to handle a single murder investigation, much less a double, and then gone on to point out that she didn't seem particularly upset about her DS's death. She'd have ended with the fact that Jasmine Woolley was already on PSD's radar, as a result of her unfortunate choice of friends: she'd been close with Ralph Streeting, who'd been a DI himself until he'd gone down for murder.

Instead, she just gritted her teeth.

"I'm sorry," she said. "If you have an issue with that, you'd better take it up with the Chief Constable."

And then she ended the call and put down her phone before she could say anything she'd regret.

CHAPTER THIRTY-FIVE

THE SMILE MARCUS had forced onto his face lasted long enough for him to walk into the team room and see DS Gaskill staring at her phone the way he'd seen people stare at seagulls that had stolen their lunch and then decorated their cars with shit just to rub it in.

It seemed he wasn't the only one having a bad morning.

She turned and saw him.

"Nothing at the house, Sarge," he said.

"I know. I've spoken to Keisha. She said you were as much use as a sandwich bag in a gunfight."

He opened his mouth to object, then thought better of it.

"No sign of his phones," DS Gaskill continued. "And the network's playing hardball."

"Want me to call around his friends, see if I can find out anything about his movements?"

There was a slight twitch around DS Gaskill's lips, and for a moment Marcus thought she was about to smile. Then she nodded, one up and one down, and her mouth was set again, and he decided he'd probably imagined it.

DI Keyes had provided a handful of names, people he remembered Bateman being friends with from years back, and his more recent drinking associates. Marcus started alphabetically, with Barry Drinkwater, and by the time he'd reached Mal Overton, four calls later, he was starting to wonder whether these people had really been Bateman's friends at all.

None of them had seen or heard from him in weeks. They were surprised to hear that he was dead, shocked, even, but none of them seemed particularly upset. They didn't know where he'd been, they couldn't imagine why he might have wanted to contact a police department that investigated other police officers, and they had no unusual behaviour to report.

"Beer and bacon crisps," said Geoffrey Morrison. "Day in, day out. If he stopped doing that, that would be unusual."

Mal Overton added kebabs and pizzas to the list, but Marcus had been in the man's house. Kebabs and pizzas weren't exactly a breakthrough.

"Real Cops," said Bill Roper, after he'd expressed the same surprise and mild disappointment as the others.

"What?" asked Marcus.

"You asked why he might have wanted to talk to you lot. I can't help you, but I know who might be able to."

"Who?" asked Marcus.

"Real Cops, like I said."

"What?" asked Marcus again, wondering if he was going to spend the rest of the call firing one-word questions at Roper and getting incomprehensible answers in return.

"His mates in the police. If he spoke to anyone about anything, it would have been those guys."

"Who were they?" said Marcus, pleased he'd at least managed another two words this time.

"I don't know, do I?"

"You don't have any names?"

"Nope. He used to say the force was full of cowards and gays."

"Right," said Marcus. He hadn't known Isaac Bateman, but he was starting to see why the man wasn't going to be widely missed.

"But there was a little group of people he called the Real Cops. Used to say they were the only decent ones left on the force."

Marcus spent another few minutes pressing Roper for more information, but that was the limit of his knowledge.

Still, it was more than anyone else had told him. He went back to the start, but none of the first four had heard of the Real Cops.

"Sounds like him, though," said Barry Drinkwater, and Marcus wasn't sure whether that was a compliment or an insult.

Jay Stephenson hadn't heard of the Real Cops, and neither had Andy Trent. But Stu Williams had.

"Yeah," he said. "Rest of the force had been taken over by disabled lesbians, he said. Hardly any proper cops left. Just that lot. Real Cops, he called them."

"Any names?"

"Nope," said Stephenson.

It wasn't much, Marcus thought. But it was a start. He told DS Gaskill what he'd found, and she sounded interested and slightly less pissed off than she had been earlier, which was something.

"I was wondering if I could ask you something," he said,

and at the same time, he heard his father's voice in his head again.

Don't piss off your colleagues.

"What?" said DS Gaskill.

She looked friendly enough. By her standards, at least. Maybe he could ignore that voice.

"I found a folder. Something about a Skeleton Key. I couldn't open it. I was wondering if you could tell me about it."

"No," she said, and turned away from him. He stared after her, feeling his cheeks burning, and when she turned back a moment later, he knew his face was red. "I'm sorry," she told him. "It's above your pay grade."

He waited until DS Gaskill was looking at her screen again, and then he closed his eyes and pictured Lolly until he felt a smile creeping its way across his face. Then he picked up his phone and called the one person who might have any idea who the Real Cops were.

Lynn Hedley had never heard of them.

"I'll look into it, though," she said. "Good work, Marcus."

It wasn't much, that. But it was the first nice thing anyone had said to him all day.

CHAPTER THIRTY-SIX

IT HAD BEEN a long time since Denise had been in a major crime team, but she'd worked closely enough with the Hub to know that there came a point in every investigation when most of what you were doing was waiting for other people to respond to the last few things you'd done.

Chuck a ball in the air, and see where it came down.

While those balls were in the air, there was time to follow up on the ones that had landed before Bateman had shown up dead. She picked up her phone and dialled Samir Rashid's number.

"Hello?" he said.

"Sergeant Rashid, this is DS Gaskill, from PSD. You were kind enough to talk to my colleagues earlier this week, and I—"

"Cut to the chase, DS Gaskill," said Rashid, and even though he was obviously trying to be unfriendly, Denise found herself warming to the man.

"Fine. We've been through your phone records, and those of PC Hanson. You called her, during her shift, shortly before the call came through about the boatyard. What did you want to speak to her about?"

"I don't know what you're talking about," said Rashid, in the tone of a man who knew precisely what Denise was talking about.

"Yes you do, Sergeant Rashid. You called—"

"I heard you the first time. And I don't remember it. You say I called her; maybe I called her. If it was important, it would have stuck in my mind."

"From what we've heard—"

"Look, I'm happy to help when you've got something sensible to ask," said Rashid. "But this is just a waste of time."

She heard a click, then the solid tone of a dead line.

Fine.

Niamh Hanson answered the phone with a weary "Yeah?" that had Denise wondering if she'd been expecting the call. She listened in silence while Denise asked her about the phone call she'd received from PS Rashid during her shift, then cleared her throat.

"I told your colleague yesterday."

"You did?" asked Denise. "Which colleague was that?"

"DC Barnes."

"You told her about this call?"

Hanson gave a tiny noise, which might have been the beginning of a laugh, then swallowed it back.

"No," she said. "I told her I wasn't willing to speak to PSD without either a lawyer or a Police Federation rep. If you have anything you want to ask me, do it formally."

"We just want—" began Denise, but Hanson was already gone. She glared at her phone, then almost dropped it when it started buzzing in her hand.

She checked the display, checked the time, and said, "Oh shit" before answering.

"I'm sorry," she said, before Dr Filey could speak.

"You missed your appointment," the psychiatrist replied.

"I know. That's why I'm apologising."

"Look, Denise, I appreciate you have a demanding job, but you can't just—"

"We're investigating a double murder. I really am sorry I missed the appointment. I'm not a person who forgets something like that. But it really has been the kind of day where you forget anything that isn't right in front of you."

"Well, I'm right in front of you now," Dr Filey pointed out. "Figuratively speaking. Can you come down?"

Denise checked her watch, then her screen, then her watch again.

"Sorry," she said.

"Sorry?"

"This case went live this morning. I can't predict what's going to happen in the next ten minutes or whether it's going to be critical or completely irrelevant. I can't risk losing an hour to—"

"Fine."

"Fine?"

"For now. But we need to reschedule, Denise. If I haven't seen you within the next three days, I'm calling it in."

"Calling what in?"

"Your clearance to work. You're only at your desk because I say you can be at your desk. If I change—"

"Fine. Tuesday, then. Half-past three."

"I'll see you then. And Denise?"

"Yes?"

"Don't forget again."

For the third time in ten minutes, Denise found herself holding a phone with a dead connection and wishing ill on the person who'd just hung up on her. She could hear Marcus Hosgood speaking quietly on the phone at his desk, but he was avoiding her gaze, like someone who'd heard something in her voice and knew what was good for him.

Maybe Marcus Hosgood wasn't such an idiot after all.

CHAPTER THIRTY-SEVEN

"Where's Harriett?" asked Carl, looking around the room.

"She had a call from Millie Tennant, boss," said Marcus. "Hanson's old friend. Went straight from the scene to meet her. She must be with her now, or she'd have joined the call."

Carl considered for a moment, then nodded.

"Fine. Can you hear me?"

Over the phone, three voices confirmed: Aaron Keyes and Tom Willis in the Hub, and Lynn Hedley in Langdale.

"Let's start with forensics. Lynn, what's the state of play on the boatyard?"

"There isn't anything useful, I'm afraid. Stella and her team had plenty of time to go over the place before... Before the second incident. Too many sets of feet over recent days, plus the killers used bleach to hide DNA. And we still don't know who the victim is."

"Right. And the..." He paused, scratched his head, and wondered how to go on. Lynn had worked with the man, after all. And Aaron Keyes had known him for decades. "The second incident," he said, taking Lynn's lead. "What about that?"

"Nothing useful at Bateman's house, sir," she told him.

"Harriett called from the scene before heading over to her meeting," Marcus added. "Looks a bit more promising. They've recovered partials from the vehicle."

"OK. Let's rewind. Where are we on the original investigation?"

"If you mean our informal look at the boatyard team," said Denise, "then both Rashid and Hanson are making life difficult."

"More than people usually make life difficult?" Carl asked.

"This isn't just a not-liking-PSD thing, boss. This call between the pair of them, they're hiding something. I'd like to push them."

Carl started to shake his head, then stopped. Just because something else had happened, that was no reason to cut off a promising line of inquiry, even if the something else that had happened was the death of a serving officer. And it *was* a promising line of inquiry.

"Go ahead," he said. "Let's see if there's any connection to Bateman, too. He wanted to talk to us, and I want you all to keep that front and centre in this investigation. And I gather we've now learned that he had friends on the force we weren't previously aware of?"

"That's right," confirmed Marcus. "The Real Cops."

"Any luck identifying these so-called Real Cops?"

"I've spoken to the Uniforms in Langdale and Ambleside." Lynn's voice sounded more distant for a moment, then closer, and with it came the rustle of paper. "No one there seems to know who they are. No one there socialised with Isaac or knew anyone else on the force who did."

"What about the people he trained with?" asked Denise.

"No luck there, either," replied Lynn. "I've managed to track down a handful of them, and they all said the same thing. Bateman was a loner. Made himself a loner, thanks to his behaviour. Not a popular man."

When they'd spoken earlier, privately, Aaron Keyes had told Carl that Lynn was an excellent officer. Carl was beginning to see why.

"So it's not just a question of how we find them," he mused, "but how Bateman had come across these people in the first place."

A silence bloomed, growing as it lengthened and nobody seemed willing to break it, stretching into the edges and corners of the room.

"Functions," said Marcus Hosgood, finally.

"Oh, good call," said Tom Willis over the phone.

"Sorry?" asked Carl.

"Police functions, boss. You know, the regional events and charity things. Cops from all over, half of them people you'd never come across otherwise. I've met other cops at those things. You see them once, have a drink, recognise them second time round, by the time you've bumped into them a third time you're friends. If Bateman went to those things, maybe we can find out who he hung out with at them."

The silence that followed this statement was shorter, and broken by quiet sounds of general agreement.

"Anyone know if Bateman had a habit of attending these things?"

"Sorry, boss," said Lynn, and Carl smiled. He'd been meaning to shake her of that 'sir' habit, but she'd picked it up just by listening. One smart DC. "I'm not aware of anything. But..."

"But what?"

"Well, these events. The food and drink, it's usually either cheap or free, isn't it?"

"Yes," confirmed Marcus and Tom at the same time.

"Ah," said Aaron Keyes. "That's Bateman, then."

"It is?" asked Carl.

"If there was free alcohol available, he'd have been there."

"Agreed, boss. Bosses," said Lynn. There was a little chuckle from Denise's desk. Marcus said nothing.

"OK," said Carl. "That's a starting point. Let's get to work."

CHAPTER THIRTY-EIGHT

WIGGIES WAS a tiny establishment tucked into a side street no more than thirty seconds' walk from Ambleside's principal tourist traps, but it might as well have been in another world. You could walk or drive through the main street a thousand times, and you wouldn't even know it was there.

Harriett certainly had. The side street itself was so quiet she wondered briefly whether she'd gone deaf, and then she pushed open the heavy glass door and realised she hadn't.

Harriett might not have known *Wiggies* was there, but plenty of others clearly did. There were five tables crammed into the middle of one small room, three or four chairs at each table, every chair taken, and four people waiting at the counter. There was a jumble of voices, all local, by the sound of it. The room was filled with steam and the combined smell of sausages and coffee, and as Harriett joined the queue she felt a gnawing sensation in her stomach and realised she hadn't eaten since breakfast, half a slice of toast chewed and swallowed on the way out of the house that morning.

She thought briefly of Tom, seeing him on the video call.

They'd be working together again, from tomorrow. They'd worked together before, but always at the Hub, not Durranhill. His place rather than hers. Now they'd be on her turf. And they were living together, too. Working together, living together, probably driving there and back together.

"I don't know what you're on, love, but I'd like it injected right into my veins," said a voice from behind the counter, and Harriett looked up to see she was at the front of the queue, and there was a middle-aged woman looking back at her with something like wonder in her eyes.

"I'm sorry?" said Harriett.

"Look on your face. Not seen a woman smile like that since Mabel over there found out her ex had died."

Harriett realised she was still smiling, wiped the smile from her face, and produced her warrant card.

"Oh," said the woman.

"I'm looking for Millie Tennant."

"Come round back, will you?"

She followed the woman through an unmarked door to a cramped stock room, where a younger woman rose with a start from the boxes she was sitting on, clumsily attempting to hide the phone she'd been looking at behind her back.

"I'll leave you to it," said the first woman, presumably the owner or manager, and Harriett introduced herself.

"Yeah," said Millie Tennant. "Niamh Hanson..." She breathed out, slowly, like a woman exhaling smoke. "Finally put a foot wrong, has she?"

"What do you mean?"

"I mean, Little Miss Perfect always thought she was too good for the rest of us, and there was no way that could last."

"Why not?"

"Because she wasn't, was she? Better than the rest of us, I mean. She's made her share of bad decisions."

Harriett was starting to think this might be a waste of time. Bad decisions didn't make someone a killer. And it was obvious there was something between Millie Tennant and Niamh Hanson that meant Tennant wouldn't be the most objective character witness.

"Like what?" asked Harriett. She tried to banish the note of impatience from her voice, but she could hear it there herself, and so could Millie Tennant. It didn't help that she could still feel the damp in her shoes, the cold around her feet.

The woman raised an eyebrow and looked down her nose, like someone about to make a point that would end the debate for good.

"Like Zack Starling," she said, and fixed Harriett with a stare.

Harriett frowned.

"Who?" she asked.

"Zack Starling." The stare slid off her face and curled into a sneer. "You know. Zack Starling."

Harriett shrugged.

"And you say you're a cop," sniffed Millie Tennant, rising from the box and glancing at her phone. "I've got to get back on shift."

"This Zack Starling," said Harriett.

"Look him up," said Millie Tennant, pushing past her and out of the room.

CHAPTER THIRTY-NINE

DI Woolley had disappeared.

She hadn't done anything as straightforward as stopping briefly in the team room to say goodbye. She'd just vanished, in her office with the door closed one moment, out of it – door still closed – the next.

Given Isaac Bateman's fate, this might have been a cause for concern, but it was normal behaviour for the DI. Lynn wasn't going to lose any sleep over it.

Instead, she was poring over the various unofficial online noticeboards and forums frequented by her colleagues in Cumbria Police. She was slipping between social media platforms, logging into her various alternative accounts on Facebook, X and Instagram, then logging out again, just in case. She was hunting down references to what Marcus Hosgood and the rest of them had referred to as 'functions' but what would no doubt turn out to be heavily subsidised, poorly organised piss-ups.

So far, she'd found two.

There was a hotel in Penrith she'd not heard of before,

the unimaginatively named Roadside Inn, which had hosted a recent event for the 'Friends of Cumbria Police', a charity whose sole purpose seemed to be raising funds to get police officers drunk as quickly and as cheaply as possible.

A brief perusal of the entertainment on offer – free drinks, free food, bar open till one – was enough to tell her it was right up Isaac Bateman's street. Penrith wasn't close, but it wasn't far away, either. Thirty miles or so. An event like that, Bateman would have crawled there on his hands and knees if he'd known about it.

Maybe he had. Maybe he'd been there.

The second event she'd spotted was worthier of the name 'function'. It had been organised by a genuine charity that had raised funds for half a century for the local emergency services, and it had been held to commemorate both that anniversary and the passing of its founder. There was a posh three-course meal and a formal dress code, which might have put Bateman off, but for all his loutishness, the man had liked his clothes. And there was free drink, too. The event had been held at the Inn on the Lake, a little closer to home on Ullswater.

Another probable, she thought.

She'd just tracked down a third, at the Bassenthwaite Manor Hotel, and was noting down the details when she sensed she wasn't alone in the room. She swivelled in her chair and gave a little gasp of surprise.

There was a man standing no more than two feet away from her.

She'd moved back in her chair without realising it, but he closed the gap, stepping towards her until his face was inches from hers.

She knew him. Not well, but well enough.

"What the fuck do you think you're playing at?" said Sergeant Samir Rashid.

"Hey," she replied. "I don't know—"

"Isaac Bateman's dead. Your own colleague. Dead." He was jabbing a finger at her now, and she realised she was pressing her back against the chair, nowhere else to go but into it.

"Yes," she said. "It's—"

"And instead of mourning him, I hear you're helping the rats in PSD hunt down your fellow cops."

"That's not fair," she objected.

"Come on, Sarge," said another voice, and she looked past Rashid's soldier to see PC Grange shaking his head, stepping forward, placing a hand on the other man's shoulder.

Rashid shook him off. She'd heard the man had a temper, but she'd never seen it in person.

"You should leave other cops alone," he said. She sniffed. Was that whisky on his breath? "And I'll tell you something else," he continued. "You want to leave my bloody team alone."

"It's OK, Sarge," said Grange. "She's only doing her job."

Rashid turned to him, but before his eyes left hers she saw a look of pure hatred form in them.

"Fucking rats," he said, turned, and pushed past Grange and out of the room.

"Look," said Grange. "I'm sorry. I'd better..."

He followed his sergeant outside, and Lynn was left staring at the empty space where Rashid had been standing, so close to her, the room still smelling of sweat and something else, not whisky, she thought, but some other spirit.

Whatever it was, it hadn't improved Rashid's mood.

DAY SEVEN

CHAPTER FORTY

Harriett looked around the room.

It hadn't been long since she'd been working in her own office, by herself. Then this team room had come along, and they'd put her in it with DS Gaskill. Harriett hadn't been sure if two people were enough to justify calling it a team room.

Then Marcus Hosgood had turned up, and three people definitely were. And now Tom was with them, occupying the spare desk in the corner and trying not to stare at everyone like an idiot. On the big screen, Harriett could see the faces of DI Keyes in the Hub and Lynn Hedley in Langdale. And DI Whaley was standing in the middle of the room, leading the morning briefing.

When DCI Branthwaite put a team together, he really did put a team together. Hopefully, none of them had noticed her bare feet. Hopefully, no one could smell the shoes still drying under her desk.

"Anything on cameras?" asked the DI.

"Nothing up near the crime scene," said DS Gaskill. "No

doorbell cameras, no CCTV. I've been through the register, and I've had a word with Uniform. It's a dead zone."

"No more than we expected. What about Bateman's house?"

"No cameras near there either, boss," said Marcus. He'd reacted warily to Tom's arrival, not that Tom seemed to have noticed.

Harriett wasn't sure he'd known that the two of them were a couple, but if he hadn't, he did now. She kept having to remind herself not to touch Tom's arm, not to rest her hand on his, or trace it down his back as he walked past. Kept reminding herself, and occasionally forgetting, and Marcus wouldn't have missed that.

He was a detective, after all.

"What about phone data?" asked DI Keyes.

"It's starting to come through," said DS Gaskill. "Slowly. I've had Tom looking through it."

"And I've not found anything useful so far," added Tom, glumly. "If Bateman had any unusual communications, either he was using a third phone, or he'd deleted them completely. And he seemed to keep his location switched off. Even managed it on his police phone. He's messed with the cell site data, too. We won't be able to track his movements that way."

"Bloody idiot," muttered the DI. "OK. Lynn, I understand you've identified some functions he might have attended."

They listened while Lynn Hedley outlined what she'd found. Three hotels, three events, each of them the sort of thing that could well have attracted Isaac Bateman.

"Good work," said the DI. "I'd like you to check them out today. You can allocate them amongst yourselves."

"I'll do Bassenthwaite Manor," said Tom, before anyone else could get a word in, and the others stared at him in confusion. "I know it pretty well," he added, in explanation.

"Alright for some," said Marcus.

"Not as a customer," Tom clarified. "Two previous cases. Both murders. Both involved the Bassenthwaite Manor Hotel."

Marcus put his hand up for the Inn on the Lake. "Always wanted to go there," he said, and Harriett didn't have any reason to argue. That left her with the Penrith venue, the Roadside Inn.

"Good," said the DI. "The post-mortem's been set for later today. Any volunteers?"

"I can go," said Lynn, before Harriett could volunteer.

For a moment, she cursed her slowness, and then she remembered she was going to the Roadside Inn.

Whatever the Roadside Inn was like, it would be better than watching Chris Robertson cut up Isaac Bateman's dead body.

"Excellent," said DI Whaley. "Does anyone have anything else?"

"There is one thing," said Lynn. "I had a visit yesterday evening. Here at the station. Samir Rashid popped in and... Well, I wouldn't say he threatened me, exactly, but he wasn't pleased that I was helping with the investigation."

"Did he call us rats?" asked Harriett. That was what he'd said right at the start of their interview with him. And there was something else, too. Something that...

She squeezed her eyes shut and tried to will the thought to come forward, but it scurried back into the darkness as Lynn replied to her question.

"Yes," she said. "He did, as it happens."

"Sorry about that," said the DI. "It happens when you work with PSD. You don't think he was actually threatening you, though? You don't need protection?"

Lynn seemed to think for a moment, then shook her head.

"I think he'd been drinking, and I can look after myself, boss."

"If you need someone to come over there, keep an eye," said Marcus, and stopped midway through the sentence, clearly aware of all the eyes on him, and all the rolling those eyes were doing.

"I'll be fine, thanks," said Lynn, diplomatically.

"Good," said the DI. "Well, if that's—"

"Sorry," Harriett said. "There is one thing, while everyone's on. I met Millie Tennant yesterday. An old friend of Niamh Hanson's, but definitely not friends any more. She wouldn't tell me much, but she mentioned someone called Zack Starling. Referred to him as a 'bad decision' of Hanson's. I've looked him up, and I can see he's not exactly a stranger to the police, but I don't suppose any of you have ever come across him?"

"I have," said Lynn, and every face turned to hers on the screen.

It occurred to Harriett that if two people hadn't seemed like much of a team in the PSD room, Lynn's current position would be even lonelier. Maybe Marcus's suggestion hadn't been so ridiculous after all.

"Go on," prompted the DI.

"He's just a local dealer. Very low-level. Not someone who features high on the radar. He tends to supply tourists at the local campsites."

"Any other connections with our investigations?"

"I don't know. I think..." She turned away from them briefly, tapped on her keyboard, scanned the results, and looked back. "Yes, I thought so. He was caught just three weeks ago with a small quantity of ketamine. Bailed for magistrates."

"Do you know him personally?" Harriett asked.

Lynn shrugged.

"I've met him a couple of times. Not for a year or two."

"Don't suppose you'd mind dropping in on him anyway?" Harriet suggested. "Ask him about his relationship with Niamh Hanson, if there is one?"

Lynn smiled. "No problem," she said, and then everyone in the room looked round as the door swung open and DCI Branthwaite walked in.

"Don't stop," he said. "Just wanted to check in on my little team."

Not so little, thought Harriett.

"Remember," he continued. "We need a win on this. I'm already getting grief from the ACC's office."

The ACC. 'Little Joe' Carghillie. The subject of their own slow, quiet investigations. Harriett glanced over at the DI, but he was staring straight at DCI Branthwaite, his expression unchanged.

"But for now at least, we've got the Chief Constable herself onside, so they can stick their complaints up their various orifices and whistle."

And with that, he grinned and turned away. He'd taken a step towards the door when he stopped and turned back again, looking down.

Looking at Harriett's bare feet.

"Keep up the good work, Zola Budd," he said, and walked out of the room.

CHAPTER FORTY-ONE

Marcus had seen the Inn on the Lake a thousand times. If you lived in Cumbria, you'd probably driven past it, or steamed past it as you crossed Ullswater. He'd assumed it was one of those boring, old-fashioned country houses.

It took less than thirty seconds for him to change that opinion.

He was greeted by a polite, smiling man who looked about sixteen, but whose smile didn't shift when Marcus showed him his warrant card and explained why he was there. Instead, he invited Marcus to wait, and showed him into an enormous room with stylish chairs set by small round tables, and windows as big as his house overlooking the lake.

He was approached by a waiter and asked if he wanted a coffee – complimentary, of course – and by the time it had arrived, the man who'd greeted him was back, with the manager a step behind, a tall woman in her thirties with long brown hair and the sort of glasses Marcus had always associated with London.

She introduced herself as Marie Stoppard and sat down opposite him, placing a tablet on the table between them.

"I understand you're interested in the function we held the month before last, for the Fells Lifesavers," she said.

"That's right. I was hoping I might be able to view any CCTV footage you have of the event. We're interested in one of the guests – potential guests, I should say."

"We can certainly provide the CCTV." She pulled the tablet towards her and tapped in a series of commands, then looked back up at Marcus. "It'll be waiting for you on a pen drive at reception. We don't have anything inside the bedrooms, obviously, but we have eighteen cameras in the bars, restaurants, common areas, the car park and the gardens. It was a foul night, from what I can recall, so I wouldn't imagine there's going to be anything to see in the gardens. But hopefully the other footage will give you what you're looking for. This guest, do you have a name?"

"Isaac Bateman," he told her. She bent back down and entered another batch of commands, frowning as she perused the results.

"I'm sorry," said Marie Stoppard, after a few moments. "He wasn't an overnight guest, but most of the attendees weren't. As for the event itself, he might have been there, he might not."

"Don't you have a list of attendees?" he asked, and she gave an apologetic smile.

"We do. But most of them seem to have used nicknames. Look."

She slid the tablet across to him, and he scanned down a column, the blank space filled with the occasional first name, but more often, with a word that was unlikely to be anyone's real name. His eyes slid past *Slapper* and *Massive*, through *TwelvePints* and *Fatty*, to *Tits* and *Bacon*.

In the box beside *Bacon*, the one for surnames, was the word *Crisps*. He stopped and looked back up at the manager, smiling.

"Isaac Bateman was here," he said, and then his smile flattened itself out as he thought back, just a handful of seconds.

He'd seen something else. Something that had lodged itself at the edge of his mind and was clinging on for dear life.

He looked back down at the list, scanning through from the top again, and he didn't see it until he was almost done.

Niamh, he read, in the first name column. *Hanson* beside it.

Probably a coincidence.

But possibly not.

CHAPTER FORTY-TWO

WHEN SHE'D VOLUNTEERED for the post-mortem, Lynn hadn't really believed she'd be allowed to attend it. There were plenty of other officers in the room, after all. More qualified officers.

But here she was, greeting Dr Robertson just inside the entrance to the mortuary at the Cumberland Infirmary.

"Not seen you at one of these before," he observed, as she followed him inside and along a series of corridors. "This is my assistant, Ruth."

There was a woman standing in front of them, wearing a mask and rolling her eyes as she held out an apron.

"Rebecca," she muttered.

"What was that?" asked the pathologist.

"Nothing," said Rebecca, and Lynn donned the apron and followed the two of them into the post-mortem suite.

Isaac Bateman lay naked on the metal table under lights so bright his skin almost glowed. Even though he was dead, it felt like a violation, seeing him like this, and Lynn looked briefly away before forcing her eyes back again.

"Not going to vomit, are you?" asked the pathologist.

"I've attended post-mortems before," she replied. No need for the pathologist to know that she'd attended precisely two post-mortems, one for what turned out to be a straightforward RTC, and the other for a horse.

No need for him to know that she'd worked with the deceased, either. That she'd sat in a room with him almost every working day for years.

"Well, let's deal with the obvious, shall we?" said Dr Robertson. He reached up to switch on the microphone above his head, and pointed to Bateman's chest, the Y-shaped incision already in place.

Here's one I made earlier, thought Lynn, and stifled the hysterical laugh that threatened to bubble up her throat and into her mouth. She watched as the pathologist parted the skin and pointed out the lungs.

"Look," he said.

Lynn took a step closer. Bateman's insides were less grey than she'd expected. More red and brown. She tried to think of them as just organs, rather than Isaac Bateman's organs, but she couldn't help it. All those crisps. All that beer.

All that fatty tissue.

"First off, if he'd drowned, there'd be foam in the airways, and if we couldn't see the foam all this time later, we'd still expect hyperinflation of the lungs."

"And there's no sign of that?" asked Lynn, trying to sound like she wasn't thinking about the living man those lungs had once been part of.

There was a pause, and she looked up to see the pathologist watching her.

"You sure you're OK?" he said. This time there was a

gentler tone to his voice, and what looked like genuine concern in his eyes.

"I'll be fine," she told him. She toyed with the idea of explaining, of telling him that these weren't just lungs, they were Isaac Bateman's lungs. But there was no point. Either he wouldn't understand, or he would, and if he did, he'd tell her to wait outside while he finished the post-mortem.

"Well," he said after a moment's silence, "no. There's no sign of hyperinflation. No overexpansion from emphysema aquosum, no signs of water as a result of pulmonary oedema. I'll be weighing these puppies later," he continued, and it took her a moment to realise he was talking about the lungs. "But I'd be surprised if they were more than four hundred grams apiece."

She knew this one. She remembered it from her reading, late nights while Gerry lay snoring beside her and she couldn't sleep.

"Heavy lungs are an indication of drowning," she said. "That's not definitive though, is it?"

She could see the smile form under Dr Robertson's mask.

"A connoisseur, I see. No, you're absolutely right. Lung volume is a better guide, and I'll be looking into that, too. But with all these indications, or more importantly, lack of indications, it's clear this man didn't drown."

"How did he die, then?" asked Lynn, and the pathologist's smile got even broader.

"Buckle up," he said. "You're about to see Isaac Bateman's brain."

When she emerged from the mortuary an hour later, blinking into the weak sun, she knew she'd never forget what she'd just witnessed, from the incision across the back of Bateman's head, through the removal of the top of the skull, to the brain itself, and the traumatic brain injury – the diffuse axonal injury, to be precise – that had killed him.

There was a small amount of foreign material around the contusions on Bateman's head. They would be sent off for analysis. The day before, Harriett had relayed the pathologist's conclusion from the scene, and he repeated it again before Lynn left, word for word.

Isaac Bateman had been smashed over the head with a blunt object, repeatedly, in the same place.

Even as she drove south towards Windermere, Lynn found herself unable to shake the image of Bateman's brain from her own. From the little she knew of Zack Starling, turning up on his doorstep wasn't going to be the most pleasant of experiences.

But it had to beat the inside of Isaac Bateman's skull.

CHAPTER FORTY-THREE

IT HAD BEEN a while since Tom Willis had been to the Bassenthwaite Manor Hotel. It was a beautiful building in spectacular grounds with its own boating lake and a restaurant that drew praise from across the county.

He hadn't missed the place. Within the walls of that beautiful building, he'd uncovered a drugs network, a blackmail ring, and a woman who'd killed the man who'd turned her into an addict.

And that was before they'd even got started on the management.

Peter Raymond, the man they'd interviewed and arrested for murder, had been released from his role as manager soon after he'd been released from custody. The owners of the Bassenthwaite Manor Hotel hadn't appreciated his management style, which seemed to involve seducing as many of the female staff as he could.

Raymond's replacement was an American named Greg – he hadn't volunteered his last name – and as he leaned back in his chair, dressed in a silk patterned shirt and a green felt jacket, his feet resting on his desk and a smile playing on his lips, Tom couldn't help thinking that at least they'd recruited someone completely different.

"So, you're after CCTV from one of our events, right?" he drawled, his accent thick enough to drown in.

Tom nodded.

"Yes. We're looking for—"

"Hold it there," said Greg, extending a single finger and then retracting it immediately, as if even that effort was too much for him. "You got a warrant?"

"Well, no. But—"

"Well, I'm not sure we can help you then, Mr Watkins."

"DC Willis," said Tom, and Greg smiled at him.

"Oops. Sorry about that, man. But still. No warrant, no CCTV."

Peter Raymond had been a lazy, uncooperative arsehole as well. Maybe the men weren't so different after all. Tom sighed.

"I can get a warrant if you insist on one. It's not like we're asking for footage of people's rooms."

"We don't do that here, DC Willis."

"I know. I'd like to think you'd want to help us solve a double murder. Of course, if you're not willing—"

"Oh, for crying out loud, fine."

Tom wasn't sure, but he thought the man had just rolled his eyes.

"You'll get the CCTV?"

"We'll get the CCTV," confirmed Greg, like a man who'd just volunteered to row single-handed across the Atlantic Ocean and didn't particularly like the sea. "What did you say the name was?"

"Isaac Bateman."

Greg leaned forward, clicked his mouse to wake up his computer, and then spent a minute or so just staring at it in silence.

"You Brits. Everything is just so goddamn slow." He clicked again, then dragged the keyboard towards him, the motion so slow and painful Tom found himself feeling briefly sorry for the man before he remembered it was just a keyboard, rather than a massive boulder.

"Bateman?" said Greg.

"Bateman," Tom confirmed.

Greg clicked again, and tapped a handful of keys. "Bateman," he muttered under his breath. "Bateman, Bateman, Bateman, Bateman, Bateman." He looked up at Tom. "How d'ya spell that, then?"

Tom spelled the name out for him, and waited.

"Yeah," said Greg, finally. "He was here."

"He was at the event?"

Greg winked at him. "At the event, and he got a room. Stayed here that night. Head office gave them a deal on rooms. He had it cheap. We'll get you your CCTV, but it'll take a bit. Come back in..." He glanced at his wrist, realised he wasn't wearing a watch, and swore under his breath. "Give me forty minutes, yeah?"

In the bar, Tom found Leo, the barman who'd been there every time he'd come to the Bassenthwaite Manor Hotel. Leo, and no one else, other than the occasional member of staff walking silently through.

"Quiet day?"

Leo looked up, recognised Tom, and grinned. "Quiet month," he said. "What brings you here?"

Tom gave him as much of the story as he could. Leo had

been helpful in the past. But his most notable quality was a complete inability to keep his mouth shut.

"Yeah, I remember the event." He took Tom's phone and spent a moment examining the photo of Isaac Bateman. "Bateman, you say? Can't say I remember him. But you know these things. They get hammered, misbehave, regret it in the morning. And there's bloody loads of them. Can't tell one pissed copper from the next."

That, Tom thought, probably wasn't true. If Bateman had been around, had done anything noteworthy, Leo would have noticed and stored it away as one of his little anecdotes.

But Bateman had been there, and stayed over, too. Tom could only hope that the CCTV would be more useful than the barman.

CHAPTER FORTY-FOUR

"Sergeant Rashid," said Denise, and heard a sharp intake of breath on the line. She waited.

"Yeah?" came the reply, a good five seconds later.

"This is DS Denise—"

"You think I don't recognise your voice?" said Rashid.

"I'd like to talk to you about—"

"Is this a disciplinary or a criminal investigation?"

"At the moment, we're just gathering information."

"Yeah, that line's got a little old, DS Gaskill, and my patience with it has well and truly run out. If you want to speak to me, go through the proper channels. And next time we talk, I'll have a lawyer with me."

And there was the click. Denise was getting used to people hanging up on her.

She stood, stretched, tried to work out the kink in her back, and failed, which made sense. If it were the sort of injury you could deal with just by stretching, she wouldn't have needed all the painkillers. And she wouldn't be waiting until she was alone in the team room before shutting the door and dialling another number.

"Christ," said Neville Warner, "you can't be running low already, Denise."

"Good to hear your voice too," replied Denise, and heard a low chuckle.

"Look, yes, it's lovely to hear from you and all that, but it's not like you get in touch for a friendly chat these days, is it? You are running low, right?"

"Yes," she admitted. "I need more."

There was a pause, which threatened to become a silence, before Denise spoke again.

"This isn't going to be a problem, is it?"

Neville made a noise, something between a sigh and a groan.

"It's not exactly by the book, what we're doing here."

"We've known each other for nearly twenty years, Nev."

"We have, Denise. Although for most of the last ten I haven't heard a thing from you. And then you need painkillers under the counter, and I'm a pharmacist, and suddenly we're—"

"OK, Nev, spit it out."

"Spit what out?"

"What exactly do you want from me? Nice friendly drink? Trip to the cinema? Boat trip on Coniston? I can—"

"Money," said Neville, and the tiny reserves of levity Denise still had suddenly went dry.

"What?"

"Money, Denise. Look, I'll sort you out this time. We're friends, or at least, we ought to be. But I'm taking a risk here. If this is going to go on much longer, I'm thinking you ought to make a contribution."

She took the phone from her ear, and for a moment she just stared at it, her finger over the red button, her mind reeling between anger and surprise.

But she needed Neville.

"OK," she said. "It won't go on much longer. I'm cutting down."

"Sure you are."

"I mean it, Nev. Look, you've really come through for me. I appreciate it. Sort me out this time and—"

"Save it, Denise," said Neville, and ended the call.

With a noise not unlike the one Neville had made, Denise turned back to her screen and commenced a background search on Isaac Bateman. It would, she thought, make her feel a little better, if only because however badly her day was going, Bateman had it worse.

Twenty minutes later, she was on the phone with Aaron Keyes.

"Have you—" he began.

"Seeing her in a couple of days," said Denise, hoping that would be enough to deflect the jab before it landed.

"I thought—"

"Been a little busy trying to find some murderers, Aaron. That's what I wanted to talk to you about anyway, not Dr Filey. I've been looking through Bateman's arrest record, disciplinaries. He wasn't a great advert for Cumbria Police, was he?"

"He was an arsehole, Denise," said Aaron.

"I've been on the web, too. The things people say about him. Accusations of brutality, fitting suspects up, even more than we usually get."

"That's because in Bateman's case, some of them were probably true. If you're looking for a suspect with a grudge against the man, you won't struggle to find one. Like I say, he was an arsehole."

Which, thought Denise, thanking Aaron and ending the call, didn't make their lives any easier. Not by a long shot.

CHAPTER FORTY-FIVE

The Roadside Inn was a long, low red brick building situated close to Penrith Castle and no more than a hundred yards from the more imposing Station Hotel. From the outside, there was something arresting about the place, and Harriett felt a sense of significance, of history, of somewhere important things would have happened over long generations.

The impression lasted as long as it took her to push open a broken automatic door and walk through a cramped and dirty reception area to a desk where two women of about her age stood, watching something on one of their phones and whispering conspiratorially together.

One of them looked up, saw Harriett waiting there, then returned to her entertainment. Harriett coughed, and with a sigh, the woman looked back at her.

"Yeah?" she said.

Harriett smiled at her and produced her warrant card.

"Harriett Barnes. Cumbria Police. We're investigating a series of murders, and we need your help."

Anything more than one could count as a series, so it wasn't like she was lying. The woman eyed her with an expression that said, 'I don't believe you' as clearly as if she'd shouted it, then stepped out from behind the desk and began to walk away.

After a few paces she turned, said, "Come on, then," and Harriett fell into step behind her. The other woman had returned to whatever she'd been watching on her phone.

The manager of the Roadside Inn, Shona Bruce, was a petite Scotswoman who listened as Harriett explained what she was there for. She was shaking her head before Harriett had even finished.

"Yeah, not gonna happen, hen," she said, her Glaswegian accent somehow jarring.

"Why not?"

"Because you're after footage of something that happened, what, three months ago, right?"

"Four," Harriett corrected her.

"Exactly. And we only keep the CCTV for a week."

Harriett felt the weight of disappointment. She'd been hoping for a result here.

"How about your guest registers? We could at least see if DS Bateman stayed here, maybe see who else was here at the time..."

The look on Shona Bruce's face told her this, too, was about to prove a mission too far.

"Sorry, hen." The manager pointed at the battered computer on her desk. "System's fucked. Can't even book anyone in right now. Maybe come back in a few days when it's all sorted."

"Maybe," agreed Harriett. She fought to keep the smile on her face until she was back in her car, and then she drove around the corner, parked up again, and swore loudly for a full minute.

She'd been wrong. Watching Chris Robertson cut up Isaac Bateman's dead body would have been better than the Roadside Inn after all.

When she'd finished swearing, she checked her inbox, hoping for better news elsewhere. Tom was still waiting for CCTV at the Bassenthwaite Manor, but it looked like Marcus had met with some success.

And Lynn finally had a hit on mispers that matched the boatyard victim.

The man's name, if it really was him, was Alexander Godwin. He was a businessman based in Formby, which Harriett had vaguely heard of as one of the posher bits of Merseyside. He had no significant other, children, or close family, and he lived alone, which went a little way towards explaining why he'd not appeared on any searches so far. He'd been reported missing by his business partner in Liverpool, after he'd not shown up for meetings two days in a row.

Imagine that. You get yourself drowned in a bucket a hundred miles from home, and no one even notices for the best part of a week.

There was something there, though. Something waving at her from the darkest reaches of her memory. Something she'd already thought, or half-thought, but not got round to fully exploring.

Harriett shut her eyes, tried to shut out the noise of the passing traffic, and waited for it to make itself known, but it remained stubbornly hidden.

It would come. She'd give it time, and it would come.

CHAPTER FORTY-SIX

"What's this about, then?"

Lynn hadn't come across Zack Starling for a year or two, but he hadn't changed. Same skinny jeans, same scrawny little beard, same startling blue eyes looking out from a pale face that seemed not to have seen the sun in decades. People said Zack Starling was good-looking, but Lynn had never really seen it.

Still, those eyes were hard to forget.

"Why don't we go inside?" she suggested, and started to walk in, but he shifted slightly to the side to block her path.

That wasn't going to work, then.

They were standing outside Starling's ground-floor flat on Oak Street, part of a three-storey seventies structure built right next to a set of older slate houses at the end of Windermere furthest from the lake itself. Starling himself was now planted firmly in the doorway, if 'firmly' was the right word for someone who twitched every few seconds, then leaned forward menacingly as if to compensate for it.

"Why don't we stay out here and you can tell me what you want?" he countered.

Fine. The remnants of something horrible lingered in Lynn's nostrils, a combination of disinfectant and Bateman's insides. The fresh air wouldn't do any harm.

"OK," she said. "Can you tell me about your relationship with Niamh Hanson?"

He turned and glanced briefly back inside, and for a moment Lynn thought Hanson might actually be in there, but that would have been stretching the bounds of probability.

There was something in there, though. Starling was nervous. And he wasn't keen on letting her inside.

Probably just drugs. Starling was a drug dealer, after all.

"Why do you want to know?" he asked.

"It really would be easier if we discussed this inside," she suggested, and made as if to move forward. He shifted again, this time towards her, and she was forced to take half a step back.

"Maybe. But it's not happening. So what's going on with Niamh, then? She missing me?"

"I'm sorry?"

He narrowed those blue eyes and looked her up and down.

"Or maybe you want some of what she had?" he suggested, and as she watched, he grabbed at his crotch and pouted.

This wasn't going the way Lynn had hoped it would go. She sighed. She'd give it thirty seconds, and then she'd walk away. Starling knew nothing, had nothing inside the flat beyond his usual stash of Class Bs, and it wasn't worth standing here putting up with this for the little she'd get out of it.

"Just tell me about Niamh," she said.

"Yeah, we were together," replied Starling, and Lynn, who'd been on the verge of giving up, blinked.

"You were?"

"That's what you wanted to know, isn't it?"

She nodded.

"When was this?"

"I dunno. Couple of years ago. Bit more, I reckon. What's this all about?"

"Why don't we go inside?"

"I'm not letting you in," he said, and she nodded. At least it was out there now.

"Why not?"

He surprised her with a sudden laugh. "Because I know what you're like. The lot of you. Fit a man up as soon as look at him, you will."

"And you've had experience of that, have you?" she asked, and his laughter dried up as suddenly as it had arrived.

"Yeah," he said. "I have, as it happens. Anything you want to know, you can learn it out here."

There was a woman walking towards them, pushing a pram with one hand while she chatted on her phone. She looked up, saw Lynn on the pavement, saw who she was talking to, and crossed the road.

"So, you and Niamh Hanson."

Starling shrugged. "We were together. Then we weren't."

"Why not?"

"I didn't realise she was a cop. Dumped her when I found out."

That seemed improbable. More likely, Lynn thought, it had been the other way round: Niamh Hanson, attracted, like some women were, to those blue eyes, unaware that the man whose face they were attached to was a drug dealer. Falling into bed, falling into some kind of relationship, falling back out again when she learned the truth. Although for a cop to be unaware of someone like Zack Starling in the first place was almost as unlikely as Starling not realising Hanson was a cop.

But whatever the ending had been, the relationship had been there. A police officer and a known drug dealer. And Niamh Hanson hadn't declared it.

Had someone else known? Had someone used the information against her?

"Who else knew about you and Niamh?" she asked, and Starling shrugged again.

"Weren't exactly a secret," he replied. "What's this about?"

Lynn was hardly going to tell him that. And she'd got what she'd come for. Still, it was worth one more try.

"I really think we should continue this conversation inside."

"And I really think we shouldn't. I'm not getting fitted up."

"Fitted up for what?" Lynn asked, taking that half step forward again, and this time he matched it with a half step back, and she really thought she'd made it inside.

Until the door swung shut in her face.

She hit it with the flat of her hand.

"Open the door, Zack," she shouted, and turned to see that the woman with the pram had stopped across the road and was staring at her.

No, not staring at her. Pointing her phone.

Filming her.

"Open the door," she said again, quieter this time, but there was no response.

Fine.

She'd taken just half a dozen steps back towards her car when her phone rang, and she answered, thinking it would be Starling, which was ridiculous. He didn't even know her number, after all.

"Yes?" she said.

"DC Hedley?" said a voice she'd heard before, and recently.

"Who is this?"

"It's Stephen Grange. PC Grange. We were—"

"I know who you are, PC Grange. How can I help you?"

There was a pause, and then Grange gave a tiny embarrassed laugh.

"I just wanted to apologise, actually."

"Apologise?"

"For the sarge. Yesterday. He was out of order."

"Oh," said Lynn.

"I don't want you to think we all think like that," Grange continued. "I know you're just trying to find a murderer. And I'm sorry the sarge acted like he did. But he..."

"He what?" asked Lynn.

"He gets a bit angry sometimes," Grange continued. "But he's a good guy, really. Look, I'd better go."

Before she could thank him, the line was dead.

CHAPTER FORTY-SEVEN

Greg had handed over the CCTV footage with ill grace, and Tom had just stepped outside into the car park when he felt a hand on his shoulder.

He turned to see a man in his twenties, wearing the uniform of the Bassenthwaite Manor Hotel, with a basket of cleaning supplies in his hands and a look of fear in his eyes.

"You're the police officer, right?" said the man, his voice low and urgent.

"Yes. Can I help you?"

"Where's your car?"

Tom pointed to it, in a row by itself at the back of the car park.

"Wait there," said the man, and disappeared back inside.

Tom had been waiting for five minutes when he glanced in his wing mirror and spotted the man approaching from the other entrance to the car park, stopping every few seconds to check he wasn't being watched, then continuing on his way. Tom leaned over to push open the passenger door, and the man slid in, his eyes fixed on the hotel building in front.

"DC Tom Willis," said Tom. "You're a cleaner here?"

The man nodded. "I'm Anton," he said.

The man's gaze hadn't shifted, and Tom found himself compelled to look in the same direction, like two men sitting beside one another on a park bench in an old spy movie, pretending not to talk, pretending not to even know one another, which was ridiculous, given they weren't on a park bench but in the front of Tom's car.

"How can I help you?" asked Tom.

"You're looking into that party, yeah? The police bash?"

"That's right," confirmed Tom. "Why don't you—?"

"Bateman. I heard that was the name you were interested in."

Tom frowned, and turned to examine the man. He had close-cropped sandy hair and a thin face. There was a tick in his jaw, an occasional movement that might have been something serious but was probably just nerves. But how could he even know...

"You were in the bar," he said, realising. "While I was talking to Leo. You heard me mention Bateman."

"Yes," Anton agreed. He looked like he wanted to say more, but stopped. Tom was going to have to play this one carefully.

"Do you know anything about Bateman?" he asked.

The man turned to look at him suddenly, and nodded.

"This was just a few weeks ago, right? Yeah. I remember Bateman."

"That's good. Is there anything you can tell me about him? Who he was with that night, what they were doing or talking about?"

Anton shook his head.

"I wasn't around that night. Just the following morning. I

went to clean his room. It was after checkout time. Should have been empty."

"And it wasn't?"

"Nope." A smile played on Anton's lips for a moment, then vanished. "They were still in it."

Tom felt a shift, a sense that he was about to learn something important.

"They?" he asked.

"Yeah. Him and the woman."

"Who was the woman?"

"I don't know her name. But he called her Eve, or something like that."

"Eve," Tom repeated. "Could that have been Niamh?"

"Yeah," said Anton. "Could be."

"Could you describe her for me?"

"Well..." Anton looked down, and kept his gaze there, on the glove compartment in front of him, as he spoke. "It wasn't really her face I was looking at," he said.

The man was embarrassed.

"Is there anything you can—?"

"But she was good-looking, right?" Anton turned to look at him again. "Thin. Tall. Fit skinny bird, maybe thirty, I reckon."

"OK," said Tom. "And is there anything else that—?"

"Her hair," said Anton. "She had curly red hair."

CHAPTER FORTY-EIGHT

Marcus had done well, he thought. He'd tracked Bateman to the Inn on the Lake, thanks to his penchant for bacon-flavoured crisps. He'd found Niamh Hanson at the same event, by virtue of her actual name, but you had to know where to look, didn't you? And he'd got CCTV footage from the night, which might establish a link between Hanson and the dead man, if he was lucky. He ran through it all with DS Gaskill, who nodded with what might, he thought, be something close to appreciation, before reminding him to enter it all onto HOLMES and the database, and to go through the actual CCTV.

That was the downside of getting hold of the footage, of course. He'd have to go through it. Hard on the eyes, boring, usually fruitless. He spent a few minutes checking shift patterns for Hanson, Grange and Rashid before he got started, but he knew he was just killing time.

There was no point. If they had some idea of Bateman's movements, they might be able to establish a time of death, but without that, it was a mess. The window was too large.

Hanson hadn't been on shift the afternoon and evening before the big team night out, the one which had produced such alarming hangovers for her and Rashid.

Bateman might have been killed during that time.

But he might not.

He turned to the CCTV footage, then paused and called the Inn on the Lake. The direct line Marie Stoppard had given him. He introduced himself, and she laughed.

"Not likely to have forgotten you already," she said. "How can I help you?"

"I should have asked at the time. Did Niamh Hanson have a room booked for the night?"

There was a short silence, broken by the sound of fingers on a keyboard, before Marie Stoppard replied.

"She did. Standard room, package rate. No complaints from the cleaning staff. All very forgettable. I hope that's helpful."

"It may well be," he said, thanked her, and ended the call. Maybe there was a link between Hanson and Bateman. Maybe he'd find it in the CCTV footage. He couldn't put it off any longer.

He could, it turned out, because there were messages on the team inbox from Harriett Barnes, who'd had no luck at the Roadside Inn, and from Tom Willis, who'd had so much luck that he'd already beaten Marcus into second place.

There was a link between Hanson and Bateman. They'd shared a room at the Bassenthwaite Manor Hotel.

"Fuck's sake," Marcus muttered under his breath, and saw DS Gaskill look up sharply.

"All OK?" she asked.

"All good," he told her, and turned to the footage.

The hour that followed was everything he'd hoped it

wouldn't be. By the time it was over, he'd watched eight hours of the footage he'd thought most likely to yield results, at eight times normal speed, his eyes were stinging, and he'd found nothing of use.

He'd found Bateman, walking here and there, usually with a pint in his hand, exchanging greetings with people, even stopping to talk to them, but he never seemed to be in the same place for long enough to figure out who was with him, and who was just the object of a passing word.

He'd seen Niamh Hanson, too, but only a couple of times – she seemed to have spent much of the evening in a poorly lit corner of the room talking to a handful of people who were no more identifiable than a single blade of grass in a field.

The quality of the images was fine. It was the people themselves who weren't playing ball, and as that hour drained slowly into its final minutes, Marcus felt himself filling with something like hatred, for Isaac Bateman, who might have been dead but who was unquestionably up to no good, and for Niamh Hanson, who might not have killed Bateman, but who knew more than she'd told them.

They were police officers. They claimed to be the servants of the law, but all they did was abuse the uniform and the rights it brought with it. For years he'd been told people were just like that, not to let it get to him, not to expect anything better, but that, he knew, was only to protect him from repeating his dad's mistakes.

But that was fine. Marcus Hosgood wasn't making any mistakes. And sore eyes or not, he'd make sure these people paid for what they'd done.

CHAPTER FORTY-NINE

Denise stared at her screen, trying to make connections, trying to break the ones already there and reform them into something that made sense.

At least they had a name. The man who'd died in the boatyard was called Alexander Godwin. The business partner who'd reported him missing was, apparently, both mystified and distraught. He couldn't think of anyone who'd have wanted Alexander dead. He knew why the man might have been in Cumbria, at least. They'd been looking at buying some land nearby.

But there hadn't been any meetings in the calendar.

They had Alexander Godwin, dead. They had Isaac Bateman, dead. They had next to nothing from forensics or pathology, but there was almost too much when it came to the PSD side of things. Too many lines of enquiry to follow them all up. Rashid and Hanson were top of the list. Then there was the dispatcher, Angela Sherman, who wasn't a person of interest at the moment, but that could always change. Grange looked clean, but that, too, was subject to anything else they discovered.

Time to cross off some avenues. She turned to Marcus Hosgood, who was staring at his screen, watching police officers staggering drunkenly around a hotel bar.

"Marcus," she said.

He didn't move.

"Marcus," she repeated, louder, and this time he turned, fast, like he'd been caught doing something he wasn't supposed to.

"Sorry," he said. "I was in another world."

"Any luck?"

He shook his head. "Not yet. But now we know there's a link between Hanson and Bateman, I'm sure it'll be here."

"Fine. Good. In the meantime, remind me, where did we get to with that insurance payout to Grange's bank account?"

"It was legit, Sarge. Company's called Havering Milton Ltd. Fully regulated."

"So why can't I see any of this on HOLMES?" she asked, and saw his face fall.

"Shit," he said. "Sorry."

She closed her eyes, counted silently to ten, then opened them again.

"It's OK, Marcus. You're doing well. Really well. I've been impressed. It's just really important that you keep the rest of us up to date, right?"

He nodded. She could see he felt bad, but that was fine. Feeling bad was fine. He had messed up, after all.

"And Claire Saunders?"

"I've put all that in, Sarge. I'm pretty sure she was on the level. I spoke to one of her neighbours and he confirmed there'd been trouble. Bins getting knocked over."

"CCTV?"

"I've asked for it, from the building manager. Might take them a while."

"Good," she said, and he smiled. "And you've looked thoroughly into her background?"

The smile seemed to flicker, then return, frozen in place.

"Thoroughly?" he said.

"Thoroughly," she confirmed.

"We know about the old soliciting caution," he said. "She's been clean since then."

"That's not thoroughly, Marcus. That's just repeating what we already know."

"Right. I'll get on it."

He turned back to his screen just as Tom Willis walked in and straight to the spare desk.

"Oh," said Marcus, then, barely a second later, added, "Oh, it's nothing."

"What's nothing?" asked Denise.

"It's just... If you go back to that period of her life, when she was... Around the time of the caution. There were concerns reported by her family."

"Hardly surprising," said Denise. "Anything else?"

She waited, then got tired of waiting and turned back to her screen, looking for more connections, but nothing jumped out at her. Harriett Barnes came in, spotted Tom at the spare desk, and walked self-consciously over to him. The two of them sat, talking quietly. Marcus was still scanning his screen, digging through Claire Saunders's background, making sure they hadn't missed anything important.

"Nothing," he said, finally, answering her question fifteen minutes after she'd asked it, as if no time had passed at all.

"Good." She raised her voice a little, and Tom and Harriett looked round. "Let's park them for now," she continued. "Saunders, Sherman, Grange, they can all go on the back burner. I want to focus on Niamh Hanson and what she's got to do with Isaac Bateman. And I don't want us forgetting about Samir Rashid. Got it?"

CHAPTER FIFTY

DECISIONS. That was what it was all about, really, being a DI. Making decisions, taking the credit for them on the rare occasions when they went well, taking the flak when they didn't. Sure, you might pop up in an interview occasionally, make a suspect nervous, use your name and rank to scare the crap out of some poor PC who'd said the wrong thing to the wrong person, but for the most part, the actual solving of crimes was done by the rest of the team.

Carl missed solving crimes. But at least the team was working well.

"Can you hear us?"

He saw Aaron Keyes and Lynn Hedley nodding in their little boxes on the big screen. Tom Willis was with them now, in the room with Harriett and Denise and Marcus.

Not such a little team. Not any more.

"OK, I just wanted a quick update and a sense of direction. As Marcus pointed out the other day, there are a lot of moving parts, and that was when we were looking into just the one murder."

Marcus Hosgood gave a tiny bow of acknowledgment.

"I've looked through your input on the database and in HOLMES," Carl continued. "I see we now have a name for the boatyard victim, and a cause of death for Isaac Bateman – thanks for attending, Lynn. But if you could all summarise what else we've learned since this morning, that would be great."

Tom Willis kicked things off with his revelation about the woman he referred to as 'Bateman's mysterious guest' at the Bassenthwaite Manor Hotel.

"Not very mysterious, is she?" said Marcus. "Rhyming name, matching hair, right sort of age. And Niamh Hanson's not only a cop, but also a regular attendee at these events. She was at the Inn on the Lake do, as well. Had a room there."

"And was Bateman with her that night?"

Marcus gave a pained expression. "Can't be sure, boss. It's not clear from the CCTV."

"Still, good work. Harriett, I gather you met with less success at the Roadside Inn."

"They have no CCTV and their systems are down. No idea if he was there at all."

"Right. What else have we got?"

"I had a word with Zack Starling," came the voice of Lynn Hedley, her mouth moving a fraction of a second behind the words. "He confirmed a previous relationship with Hanson a couple of years ago. Said he'd ended it when he realised she was police, but there's just as much chance it was the other way round. He seemed nervous, though."

"Nervous how?"

"Edgy. Aggressive at times. Referred to being fitted up, more than once. And he wouldn't let me in the house."

"You didn't have grounds to enter," Carl pointed out.

"No. But we were standing outside having this loud conversation. Most people would have wanted to take it somewhere private. My guess is he's got drugs in there."

"Fitted up," said Denise, with the air of someone thinking as she spoke. Carl waited a moment, and she went on. "I checked Bateman's arrest history and a few snippets online. There's a history of allegations. Brutality, framing suspects, the usual."

"Aaron," said Carl, turning back to the screen. "You knew the man. Is this plausible?"

Aaron Keyes nodded.

"Eminently plausible."

Carl took a moment, allowing the idea to settle, before he went on.

"So we've got a drug dealer who might have reason to be angry with Bateman, who's paranoid about being fitted up, and who happens to have a previous undisclosed relationship with the same woman we're looking at because she decided not to stop at the scene of a murder a few days earlier. A woman who's now refusing to cooperate with the investigation, and who might also have had a relationship with Bateman himself."

"And there's the payment into her bank account," added Harriett. "Two hundred and fifty quid from a company based in the Cayman Islands, and no reason for it as far as we can see. That, and the call from Rashid a few minutes before the boatyard shout, which neither of them wants to talk about."

"And Rashid's behaviour towards Lynn," said Marcus. "Threatening."

A phone rang somewhere in the room, and Carl looked

around to see Denise checking the display on her phone and switching it off.

"Grange called me earlier to apologise," said Lynn.

"Isn't Grange who owes you the apology," replied Marcus, but Carl's attention was on Harriett, who was staring at her screen with her mouth hanging open.

"What is it?" he asked.

"Rashid," she replied. "I need to... Hang on a moment."

She turned to her screen, brought up a file, scanned it for a moment, then turned back again.

"Sorry," she said. "I was just checking the transcript."

"What transcript?" asked Carl.

"Rashid's interview. Here."

She tapped a key, clicked on her mouse, and a third box appeared underneath the boxes containing the faces of Aaron and Lynn. This one was filled with text. As Carl watched, a red circle appeared around a line.

"'Not sure why you're bothering with all this just for some dead Scouser, anyway.'"

"I thought that was what he said," said Harriett.

There was a brief silence. Carl saw the point after a second or so, and spent the next thirty seconds watching the room, watching eyebrows raise as each team member realised the implications.

Marcus was last.

"How did...?" He looked around, realised everyone was looking at him, and fell silent.

"Harriet," said Carl. "It was your spot. Enlighten us."

"Alexander Godwin was from Merseyside. But we didn't have his identity until today. So how did Samir Rashid know he was from Liverpool?"

Carl waited again, but no one seemed to have anything to add.

"Excellent. So, we can park Grange for the moment, and the dispatcher, Angela Sherman. It's Hanson and Rashid in the spotlight. We'll bring them in tomorrow. Marcus, can you set things up with Hanson?"

"She won't want to come in," Marcus pointed out.

"This time it's not a nice little chat we're after, so she won't have much choice. She can bring a lawyer if she wants to. And we'll ask for permission to search her property while she's in. Harriett, can you line up CSI?"

"Will do, boss," replied Harriett. "What if she says no?"

"If she refuses, we'll consider arresting her or applying for a warrant. Now, who wants to handle Rashid?"

One hand shot up.

"You sure?" he asked.

"I'm sure," said Denise, and Carl reckoned that of the two people in the interview room when Rashid came in, it would be Denise who'd be the scarier one.

Even if Rashid turned out to be a killer.

DAY EIGHT

CHAPTER FIFTY-ONE

"Long time no see," said Paula Vernon.

Carl smiled at her, but he wasn't sure she was joking. That was the thing about Paula Vernon. She was a good lawyer for her clients, and she didn't piss about and play games, so he was always relieved when he walked into an interview room and saw her there.

But she was inscrutable, too. On a handful of occasions, he'd caught her in what he thought might be the beginnings of a smile, a slight movement of the lip that was gone before it was really there, but he was never entirely sure whether he'd imagined it.

Anyway, it hadn't been a long time. There weren't many lawyers equipped to represent police officers accused of Misconduct in a Public Office, or whatever else they were about to throw at Niamh Hanson. Paula Vernon was one of them. She'd acted for Streeting less than a year earlier, and Carl had come across her since on smaller, less life-changing cases.

"Get on with it," said Niamh Hanson.

Carl gestured to Marcus, who ran through the formalities and commenced the recording.

"Are you willing for your property to be searched while you're here?" asked Carl.

Hanson gave him a wary look.

"What do you mean by property?"

"Car, house, anything else we want to take a look at."

"What happens if I say no?" asked Hanson, and Paula Vernon bent over and whispered something in her ear.

Hanson sat back, arms crossed.

"Fine," she said. "Go ahead."

Marcus paused the interview for the time it took to call Harriett and tell her she could get started, and then they were on again.

"Tell us about your relationship with DS Isaac Bateman."

"Bateman?" repeated Hanson.

"You knew him, yes?" prompted Carl.

"Of course I knew him. Everyone knew him. But..." She turned to her lawyer. "I didn't think this was about Bateman. I thought you wanted to talk to me about the boatyard."

"We'll come to that," said Marcus. "But the two matters are linked. Tell us about your relationship with Bateman."

"Relationship?"

"Yes. We understand you were sleeping with him."

Hanson's mouth fell open.

"What?"

"You. Bateman. We understand you had a relationship with him. Or maybe just a one-off. Either way, we'd like to know about it."

"I don't know what you're talking about."

"There's no point in messing us around, PC Hanson,"

said Marcus. Carl could see the colour rising in his face, and stepped in.

"Are you telling us you didn't have a sexual relationship with Isaac Bateman?" he said.

"Of course not. I knew him, of course I did, he was local police. But I couldn't stand the man. Him or the rest of them."

"The rest of them?"

"The police he liked to spend time with. Bunch of racist, sexist Neanderthals, the lot of them."

"So you didn't spend time with him at police functions? I'm thinking about two in particular, one at the Inn on the Lake, the other at Bassenthwaite Manor."

There was a pause, Hanson frowning, opening her mouth to answer, then closing it again.

"No," she said eventually. "I mean, I was at the one at the Inn on the Lake, but so was half of Cumbria Police. I remember that one, because I splashed out on a room. Big deal, on a PC's pay. I don't know if DS Bateman was there, and if he was, I might have chatted to him for a minute, maybe even two minutes. I certainly didn't..."

The look on her face was enough to complete the sentence.

"And the Bassenthwaite Manor one?" asked Marcus, who seemed to have recovered his composure.

She turned to him and shrugged. "I've been to events there before, but not for a while. I don't remember when the last one was. I'd have to check my diary."

"Tell us about the phone call," said Carl, and she turned back, confusion on her face.

"What phone call?"

"The one you took from PS Rashid shortly before you

decided to ignore a call regarding a disturbance at a boatyard where a man was being murdered."

"I don't want to talk about that," she said.

"PS Rashid's been invited to answer questions about that call, Niamh. He's coming in today. If you don't tell us, I'm sure he will."

She shook her head.

"And that decision, again," prompted Marcus. "Why precisely did you choose not to stop at the boatyard?"

"I don't know," she said, a catch in her voice.

Her eyes were wet, Carl saw, and there might have been times, at the start of his career, when he'd have thought that meant something.

But he'd seen too much to fall for it now. He glanced to his side, to see Marcus watching her, suspicion written all over his face.

Good.

It was nice to think well of people, nice if you could imagine everyone was just trying to get on with their lives and not bother anyone else. It was a lovely notion. But it was a notion that would be smashed into sad little slivers the moment it came up against the reality of a career in PSD.

And if Marcus already knew that, so much the better.

CHAPTER FIFTY-TWO

Samir Rashid was due in Durranhill at ten, in fifteen minutes, which wasn't enough time to get stuck into anything useful, but too long to spend doing nothing.

Denise spent five minutes on the phone with Nikolas Costas, the man from Bateman's phone network, who confirmed that the dead man had kept his location switched off and scrambled the cell site data which might have told them where he'd been, two things Denise already knew. As for anything useful, he couldn't help her. Not yet.

"It's coming, DS Gaskill," he told her. "Be patient."

It was a good thing for Nikolas Costas that he wasn't there in the room with her. She'd woken without too much pain, but it was growing now, and she didn't know if that was just natural, or something Costas had achieved all by himself.

"Any luck?" asked Tom Willis from the spare desk. His eyes were still on his screen, and she rose from her chair to stand behind him and pretend she was interested in what he was doing.

It was the best way to stretch your back without anyone realising quite how much you needed to stretch your back.

"No, not yet, which saves you from going through more of Bateman's pointless phone data and keeps you on... What *is* this?"

"Worse than Bateman's phone data," he replied. "I'm going through the footage from Bassenthwaite Manor. Look, there's Bateman."

The screen paused, a grey wash over a handful of blurred figures with bulbous heads and elongated bodies.

"They've got one of those weird fisheye lenses on the camera," Tom explained. "And they haven't cleaned it in a while."

"Looks like someone's been burning something underneath it," Denise complained, as she followed his finger to a man leaning against what she assumed was a bar. There were other men near him, but they seemed to move away from time to time, and when they returned she couldn't be sure if they were the same men or different ones.

All men, though. That much was clear.

"Any idea who they are?" she asked.

"I'm guessing they're human," he replied. "That's about as good as it gets. And no sign of Niamh Hanson coming anywhere near him. Back giving you trouble?"

"It's fine," said Denise, who'd carried on stretching without really thinking about it, even after Tom turned to look at her. She returned to her desk, cast an eye over the overnight updates, just in case anything relevant had come in, and when she saw it hadn't, cast the same eye over the investigation database.

It caught on an update Marcus had made the previous

day. The note on Claire Saunders. "Concerns reported by her family," he'd said, and she could see the details now.

It was an email from Claire's sister to the local police station, dated four months after Claire had received her caution for soliciting. A chunk of it had been redacted, which wasn't standard procedure, even if nothing had come of the complaint. But she could always request the full version if she wanted to see it.

The wording that remained seemed a little odd.

I have concerns about my sister, Claire.

What precisely were these concerns?

Denise might have assumed they were just around Claire's lifestyle: the work she was doing, the people she was mixing with, the path she was on. But if that was the case, what did she think the local police station could do about it?

She tapped in a request for the full document, and dialled the number Marcus had left for Claire Saunders.

"Yeah?" said the woman. She sounded half asleep, and Denise glanced at the clock on her screen.

It was five past ten. Rashid was late.

"DS Gaskill, Cumbria Police. Sorry if I woke you."

Claire yawned. "No worries. Bad night. Need to be up now anyway. How can I help you?"

Denise explained why she was calling, and waited for Claire Saunders to deliver the bombshell that would blow the case wide open, but instead the woman just yawned again.

"Yeah," she said after a particularly loud one. "I was a bit wild back then."

"But your sister contacted the police station," Denise pressed. "Why do that? Why not intervene directly?"

"Oh, she did that." A laugh broke through the latest

yawn. "If she wasn't on the phone she was at the door, telling me to grow up and take a look at myself. Wouldn't stop going on at me. Suppose it worked in the end, because... Well, I'm different now."

Claire stopped, and Denise waited for her to say something else.

Something useful.

"Look," said Claire, finally. "I didn't even know about this email. But she was worried about me. She did everything she could to sort me out. I guess that included emailing the police. I'm sorry I can't help you, but I really don't know anything else, and I doubt Emily does, either."

Denise thanked her and ended the call, then checked the clock again.

Quarter past ten. And still no sign of Samir Rashid.

CHAPTER FIFTY-THREE

NIAMH HANSON's home was a modern terraced cottage situated high above Ambleside just off the road out towards Stock Ghyll Force. There were twelve almost identical houses and two larger detached ones at the end, all of them clearly well looked after, with big windows and whitewashed stone with a layer of slate beneath it. Harriett stood outside for a few minutes, taking in the views of steep hills and scattered woodland, as she climbed slowly into her forensic suit and wondered how a local PC could afford a decent place in an area full of money and second homes.

Family money or dumb luck, a good purchase at the right time, hard work and a good attitude towards money and saving. They were all reasonable possibilities.

As was Niamh Hanson supplementing her police income with something else.

She turned a full circle, smiling at a neighbour who was staring at her from the other end of the short street, then approaching the man, whose expression suggested he was terrified at the apparition walking towards him dressed entirely in white.

"DC Barnes, Cumbria Police," she said. "Do you know the woman who lives here?"

She pointed back at the house. There was an upstairs window open now, she saw, with Keisha Middleton's masked face framed in it.

The man frowned.

"Niamh? She's one of yours, isn't she? Lovely girl, Niamh. Is she alright?"

Harriett smiled again, ready to reassure the man, as Keisha's voice boomed out.

"Oi! Barnes! Get up here! Looks like someone's been a naughty girl!"

"She's absolutely fine," said Harriett, then turned and headed back to the house, slipping on her mask as she went inside, careful to keep her feet on the boards Keisha had laid out. They didn't really know what they were looking for here. But if anyone could find it, Keisha could.

And she had. Keisha was muttering as Harriett entered the room.

"Naughty, naughty," she heard. "Very naughty."

"What have you got?"

Keisha looked up.

"I've got this."

She was standing by an open wardrobe, one side full of clothes on hangers, the other with drawers. One of the drawers was open. Keisha was pointing at it. Harriett approached.

More clothes, she saw. Tiny strappy tops folded over ready for the summer. And something else at the back, behind them all. A small, plain wooden box, which Keisha had opened to reveal about a tablespoonful of a rough, grey powder.

"Is that...?"

"Ketamine, at a guess," said Keisha.

Ketamine. It was a popular drug, but a big risk to take if you were a police officer.

Most importantly, it was the same substance Zack Starling had been caught in possession of just three weeks earlier.

Zack Starling, the man Niamh Hanson had been in a relationship with, and failed to declare. The man who'd complained about being fitted up and refused to let Lynn inside his house.

Niamh Hanson had questions to answer.

CHAPTER FIFTY-FOUR

"PC Hanson," said Marcus, "tell us about Wednesday afternoon. And evening, if you don't mind."

He fixed her with what he hoped was a friendly smile, which was probably a waste of time, given the questions he'd already thrown at her.

"I need to see my notebook," she replied.

"If it helps," Marcus told her, "that was the day before you first came in to see us. The night you were all out for team drinks."

"Well, yeah, then," she said. "We had the team drinks."

"Before that," said DI Whaley.

Marcus glanced over and saw the boss wasn't bothering with a smile. Maybe they were past the point of smiles. Niamh Hanson certainly wasn't smiling.

"You weren't on shift," Marcus reminded her.

"I was at home," she said. "All afternoon and into the evening."

"Anyone else see you there?"

"No," she replied. "I was alone."

"And what did you know about Isaac Bateman's plan to approach PSD?" asked the DI, and Hanson's eyes narrowed, her forehead creasing as if she couldn't quite understand the words.

"What?" she said.

"DS Bateman intended to come in and talk to us. He'd made plans to discuss it with a colleague. What do you know about that?"

"I told you," she replied. "I don't know anything about Bateman. I hardly knew the man."

"So you've told us," said the DI. "But that's not the case when it comes to Zack Starling, is it?"

Hanson's mouth fell open for a moment, before it registered and she pulled it shut.

"What?" she said. She seemed to say that a lot.

"Zack Starling." Marcus took up the thread. "We understand you were in a relationship with him."

Niamh Hanson stared at them in silence, then turned to her lawyer.

"I've got to ask," said Paula Vernon. "What's the relevance of this line of questioning?"

DI Whaley nodded towards Marcus, who addressed the lawyer.

"We understand your client was in a relationship with this man, Zack Starling," he said. There was a tablet on the table between them, face down, and now he flipped it over to reveal Starling's mugshots from his most recent arrest. "Zack Starling is a known drug dealer. We believe this relationship speaks to motive."

"And this relationship, when's it supposed to have occurred?"

"A couple of years ago, we're told," said Marcus.

"Not much of a motive, if you don't mind me saying, DC Hosgood," said the lawyer.

Marcus had come across his share of defence lawyers in his short time in the force. Most of them had been so obviously inept or lazy he'd almost felt sorry for their clients, and the ones who knew what they were doing tended to have some other personality disorder that made them hard to like. They were aggressive, or sarcastic, or patronising – that was the worst of it, being called 'young man' by some paper-pushing slob only five years older than he was.

But he couldn't help liking Paula Vernon. She was switched on, and polite, and she'd remembered his name, which was more than could be said for most of her colleagues.

And she seemed to be doing a decent job for her client.

"Starling was – is – a drug dealer," said the DI.

"And?" asked Paula Vernon.

The DI addressed Niamh Hanson. "Do you mind telling us about the drugs found at your house?"

The PC's mouth fell open again, and this time it stayed that way for a good five seconds, while Marcus tapped on the tablet until it displayed the photo Harriett Barnes had just sent over: a small wooden box, its lid open, a greyish powder inside.

They waited.

"I've never seen this before in my life," said Hanson eventually.

"It was found in your drawer, inside your wardrobe, behind your clothes," said the DI.

"No." She shook her head firmly. "No. I'm being set up here."

"You sound like Zack Starling," said Marcus. "He said something similar to our colleague yesterday."

"No," said Hanson, again.

"This substance will be analysed by our colleagues in the lab," the DI said, his voice gentle but insistent. "But the initial view is that it's ketamine. Zack Starling was found in possession of a quantity of ketamine just three weeks ago. Now, you haven't told us anything about your relationship with Starling, but I'm starting to wonder if it really did end two years ago after all."

"I don't know about any of this," said Hanson.

"This was inside your house." Marcus pointed at the image.

"Look at it from our point of view," said the DI. "This can't be a coincidence, can it? So why don't you tell us the truth?"

"I have told you the truth," insisted Hanson.

"Is he your supplier?" asked Marcus. "Or are you helping him shift drugs?"

"I'm not having this," said Hanson, staring right at him now, a fire in her eyes he hadn't seen there before.

"If you just—" began the DI.

"No," said Hanson. "I'm being set up. It's obvious. I'm not saying any more."

Marcus looked over at the lawyer, who gave a tiny shrug. If her client wouldn't talk, there wasn't much she could do about it, not there in the room with the men who were questioning her. Maybe if they gave the two of them some time alone, she'd come around.

Marcus didn't think so, though.

"You won't answer our questions?" said the DI.

Hanson shook her head.

"Fine," said the DI. "In that case, Niamh Hanson, I am arresting you in connection with the possession of and intent to supply ketamine in contravention of the Misuse of Drugs Act 1971."

CHAPTER FIFTY-FIVE

Denise had only stopped by to see if the interview was still going on. As she turned the corner, she saw the door open and Marcus Hosgood emerge, walking towards her. Behind him was the lawyer, Paula Vernon. Niamh Hanson followed, and the way DI Whaley walked behind her, close, but not too close, was enough to tell Denise that things had moved quickly in there.

She hadn't expected to see Niamh Hanson under arrest already.

"What happened?" she asked quietly, as Marcus drew level with her.

"The drugs," he whispered back. "She wouldn't talk about Starling, so the boss arrested her over the drugs."

She watched as the DI applied a gentle touch to Hanson's back, steering her down another corridor, where she'd go through the custody formalities. Where she'd have her possessions catalogued and her rights explained, and eventually, her blood taken and sent to the lab for testing.

Shit.

Denise had seen it happen a hundred times. It wasn't always part of the post-arrest procedure, but it was particularly important when a police officer was the one being arrested. Drug addiction remained the easiest way to blackmail a cop. Get them hooked, make them do whatever you wanted them to.

Hence the blood tests.

And Denise didn't like to think what would happen if her own blood got tested. *When* her own blood got tested. It had been a while, since the last random sampling. It could come at any time.

She'd have to get herself clean by then.

She returned to her desk. Still no Samir Rashid. She called him, and it went straight to voicemail, which might mean he'd switched it off because he was preparing for an interview with PSD, or might mean he'd been murdered and dumped in a river, like Isaac Bateman.

Probably the former, but you never knew.

There was a number on the system for Claire Saunders's sister, Emily, the one who'd made the complaint, or expression of concern, or whatever it was, and Denise dialled it.

Another voicemail.

She left a message, explaining who she was and stressing that Claire wasn't in any trouble. "I'm just looking into a local matter that dates from around the time you sent your email," she said. "It's probably nothing, but I'd love to speak to you and get a little background."

She smiled as she put the phone down. She could still talk like a normal human being when she had to.

At half past ten, half an hour late, she got the call that Samir Rashid had finally turned up and been taken to one of the interview rooms, where he was waiting for her.

"Who's his lawyer?" she asked the desk sergeant.

"He's by himself."

She took the stairs slowly. Rashid had kept her waiting long enough, after all. When she pushed open the door, she expected to see someone sitting with Rashid, but no, the desk sergeant hadn't been mistaken. Samir Rashid was alone.

He stood as she came in, a big smile on his face, and walked towards her with his hand out.

She ignored the hand.

"Sit down," she told him.

"Good to see you," he replied.

"I'm going to caution you now," she said.

"Oh," he replied. "I thought this was just, you know, an informal chat sort of thing."

"You had your chance for an informal chat, Sergeant Rashid. Instead, you told us we were rats and refused to say anything helpful. Now, if you want to get yourself a lawyer, that's fine. But one way or another, we're getting some answers out of you today, and we're getting them on tape. OK?"

Rashid sat down and gave a solemn nod.

"OK," he said. "And no, I don't want a lawyer. For now."

"Good. Let's get started then, shall we?"

CHAPTER FIFTY-SIX

BACK OUTSIDE HANSON'S HOUSE, Harriett was finding a shortage of neighbours. This wasn't really second-home territory, not in this street. These were just normal people with normal jobs, which meant they weren't likely to be home at eleven on a Monday morning.

Some of them had doorbell cameras, but a brief examination of the angles was enough to tell her Hanson's house wouldn't be caught on any of them. So the woman's claim that she'd been home alone in the hours leading up to her team night out couldn't be verified.

Harriett wasn't sure that really mattered. Bateman could have died at almost any time from the call he'd made to DI Keyes to some point a day or so before his body had been discovered. As windows went, it was wide enough to drive a truck through.

"Oi!" she heard, and turned to see Keisha's head at the window again.

"Yes?" she shouted back, then scurried back towards the house. Whatever Keisha Middleton was about to tell her, it probably wasn't the sort of conversation they should be conducting in the middle of the street. Not all the neighbours were out, after all.

"Up here," called Keisha, and she followed the voice back to the same room they'd found the drugs in. Keisha was standing at the same wardrobe, too, but the other side of it this time, her gloved hand thrust between the hanging clothes, holding items apart.

"Look at this," she said.

"What?" asked Harriett, stepping forward for a closer look.

At the far end of the wardrobe, almost obscured by the open door, were what Harriett assumed were Hanson's less important clothes, or at least, the ones she didn't wear much and didn't mind getting a little dusty. There was a dress, a severe, prim-looking thing that Hanson had no doubt been obliged to wear for some formal occasion she hadn't had cause to repeat. Past that, there was a thin waterproof coat, and then a puffer jacket, and then another coat.

"Here," said Keisha.

Beyond the second coat was a third, similar to the first two, and on the same hanger, a pair of brown walking trousers. Keisha was indicating the items, and even from close range, Harriett struggled to make out what she was pointing to.

And then she saw it.

"Fibres?" she said.

Keisha nodded.

"Blue fibres. Again, it'll need to be tested, but I can tell you that's denim."

"Right," said Harriett, her eyes scanning across the rest of the wardrobe, and the handful of items scattered elsewhere in the room.

"Save yourself the bother," Keisha told her. "There's only one bit of denim in this house, and it's a black skirt that would look pretty damn good on me. Nothing blue."

"Right," said Harriett, who was starting to see where Keisha's thoughts were heading.

"Thing is," Keisha said, "I do know one particular arsehole who's always in a lightweight denim jacket of that exact shade. A dead arsehole now, but still an arsehole."

Harriett nodded and pulled out her phone. She navigated to the team inbox and the photos Keisha's colleague Caroline had taken from the crime scene.

The photos of Bateman in the car, hanging upside down.

"Yes," she said.

"Thought so," said Keisha.

Isaac Bateman had died wearing a denim jacket of precisely the shade of blue that had somehow found its way into Niamh Hanson's wardrobe.

CHAPTER FIFTY-SEVEN

Samir Rashid was smiling again as Denise ran through the formalities and commenced the recording.

"Just you, is it?" he asked.

"Just me. And I should let you know that your colleague, PC Hanson, has just been arrested."

The smile dropped from his face like it had been picked out and shot.

"Sorry?" he said.

"Niamh Hanson. Arrested."

"What for?"

Denise simply shook her head. "Now, we've been going through the interview you granted us the other day, Sergeant Rashid, and we've noticed something rather interesting. How did you know the victim of the boatyard murder was from Liverpool?"

"Eh?" said Rashid.

"You're going to have to be a little more eloquent than that, I'm afraid." She leaned forward and looked him in the eye. "Look, between you and me, Sergeant Rashid, it's like this. We've just got a name for the body in the boatyard. He's a Merseyside businessman called Alexander Godwin."

She watched him carefully as she spoke, but there wasn't a flicker. Maybe he knew this already. Maybe he didn't.

"But the thing is," she continued, "we've only just found this out. Well, yesterday, to be fair. But that's still several days after you said, in interview with my colleagues, 'Not sure why you're bothering with all this just for some dead Scouser, anyway.' So would you care to explain how you knew the victim was from that area of the country?"

Rashid's eyes had gone wide.

"Sergeant Rashid?"

"Sorry," he said. "I don't... I don't remember."

She sighed.

"That's not very helpful," she told him.

"I really don't." He gestured helplessly, palms out, the picture of innocence, if innocence had been drawn by a toddler in cheap marker pen. "I thought everyone knew. Maybe..."

He scratched his head, and Denise decided she might as well pretend to believe in all this – the confusion, the head-scratching, the trying *so* hard to remember.

"Maybe Niamh told me," he said, finally. "Someone did."

"Niamh Hanson?"

He nodded.

"Must have been her." He was frowning. "I mean, I'm not sure I remember. We were talking about it."

"We?"

"At the pub. Me and Stevie and Niamh. Maybe one or two others. It's all a bit of a blur, to be honest."

"Perhaps you can think a little harder, Sergeant Rashid. See if anything comes into focus."

He shrugged. "We were drunk. I was drunk. She was even drunker."

"PC Hanson?"

He grinned, and then remembered himself and turned serious. "Yes. Stevie gave her a lift home. We both had to help her to his car, the state she was in."

"Right. But you remember discussing the fact that the boatyard victim was from Liverpool, yes?"

"Yes."

"And someone raised it that night?"

"Reckon so, yes."

"And you think that was Niamh Hanson?"

"Yes. I mean, it might have been. Yes."

Not exactly conclusive.

"Moving on, Sergeant Rashid, we still haven't had an explanation of why you called PC Hanson during her shift, shortly before the dispatcher contacted her about the disturbance in the boatyard."

"What do you want me to say?"

"I want you to tell me what you discussed."

"I mean, I don't know. I don't remember."

"You don't remember that, either?"

Again, that shrug, and for a moment, Denise contemplated standing up and arresting the bastard. There had to be something she could arrest him for, misconduct or perverting the course of justice or even assisting an offender. And there had to be something in that head of his, too.

But only for a moment. There wasn't enough to arrest the man, and there certainly wasn't enough to charge him. Not yet.

"Thank you, Sergeant Rashid," she said, and stood up.

"Sorry?"

"You can go now. Thanks for your time."

"Oh. Right." The smile was back, but it was a lot more unsure of itself than it had been when they'd started.

So the whole thing hadn't been a complete waste of time.

CHAPTER FIFTY-EIGHT

NIAMH HANSON BEING under arrest didn't really change much. She couldn't walk out, but Carl couldn't force her to answer his questions any more than he'd been able to force her to before.

And now the clock was ticking. Charge or release.

Her face looked different when she came back into the interview room. Shiny. The sign of someone who'd scrubbed off all evidence of tears, leaving just the clear evidence that tears had been there, because there wasn't anything else for her to scrub.

"Tell me about the payment in your bank account," said Marcus.

"What payment?"

"The two hundred and fifty pounds. It was made by a company called Winterburn, registered in the Cayman Islands, which means we can't touch it, but the thing about companies in the Cayman Islands is that they're there for one of two reasons, and neither of them's the weather."

Hanson stared at him blankly, and he continued.

"One's to avoid tax. The other's to avoid having to tell anyone who actually owns them, or runs them. So I'm sure you'll appreciate that when someone we're looking into receives a payment from a Cayman Islands company, we sit up and pay attention."

"Two hundred and fifty quid?" said Hanson.

"That's right," Marcus confirmed.

She laughed, now, a short, bitter laugh that took Carl by surprise.

"You think I killed Bateman for two hundred and fifty quid?"

"Are you saying you were paid more than that?" said Marcus, and Paula Vernon leaned forward.

"Hang on," she said. "You can't—"

"No, you're right. Getting ahead of myself here. Apologies."

Niamh Hanson was shaking her head, sporting a sardonic smile hanging over from the laugh. "You think I managed to move Bateman's dead body around by myself?"

"How did you know it was moved?" asked Carl.

"Oh come on, DI Whaley. One of our own gets murdered, we make it our business to find out the details. Word gets around. He was beaten on the head and shoved into his car. You've seen the size of the man. You think I could do that?"

"Maybe you had help," suggested Marcus. "Maybe it was your old boyfriend, Zack Starling. We know you're still close to him."

"Not this again," said Hanson.

"Fine." Carl lifted a hand, and Marcus nodded at him.

Point taken. Time to move on.

"I'd like you to look at these images," said Marcus,

tapping on the tablet to reveal a series of photographs. "They show items of clothing in your wardrobe."

He waited.

"Yeah," said Hanson.

"Do you recognise the clothes?" asked Marcus.

Hanson pulled the tablet closer, lifted it and squinted, then put it back down and nodded.

"Yes."

"These are close-ups of the same clothes." Marcus reached across and tapped again, and another series of images appeared. "As you can see, there is a significant presence of blue fibres that don't match the clothes they're on, and don't appear to match any of the clothes in your house."

"Right," said Hanson, frowning, clearly unsure where this was going.

"Can you account for the presence of these fibres?" Marcus asked.

"What?" said Hanson.

"We're having them examined, but the crime scene investigator is convinced they're a match for the denim jacket worn by Isaac Bateman when he was, as you put it, beaten on the head and shoved into his car."

"What the fuck?" said Hanson, shaking her head. "No. Sorry. I've never seen these before. No idea how they got there."

"One more thing, for the moment," said Carl. "We understand you told colleagues that the victim of the boatyard murder was from Liverpool."

"I did what?"

"You told colleagues—"

"I heard you. I just don't know what you're talking about."

"That's not what we're hearing. How did you know, Niamh? How did you know Alexander Godwin was from Liverpool?"

"Who?" said Niamh.

"We'll leave it there," replied Carl.

They'd thrown a lot at her. Enough for her to have a quiet conversation with her lawyer, and maybe, just maybe, enough for her to start telling the truth, now she knew what she was up against.

CHAPTER FIFTY-NINE

DI Whaley waited until DI Keyes and Lynn were on-screen, then kicked things off.

"Niamh Hanson's not telling us anything," he said.

"Want me to have a crack at her?" asked DS Gaskill, and the boss shook his head.

"Marcus has gone in hard, gone in gently, played it every way possible. If she was going to talk, she'd have spoken to him."

Harriett glanced at Marcus, but he was staring at his screen, frowning in concentration. She wasn't sure he'd even picked up on the DI's praise.

"We've confronted her about Starling," he was saying. "Him, plus the payment, the drugs, the fibres, and the phone call. And the Liverpool line. She's not talking. Speaking of which..."

"Rashid claims he doesn't remember it," said DS Gaskill.

"But he does remember Hanson telling him the boatyard victim was from Liverpool?" asked Harriett, and the DS pulled a face.

"Not really. He *thinks* he does. Someone told him. Someone told the lot of them, apparently."

Starling, the payment, the drugs, the fibres, the phone call, the Liverpool line. Any one of those, in isolation, would be enough to make PSD twitchy. All of them, though?

Niamh Hanson was in a lot of trouble.

"Talking of the victim," said Lynn, her lips now synched so perfectly with her voice it was like she was in the room with them, "I've got a little more information from the business partner. They were looking to buy some land north of Keswick."

"Right. I think we knew that," said DI Keyes, also on the screen.

"But what we didn't know was that a local consortium was interested in the same plot of land."

"Right. So what, you're thinking motive?" asked DS Gaskill.

"It's possible," said Lynn.

"It is," agreed the boss. "See what you can find out about this local consortium, Lynn. Starting with who the hell they are. We can mention them to Hanson when we speak to her next. OK, Marcus?"

There was a silence, during which all eyes turned to Marcus, still squinting at his screen. Harriett thought she could hear something, too, a tinny, high-pitched noise.

Was Marcus watching a video during the boss's briefing?

"Marcus?" said DI Whaley.

"Yeah, boss. Sorry. Will put it to her in interview. Got it."

"Right." DI Whaley turned to address the rest of the room. "We'll let her stew overnight, see if that loosens her tongue at all. And we need to be ready to pick up Starling, too, given the way he acted when Lynn went to see him, and the drugs Keisha found at Hanson's place."

"Have you got anywhere identifying Bateman's police friends?" asked DI Keyes on the screen.

"No," said the boss. "And thanks for reminding us. I want to broaden things out from Hanson. She's looking like our best bet, but if we can find these people, we might get an idea of why Bateman wanted to come in and talk to us, which, in case you need reminding, is the main reason it's us running this investigation rather than Jasmine Woolley."

"And we might get a clearer sense of his movements before he died," added DS Gaskill. "But unfortunately, nobody seems to know who Bateman's friends were."

"True," said DI Whaley.

"I'm not so sure about that," said Marcus, and once again, every eye turned in his direction.

"What?" asked the boss.

"Listen to this," Marcus replied. He tapped on his screen, and another box appeared on the big screen, underneath the ones with DI Keyes and Lynn in them.

Inside it was a still from Niamh Hanson's interview, the first one that morning, and as they watched, Marcus tapped again, and it started moving.

"Of course not."

Niamh Hanson's voice boomed out of the speakers with a force that had Harriett physically recoiling in her chair. Marcus tapped again, and the sound fell to a more tolerable level.

"I knew him," Hanson was saying. "Of course I did, he was local police. But I couldn't stand the man. Him or the rest of them."

"The rest of them?" asked Marcus.

"The police he liked to spend time with. Bunch of racist, sexist Neanderthals, the lot of them."

Marcus reached over and tapped to stop the recording, and Harriett turned to see a smile forming on DI Whaley's face.

"Looks like we'll be paying PC Hanson a visit sooner than I thought," he said.

CHAPTER SIXTY

MARCUS COULD FEEL his eyes beginning to lose focus. He looked up at DS Gaskill, knocking back her third coffee in fifteen minutes, and wondered how two creatures from the same species could react so differently to the same thing.

If he risked coffee now, even half a weak cup, he wouldn't get to sleep until four in the morning. And he wouldn't even have Lolly to keep him company.

They'd had to wait nearly an hour, because Paula Vernon had left and made it most of the way home before she was called back in. Home for Paula Vernon was Kirkby Lonsdale, which was basically Yorkshire, as far as Marcus was concerned, even though technically it was still Cumbria. The important thing, though, was that it was sixty miles, and Niamh Hanson was refusing to talk to them until her lawyer turned up.

Part of Marcus was annoyed at being made to wait. But he could see Hanson's play here. She had something they wanted. If she was going to get anything for it, she'd want her lawyer on hand to make sure every 't' was crossed and every 'i' had the dot in the right place.

"I'm so sorry," said Paula Vernon, hurrying into the interview room and out of her coat. "I was almost home when I heard."

"That's OK," said DS Gaskill. She was smiling, and the smile didn't look right on her face.

Neither did the patience.

"Let's get started, then," Marcus suggested, and once they'd started recording, DS Gaskill gestured for him to open things up.

"When we spoke this morning," he said, "you mentioned DS Bateman's friends. On the force, I mean. You referred to them as sexist Neanderthals—"

"I believe my client called them 'racist, sexist Neanderthals'," said Paula Vernon, and Marcus suppressed a smile.

"Racist, sexist Neanderthals. You're quite right. As you know, Isaac Bateman was planning to come in and talk to us in PSD, and we are of the belief that this decision is connected with his murder. You claim not to know anything about this proposed visit—"

"And I don't," said Hanson.

"Fine. Well, maybe his friends on the force do. But we're struggling to identify them."

"Not a popular man, Isaac Bateman," added DS Gaskill.

"So," continued Marcus, "if you could give us some names, it might get us there sooner rather than later."

"Names?" said Hanson.

"Yes. Bateman's friends. The ones you referred to as racist, sexist Neanderthals."

"What's in it for me?" asked Hanson.

Marcus glanced over to DS Gaskill, who gave a tiny shake of the head. They'd discussed this already, between them, but he wanted to be sure she hadn't changed her mind.

"You say you have no idea about any of this, Godwin, Bateman, the drugs, the fibres?"

"Yes."

"Which means someone else has been setting all this up?"

Hanson shrugged. "It seems likely, doesn't it?"

"Well if that's the case, I'd have thought you'd be keen to help us track down the real culprits as quickly as possible, because given the weight of the evidence against you, that's the only way you're going to exonerate yourself."

"I'm not sure that's true, DC Hosgood," said Paula Vernon, and he could sense the steel behind her smile. Maybe she was right. She looked like someone who could demolish all that evidence in court without breaking a sweat.

"Maybe," he conceded. "But either way, it has to be in your interest for us to find the real killers."

"I need a few minutes with my lawyer," said Hanson.

Twenty minutes later, Paula Vernon's head appeared in the canteen.

"We're ready," she said.

Back in the interview room, Hanson laid out her demands.

"I'll tell you what I know if you release me immediately, with a full apology, and ensure that there's no record of this affair on the system."

"We can't do—" Marcus began, but DS Gaskill was speaking at the same time.

"What is it you know?" she asked.

Of course. At least find out what the suspect has before

you tell them you're not giving them anything for it. The knowledge of what they weren't telling you was better than no knowledge at all.

"Names," said Hanson. "Bateman's friends."

"How many?"

"Do we have a deal?" asked Paula Vernon.

"I'm afraid not," said DS Gaskill.

"What?" said Hanson.

Vernon raised one eyebrow, but unlike her client, she didn't seem particularly surprised.

"We can't release you until you've given us an adequate explanation for the money, the phone call, the fibres, the drugs, and your knowledge about Alexander Godwin, and we're happy with your relationship with Zack Starling." DS Gaskill spoke gently but clearly, without emotion.

"Then I'm not telling you anything," said Hanson.

Marcus looked at the lawyer, who seemed uncomfortable for the first time that day.

"It really is in your interest—" Marcus began.

"I'm telling you nothing," said Hanson, louder this time.

"Why don't we have a quick chat, just the two of us?" suggested Paula Vernon, but Hanson shook her head.

"Nope. This is a joke, all of it. Give me what I've asked for, or I'm telling you nothing."

DS Gaskill gave a sad, weary sigh, and stood up.

"I guess you're telling us nothing, then."

DAY NINE

CHAPTER SIXTY-ONE

THE FACT that Hanson had changed her mind overnight wasn't much of a surprise. The fact that she'd changed it quite so dramatically was more than Denise had expected, though.

"Three names," she said.

"Go on," replied Denise. She'd had a bad night, her back and neck alternating roles as host for the ugliest of the pain. But whatever she'd been through, Niamh Hanson had had it worse.

The woman slumped in her chair, her eyes red, her face no longer shiny but a patchwork of red and white blotches, her mouth curled into a pained smile that kept fading as she forgot to hold it in place, then remembered and pasted it back on again.

"Darren Chisholm."

Denise waited. Hanson looked over at Paula Vernon, who nodded.

"Harvey Grey," she continued. "John Illingworth."

She stopped and just looked at them. There wasn't

enough energy in the look to call it a stare. Her eyes were open, and Denise and Marcus were sitting in front of her. That was as far as it went.

"These men are – were – Bateman's friends on the force?" asked Marcus.

"Yes."

"Tell me about Zack Starling," said Denise. The woman was in a sharing mood, after all.

Hanson looked at her lawyer again, and again, Paula Vernon nodded at her.

"Yes," she said.

"Yes, what?"

"Yes, we were in a relationship. Me and Zack. Years ago. It ended when I became aware of his criminal activity, though."

"Really?" asked Marcus, the scepticism Denise felt dripping from the single word.

It wasn't exactly likely. Hanson had been a cop. A local cop. Someone like Starling, everyone knew what they were like. No one more than a local cop.

"Really," insisted Hanson. "I know what you're thinking. Zack was trouble, how could I not have known? But he wasn't. He was so far down the food chain he was barely there at all."

"What do you mean?" asked Denise.

"Yes, he dealt a little. But hardly anything. Small amounts of weed, to the tourists in the campsite. If there was ever anything bigger than that, he was fitted up."

"He was caught with a supply of ketamine three weeks ago," Marcus pointed out.

"That's now. I'm talking about then. And me and Zack,

it's been over for a long time. Ended two years ago. I've had nothing to do with him since."

"Why didn't you report the relationship at the time?" asked Denise, even though she knew the answer.

"I didn't want that on my record, did I?"

"What sort of man is Zack Starling, then?" asked Marcus.

"I told you, I don't know him any more."

"OK," Marcus said. "Let's say that's true. What did he think of Isaac Bateman?"

For a moment, Hanson looked even more miserable than she had at the start of the interview, something Denise wouldn't have thought possible if she hadn't seen it.

"He didn't like him," she said. "Insisted Bateman was always on his case. Fitting him up."

"You realise how this looks?" said Denise.

"But I've got nothing to do with Zack any more!" Hanson slammed her fist on the table in frustration, and Denise saw Marcus flinch in surprise. "And he's not a violent man, either."

"Zack Starling? Not a violent man?"

"No," said Hanson. Denise tried to remember what she'd seen of Starling's record. She couldn't recall any violent offences there.

"Thank you," she said. "You've been really helpful. Now, there are a few other items we'd like to discuss. Again."

Hanson sighed.

"This payment into your bank account."

"I've told you, I don't know anything about it."

"Fine," said Denise. "How about your relationship with Isaac Bateman?"

"There was no relationship. I couldn't stand the man."

"You were seen in his room at the Bassenthwaite Manor Hotel."

"Jesus Christ!" said Hanson. She looked like she was about to cry. "I don't get it. Am I supposed to have hated Bateman, or slept with him?"

"Why not both?" asked Marcus.

Hanson just glared at him.

"Tell me about the call you took from Sergeant Rashid," said Denise.

"Leave Sammy out of it," replied Hanson.

And that, thought Denise, was as much as they were going to get.

Which was still more than she'd hoped for.

CHAPTER SIXTY-TWO

Lynn had come across groups who called themselves a 'consortium' before. A handful of low-level drug dealers, a semi-organised set of football hooligans, and, on one memorable occasion, a gang of teenage girls who'd developed a surprisingly sophisticated car theft routine.

This was the first one that was worthy of the name, though.

She could see the plot of land north of Keswick, on the edges of Skiddaw. She'd found it on an auctioneer's website, called them, and confirmed the names of both bidding parties. The Godwin Land Partnership was out of the running now, for obvious reasons.

The Cumbria Estate Facilities Servicing Group was the last man standing.

It was a hell of a mouthful, a random jumble of corporate words preceded by a location, forgettable the moment you read it, but it was real. It had articles of incorporation and a registered company number, and directors, who were also companies, and shareholders, who were other companies.

Fifteen minutes of digging into the shareholders of the directors and the directors of the shareholders told Lynn what she'd suspected the moment she saw the name, which was that the people who really owned The Cumbria Estate Facilities Servicing Group were happy to remain very much in the background.

She heard footsteps behind her and turned, expecting, unaccountably, to see Isaac Bateman's face looming over her, but it was just DI Woolley, looking at Lynn like she was something she'd just wiped off her shoe.

The usual look, then.

"Solved your murder yet?" she asked, and walked off without waiting for a reply. Beyond her, in the corridor, Lynn could see more figures, and for a moment she froze as she locked eyes with Sergeant Rashid. There was something in that look, something raw and so obvious it was easy to overlook when you saw it in real life, which was why it took her a moment to recognise it for what it was.

Hatred.

On the whole, Lynn thought she preferred the something-wiped-off-the-shoe look she'd just got from DI Woolley.

Rashid looked away and carried on along the corridor. Behind him came Stephen Grange, who offered a shrug and a sheepish grin before he, too, was gone.

Lynn returned to her work, trying to focus on the numbers and names and ignore the afterimage of Rashid's eyes, which seemed somehow burned into her own.

The auctioneer, Davis Holroyd, was friendly enough, but he couldn't really help.

"I've not met the bidders themselves," he told her. "You don't, usually. Just the lawyers."

"And who are the lawyers?"

She noted down the name, Millett Weald, a local firm, thanked him, and called the lawyers.

"I don't think so," said the person who answered, a man who sounded about sixteen years old and spoke with a lisp he seemed proud of.

"This is a murder investigation," she told him.

"In that case, once we've seen the proper documentation, I'm sure we'll be happy to release all the information we can. But until then, DC Hedley, our files will remain sealed."

The word remained stuck in her head, the way he said it, *thealed*, alongside Rashid's eyes, which in her clearly mistaken memory were now a deep shade of red. The lawyers wouldn't help, but someone would have paid for the land registry searches.

It took half an hour to establish that someone had indeed paid for the land registry searches, but that someone was Millett Weald, footing the bill on behalf of their client. And Millett Weald's files were sealed.

Thealed.

Davis Holroyd had emailed her all the information he had, but there was nothing helpful in there. At least he was trying. She called him, racking her memory at the same time, trying to recall what you had to do when you bought land. It had been years since she and Gerry had bought their place, and she couldn't get past the lawyers and the bank.

"Of course," said the auctioneer, "they organised a survey."

The surveyor. Hers had saved them a fortune. How could she have forgotten the surveyor?

"I don't suppose you have the name?" she asked.

"Give me a minute."

Davis Holroyd was as good as his word, returning a

minute later with a name she wasn't familiar with and a Carlisle phone number.

The phone at Willis Carmichael was answered on the first ring by a man who gave his name as Mike and was familiar with the survey, since he was the one who'd conducted it.

"I was hoping you might be able to tell me a little more about the place," she said.

"It's a shithole," he said, his voice still pleasant and friendly.

"How so?"

"You can't really put anything there. Not anything useful, anyway. Not anything *good*. They... Hang on."

There were voices in the background now, one male, one female, raised in what sounded like argument. As they drew closer, the tones became shriller, and Lynn had the uncomfortable sensation that they were talking to her.

They weren't, though. They were talking to her new friend, Mike, and they didn't sound very happy with him.

"Better go," said Mike, and cut the call, and that was the end of the most promising conversation Lynn had managed all morning.

Her phone rang half a second later, and she answered immediately, thinking it might be Mike calling back already.

"Talk to Zack Starling," said a voice, neither male nor female, distorted through so much software it was barely human at all.

"Who is this?" she asked.

"Talk to Zack Starling," repeated the voice. "Check his phone."

Then the line went dead.

CHAPTER SIXTY-THREE

THERE WERE THREE FOLDERS, freshly filled with intelligence profiles, on the desk in front of Harriett. There were five boxes open on the big screen. From three of them, six eyes stared out into the room.

"You sure this is the best way?" asked Tom.

Pushing down her annoyance, Harriett turned to him with a smile.

"It's worth trying, isn't it?" she said.

She'd have a word with him later about questioning her judgement in front of her colleagues like that.

"OK." He shrugged.

Marcus looked from one of them to the other, waiting.

"So," she said. "The three men Hanson gave us. These are their images, from the internal systems. They're all in Cumbria, so it makes sense."

"You think she was telling the truth?" asked Tom.

"It felt like it," said Marcus. "But she could just be a good liar. Ugly bunch, aren't they?"

It was true, and Harriett was glad someone else had said

it first. Darren Chisholm was an overweight middle-aged man with a pronounced brow and a face that looked confused by the concept of the camera. Harvey Grey had one long eyebrow and no other hair at all, which might have been fine if it weren't for the unfortunate, almost conical shape of his skull. John Illingworth was the most normal-looking of the three, with thick glasses on a round face, a poorly shaved beard, and a crooked smile revealing at least two missing teeth.

"So," Harriett continued, "if we keep those images up on the screen, in those three boxes, and focus on the footage from the Inn on the Lake and the Bassenthwaite Manor Hotel in the other two boxes, hopefully we'll be able to identify them at these events."

"And if we can?"

"If we see them with DS Bateman, any real contact with him, then I think we can assume Hanson was telling the truth. At least, enough to call them and have a word. But without any supporting evidence..."

She waited, and after a moment both Tom and Marcus nodded in agreement.

"OK," she said. "Let's go."

The first hit came no more than ten minutes later, the distinctive shape of Harvey Grey's head proving surprisingly useful. It was Tom who spotted him, leaning against the bar in the Bassenthwaite Manor Hotel. The image was smudged, and the fisheye lens made Grey's head seem even longer than it was, but it was so much longer than everyone else's in the footage, it could only be him.

They'd already identified Bateman, and it took just five more minutes for them to spot the two men together, chatting at the bar, arms on shoulders as they greeted one another, the physical contact of people who were familiar with each other.

If the Real Cops existed, it was a safe bet that Grey was one of them.

Darren Chisholm appeared fifteen minutes after that, strolling in through the door at the Inn on the Lake like he owned the place.

That wasn't all he seemed to think he owned.

"Did you see that?" said Harriett.

"I did," confirmed Tom.

"Yes," said Marcus, in a tone of weary disgust.

"He put..." said Harriett.

"He did," agreed Tom.

"He put his hand on that girl's bum. The one walking past with the tray of empties. Looks like she gave him a mouthful, at least," said Marcus. "Lucky she didn't glass him."

"And these are the people who call themselves Real Cops," muttered Tom.

Now they'd identified him, spotting Chisholm with Bateman was a simple enough matter. They spoke at the bar briefly, then drifted apart, and were together again a little later, sitting at a table by a window overlooking the lake.

Two down. One to go.

Illingworth proved a tougher catch. In the end, it was Harriett who saw him, his face turned for a fraction of a second towards the camera near the bar in the Candleroom at the Inn on the Lake. She paused it, so they could take in his clothes, which might make him easier to spot again.

Having shown up once, Illingworth now seemed to be everywhere, but unlike Bateman and the other two, he seemed to know everyone, too. He stopped and chatted every few minutes, shaking hands, smiling, acting, on the whole, like an entirely normal human being. It was nearly half an hour before they saw him with Bateman, and they had to rewind and watch the brief interaction four times before they could be sure the two men knew each other.

"They're definitely talking," said Marcus.

"Look." Harriett froze the footage again and approached the screen, pointing out Illingworth's arm, his hand out to touch Bateman's shoulder.

"They know each other," said Tom. "That's it. All three. What next?"

"Next," said Harriett, "we call them."

CHAPTER SIXTY-FOUR

"Harvey Grey?" said Marcus.

"Who's calling?" said the man.

"This is DC Marcus Hosgood, Cumbria Police. Is that Sergeant Grey?"

"It is. How can I help you, young man?"

Marcus turned and gave a thumbs-up. Harriett Barnes was already putting the phone down and shaking her head. He hadn't heard her speak. Darren Chisholm hadn't even answered his phone, by the sound of it.

"I'm calling to talk to you about someone I think you know. A colleague."

"Right," said Grey, drawing the word out, a note of uncertainty entering his voice.

After seeing what he'd done to the waitress at the Inn on the Lake, Marcus had offered to call Chisholm himself. So had Tom Willis. But Harriett had insisted, and even though all three of them were the same rank, Harriett seemed to be in charge.

It was probably a good thing for Chisholm he hadn't answered the phone.

"Sergeant Isaac Bateman, based in Langdale Station."

"I know him," said Grey. "Knew him, I should say. What's your interest in this?"

"I'm calling from Carlisle. Durranhill. Seems you're aware that Sergeant Bateman's no longer with us."

There was a short pause, and then the quality of the sound changed, as if Grey had moved into a different room. Tom Willis had gone for coffee, and Harriett Barnes was on the phone again already.

"In Carlisle where, exactly?" asked Grey.

It was always going to come out. Marcus had just hoped it would come out a little later.

"PSD," he said.

"Oh, no," said Grey.

"Sergeant Grey, I think—"

"Look, I don't want to talk to you, OK?" said Grey. The uncertainty in his voice had been replaced by something sharper.

Something that sounded a lot like fear.

"I think things have got past the point where—"

"Don't call me again," said Grey, and ended the call before Marcus could finish what he was saying.

"Stupid bloody idiot," Marcus muttered. Harriett Barnes was still on the phone, talking quietly, nodding, even though no one except Marcus could see her, a serious expression on her face.

By the sound of it, she was having more luck with John Illingworth than Marcus had had with Grey.

He put down his phone and pulled up the latest updates on his screen. There was nothing new there, nothing he didn't already know, but it wouldn't hurt to see it all again. All those moving parts. Maybe he could finally slot one into place.

For ten minutes, he stared at the screen, tapping between reports and transcripts and notes, and by the end of it all, it made no more sense than it had when he'd started.

But something was beginning to crystallise in his mind.

The idea that Niamh Hanson might not be guilty after all.

There were so many elements pointing to her. But he couldn't shake the sense that she might be telling the truth. In those interviews, she'd been helpful, she'd been obstructive, she'd ranged between resignation and anger and despair. The one constant was that every time, she'd been convincing.

There was a note on the screen in front of him from Harriett Barnes, the record of her meeting with Millie Tennant. Marcus read through it for the third time, then picked up his phone.

"Yeah?" said the woman.

"Millie Tennant?"

"Speaking. Who's this?"

"DC Marcus Hosgood. Cumbria Police."

"Bloody hell, another one?"

He gave an apologetic laugh. "I know. I'm sorry to bother you. And thanks for meeting with my colleague. I just wanted to ask you a couple of questions."

"OK, but it'll have to be quick. I'm supposed to be on stocktake."

"OK, then. Why were you so keen to talk to the police about Niamh Hanson?"

"What?"

"It's a simple question, Miss Tennant. We're grateful for

the information you've given us. But I was wondering why you chose to give it."

"As I recall," said Mille Tennant, "you were the ones who came looking for me. Left a message on my phone, came to my place of work."

"Yes, that's true. But you've been very forthcoming about someone who was apparently a friend of yours at one time. Why is th—?"

"Fuck it," said Millie Tennant, and for a moment Marcus thought someone else was about to hang up on him, but he waited, and she gave a long sigh, and continued. "Yes. Well, we were mates. It's true. Since we were schoolgirls. Then years later, she starts going out with my brother, and I told them both, I don't want to get in the middle of this, but it seemed fine, it was all quite serious. And then suddenly she dumps him for that fucking waster."

"Zack Starling?"

"One and the same."

"And your brother?"

"Near enough destroyed him. He's alright now, though. Married. Happy enough. He's the forgiving sort."

"And you're not?"

She laughed.

"No, I suppose I'm not. But it's not like I've lied. I've only told you the truth, and it was what you wanted to know. I mean, it would have been wrong of me to hold back, wouldn't it?"

"It would, Miss Tennant. Thank you for your honesty."

He ended the call and sat, thinking hard. Everything she'd said was true. There was nothing unusual in her involvement.

And yet he couldn't help feeling that something was out

of place. Unnatural. He closed his eyes and tried to remember when her name had first come up. It was in the notes somewhere, but it came back to him before he'd opened a file.

Grange. It was Stephen Grange who'd put them onto Millie Tennant. He turned to Harriett to discuss it with her just as she put down her phone.

"He's agreed to meet me," she said.

"Illingworth?"

She nodded. "Tonight. At The Bitter End, in Cockermouth."

"You want company?" he asked, just as Tom Willis walked in carrying the coffees. "Safety in numbers?"

She smiled at him and shook her head, looking past him at Willis.

"It's OK," she said. "I'll be fine."

CHAPTER SIXTY-FIVE

"Going well?"

"Going well, sir," Carl said. He sat uncomfortably in the chair opposite DCI Branthwaite's paper-strewn desk and hoped this would soon be over.

It wasn't that he didn't like the DCI. It wasn't that he didn't appreciate his qualities as a boss. But he was trying to run two murder investigations with a team that had never run a murder investigation before, and every second away from that team had him worrying that something had gone horribly wrong.

"And the team? They're performing?"

Carl nodded. His worries were ridiculous, he knew. They'd all worked murders alongside Zoe's team – he felt a sting as her name passed through his mind, but the sting was getting softer. All of them except Marcus, at least. Denise was perfectly capable of running things in his absence. And if they missed anything, Aaron Keyes would be there to make sure it got picked up before it was too late.

"The new lad? Marcus?"

Carl opened his mouth to reply, then started at a knock on the door. He turned to see a head appear, an assistant from one of the other teams, then duck back out again with a mumbled apology. When he turned back to DCI Branthwaite, the man was smiling at him and...

Was there something missing from the desk? Carl could have sworn there'd been more paper on it when he'd walked in.

"You were telling me about Marcus," the DCI prompted him.

He must have imagined it. He blinked and reminded himself there were enough problems in front of him without making up new ones.

"He seems fine, sir," he replied.

"Bit of a brainbox, I hear. Tendency to rub people up the wrong way, by all accounts."

Carl smiled. He'd noticed that, too.

"He's doing really well. Excellent in interviews with the suspect."

"Ah, yes. The suspect." The DCI must have seen something in Carl's eyes, because he raised an eyebrow. "Hope I'm not boring you, Carl. But I think I'm within my rights to keep a close eye on things. It's my neck on the line here."

Another flash, another memory, another tiny knife in the guts. *My neck on the line.* Zoe had complained about her old super saying the same thing, time after time, but Fiona Kendrick had always come through for her.

Doug Branthwaite seemed to be cut from the same cloth.

"I'm sorry, sir. It's just—"

The DCI grinned and shook his head. "Go on, trot off to your team. Let me know if anything big happens."

Back in the team room, nothing big had happened, but the small things were mounting.

"I don't like Hanson for all this, boss," said Marcus, before Carl had even got in.

Harriett and Tom exchanged a look. Denise just shook her head.

"The evidence likes her though, Marcus."

"It's too convenient," he insisted. "And the state of her... She really seems shell-shocked by all this."

Carl had to admit the lad had a point. But Denise had a point, too, and hers was stronger.

"Meanwhile, I've been trying to get hold of our friend Rashid," she added. "He's not answering his phone."

"We should bring him back in," said Marcus, and now Carl had to intervene.

"One thing at a time, OK? We've got a suspect downstairs. Custody extension has been approved by Detective Superintendent Carnegie, so we don't have to let her go for a little while yet. She's given us some names, and from what I understand, Harriett's set up a meeting with one of them. Is that right?"

"Right, boss," confirmed Harriett.

"So let's see what comes of that. If we decide we want to take another look at Rashid, we know where to find him. Lynn, have you got anything on that consortium you were looking into?"

"No," said the face on the screen. Just the one face, this time. He could brief Aaron Keyes privately if he needed to, but from what he'd seen, Aaron was keeping himself on top of everything without any help from Carl. "But there is something, sir."

"Yes?"

"Zack Starling."

"What about him?"

"I had a call, sir. Anonymous, voice disguised, and the number's a burner. Whoever it was, they said to talk to Zack Starling. Talk to him, and take a look at his phone."

Starling. Could he hold the key to all this? The man was intimately connected with the prime suspect, had a criminal record and a grudge against at least one of the victims, and then there were the drugs at Hanson's house...

"Any idea who it was?"

"Not a clue, sir. Sorry."

"And they didn't say anything else?"

"Just that," Lynn replied. "Talk to Zack Starling. Check his phone."

Carl looked around the room. Every eye was on him. The call alone wasn't enough, not for an arrest, but Hanson's lies and Starling's history could push it over the line.

"Well," he said, "we'd better do what the dodgy anonymous caller's telling us to do, hadn't we?" He turned to Harriett. "Get onto Uniform. Let's bring Zack Starling in."

CHAPTER SIXTY-SIX

DENISE TOOK the stairs like a woman heading for a date with a potbellied man with bad teeth, each foot planted firmly on a step before she slowly reached out for the next. She'd checked her messages, seen there was nothing back from Rashid, or from Claire's sister, Emily Saunders.

She'd checked her watch, seen she was five minutes late, and spent another five minutes on the phone with Nikolas Costas, from the network, who seemed to be drip-feeding Bateman's phone data through like a man engaged in a science experiment.

And then she'd taken the stairs, as slowly as she practically could, until she reached the first floor.

Dr Filey kept a room here, in addition to the room she used at the Hub and another in Penrith. There were a lot of cops with psychological problems, it seemed, and Denise didn't think she was one of them. Not unless a powerful aversion to seeing the police psychiatrist counted as a psychological problem.

There were the painkillers, too, but she could handle that all by herself.

"About time," said Dr Filey, pointing to the reproduction Bauhaus chair by the small round table in the middle of the room. No couch for Adrienne Filey. Everything had been chosen to create a very specific effect, from the chair, which was more comfortable than it looked, to the prints on the wall, to the tablet on which Dr Filey took her notes.

"Look," said the psychiatrist, once Denise was settled. "I can see you're doing everything you can to get out of these appointments."

Dr Filey paused. Someone else might have used the moment to object, politely, but Denise Gaskill wasn't someone else.

"I do understand," the psychiatrist continued. "It's clear there are things you don't want to talk about."

"It's more that there are things I'd rather be doing," Denise pointed out. "Mostly, my job."

Dr Filey smiled. During her first appointment, Denise had thought she'd grow to hate that smile, but by this one, her third, she was used to it. The thing was, the woman was clearly good at her job. Brilliant, if Aaron Keyes was anything to judge by. She'd taken him from a shell of a man to a piece of flesh and bone so solid, mentally, that it would take a wrecking ball to break him open. And she was pleasant, too. Time spent in her company might even have been enjoyable.

If it weren't for the fact that Denise would rather be almost anywhere else in the world.

"Your job," said the psychiatrist. "Which you won't be able to do properly if you don't open up. At the moment, you're probably functioning at around eighty per cent."

Denise opened her mouth to object, but Dr Filey held up a hand to silence her.

"I know you think you're on top form, but there's absolutely no chance of that. Not with the trauma you've been through. And unless you acknowledge it and deal with it, that eighty is going to slowly slide down to seventy, sixty, fifty, until you're one of those cops who... How did you put it?"

"One of those cops who's as much use as a pig at a chess tournament," Denise replied. It was a comment she'd made during their first appointment. Clearly it had stuck in the psychiatrist's mind.

Dr Filey smiled at her.

"I understand," Denise continued, thinking about what she was going to say, about how to put it, what she should reveal, what she shouldn't. "I understand you really believe this, which is why I've agreed to come to these appointments."

"Which is an excellent first step," said Dr Filey.

Now it was Denise's turn to smile, to acknowledge a small hit.

"But I have work to do. There are things that need looking into in half the police stations in Cumbria. And you keep asking me to come in here and talk about the incident, the pain, the fear, and the fact is, I don't remember the incident, because I was unconscious for most of it, and I don't remember the fear, because during the bit I might have been scared, I was in an induced coma. And the pain's something I've just had to come to terms with. It's not some huge trauma I can't bring myself to face. It's just bad luck."

Dr Filey gave her a look that she recognised, and it took

Denise a moment to figure out where she'd seen it before. When it came to her, she smiled again.

Her own face. It was the look she gave suspects when she didn't believe a word they were saying. She'd seen it when she watched video recordings of interviews she'd conducted.

"I wish I could remember more," she said.

"Do you?" asked Dr Filey. "Is that really true?"

Denise nodded, and opened her mouth to say yes, it was, and then something happened, a sensation, something physical and so real that it took all her willpower not to jump from her chair and shout.

It was heat, and cold, at the same time, the sense that half her body was freezing and the other half was burning, and the noise, a vibration, loud, then quiet, then loud again, then quiet...

She closed her eyes and hoped it would go away, and after a moment, it did, and she was back in the real world, with Dr Filey sitting opposite her, wearing an expression of deep concern.

"Are you OK?" asked the psychiatrist.

"Yes," said Denise. The word didn't sound right in her mouth. Like someone else had put it there. "Why?"

The psychiatrist pointed to her eye, and Denise frowned, before lifting her hand to her own eye, the right one, and feeling something wet.

Feeling it coursing down her face, dropping to her chin, dripping onto the chair.

"I don't understand," she said.

"You're crying," Dr Filey told her.

"I know that," she said. "I don't understand why."

"Just tell me what you can remember," the psychiatrist

said, her voice so low, so patient, so gentle, that Denise found herself replying.

"It was weird. Just now, I mean. I could feel it. Hot and cold, and yes, I think there was pain, but it was there and gone so quickly I'm not sure I didn't imagine it."

"You didn't imagine it, Denise. You *remembered* it. It was real."

"I don't... I'm not sure I want to go on with this."

Dr Filey nodded.

"That's fine," she said. "I know you won't think so, but this was a breakthrough, Denise. You can sit here in silence for a few minutes, or you can go back to work. But either way, you're making another appointment to see me next week. Whether you want to or not. OK?"

"Fine," said Denise, and even though she made sure to inject the usual annoyance and cynicism into her voice, for the first time, she wasn't entirely sure she felt it.

CHAPTER SIXTY-SEVEN

TALK TO ZACK STARLING. *Check his phone.*

Had Lynn recognised that voice? She tried to play it back in her mind, but all she got was a weird, alien-sounding noise. It had been run through distorting software. Anything human in it had been entirely erased.

They were picking up Starling. It might come to nothing. But it couldn't hurt.

Her phone rang, and she checked the display before answering. A familiar number, but she couldn't place it.

"Is that Lynn Hedley?" said a male voice. Definitely human this time, and one she'd heard before. Heard that day. Who was it?

"Yes, who's this?" she asked.

"It's Mike. From Willis Carmichael. I think we spoke earlier?"

Lynn sat up.

"We did," she confirmed.

"Thank fuck for that," said Mike. "Sorry. But all I knew was that you were called Lynn, and you were with the police.

You're the third Lynn I've tried. The other two... They weren't very patient. Didn't seem to believe me when I told them I was after a police officer called Lynn who'd called me earlier."

Lynn laughed.

"It's not funny," said Mike. "One of them called me a pervert."

It *was* funny, really. And there was a break in Mike's voice that told her he thought so too.

"Thanks for persevering," Lynn told him. "It sounded like you had to get off the phone in a hurry when we spoke earlier."

"Yeah. Well, the partners aren't happy with me already. If they knew I was talking to the police about their clients, they'd probably have me fired."

"We're investigating two murders, Mike. Mike..." she said it twice, out loud, and it seemed odd, the single word, in isolation like that. Orphaned, somehow. "What's your surname?" she asked.

"McKenzie. Mike McKenzie. Just flows off the tongue, doesn't it? And yes, I know you're investigating two murders, that's why I've called, but as far as Willis Carmichael's concerned, client confidentiality is sacrosanct."

"And you don't agree?"

"Not when you're dealing with pricks like these," he said.

She waited for him to go on.

"Look, I can chat now, because they're not here, but if anyone comes back..."

"If anyone comes back, you know which Lynn I am now. We can talk when you have a bit more privacy."

"Right. Yes. Well, this bit of land, like I said, it's not

much good for anything, but as far as I can see, these people just want to use it to bury waste."

"I see."

"I'm not sure you do. If they get their way, there's going to be truckloads of crap from all over the country making its way to the Lake District to get buried under Skiddaw. Not exactly what we like to boast about in the National Park, is it?"

"Surely they won't be allowed to do that?" Lynn said.

"Oh, there's always ways, as long as you know the right people and you're prepared to pay the right price. As it happens, they haven't said that's what they're planning. But I can't see any other way they can make money out of it."

"Right. And I don't suppose you know who they are?"

"They?"

"The consortium. The people we're talking about. Do you have any names?"

"Oh, right. No. I didn't speak to anyone. And my contact was just a generic email address with a company that calls itself Cumbria Estate Facilities Servicing Group."

"Never mind," said Lynn, but the disappointment must have come through in her voice, because Mike was talking again immediately.

"But I can tell you who I invoiced for the survey," he said. "And that wasn't Cumbria Estate Facilities Servicing Group."

"Who was it?" she asked.

"Local business. A real one. You might be familiar with them, actually, they've done some work round your way. They're called Conway Developments."

It was a good thing Mike couldn't see Lynn's face,

because her mouth fell open and stayed that way for a good ten seconds before he asked if she was still there.

"Yes," she said. "Sorry. And thank you," she added, before saying goodbye and ending the call.

Conway Developments. She'd come across them before. Sinead Conway, the company's owner, had cropped up in one of DI Keyes's old investigations. And then she'd cropped up again last year, when a protester objecting to one of her projects had been murdered.

Sinead Conway hadn't been involved in that murder, as it turned out. But there were incidents in her past, dark happenings that clustered around Sinead Conway and her business like iron filings drawn to a magnet.

Lynn spent a few minutes updating HOLMES and the case file, and was thinking about heading home when her phone rang. She checked the display. Not Mike McKenzie this time, but someone else she knew.

Why would Caroline Deane from the CSI team be calling her so late in the working day?

CHAPTER SIXTY-EIGHT

John Illingworth had asked to meet Harriett at The Bitter End in Cockermouth. Harriett spent most of the journey there arguing with Tom on the phone, him insisting she shouldn't be doing this by herself, neither walking into a pub without backup nor listening to whatever Illingworth had to say without someone to corroborate it, and her replying that if there was any chance of making Illingworth talk, surprising him with one extra cop would blow it away. By the time she reached the pub, a few minutes early, she thought she'd won the debate.

The Bitter End was a quiet pub with banquettes and chairs in dark shades of red and orange, situated on a residential street in an attractive part of town just off the main road. She ordered a half pint of non-alcoholic beer and found a table to wait at, and spent ten minutes scrolling her phone, noting Lynn's latest updates and replying to Tom's anxious messages, before a man approached her, staggering slightly as he walked.

"You by yourself, love?" he asked.

"I'm meeting someone," she told him, squinting at his face as she tried to work out if the enormous waxed moustache that spread from under his nose like an ancient tree was real, or part of some fancy dress.

"Sure I can't change your mind?" he said.

She sensed movement beyond him and saw the barman looking her way, a question in his eyes.

Do you need help?

She shook her head, at both of them. She could feel her body tensing, ready to make her response clearer if she had to, but he nodded and started to walk away. Then he stopped and turned.

"It's real, by the way," he said, and walked out of the pub.

By the time Illingworth was twenty minutes late, Harriett was becoming concerned. She called him, and the phone went straight to voicemail.

After thirty minutes, with Illingworth still not answering, she phoned the DI.

"Hello?" he said. "Everything OK?"

She could hear the low hum of his engine. He'd be on his way back home. Still living in Whitehaven, like she was, only she had a reason for being there, what with Tom's usual base of operations being the Hub. DI Whaley's reason had been DI Finch, and she was nearly four hundred miles away now.

"Illingworth hasn't turned up," she told him. "And he's not answering his phone. I'm heading round to his address."

"Wait," said the DI. "Think about it."

"I am thinking about it, boss. After what happened to Bateman, I'm worried. He sounded happy to meet earlier. Maybe not happy. But definitely willing. Not like someone who'd just change his mind. And definitely not like someone who'd forget."

"Exactly. If something's happened to him, I don't want you walking straight into it. Wait for backup, please."

"Is that an order, boss? Because if Illingworth's in danger, then me turning up might make a big difference."

There was a pause.

"OK. Head straight there if you're worried, but I'll call in backup. Just be careful."

"Will do," she said, knocked back the last sip of her beer, and headed out into the evening gloom.

CHAPTER SIXTY-NINE

There were people who'd have found it lonely, being the last one in, when the room had been filled with more police than Marcus had ever seen on one team. People who wouldn't have enjoyed it when the lights went out and they had to gesture, stand up, and finally walk around to get them back on again.

Tom Willis had gone home. DS Gaskill had gone home, and so had the boss. Harriett Barnes was meeting Illingworth in some pub, and wherever Lynn Hedley and DI Keyes were, they weren't in the room with him.

Marcus was in his element.

Within ten minutes of Tom's departure, the news had come in that Zack Starling wasn't home, and over the next hour, his usual haunts drew the same blank. At the end of that hour, Marcus took a call from a man he wasn't familiar with, an Inspector Keane from the Hub, who asked him what he wanted to do now.

"What are my options?" asked Marcus.

"You can drop it, see if he shows up overnight, and try again in the morning."

"Right," said Marcus, thinking that was probably what he'd end up doing.

"Or you can order a wider hunt. Mobilise the kind of numbers that might find someone who's trying not to be found."

"You think he's trying not to be found?" Marcus asked.

"Do you?" replied Inspector Keane.

Marcus was inclined to think that yes, Zack Starling was trying not to be found. The little they knew of him suggested he was a man of habit. And with the net closing in the way it was...

"Yes," said Marcus. "I think we should do that. The wider hunt."

"You'll need authorisation from someone with a rank of inspector or above, of course."

Marcus thought that over, and considered who he was talking to.

"Someone other than me," clarified Inspector Keane.

"OK," said Marcus. "I can get it. Can you get things started in the meantime? I'll have approval for the PNC by morning."

It wasn't entirely a lie. But it was said with a lot more confidence than he felt.

Once he'd finished with Inspector Keane, Marcus returned to the person who'd put them onto Starling in the first place. Millie Tennant. And it was Grange who'd put them onto Tennant.

That had been bugging Marcus since he'd spoken to her earlier.

Was there a connection between Grange and Tennant? Or had the PC just had a useful name up his sleeve?

This time, Millie Tennant didn't answer her phone, and for the briefest of moments, Marcus wondered whether he should order a hunt for her, too, before realising he was getting ahead of himself.

Keep it calm.

Another one of his dad's little mantras, not that keeping it calm or not pissing off your new colleagues or not letting them see you cry had done him much good in the end.

He picked up his phone and dialled a number.

"Elias Hosgood," said the old man, a moment later. He'd have seen Marcus's number, known who was calling, but that was the way he answered the phone, and it didn't matter who was on the other end.

"Dad," he said.

"About time," replied Elias. "They sacked you yet?"

"Not yet. How are you?"

The old man laughed, a burst of surprising vitality, and it struck Marcus that he wasn't that old, really. He just had an air of age beyond his years.

And he hadn't answered the question.

"That bad?"

"Nothing a good drink can't fix."

It had been 'a good drink' that had got Elias Hosgood where he was – divorced, friendless, getting by on his pension and what Marcus could spare. But Marcus had wasted a decade arguing with his dad about the drink. It hadn't got either of them anywhere then, and it wouldn't get either of them anywhere now.

"How's Lolly?" he asked.

"Missing you, I think," replied Elias, and then Marcus's phone buzzed with another call coming through.

"Got to go," he said. "Bye, Dad."

He answered the other call without waiting for his dad's response, hoping for news on Starling. If they'd found the man already, he could probably fudge the search authorisation, suggest it hadn't really been needed after all.

It wasn't news on Starling. It was Lynn Hedley.

"Are you the only one there?" she asked.

"Yes," he confirmed.

"Right," she said, and there was a short, uncomfortable silence during which he realised that she'd only called him because she couldn't get hold of any of the others, and that she'd realised he knew it, too. "I've got Caroline Deane on the line. From CSI."

"Yes," he said again, trying to sound normal and not a tiny bit hurt.

"Hang on."

A moment later all three of them were connected, and he listened as Caroline outlined her latest findings.

"These fibres," she said. "The ones Keisha found on Hanson's clothing."

"What about them?" Marcus asked.

"Well, the first thing is that we've confirmed they are from Isaac Bateman's jacket."

That was it, then. It didn't put Starling in the clear, but it certainly put Hanson in the firing line.

"But," continued Caroline, "they're very neatly positioned. Almost uniformly over the coat and walking trousers."

"Eh?" he said.

"The fibres. They're not present in the places that would

have made the most contact if you were attacking someone or moving a body. No, that's not right. They are present there. They're just present everywhere else, too, in the same sort of quantities."

"What do you mean?" he asked, although what she meant was slowly filtering through his brain.

Maybe Hanson wasn't in the firing line after all.

"Hello," said someone else, and Marcus recognised the voice of Stella Berry, the crime scene manager.

"Hi," he said, unsure what to say next. All he knew was that he definitely didn't want to say the wrong thing. He'd not met Stella Berry before, not in person, but he had met Keisha Middleton, and the rumour was that all the attitude and impatience the younger woman had, she'd picked up from her mentor.

"Let me spell it out for you," said Stella, "because it sounds like you're the sort of person who needs things spelled out."

This, when he hadn't said much more than 'Hi'. He decided to stay silent while she continued.

"What this means is that if someone – defence counsel, for instance – wanted to stand up in court and claim that these fibres were deliberately placed on PC Hanson's clothes, I wouldn't have much of an argument against the hypothesis."

"So you're saying they *have* been deliberately placed there?" he asked, unable to remain silent after all.

He heard a sigh. "Not necessarily. I'm just saying they might well have been."

"Right," he replied, thanked her, and Caroline Deane, and Lynn Hedley, and ended the call feeling a lot more confused than he had been five minutes earlier.

CHAPTER SEVENTY

John Illingworth's flat was on the second floor of a new block situated opposite a supermarket in the dead centre of Cockermouth. Like the pub he'd chosen to meet her in, it was smarter than she'd expected from the little she knew of the man. Harriett hit the buzzer for number twenty-one and waited a minute, but nothing happened.

Thirty seconds later, just as she was about to start hitting the other buzzers, she heard footsteps behind her and whirled around.

"Didn't show up, then?"

It was the man she'd seen in The Bitter End. The one with the moustache. In the faint light of the pub, he'd looked older, but now she realised he was probably her own age, and just a little drunk.

"Sorry?" she said.

"You said you were meeting someone. Damn fool, if he stood you up."

Damn fool? What with that and the moustache, it was like she was talking to someone from the nineteen-fifties.

"I'm Teddy, by the way. Edward Standen."

"DC Harriett Barnes." She flipped open her warrant card. "Cumbria Police. Do you live here?"

Edward Standen dropped the time-traveller act like it was on fire.

"Shit," he said. "Is everything OK?"

Harriett had the strongest sense that things weren't OK, but she kept a calm face on as he opened the door for her and directed her to the second floor. Number twenty-one lay at the end of a short corridor, and as she approached she could see the door wasn't shut.

She pushed it, and it opened onto the sort of scene she'd imagined, and feared, and hoped she wouldn't see.

"Fucking hell," said Edward Standen, the fifties routine now a distant memory. She hadn't realised he'd followed her all the way here.

She stared into the room, and the lifeless eyes of John Illingworth stared back at her.

He was hanging from a light fitting beside a small table in the middle of what looked like a living room.

"Fucking hell," said Edward Standen, again.

"Don't move," she told him, and walked into the room.

Preserving the scene was vital, but nothing was more vital than preserving life. Still, she took care to avoid touching anything she didn't have to touch.

She had to touch John Illingworth. Had to check his pulse. See if there was any way he might still be alive.

There wasn't.

She turned to see that Edward Standen had taken a cautious step into Illingworth's flat.

"Stay back," she said, and he retreated.

She had gloves and a suit and everything she needed in

the car, but that could wait until backup arrived. The important thing was to make sure Edward Standen stayed out of the room, and no one else came in.

Her eyes were drawn to the body, swinging gently in the breeze from the open door. Illingworth's eyes were swollen, his tongue protruding, his face mottled and dark, but she'd never seen him in real life, in the flesh. Maybe his face was always like that.

He'd used electrical flex. He'd managed to get enough height, at least: it might not have been quick, but it wouldn't have felt like it was going on forever. She looked down to see drag marks in the carpet. He'd moved the table so he could stand on it, put everything in place, then stepped off.

There were a couple of items on the table, and with a warning glance back at Edward Standen, she approached it again, careful to step in the faint marks she'd already left in the carpet.

A mobile phone lay beside a scrap of white paper. Was that writing on the paper?

She took another step closer and bent over it, trying to ignore the feet dangling inches from her face.

There were no words on the paper. Instead, there was an arrow, drawn in blue pen, pointing to where the mobile phone sat beside it.

And underneath the arrow, a series of numbers.

'031426'.

DAY TEN

CHAPTER SEVENTY-ONE

"To lose one cop," Branthwaite had said first thing, "may be regarded as a misfortune. Two looks like carelessness."

Carl couldn't help wondering if perhaps the DCI was right. But for now, he had to keep things under control. Or at least give the appearance of control.

"OK," he said, walking into the middle of the team room. "Let's get started. Tell me about the crime scene."

The screen was on, the two usual faces in their usual boxes, and the flesh-and-blood humans sitting at their desks around him.

There were two new boxes on the screen this morning. One of them displayed the face of Keisha Middleton, looking bored. The other was a photograph of the crime scene.

"It's not a crime scene," said Keisha. "I've been concentrating on the phone, but Caroline's been in the flat, and she doesn't think anyone was in that room other than the dead man and Harriett. And Harriett's moustachioed friend, but he stayed by the door."

Harriett coloured as Keisha gave an exaggerated wink.

"What does the pathologist say?" asked Carl.

"Post-mortem will be this afternoon," Harriett told him. "But the initial view is this was death by respiratory asphyxia. No defensive injuries, no injuries at all other than the one that killed him. We'll have to wait for toxicology, but..."

"But it was suicide," said Carl. He wasn't sure if that was worse or better than murder.

Better, probably.

"Tell me about the phone," he continued, addressing Keisha.

"I've already sent through the data," she replied, and he nodded. He'd seen it. And he hadn't enjoyed the process. "Illingworth left it unlocked. The only things on it were a handful of contacts, a few photos, and Telegram."

"It's a messaging app," added Marcus. "High levels of encryption."

"Thanks for telling us all what we already know," added Keisha, and now it was Marcus's turn to go red, much redder than Harriett had gone. Closer to the colour of the dead man in the box beside Keisha's face. "Anyway, he had it, and the password for it was handily written down for us on a piece of paper."

"Thank you, Keisha." Carl took over again. "I've looked through these messages. They're mostly dominated by a single group called Real Cops."

"It was true, then," said Denise.

She looked surprised. Working in PSD as long as she had, she was probably used to doubting everything she was told.

"It was. In normal circumstances, I'd say you don't want to read the stuff they wrote on there. But I've downloaded it to the team files, and if we're going to solve these murders, you're going to have to go through the lot. All of you. Now, moving on to other matters—"

"Can I go now?" asked Keisha.

"I'm sorry?"

"Well, you wanted me to talk about the phone, not that you actually needed me to say any of that, but I'm done now, aren't I? So can I bugger off?"

"Go ahead," he said, and the box disappeared. There were a couple of quiet chuckles as he turned to address the room.

"Moving on," he said, again. "Our friend Zack Starling was tracked down first thing this morning at the railway station in Penrith. He was waiting for a train south."

He was staring at Marcus as he spoke, but the DC wouldn't meet his eyes.

"He put up a bit of a fight, and he was arrested. They're bringing him here as we speak. Marcus, you're a lucky lad."

Marcus turned now, and Carl saw a pained expression on his face.

"I'm sorry," he said.

"Want to tell the room what you're apologising for?" said Carl, and even as he spoke, he felt a little guilty for doing this in public.

But you had to teach people. They had to learn.

"I ordered a full-scale manhunt without getting approval from an officer of the rank of inspector or above," said Marcus, reciting the regulation as if he'd known it all his life.

"You did," agreed Carl. At least he hadn't sugar-coated it. "And you shouldn't have done, and there was no way you'd have got away with it, which at least shows you're willing to face the consequences of your actions. As things stand, those consequences are limited to me embarrassing you in a team briefing. We've got Starling, and we've got Starling's phone, so I should say 'well done', but all you had to do was call me and I'd have given approval."

"Can I—?" began Marcus.

"Yes," said Carl. "You can interview him, but I'll be asking Denise to keep an eye on you. Make sure you don't do anything illegal. In the meantime, Hanson's custody has been extended by the magistrate. The clock's ticking, though. We've got just over a day."

"This news," said Marcus, "about the fibres. I was already worried about the evidence against her, but this points to her telling the truth, doesn't it?"

Carl suppressed a smile. The DC was certainly resilient.

"You make a good point," he replied. "And we're keeping it in mind. But however weak that evidence might be, right now Niamh Hanson is the only person with any real evidence against her at all. So for the time being, we're going to keep her in. Anything else?"

"Conway Developments," said Lynn Hedley on the screen. "They're involved in the consortium."

Carl saw Aaron Keyes's head jerk up.

"Thanks for reminding us," said Carl. "What with everything else, there was a danger of that getting lost."

"Is it something we should be looking into?" asked Lynn.

"Aaron?" said Carl. "You know these people better than anyone else does."

Aaron Keyes frowned, then shook his head.

"Not directly," he said. "The thing about Sinead Conway is she keeps turning up at the edge of things, and we waste time looking into her, and it turns out she's got nothing to do with anything. But the number of things she's turned up at the edges of..."

"So, what, we should keep digging, but keep it low key?"

Aaron nodded.

"Exactly. Don't let it distract you from anything else, but Lynn, it might be an idea to keep an eye out, without letting them know you're interested. Just quietly find out if there are any other connections with any other element of the investigation."

That made sense, Carl thought. There were too many elements in this investigation to keep on top of all of them, after all.

CHAPTER SEVENTY-TWO

Marcus couldn't tell if Zack Starling was just tired, or if he always looked like that. If it was the latter, the man needed to get out more; his face was pale enough to land planes by.

"Not been in here before," observed the lawyer, an innocuous-looking man who'd introduced himself as Stan Basham and asked Marcus if he was as dumb as he looked. "It's like the Hub, just a bit shitter."

"Why don't we get started?" suggested DS Gaskill.

"Yes," agreed Basham. "I've got more important things to do today. Spot of gardening." Starling turned to face the lawyer, staring at him in confusion and disappointment. "No offence," added Basham cheerfully.

"Where were you heading, when our colleagues found you this morning?" asked Marcus.

Starling turned to him, and Marcus was briefly surprised by the intensity of his gaze, by the deep blue of his eyes in such a worn and weary face.

"No comment," he said.

"Come on, Zack," said DS Gaskill. "I know your lawyer here's told you saying 'no comment' is the best way to stay out of trouble, but you might want to ask him just how well that's worked out for his clients lately. You'll be surprised by the answer."

"Hey," said Basham. "I don't criticise the way you lot do your job, do I?"

DS Gaskill turned an incredulous look on him, and he laughed.

"Fair enough, maybe I do. But it's not like you don't deserve it. Please, do continue."

"Tell us about the drugs," said Marcus.

"No comment," replied Starling.

"Isaac Bateman," said DS Gaskill. "What's your connection to him?"

Starling just stared at her, silent.

"Come on, Zack," said Marcus. "He fitted you up, didn't he?"

"Course he did," said Starling.

"Shut up," said Basham, and Starling fell silent again.

"He fitted you up, and you weren't happy with him," Marcus continued. "Been seething ever since, haven't you?"

Starling shrugged but didn't speak, and then there was a knock at the door, and Harriett Barnes appeared, gesturing at DS Gaskill.

The interview was paused while she left the room, and the three men sat in uncomfortable silence for five minutes waiting for her return.

When she did, she was smiling.

"You should have locked your phone, Zack," she said when they resumed.

"Eh?" he replied.

"Not much of a master criminal, are you?" she continued.

Marcus wasn't sure what she was driving at, but she looked very happy, and Zack Starling looked more worried than he had been a few minutes earlier.

"I don't understand," he said.

"Shut up," Basham told him.

"You didn't lock your phone, you didn't turn off location data, you didn't even delete your satnav searches."

"Oh," said Starling.

"Which means we can now place you on the very spot where Isaac Bateman's body was found, right in the middle of nowhere, and bang in the middle of the window for his murder."

"Shit," said Starling.

"Care to explain that?" said Marcus.

Starling took a couple of deep breaths. There was a little colour in his face now, and Marcus thought he could see a vein throbbing in his forehead. He glanced down at the man's arms and saw them braced against the table, the muscles tensed, and then he looked back up and saw the same tension throughout Starling's body.

He looked like a man about to unleash.

Trying to minimise his movements, Marcus prepared himself, edging back a little, giving himself the space to get up and close the gap in his own time, on his own terms.

"Don't be an idiot, Zack," said DS Gaskill.

"What?" said Starling.

"You. You look like you're about to take us both on. I've not long recovered from a coma and I'm probably ten years older than you, but if I had to, I could snap you like a twig.

And Marcus here was a professional boxer before he joined the force."

"Right," said Starling, and his whole body seemed to relax. "Yeah."

A professional boxer.

Marcus was struggling not to laugh. He'd punched someone once, but he'd been about nine at the time, and the kid had nicked his schoolbag. He'd got the bag back, but he'd hurt his hand more than he'd hurt the other boy.

"Tell us what you were doing there," said DS Gaskill.

"No comment," replied Starling, and his lawyer sat back, arms folded, wearing the smile of a man who'd forgotten about his gardening and would happily sit there like that all day if he had to.

As long as he was getting paid.

CHAPTER SEVENTY-THREE

Starling had just been promoted to joint lead suspect, but that didn't mean all the other leads had gone dry.

Denise returned to her desk and switched her phone back on to find a message from Emily Saunders, Claire's sister. She played it, then played it a second time.

"Look," said Emily Saunders. "I only want the best for my sister, but I don't know if I can trust the police. No one ever followed up last time round."

Meanwhile, her request for the full details of Emily's complaint had been processed. All Denise had seen was the edge of a complaint, *I have concerns about my sister Claire.* The rest of the document had, unusually, been redacted.

And now, it seemed, the document had been lost. Denise had been in PSD long enough to know how easy it was for things to get lost deliberately, if someone didn't want you to find them. But she'd been a functioning human being for long enough to know that when it came to a toss-up between incompetence and corruption, the answer was usually incompetence.

She dialled Emily's number, but it went straight to voicemail.

There had been a high point, not half an hour earlier, when she'd seen what had been found on Starling's phone and thought they had their killer. But Starling hadn't told them anything new, and now she was being stalled by a missing document. She called Nikolas Costas, who told her he was still progressing her request for Bateman's phone data, and relieved a little of her frustration by comparing him to a tortoise out loud, and to a Nazi camp guard in her head. She knew it was petty and out of all proportion, and she knew it wouldn't make him move any faster, but it made her feel a tiny bit better, so it was worth it.

She spent the next half hour sitting with Harriett Barnes, Tom Willis and Marcus Hosgood, going through the 'jokes' that seemed to form the majority of the communications on John Illingworth's phone. They were all repulsive, not just sexist and racist and homophobic, but stupid, too, with all the sophistication of a street fight outside a kebab house. After ten minutes she thought she'd found one that was funny enough to raise a smile, but on a second reading, it became clear that the only clever line in the joke was a typo.

She wasn't there for the jokes, though. None of them were. They were there for the names, for what they could glean from the combination of phone numbers, contact details, and the grains of personal information dripped infrequently into the conversation.

They had two names already, Darren Chisholm and Harvey Grey, and within twenty minutes they'd confirmed both men were in the group, along with Illingworth himself, and, of course, Bateman. Chisholm had been stupid enough to use his police-issue mobile. Grey had joined under the nickname 'Skullhead'. Subtlety clearly wasn't their strong suit.

By the time the half hour was up, they had another two: James Borman and Craig Underwood. There were three more people in the group, but they didn't have anything as useful as real names, or even nicknames that might lead somewhere. Just handles – Simon, Wilf, Pete – and phone numbers, which didn't show up on the system, or anywhere else.

Harriett put in information requests with the network providers, but everyone knew that would be a long and painful process, if it got them anything at all.

Still, it might provide an excuse to shout at Nikolas Costas again.

They divided the names they had amongst themselves. Marcus wanted Chisholm, and Grey was at the same station in Kendal, so he could pick up a pair for the price of one. Tom took Borman, who he didn't know, but who was based at the Hub. Harriett wanted to stick around and work through Illingworth's phone, which left Denise with the long drive to Barrow-in-Furness, where Craig Underwood would be starting his shift in a couple of hours.

This time, there would be no warnings. Not after what had happened with Illingworth.

Denise was pulling on her coat, with Marcus and Tom already at the door, when Harriett called out.

"You might want to see this," she said, and all three moved to stand by her screen and read the notification that had just landed.

It came from Stella's lab. The analysis on Bateman's car was complete, and there was a match on some of the partials that had been found on the door handle.

The name those prints belonged to was Zack Starling.

CHAPTER SEVENTY-FOUR

Harriett had been looking forward to an hour or two alone in the team room, working her way through Illingworth's phone, trying to figure out how a series of off-colour jokes had led to the deaths of two men.

Three, if Godwin was somehow involved in all this.

But now that Starling's prints had turned up on Bateman's car, everything had changed. She was itching to get in the room with the man, sit down alongside the DI, and see how he could account for this. The satnav searches and the location data were good. But this was damning.

Unfortunately, Stan Basham, Starling's lawyer, had decided to disappear at just the wrong time. He was on his way back, apparently. He'd be there in due course.

But he couldn't put a time on it. Which meant Harriett was stuck there with the data from Illingworth's phone until Stan Basham decided to show up.

The jokes were bad. Harriett decided she'd heard worse, and then she carried on through and decided she hadn't. There were nearly two years of them, not a single one good enough to raise even a chuckle. Sometimes they came thick and fast, a dozen in a day. Sometimes there would be a break, two, three, once even four days of silence, before someone threw in a distasteful comment about a disabled athlete or a black politician, and the whole thing kicked off again.

In some ways, it was like a normal chat group. Just a lot worse.

Over recent weeks, though, the Real Cops had fallen quiet. Only one of them had had anything to say, and what he said was very different to everything else she'd seen in the group.

Simon had been blackmailing them.

The first message came after a flurry of abusive one-liners about victims of sexual violence. It was very simple.

Simon says, do as I ask, or this group and your participation in it will be made public.

What Simon had asked, at that point, was for someone to trace a car registration for him.

No one had replied, but half an hour later, Simon had been back.

Thanks for that, Craig. Replying privately is fine, by the way.

Harriett stopped what she was doing and worked backwards again. She hadn't noticed anything from Simon beyond the occasional laughing emoji or a *good one*. He hadn't made a single joke.

And he'd been there all along. Since before Illingworth had joined the group, at least.

She scanned forward until she reached the next task. This time Simon was asking for information on criminal records. Like the registration plate search, he could have done this himself if he was really a cop. But maybe he wasn't.

It would have been the greatest irony of all if one of the Real Cops wasn't a cop at all.

Of course, he could well be a cop. If he was, and he'd carried out these searches himself, someone might have found out. So either he wasn't a police officer, or he was, and he was being careful to cover his tracks.

There were more requests for registration plates and criminal records, a couple for shift patterns at Penrith and Kendal. As far as intel went, it was on the less sensitive side, but it was still more than enough to get anyone fired, and probably facing charges.

The tasks continued, no big step changes, just information, small things, until Harriett's eyes caught on one particular message.

It had been sent the morning of the boatyard killing.

If any of you are scheduled to be on shift tonight, steer clear of Waterhead. If you hear anything, ignore it. Pass this on to anyone who'll listen to you. Waterhead's off limits until tomorrow morning.

There was no response to that. There were no further messages at all, from anyone, until three days later, Isaac Bateman had finally grown a pair and said something.

This has gone too far. If the rest of you aren't going to do anything about it, I am.

That, Harriett realised, was the same day Bateman had contacted DI Keyes, asking about PSD, and referring to a delicate local matter.

At least they knew what he'd wanted to talk about now.

And Harriett was pretty sure she knew why he'd died.

CHAPTER SEVENTY-FIVE

THE TIMING COULD HAVE BEEN BETTER.

Marcus sat in the front of a police van parked just feet from the war memorial, right in the middle of the market-place off Stricklandgate, the main shopping street running through the centre of Kendal. From the back of the van, he could still hear the high-pitched bleat of Harvey Grey, the man who'd called himself 'Skullhead', insisting that he didn't know what they were talking about and complaining that they'd hurt his arm when they'd put him in the van.

That was a lie. Marcus had watched it happen, watched the man walk out of the police station with a smile on his face, towards his car, and be intercepted by the uniformed officers from Carlisle that Marcus had brought with him. They'd been as gentle as lambs.

Marcus might have used a local team. But Chisholm and Grey *were* the local team.

Darren Chisholm was supposed to be with Grey, but it turned out he'd switched shifts with someone else, and that was where the timing had gone wrong. All this, it was supposed to be quiet.

Marcus had the feeling it wasn't going to be quiet.

A voice came through on the radio, Mel Cunliffe, one of the PCs he'd brought with him.

"He's coming," she said.

Marcus stepped out of the van, two more PCs following close behind him, and walked through a crowd of ambling shoppers up the marketplace towards a narrow, paved alleyway. Even as he reached the point where it joined the main thoroughfare, Chisholm emerged.

Shit.

The idea had been to grab him in the alley, where it was quieter.

Chisholm seemed fatter than he'd looked in his photo and in the CCTV footage. Maybe he'd been enjoying all that free food and drink a little too much. He looked up, his eyes sliding past Marcus to the PCs behind him, registering them, a frown slowly forming on his face.

If there were uniformed police on the streets of Kendal, he'd have expected to recognise them.

They'd almost reached him by the time he realised it was him they were heading for, and that realisation moved across his face like a slowly rolling wave, first surprise, then fear, then anger. He stopped walking and took a single step back, glancing both ways, noting that the only way he could run was the way he'd just come.

Marcus was almost on the man now. His stomach hung down below his belt. He didn't look like a runner. He stared Marcus in the face.

"Who the fuck are you?" he said.

"Darren Chisholm?" asked Marcus, speaking as quietly

as he could, but not quietly enough – the movement around them had stopped, suddenly, an awareness spreading through the crowd that something unusual was happening, and something close to silence had descended.

"Yeah," said Chisholm. "So you know me. But I don't know you."

"I'm DC Marcus Hosgood. PSD," he added, a little quieter, hoping for at least an element of subtlety.

"PSD. Might have fucking known," snarled Chisholm, and then he was on them, arms whirling, moving with surprising speed for a man of his size. Marcus stepped back and feinted left, catching a glancing blow to his shoulder, then pivoted, ready to counterattack, but there was no need.

Chisholm might have taken him by surprise, but it was four against one. He'd seen the three in front, but he hadn't spotted the fourth, behind him, and now he was on the ground, still snarling, but in a mixture of resignation and pain, and Mel Cunliffe was holding his arm at an angle that more than accounted for the pain.

"Darren Chisholm," said Marcus, bending down and speaking into the man's ear. "I'm arresting you for misconduct in a public office."

And misconduct in a public office, he thought, was just the start of it.

CHAPTER SEVENTY-SIX

"NICE OF YOU TO JOIN US," said Stan Basham, the lawyer who'd kept them waiting for well over an hour and finally turned up five minutes earlier.

Carl pushed the toes of his right foot hard against the end of his shoe, and just smiled. He'd heard all about Stan Basham from Zoe. He'd heard about him again that day, from Denise and Marcus. He'd warned Harriett, but Harriett was the sort of person who stayed calm, whatever the crisis.

Basham wouldn't be getting a rise out of either of them. Carl didn't even bother answering, just waited while Harriett ran through the formalities. And then he went in hard.

"We've found your fingerprints on Isaac Bateman's car, Zack. On the door handle. The evidence on your phone was damning enough, but this?"

Basham turned to his client, a look of weary disappointment on his face.

"Unless you can explain what you were doing there," Harriett said, "you're looking at a murder charge."

"Shit," said Starling.

"Shut up," said Basham.

"No, but this isn't right," said Starling.

"Don't tell me," said Carl. "You're being fitted up, right?"

"Yeah," said Starling, but then he must have seen the look on Carl's face, the look of a man whose patience had run out at just the moment he found himself holding all the cards. "Yeah, but not like you think. I mean, the phone, the prints, that's true. I was there."

"I said shut up," said Basham, but the fear and the fingerprints had done the job.

The sullen, uncooperative Starling who'd been interviewed earlier by Marcus and Denise had been replaced by a man eager to talk, and no longer willing to listen to his lawyer's unchanging advice.

"I was there," Starling told them, fixing Carl with those intense blue eyes, then turning to Harriett and doing the same thing. "I was called out there."

"Who by?" asked Harriett.

"I don't know. It was a WhatsApp, wasn't it? Told me to meet 'em up on that spot at four and bring everything I had."

"You mean drugs?"

"Well I don't mean fucking clown shoes, do I?"

Basham sniggered, then said, "Shut up" again.

"There's no sign of this message on your phone," Harriett pointed out.

"No. Course not. It's been deleted by the sender, hasn't it? And no," Starling continued, "before you ask, I don't remember the bloody number, either."

"You're asking us to take a lot on trust here, Zack," said Carl, and for the first time, the man looked genuinely frightened.

"I promise it's the truth," he said. "I turned up there, five to four, coz I like to be early, check out the scene. There was no one there, so I waited around, ten, twenty minutes, and it wasn't till I was about to give up that I turned and saw the car in the water."

"Twenty minutes of checking out the scene, and you don't notice a car upside down right next to you?"

Now Starling looked embarrassed as well as frightened. "I might have been a bit high," he said. "And it wasn't that easy to spot."

"For Christ's sake," said Basham. The lawyer was leaning forward, his head in his hands, rocking gently as his client did the opposite of what he'd advised him to.

"It's true," said Harriett, gently. "From the main track, you wouldn't necessarily see it straight away. What happened after that, Zack?"

"I scrambled down, tried to get the door open, couldn't. But I got a proper look inside. Saw a fella in there. I couldn't see who it was, but it was obvious he was dead."

"Obvious how?"

"He was hanging upside down and his face was basically in the water. I'd been there twenty minutes. Christ knows how long he'd been there, but it was long enough for a man to drown."

"Isaac Bateman didn't drown," Carl told him. "He was murdered, then he was put in his car."

Starling held up his hands.

"It wasn't me. I didn't even know it was Bateman till I saw it on the news. Thought maybe I'd got away with it, then your mate came sniffing round, asking questions."

"Lynn Hedley," said Carl.

"Yeah. Her. She didn't mention Bateman, but it couldn't

be a coincidence, could it? I held out a couple of days, and then I thought, what's the fucking point?"

"What do you mean?"

He gestured at himself, at the room. "All this. I could stick around and wait for you lot to turn up, tell you the truth, but you're not gonna believe me, are you? Whoever did this, they knew what they were doing. So I thought, better run." He laughed, a low, bitter puff of air. "Much good that did me."

Carl thanked him and terminated the interview. On the way back upstairs, he compared notes with Harriett.

She thought the same as he did. The evidence was overwhelming, and the story was poor. A missing WhatsApp message, a pointless attempt to save a dead man, and then the decision to run. If he'd read it somewhere, he'd have put every penny on it turning out to be a lie.

But reading it somewhere wasn't the same as being in the room with the man. And Starling, like Niamh Hanson, had seemed desperate.

Of course, desperate people could still lie. But there was something about the way Starling had broken, finally, that had Carl thinking twice.

CHAPTER SEVENTY-SEVEN

Harriett had hoped for some time to go through the interview and see if they could reach a conclusion between them, but the minute it took to walk back to the team room was all she got. By the time she'd pushed open the door, her phone was ringing.

"Hello?" she said.

"Harriett, it's Caroline Deane. I'm at Hanson's house."

The search was continuing there. The more evidence they found, the more obvious it looked that Hanson was involved, the greater the justification for hunting through every last square inch of her house. Starling might have been Hanson's accomplice, or the man she'd picked to take the fall, but either way, Hanson was still in the frame.

"Found anything?"

"Very much so. Have a look at your inbox."

Harriett sat at her desk and tapped open the team inbox. There was a message there from Caroline, with a link to a handful of images she'd already uploaded to the file. She clicked open the first of the images and frowned at it.

"What's this?" she said.

"It's a phone," Caroline replied.

"I can see that. But... Where was it?"

"It was under a loose floorboard, under a rug in the bedroom. We should have found it earlier, to be honest."

"Have you—"

"It's all in the notes, Harriett. But it looks like a burner."

It would be. Harriett leaned forward, rubbing at her head.

"Do you think you'll be able to get it open?"

"No need. It wasn't locked."

Harriett sat back up.

"Seriously?"

"Seriously. Data's being uploaded as we speak, so you can take a look at your leisure, but there's not much on it."

"Don't tell me. Telegram."

"Precisely. The app, but none of the messages. Just places where messages were sent and received, then deleted."

"It's not looking good for Niamh Hanson, is it?" Harriett said.

"Well..." said Caroline, then paused. "Have you heard from Keisha?"

"Isn't she there with you?"

"No. She's at the lab. She wanted to talk to you."

Harriett held her phone out and checked the notifications. Sure enough, there were three missed calls from Keisha Middleton, all while she'd been interviewing Starling.

"Do you know what it's about?" Harriett asked.

"Call her," said Caroline, and Harriett thanked her and ended the call.

Keisha Middleton answered on the third ring.

"Thought you might be dead or something," she said.

"Just interviewing a suspect," Harriett replied drily. There was no point engaging Keisha, trying to justify yourself or anything as rational as that. She'd just move on before you'd even got started. "What have you got for us?"

"Hanson's tests. They've come back."

"Drugs?" asked Harriett. If there was ketamine in her system, or anything else that could reinforce the link between Hanson and Starling, her defence would take a serious hit.

"Yep. And no prizes for guessing which one," Keisha told her.

"Ketamine?"

"I said no prizes. But yes."

"I thought it only stayed in your blood for a day or so."

"And you thought right," Keisha agreed. "But we didn't find it in her blood. We found it through the hair she gave us voluntarily. Stays there for months. And we couldn't find it in the older samples we pulled from the brush in her house. Which suggests she started taking it relatively recently."

The case was moving quickly now, with no time to adjust to a piece of evidence before a new one came in. And Niamh Hanson's story was sprouting so many holes, it was starting to look more like a sponge than a defence.

CHAPTER SEVENTY-EIGHT

Craig Underwood was the sort of man you could walk past a hundred times and still not recognise. Average height, medium-length brown hair, eyes of a colour you couldn't quite put a name to, but only because it wasn't interesting enough to have its own name, a dull, pasty face that was neither ugly nor good-looking. He walked into the interview room at the Barrow Central Police Station wearing one of those diffident smiles that hid a person who wasn't sure what they were about to encounter, but wasn't enormously worried by it, either.

Denise had read the comments and jokes Underwood had made in the Real Cops Telegram group. If he wasn't worried now, he would be in a minute.

"How can I help you?" he asked.

He'd been told there was someone there who wanted a quick chat. There was a uniformed officer from Carlisle outside the door, and another one a little further down the corridor, but Denise hoped she wouldn't need them. Her plan had been to go gently, to coax him into telling her what he could before she told him how much trouble he was in.

It had been a long drive from Carlisle, south on the motorway and then west to the southern tip of Windermere, almost blinded from time to time as she turned a corner and found herself driving towards the sun. At Ulverston she'd realised she was going to be earlier than she'd intended, and decided to cut south again towards Birkrigg Common, the narrow road lined by tall hedges that fell away suddenly as she approached the coast, revealing distant hills and finally the sea itself, grey and blue before her. The Coast Road supplied marshy lowland to her left, trees and fields to her right, and of course the sea again, now glinting in the light of a sun that remained conveniently outside her direct line of sight. She reached Barrow in a better mood than she'd set out in. Even the pain in her neck seemed to have receded. Craig Underwood was in all kinds of trouble, but Denise was inclined to make it as easy as she could for the man.

But that smile had pissed her off. That smile, on the face of a man who had the good fortune to work in one of the brightest, shiniest police stations she'd ever seen, a place with a three-storey reception area shaped like the inside of a bloody ship, and chose to abuse that good fortune in the way Underwood had...

"Tell me about the Real Cops Telegram group, Craig," she said. She hadn't bothered introducing herself, hadn't done anything formal, yet.

This was just a chat, after all.

The smile faltered for a fraction of a second before he recovered. "I don't know what you're talking about," he said.

Well, she'd gone in gently. She'd given it her best shot.

"I'm going to caution you now," she told him.

"What?"

"You already know Bateman's dead, Craig. You probably don't know about Illingworth."

"What about him?" said Underwood, then, a moment later, "Who's Illingworth?"

If she hadn't read those messages, Denise might even have felt sorry for the man.

"When we've finished this little chat, I'm going to arrest you for misconduct in a public office, Craig. That's happening. Whatever you tell me next, that's happening, and frankly, you should be pleased about it, because the people in your little group are dropping like fat men on a fun run, and the safest place for you right now is in a cell."

"I don't know what you're talking about," he said again.

By the time she'd cautioned him, reminded him about Bateman, and told him they'd recovered Illingworth's unlocked phone alongside his dead body, Underwood had decided he did know what Denise was talking about after all.

"Yes," he said. "I was in the group."

"You sent these messages?" she asked, showing him a printout of a selection that made that dull, pasty face turn redder than a Scotsman in Tenerife.

And they weren't even the worst of the bunch.

"Yes," he said. "But I didn't mean any of it. I didn't—"

"Save it. Tell me about the blackmail, Craig."

He nodded.

"I gave him shift patterns, looked up a couple of records. Oh, he wanted to know where some evidence was being stored. There's a separate chat. He probably had one of them with each of us."

"I'll need to see your phones," she said.

He nodded again, reached into his pocket, and passed her two phones.

She waited, and he reached into a second pocket and handed her a third.

"And I'll need your passwords."

He paused, and for a moment she thought maybe he'd found a backbone somewhere, and was about to ask for a lawyer or a rep, but he must have seen something in her face that told him not to bother. He gave her the passwords.

"Do you know who Simon is?"

He shook his head.

"How about these two?"

Wilf and Pete, he knew. He gave her their names, and she sent an urgent message back to the team.

"Who set up this group, Craig?"

He shook his head.

"No point not telling me. We'll find out soon enough."

"I don't know. It wasn't me."

None of the men Marcus and Tom had picked up knew, either; Denise had taken a moment to check the latest updates before Underwood had walked in.

"What about Isaac Bateman?"

"I don't think he set it up," Underwood said. "He's not the sharpest."

Which, coming from a man who'd been caught sending the sort of messages Underwood had sent, was certainly saying something.

"I mean, did you know him?"

Underwood nodded.

"What about Samir Rashid?"

He frowned and shook his head.

"Niamh Hanson? Stephen Grange?"

"No," he said.

"Angela Sherman," she tried, finally, and again he shook his head.

"What do you know about Bateman's relationships with his fellow officers?" she asked.

"What do you mean, relationships?"

"I mean, we understand he was sleeping with a female PC who didn't work far from his station."

Underwood started to laugh, saw her glare, and stopped.

"No," he said.

"We have evidence that he slept with this officer at a police function. At the Bassenthwaite Manor Hotel."

"Not a chance," said Underwood.

"Why not?" asked Denise, and then, in an instant, it came to her. "Bateman was gay, wasn't he?"

Bateman being gay would explain a lot. He'd been the sort of man who could never have admitted it. A man who'd easily have succumbed to blackmail, who'd have done anything rather than let the world know.

"No," said Underwood, again. "Bateman was straight. I'm not saying he wouldn't have slept with some bird at a party. He'd have slept with anything if it was female and alive."

"Right," said Denise, disappointed.

For a moment, it had all seemed to make sense.

"I'm just saying that if he *had* managed to pull some bird at a party, there's not a chance in hell he'd have kept quiet about it."

CHAPTER SEVENTY-NINE

A BIT of healthy debate wasn't a bad thing, but you had to stay focused and not let your emotions get the better of you.

Carl had experienced every side of that over the last year or two with Zoe: the things she'd done without telling him, the rows they'd had about whether you could cross the line. The argument raging in the team room was on the verge of spilling over into something more than healthy debate.

"OK, shut up, and let's discuss this rationally, shall we?" he said. Shouted, more than said, and they fell silent.

Marcus was on one side of the ring and Harriett was on the other, and Denise, who'd just returned from Barrow-in-Furness, seemed content to sit back and throw little jabs at either protagonist whenever an opportunity presented itself. Tom Willis was keeping his mouth firmly shut. Aaron Keyes had chosen to sit this briefing out, and Carl was beginning to wonder if he might have known what was in store.

"Good," he continued. "Now, Uniform should be bringing in the last two members we've identified from the Real Cops group. But based on the interviews with the ones we've already got, none of them knows how the group was set up, or who invited people in."

"Borman said it all seemed a bit organic," said Tom.

"Chisholm said much the same," agreed Marcus. "In fewer syllables."

There was a mumble of assent from Denise.

"So," Carl went on, "while it's possible one of them's lying, the likelihood is we're looking at someone else, this so-called Simon, who set the whole thing up, used it to get blackmail material on the rest of them, and then started applying the pressure."

"It's Hanson," said Harriett, and that was it, the debate, or argument, the same points round and round until they didn't make sense any more.

"I'm telling you," said Marcus, "it's not her. None of them know anything about her. Not even heard of her."

"But she knows them," Harriett shot back. "She gave us their names."

"Exactly." Marcus sat back, a smug smile on his face that made Carl hope, briefly, that he'd lose the argument, and lose it painfully, just to wipe that smile away.

"What do you mean?" asked Tom.

"Why would she give us the names if she was the one behind it all?" Marcus replied.

"No," said Harriett, apparently unaffected by Marcus's smile. "She gave us the names after a night in the cells. She didn't *want* to give us the names. She was looking for a way out. And," she continued, silencing an open-mouthed Marcus before he could interrupt, "there's everything else. There's the phone, to start with."

"Tell me about this phone," said Carl.

"Unregistered burner," said Harriett, who'd been looking

into it for the last half hour. "I've traced it to a bulk purchase from nearly three years ago. And some of the other phones from that purchase have been linked to other crimes. We've got a murder in Northumbria, an armed robbery in London, and a drugs ring in Dorset."

Dorset. Where Zoe was now. Carl turned the word over in his head. To his surprise, it didn't sting.

Maybe he was finally going numb.

"Do we have any idea who made that purchase?" he asked, and Harriett shook her head.

"No. And we're not likely to get one. The officers looking into those other crimes have been all over it for years."

"So what's on Hanson's phone?"

"The messages she sent to the Telegram group have been deleted and can't be recovered," Harriett said. "But the metadata's still there."

"Meaning?" said Carl, but Marcus was already objecting, like a defence lawyer in court.

"We don't know it was her that sent them."

Harriett ignored the interruption, answering Carl's question instead.

"Sorry, boss. Meaning that we know *when* the messages were sent, and we know the groups and conversations they were sent to. And the timings coincide with the ones sent by the person who called themselves Simon."

"She's got to be Simon," said Tom, finally weighing in on his girlfriend's side.

"It's too easy," said Marcus. "Why leave the phone unlocked? No prints have been found on it, right?"

"Right," said Harriett, warily.

"So if it's Hanson, do we really think she's smart enough

to use gloves or wipe it clean, and hide it under a floorboard, but then leave it unlocked?"

"Illingworth's phone was unlocked," Tom pointed out.

"Exactly," said Marcus. "Because Illingworth *wanted* us to see what was on it. Why would Hanson wipe this thing clean, go to the trouble of hiding it under the floor, and not even bother locking it?"

There was a short silence. Carl looked around the room, but no one seemed to have an answer.

"What about the ketamine?" said Harriett. "Starling's supply, in her house, in her system."

"Taking ketamine doesn't make you a murderer," Marcus countered. "And then there's the fibres," he added. "Stella's team told us they might have been placed there deliberately."

"Might," said Harriett. "Look, you're right, there's a lot of room for doubt with the evidence we have on Hanson. But there's a lot of evidence there in the first place. Don't forget, Starling was there, on the scene, with a motive and his fingerprints on Bateman's car."

Marcus fell silent. He'd made some good points, but there was no doubt Harriett was right, too. The evidence against Hanson was piling up faster than a bank holiday traffic jam. Every time a problem was found with one piece of evidence, a new piece of evidence turned up to replace it.

If anyone was going to fight Hanson's corner, they'd need more weaponry than they had right now.

CHAPTER EIGHTY

THE TROUBLE WAS, thought Marcus, Harriett was right. And Niamh Hanson wasn't exactly helping herself.

He was sitting opposite her, with DS Gaskill beside him and Paula Vernon wearing a look of quiet resignation on the other side of the table, and she still wouldn't tell him what he wanted to know.

"Why did Rashid call?" he asked. "What did he have to tell you, just a few minutes before the boatyard call came in?"

Hanson shook her head.

"OK," said DS Gaskill. "Let's go back a bit. Tell us about this phone."

They'd shown her the phone, or the images of it, at the start of the interview. She continued to deny any knowledge of it.

"It was found inside your house, Niamh," Marcus reminded her.

"Then someone put it there."

"Tell us about this Telegram group. Real Cops."

"I'm not even sure what Telegram is," she said, and the DS gave a sigh of impatience.

"We've been through this. It's an encrypted messaging app. The encrypted messaging app you used to communicate with the rest of the group, and to blackmail them."

"This is ridiculous," said Hanson. And it was.

"You can make all this go away if you'll just come clean," said Marcus. He could see why DS Gaskill was feeling impatient.

"I've told you everything I know."

"You haven't told us about the call from Rashid."

And so it began again. A cycle, through the phone call from Rashid and the decision not to stop at the boathouse, to the Telegram group, the ketamine, the relationship with Starling, the mysterious payment, the night in Bateman's room, and back around again to the phone call from Rashid.

She'd stared at them blankly for a minute when Marcus had told her about the ketamine they'd found in her hair. She'd denied taking it. DS Gaskill had all but laughed at the denial.

"Are you saying someone's drugged me?" she asked.

"We're saying there's an illegal drug in your system," replied the DS. "The same illegal drug we found in your house. Why did Rashid call you?"

"I've told you, I'm not discussing that."

"Was he reminding you not to go near the boathouse?" asked Marcus. "Is he Simon? Is he the one who's been giving you instructions?"

"I don't know what you're talking about."

"I think you do," said the DS. "But on the whole, I think it's more likely you're Simon. You cooked this whole thing up yourself, didn't you?"

"You're just speculating now," said Paula Vernon.

"We wouldn't have to if your client would just tell us the truth."

"I *am* telling you the truth."

And round and round and round again.

There was a moment where she faltered, when Marcus told her about Starling.

"Your ex was on the scene when DS Bateman died," he said.

She shrugged.

"We've got his prints on Bateman's car. We showed him the evidence, and he admitted it."

That was the moment. A look of shock passed across her face, and she turned to her lawyer, who looked back at her, impassive, nodding gently.

Paula Vernon knew Marcus wouldn't have said it if it hadn't been true.

Marcus exchanged a glance with the DS, and went in for the kill.

"Did you do it together?" he asked.

"What?" she said.

"Kill Isaac Bateman. You both had motive. Bateman was about to expose you as Simon, and Starling resented him for supposedly framing him."

"No," said Hanson, shaking her head, but she looked more confused than certain now.

"Did you rope Starling into your plan?" asked the DS. "Or was it the other way round? If he was forcing you to do this, Niamh, you just have to tell us."

"No," she said again, and then fell silent, and nothing they could say would make her speak.

DS Gaskill terminated the interview, and they walked

slowly back upstairs. On the turn halfway between the first and the second floor, she stopped.

"I think the CPS would agree there's enough to charge her now," she said.

Marcus wanted to argue, but she was right. Enough to charge her, and not far short of enough to convict.

"But," she continued, "we've got a bit more time. And I'm still not sure."

"Neither am I," he said, and she smiled at him. Marcus wasn't sure he'd seen DS Gaskill smile before.

"We know that, Marcus," she said. "You've made that abundantly clear. We'll hold off charging for a little longer, then. Let's see what we can dig up."

CHAPTER EIGHTY-ONE

Harriett looked up at the sound of the door opening. DS Gaskill nodded as she walked in. Behind her, Marcus marched straight to his desk, head down, face creased into a frown. Harriett wasn't sure if she was imagining it, but it felt like he was avoiding her eye.

Clearly, he hadn't got what he'd wanted out of Niamh Hanson.

She took a moment to run through the argument they'd had, the debate on Hanson's guilt. She was convinced she was right. Marcus was convinced he was right. Maybe things had got a little overheated. Two men had been murdered, and a third had killed himself. A little anger wasn't the end of the world.

But she could see it from Marcus's point of view, too. Not that he was right – he wasn't right, he was just blinded by the need to see something more complicated than the simple fact of Hanson's guilt – but he was new here. Unfamiliar with the people, the place, the process. Even the people they'd drafted in from the Hub were Harriett's people

– the DI she'd worked alongside when she was undercover, and the man she was living with.

Marcus would be feeling like he was fighting on his own. Harriett had been there herself. If it didn't make you back down, it made you bite back, even harder.

She was wondering whether to say something to him, maybe just offer him a coffee, when her phone rang. The number looked vaguely familiar, but she couldn't place it until she answered and heard the voice.

"Is that DC Barnes?"

"PS Rashid?" she said. "Yes, it's me."

"Sorry to bother you," said Rashid. "I..."

He gave a small laugh, then fell silent.

"What is it, PS Rashid?"

"Look," he said. "I might have made a mistake."

"Is this about the phone call?" Harriett asked, and sensed movement to her side. Marcus was watching her now, a look in his eyes she couldn't quite name. Hunger, almost.

"Enough about the fucking phone call," said Rashid. "I don't remember any bloody phone call, right? No. This is... Well, it's probably not important. But I think I might have got something wrong."

Harriett had been told a hundred times that you could hear a smile in a person's voice. She knew you could hear a scowl. She fought off her own impatience, wiped the scowl away, and put a smile there instead.

"What is it you think you've got wrong?" she asked.

"Liverpool," he replied.

She lifted the phone from her ear and looked at it in bemusement for a moment.

"You'll have to be a little clearer than that," she said.

"I said it was Niamh who mentioned something about the boatyard victim being from Merseyside."

"You did," Harriett agreed. It was yet another piece of evidence Hanson had knocked back, unconvincingly.

"Yeah, well, I think I might have remembered that wrong."

"You do?"

"Yeah."

She waited.

"I'm assuming there's more to this, PS Rashid," she said, after ten silent seconds had gone by. "If Hanson didn't tell you, then who did?"

"I was drunk," said Rashid. "I'm not sure."

"But you've an idea, haven't you? You must have remembered something, or you wouldn't have called."

There was another silence, and this time Harriett allowed it to lengthen, to push itself into Rashid's mind and force out the words he seemed so reluctant to say.

"Look." His voice was strained, the voice of someone ending a marriage that had lasted decades, or telling a loved one they had a terminal disease. "I think it was Stevie."

"PC Grange?"

"Yeah. I'm not sure. I was—"

"You were drunk. Yes."

"But I think it was Stevie. I think he told us the man had a Liverpool tattoo."

"PC Grange told you the man had a Liverpool tattoo." Harriett repeated Rashid's words back to him, waiting for him to correct her, or retract it. He didn't.

"It doesn't mean anything, though," insisted Rashid.

"No," Harriett agreed. She wasn't sure she meant it, though.

"He must have read about it in the post-mortem report," said Rashid.

"Thanks for your information," Harriett told him. "If you can think of anything else, please let me know."

When she looked back round, DS Gaskill was gone, and Marcus was putting down his own phone and typing furiously on his keyboard.

"What are you doing?" she asked.

"I heard all that," he replied.

"And?"

"And I'm requesting more information on Grange's shift patterns." He fixed her with a stare of such utter determination she almost looked away.

Almost, but not quite.

"It might not mean anything," she pointed out, aware that she was echoing Rashid's words from a minute earlier, and aware, too, of how weak they sounded.

"Maybe," said Marcus.

But she knew he'd be thinking the same thing she was. Asking himself the same question.

Why, given the nature of his job, would PC Stephen Grange have read Alexander Godwin's post-mortem report?

CHAPTER EIGHTY-TWO

THIS TIME, Aaron Keyes had joined them on-screen, and Carl was grateful for his presence, albeit virtual. Hanson and Starling had both gone quiet, but the same couldn't be said for Carl's team.

"I'm telling you," Marcus said, "it's Grange we should be looking at."

He looked around the room, a belligerent expression on his face, daring anyone to disagree. Carl couldn't remember being quite so sure of himself as a DC, but he'd forgotten plenty since then, and the young always thought they knew what was what.

A pity for Marcus Hosgood, then, that the opposition came from someone as young and confident in her opinions as he was.

"Hanson's the priority," said Harriett.

Beside her, Tom Willis grunted quietly in agreement, but didn't say anything.

Wise man.

"Denise?" asked Carl, and she shot him a look that told

him she didn't relish being shoved into the middle of this particular debate.

"I'm happy to look at Grange," she said, and Marcus smiled, before she went on. "But Hanson's still the priority." The smile dropped from Marcus's face. "She's the one in custody, and the evidence might be open to challenge, but there's a lot of it, and it all points in her direction. We've not got long before we have to talk to the CPS about charging. She should be our focus."

"What about Rashid?" Carl asked.

"He might be involved," said Harriett. "But I'm still convinced Starling and Hanson are in this together. That's where the evidence points."

Another smart move. Echo what the DS just said, and it'll look like you're not the one who made the point in the first place.

"Fine," replied Marcus. "Let's look at this so-called evidence, shall we?"

"OK," said Carl. Clearly, Marcus's intention was to shoot it all down, but a review of what they had on Hanson, good and bad, was exactly what was called for.

"Motive-wise," Marcus continued, "we've got two things. There's an apparent affair with Bateman, which she denies, and there's a previous relationship with Zack Starling. She admits to a relationship with Starling, and we know Starling was on the scene. We also know Starling didn't like Bateman."

"That's quite a lot," Harriett pointed out. "More than enough to go on. And you've forgotten the other motive."

"What?"

"Maybe Bateman knew she was Simon. Maybe she killed him before he could expose her."

"She's not Simon," Marcus replied. "That phone's been planted."

He paused, but not for long enough for Harriett to counter.

"As for the other stuff, it's two separate things, isn't it?" he said. "If she's sleeping with Bateman, what's that got to do with Starling's revenge? And the thing with Starling, that was years ago."

"So she says," muttered Tom.

"Who put us onto Zack Starling?" asked Marcus, with the air of a man who knew the answer and was looking forward to hearing it.

"An anonymous call," said Lynn, from the screen.

"Millie Tennant," said Harriett, in the room.

"And who put us onto Millie Tennant?" asked Marcus.

"Grange," said Denise, when no one else had spoken for a few seconds. She turned to her keyboard, tapped a couple of keys, and brought up a new box on the big screen. "I'm calling her," she said.

"I'm not sure..." began Harriett, but the phone was already ringing, and three seconds later the new box was filled with Millie Tennant's face. In the background, Carl could see cardboard boxes and plain white walls. It looked like Millie Tennant was at work.

"Hello?" she said, peering at her own screen, frowning at what probably looked like half a dozen shadowy figures in a poorly lit room.

Denise introduced herself and explained why she was calling.

"I don't have much time," said the woman.

"We won't keep you long," Denise told her. "Can I just ask, do you know Stephen Grange?"

"Yes," said Millie Tennant.

"Did he ask you to talk to us?" said Marcus.

"Who's that?" asked Millie Tennant, and now Marcus had to introduce himself again. "Bloody hell," she said. "How many of you are there?"

"Did he ask you to talk to us?" Marcus asked again.

"It's not like that," said Millie Tennant.

"It's not?" said Denise.

"No it bloody well isn't. He just... Stevie spoke to me, yeah."

"And what did he say?" asked Marcus. He was keeping his cool, Carl was pleased to see, even as Millie Tennant grew more defensive.

And there was something else, too. Had the woman blushed when she'd said Grange's name?

"He just suggested that if the cops got in touch, I should agree to speak. That's fair enough, isn't it?"

"It is," agreed Denise.

"I mean, you don't keep secrets from the police, do you?" Millie Tennant continued.

"Absolutely not," said Marcus. "And we'd like to thank you for all your help."

Smooth, thought Carl.

When the call was over, there was a brief silence in the room, and then everyone seemed to start talking at once.

"Shut up!" he shouted, and they fell silent. "OK, team. We've all seen the same thing. If I had to guess, I'd say Millie Tennant has a soft spot for our PC Grange."

No one disagreed.

"But there's nothing conclusive there. Either way. Which means Hanson's still our chief suspect, and the evidence we have against her still leaves a lot to be desired. It's clear we're not getting anything more out of Hanson or Starling tonight, so I'm going home. We've got half a dozen cops in custody, plus Starling. Hopefully one of them will have remembered something useful by morning."

He turned and left the room, and he could hear the argument starting up again before the door had swung shut behind him.

CHAPTER EIGHTY-THREE

FORTY MINUTES LATER, no one had come close to changing their mind.

Harriett Barnes had stopped on her way out of the team room and turned around, her movements considered and deliberate, as she walked over and stopped again in front of Marcus.

"What?" he asked.

"It's nothing personal," she said.

"Tell that to Niamh Hanson," he replied, and then she turned and walked away again, Tom Willis a silent step behind her, leaving him to feel like the worst person in the world.

Now it was just him and DS Gaskill, who was watching him like you'd watch a tiger that was getting worryingly close to the edge of its enclosure.

And this was Denise Gaskill. He'd heard about her, over the years. He'd seen how she operated first hand. Of the two of them, it wasn't him that was the dangerous wild animal.

Was it?

Brushing his doubts aside, he picked up his phone and called Rashid.

The man didn't sound pleased to hear him, but he hadn't joined PSD to be greeted like a friend.

"What is it?" Rashid asked. "I've got a life outside answering questions from PSD, you know."

If he was trying to hide his wariness under a veneer of impatience, it wasn't working. Again, Marcus felt a little stung.

Was he really the tiger?

Maybe he was. You became the person other people treated you like. If people were going to treat him like the tiger, they could face the consequences.

"Tell me about your team night out, PS Rashid."

"Why?"

"Because so far three men have died and I wouldn't like there to be a fourth."

Rashid was silent for a moment.

"It was just drinks," he said eventually.

Marcus pushed on. "You were supposed to be buying. I understand PC Hanson ended up using her card to fund your purchases."

"My phone wouldn't work on the machine there, so she paid, and I transferred the cash. Not very complicated."

"And those were all the drinks your party bought?"

Another pause.

"No," said Rashid. "Stevie was up and down at the bar all night."

Marcus sat up straighter.

"This is PC Grange?"

"That's right."

"He was the designated driver, though. He didn't drink."

Rashid gave a small laugh.

"Didn't stop him throwing the booze down Niamh's throat, though."

"Are you saying he was buying drinks for PC Hanson?"

"Her and me, yeah. But mostly her. I thought maybe he was trying it on with her, but Niamh's old enough to look after herself, so I decided to just get drunk and enjoy myself."

Now it was Marcus's turn to fall silent and ponder what he'd just heard.

Grange had been buying drinks for Hanson. Getting Hanson drunk.

Drunker, at least.

"PS Rashid, I know you were drunk yourself, but this is important. Is it possible that Hanson was given something else, in the drinks?"

"What do you mean?" The wariness was back in Rashid's voice. "Stevie was buying drinks. That's all."

"You're sure of that? Is it possible something might have been slipped into one of those drinks?"

"Like what? What are you implying?"

Marcus sighed, and switched tactics.

"PS Rashid, between you and me, we've found traces of ketamine in PC Hanson's system. Is it possible that it was administered to her through the drinks she was bought, without her knowing?"

"That's not how you take ket," said Rashid.

"Not usually, but it can be," Marcus told him. "Is it possible it happened that night?"

"No," said Rashid, immediately, and the sense of anticipation that had been growing inside Marcus withered and died in an instant.

"Are you—?"

"I mean, I suppose it's possible," Rashid continued. "Theoretically. But Stevie wouldn't do that."

Marcus thanked him and ended the call, and when he turned around, DS Gaskill was standing next to him.

"Did you hear that?" he asked.

She nodded. "I did. And it's good work. But you're not Hanson's lawyer, and it's not conclusive. I'm going home. If I were you, I'd do the same thing."

"I will shortly," he told her, and he could see from the long look she cast his way as she headed out of the room that she didn't believe him.

While he'd been on the phone with Rashid, the shift information he'd requested earlier had come in, and he spent five minutes scanning it, trying to spot differences between the patterns that had been set in advance and the reality of who had worked when.

It was perfectly normal for those patterns not to match. Problems arose. Someone might be taken ill, or just have plans they'd forgotten about, and arrangements were made behind the scenes, favours traded, and the problems disappeared. You could track the reasons, but it took time, and it wouldn't appear here, in the raw data, which just showed you the basics, like who'd been put on a shift and who'd ended up working it, and...

"What's this?" he said, before remembering he was the only one left in the room.

Last man standing.

He looked through it again; the original shift pattern, and the detail on the shift itself.

Stephen Grange hadn't been slated for the shift with Niamh Hanson the night of the boatyard shout. Someone else was supposed to be there, D Etherington, a name

Marcus hadn't come across, and if this went any further, he had a feeling he'd be making D Etherington's acquaintance.

But it wasn't a case of D Etherington requesting someone else to cover the shift. There was an Easter egg here, a surprise bonus he hadn't expected to find in all the data.

A request, from Grange himself, to work the shift.

CHAPTER EIGHTY-FOUR

Gerry being away with work again was annoying, and Lynn missed him, but Gerry was away so much these days that she was used to it. And there were positives, too. She could spread out in bed, in her pyjamas, with a glass of Baileys over three ice cubes, sheets of paper scattered over the duvet, and her laptop open in front of her.

Lynn had learned, over years of patient experimentation, that a glass of Baileys was good for her concentration. Two glasses had a negligible effect. Three, and things started to turn the other way. But one worked nicely.

If other people didn't understand that, that was their problem.

A glass of Baileys also made boring work slightly less boring, and the work she was doing at the moment was definitely boring. She was trying to find out the names of the real people behind the consortium that was now the sole bidder for the land Godwin had been looking to buy before he'd been killed. She had one name, Sinead Conway, but Sinead

Conway had a habit of wriggling out of things. There had to be others, too. Multiple companies, multiple people.

That was what a consortium was, right?

She was dragged from the depths of a set of corporate accounts by a ping, the sound of a text coming through. She closed down the accounts, feeling an odd mixture of disappointment and relief.

It was probably Gerry. She hadn't heard from him today, which wasn't uncommon. She flicked open her phone to see a message from Mike McKenzie, the surveyor from Willis Carmichael.

Sent you an email, it said.

The email contained a couple of attachments: the invoice for Willis Carmichael's services, made out to Conway Developments, and a remittance advice from the client, showing the payment made.

She read the invoice, glanced at the remittance advice, blinked, then looked again.

She picked her phone back up and called Mike McKenzie.

"Hello," he said. He sounded tired. That or drunk, and either was reasonable, at this time of the evening. "Get my email?"

"I did. Thanks for sending it through. But I just wanted to check the remittance advice. The numbers correspond. That's definitely the payment made for the survey you did on the Skiddaw site?"

"It is, yes."

"But I thought you said it was paid by Conway Developments. The invoice is made out to them."

"It is, yes."

She took a moment, frowning at the screen in front of her. Had she misunderstood something?

"But the payment wasn't made by Conway Developments," she pointed out.

"Oh, yeah." Mike McKenzie laughed. "Sorry. Been a long day, not entirely with it."

"The payment was made by a different company," she said. "An insurance company. What have they got to do with Conway Developments?"

"You're right," replied Mike McKenzie. "It's not them. It's one of the others in the consortium."

"But it's an insurance company," she said again.

"It's a captive," he replied – just that, three simple words, as if they made any sense at all.

"I'm sorry?"

"A captive insurance company. It's owned by Headland Stamp Construction."

"Who are they?"

"Beats me. They're in the consortium, but I've never come across them before. And yes, before you say it again, it *is* an insurance company, properly regulated and everything, with all the risks reinsured and capitalised, but it only insures for incidents on Headland Stamp sites."

Only half of what Mike McKenzie had just told her made any sense at all. But it was the important half.

The half, she thought, that might turn everything they knew about the case on its head.

"Is that normal?" she asked. "This captive insurance company thing?"

Mike McKenzie assured her it was all completely normal, and she thanked him and said goodbye.

"Hang on," he said.

"Yeah?" she asked, wondering if he was about to turn everything on its head again.

"I was thinking," he said, then stopped.

"What?" she asked.

"I don't suppose you'd like to go for a drink sometime?" he said.

She laughed.

"You don't know anything about me," she pointed out.

"I do. I had to look up every Lynn in Cumbria Police when I was trying to track you down. I know what you look like."

"And you've asked me out for a drink. That's very flattering, Mike, but I'm married."

"Oh," he said. "Shit."

"Yeah. They don't put that on the bio. And besides, I don't know what you look like."

"Doesn't really matter, does it?" he replied, and said goodbye.

Lynn glanced at the time, put her phone down, updated HOLMES and the case file with what she'd just learned, and put in a request for more information on Headland Stamp Construction.

This was big.

She poured herself another Baileys and waited. It was late, but there was always a chance someone would see her update and call her to discuss it. She'd left a note with the information, saying she'd be up for a while and was happy to talk it through.

She sipped at her Baileys and waited, but no one got back to her.

Maybe they were all out, arresting somebody. Maybe

Niamh Hanson had confessed. Maybe they'd given up and gone to the pub.

Lynn finished her glass of Baileys and poured another, checked the system again, and saw that no one had opened her update.

This *was* big, wasn't it? She hadn't just imagined it, had she?

She hadn't. And she was far too excited to sleep. She sipped at her drink and smiled to herself.

Mike McKenzie had asked her out for a drink. He'd looked her up, seen what she looked like, and he'd asked her out for a drink.

She finished the glass and poured herself another – her fourth, she thought, or was it her fifth? – and checked the system yet again. Nothing. While she was at her keyboard, though, she opened a browser and found the website for Willis Carmichael, the surveyors.

It was a bland enough website, but when she opened the menu, the page she was looking for was there.

Our People.

She clicked it open and found the link she was hoping to find, and sipped at her drink, and clicked again.

She was far too excited to sleep.

Mike McKenzie was a good-looking young man, with the emphasis on the young. He had a mop of unruly dark hair, green eyes, and a mischievous grin, and he didn't look older than twenty-five.

Too young for Lynn, surely. And besides, she was married.

When she fell asleep five minutes later, the half-empty glass falling from her hand and the drink running out onto the bed, it was with the green eyes of Mike McKenzie watching over her.

CHAPTER EIGHTY-FIVE

Once you found one interesting thing, the world was suddenly full of them.

Stephen Grange's shift patterns, for instance. He hadn't been on shift the night before he'd been called into PSD for the first time, because that was the evening of the notorious team night out.

When someone might, just possibly, have slipped a dose of ketamine into Niamh Hanson's drink.

But Grange had been on shift during the afternoon that preceded the night out. This was within the window for Bateman's murder – it was, in fact, the same period during which Hanson had been at home alone, without an alibi.

But Grange didn't have an alibi either. He hadn't just been on shift. He'd been on a solo shift.

It wasn't Grange's shift that was the interesting thing, or that he'd done it alone. It wasn't even the fact that, according to the records, it had been as quiet a shift as anyone could hope for.

It was that the tracker on Grange's car wasn't fully operational at the time.

And neither was the Airwave radio terminal attached to the car.

And, for some reason, the location tracker on Grange's phone hadn't been working, either.

There was bad luck, and there was coincidence, and then there was the kind of bad luck and coincidence that involved three pieces of equipment with the same function but different hardware and networks, all breaking down at the same time.

Marcus thought he had a pretty good idea where that car had been, but there was no way of knowing for sure.

Or was there?

He highlighted the details he needed, opened another window, and found the page he was looking for.

He stared at it for a minute. He'd moved so fast on this, all the pieces falling into place. But now, suddenly, he was unsure of himself.

He didn't enjoy the sensation.

He carried on staring at the screen. He could wait. That would be the sensible thing to do. Wait until morning, talk it over with the rest of the team, come to a joint decision. Even Harriett Barnes would agree with him when she saw what had happened to Grange's tracking systems.

But what if Grange realised Marcus was onto him?

It wasn't as if there was much evidence against the man. No evidence at all, really. Just a weakness in the evidence against Hanson, and the sense that things led back to Grange.

There would be evidence somewhere. But if Grange

figured out Marcus was looking for it, that evidence would be gone long before anyone could find it.

He reached for his keyboard, copied the details he'd highlighted earlier, entered his own information, entered DI Whaley's information, and tapped submit.

Then he put his phone on the desk in front of him and waited.

It rang less than a minute later.

"Is that DC Hosgood?"

"It is."

"This is Errol Winter, from Rosebank."

Rosebank was the site in Whitehaven where the CSIs were based. He'd worried that the call would come from Stella Berry or one of the team he'd worked with, which might have screwed things up, but he'd taken the chance anyway.

He'd never heard of Errol Winter, which meant Errol Winter had probably never heard of him. It looked like that chance had paid off.

"You're calling about the search request?"

"That's right. Just to be clear, you want us to go in and impound a police vehicle, carry out an emergency analysis, and keep you updated with the results in real time?"

"That's right."

"And I can see you've given us access to the case file so we can prioritise searches for traces of individuals who are named in there."

"Yes. Not Grange or Hanson, though. We already know they'd both been in that vehicle in recent days."

"Understood. You're aware this needs to be authorised by an inspector?"

"DI Whaley has already cleared it," said Marcus.

"We'll need to check this with him personally."

"Ah," said Marcus.

"Ah?"

"Might be a problem. He's not here."

"Well where is he, then?"

"I can't say, Errol. It's sensitive."

Marcus waited. Everything hung on this.

"He has cleared it, though?" said Errol after a minute.

"You can see his details on the request," Marcus replied, failing to mention that he'd added those details himself, and that they didn't include anything more than the DI's name and phone number.

"Fuck it," said Errol. "We'll get cracking."

Marcus thanked him and sat back, heart pounding, aware, suddenly, that it wasn't just the case that hung on whatever Errol and his team were about to unearth.

After what he'd just done, it was make-or-break for Marcus's career, too.

CHAPTER EIGHTY-SIX

Carl was listening to Adam Ant on the tinny little smart speaker, missing his turntable, which was in one of the boxes they'd never got round to unpacking, and in the mood for something a little stronger than beer.

Zoe hadn't been a drinker. Still wasn't a drinker, as far as he knew. It had seemed wasteful, opening a bottle of wine just to drink it by himself. He'd always enjoyed it when they'd been with other people, enjoyed the excuse, the opportunity to pop a cork or mix a few gin and tonics.

He hadn't done that in a while now. Why exactly was that?

He pulled open the door to the sideboard they'd bought together shortly after they'd moved in here. It was all there, still, all the furniture they'd shared, all the plates and cutlery and ornaments, the TV, the prints on the wall. He'd have to get rid of some of it when he moved, and that was coming sooner than he wanted it to, but he couldn't hang on here by himself forever.

There was the gin, barely touched, its black cap winking up at him like a single eye with a cheeky little message.

Drink me, it said.

Carl was reaching for the bottle when his phone rang, and for a moment, he thought he'd ignore the call, but only for a moment.

They were investigating a double murder, after all.

"How's tricks?" asked Jake.

Carl backed away from the sideboard, pushed its wooden door shut, and sat on the sofa, leaning back and closing his eyes.

"Not bad," he replied. "You?"

"I've been hearing things about two recent events and the possibility that they're linked, Carl."

Carl's eyes shot open.

"You're not going to write about them, are you?"

Jake Frimpton was a journalist at the *Whitehaven Chronicle*. He was a good journalist, both in the quality of his output, and the fact that he avoided publishing the sort of information that might stir up too much trouble.

But more importantly, Jake was a friend. He'd been a friend of Zoe's first, but he'd become Carl's friend, too.

And Zoe wasn't here any more.

"Course not. I just... I understand that the road traffic accident over Rydal way might not have been an accident after all."

Carl thought about lying, and simply couldn't be bothered.

"You understand right. And yes, we're exploring the possibility of a link with the boatyard murder. I don't know where you get your information, Jake—"

"And I'm not going to tell you, but you know that. Don't

worry. It's between us until you say otherwise. How are things?"

Again, Carl thought about lying. He closed his eyes and ran through the day, the last few days, the hangovers and the bottle of gin winking at him from the sideboard. He saw Marcus snapping at Harriett. He saw Harriett snapping back and Denise keeping well out of it, which was unusual for her. He saw Branthwaite inviting him for a drink, saw Branthwaite's desk, saw himself looking away, then back again, and yes, he was sure of it now, there *had* been something missing from Branthwaite's desk. Something the DCI had removed while Carl's back was turned.

What was it?

He squeezed his eyes tight, and thought he saw a sheet of paper, with handwriting on it, and...

"Carl?" said Jake.

"Sorry, mate," said Carl. "I was miles away."

"Are you sure you're OK?"

Jake knew Carl better than almost anyone else in Cumbria did. But he still didn't know him well.

"I'm fine," Carl lied.

"Good. In that case, I've got a request for you. You know we've merged?"

Carl had been hearing about this for a while. The merger of the *Whitehaven Chronicle* and the *Ambleside Gazette*, with half a dozen even smaller titles thrown in for good measure. The whole joint operation had been bought up by someone new, and Jake had been concerned about the effect it might have on the work he did.

"Yeah. How's that going? As bad as you feared?"

"The opposite, actually." Carl could almost hear the smile in Jake's voice as the other man went on. "They've got clear ideas about the sort of thing we should be publishing, and they're ideas I can get on board with."

"Good for you," said Carl, and hoped the words didn't sound sarcastic. He hadn't meant them to be sarcastic.

"Anyway," Jake continued, clearly untroubled by Carl's tone, "the new proprietor, Terri Burscough."

"The Scotswoman," said Carl, anxious to prove he'd been listening all those times Jake had raised the subject.

"That's right. She says she's keen to put an end to irresponsible journalism practices."

Carl said nothing. Anything he did say in response to that would *definitely* sound sarcastic.

"Her son, Cameron. He's getting involved. He's told me they'd like to meet you."

A meeting with a millionaire newspaper magnate and her spoiled offspring?

"Lovely idea," replied Carl. "I don't suppose it can wait until we've cracked our double murder?"

That one had come out sarcastic, and he didn't care.

"Of course," agreed Jake. They chatted amicably enough for a minute or two, before Carl made his excuses and ended the call.

He could still see that bottle of gin, winking at him even through the closed wooden door.

DAY ELEVEN

CHAPTER EIGHTY-SEVEN

IT WAS NONSENSE. Harriett was sure of it. She lay on her back, eyes open and fixed on the darkness above, Tom snoring quietly beside her, and reminded herself it was all nonsense.

Marcus was being an idiot. Maybe he had a thing for Niamh Hanson, but more likely he just wanted to prove himself, say something different from what everyone else was saying, and then try to rearrange the world to make himself right.

Unfortunately for Marcus, the world didn't work like that. His ideas made sense in isolation, but they just weren't realistic.

She nodded quietly to herself, turned onto her side, and tried to get back to sleep.

Ten minutes later, she was on her back again.

Niamh Hanson had drugs in her system and drugs in her house. She had a phone with deleted Telegram messages; she had fibres from Bateman's jacket; she had a relationship with Starling, who'd been there at the scene of Bateman's death, and another relationship, possibly just a one-nighter, with Bateman himself. She had a mysterious payment into her bank account and a mysterious phone call from PS Rashid.

The idea that Niamh Hanson was innocent was preposterous.

Why, then, was Harriett lying on her back, staring into the darkness at four o'clock in the morning, unable to get back to sleep?

It was the link between Bateman and Hanson, she decided. It didn't seem to fit in with everything else.

The two of them had hooked up at the Bassenthwaite Manor Hotel, but what was behind that? If Hanson was Simon, had Bateman known?

If he hadn't, maybe that night had been Hanson's way of exerting a little more control over him. If anyone was going to break ranks and destroy the carefully executed blackmail plan she'd set up, it would have been Bateman. It had been Bateman, in the end, who'd decided to go to PSD. Had she seen that tendency in him and decided to keep a closer eye?

Or had Bateman known she was Simon all along?

Maybe he'd been in on it with her. She felt her mouth curl, as if she'd eaten something unpleasant. She didn't like that idea.

She had a better one, though.

Maybe Bateman had realised that Hanson was Simon, somehow, and forced her to sleep with him in exchange for keeping her secret.

That made sense. Harriett smiled to herself and rolled back onto her side. It gave Hanson a motive for sleeping with Bateman, and a motive for killing him that slid in nicely alongside Starling's motive for killing the same man. She closed her eyes and willed the sleep to come, and ten minutes later, she sighed and poked Tom in the side.

"What?" he groaned, opening one eye.

"Wake up, Tom."

"I am awake. What time is it?"

"I don't know." She reached for her phone and squinted at the display. "It's nearly half past."

Tom sat up, shaking his head like a wet dog.

"Half past seven?"

"No. Half past four."

He frowned and stared at her for ten long seconds, mouthing a series of words, none of which made it out with the sound attached.

"What," he said, finally, "are we doing up at half past four in the morning?"

"We're paying a visit to the Bassenthwaite Manor Hotel," she said, and got out of bed.

CHAPTER EIGHTY-EIGHT

The place was in darkness, not just the team room but the whole corridor and most of the stairway. There were people milling about the ground floor – Durranhill was a fully operational police station, after all – but up here, you could feel like you were the only person on earth.

If he was the only person on earth, that was fine with Marcus. It seemed he was the only person willing to sacrifice a little sleep to make some sense of their investigation.

The first thing he checked was the custody records, but nothing had happened there, not with Hanson or Starling or any of the so-called Real Cops. No one in the cells downstairs had fallen ill or had a sudden attack of conscience and confessed to everything.

And no one would, he thought. Because none of them had done it. It was all so neat, Hanson and Starling and their lack of alibis and their mixed-up motives.

It was too neat.

Real life wasn't like that. Real life was a dry-stone wall,

with bits sticking out in weird places, and cracks running from top to bottom, and angled overhangs that looked like they'd bring the whole thing down, but somehow didn't. If you tried to build a dry stone wall and made everything perfectly even, it wouldn't last through the ages the way a proper wall did.

That was another thing his dad had told him. It had seemed like a load of bollocks at the time. But now, alone in the team room, the darkness broken only by the glare of Marcus's screen, it made sense.

The next thing he checked was the news from forensics, but they hadn't sent him anything yet. He hadn't been woken in the night by a summons from the boss or the DCI, and a quick firing for exceeding his authority and lying about it, but that was coming, he knew.

At least, it was coming if he couldn't figure all this out.

Time to head back to the start, he thought. The first thing that had happened.

He pulled up the notes they'd made when they'd first become involved. Angela Sherman had still been on the radio with Hanson and Grange, so the conversation had been recorded and made it onto the transcript.

PC8436G: *You want to bother with that?*

PC1453H: *Nah, leave it till morning shift.*

PC8436G was Grange. PC1453H was Hanson.

Why hadn't she wanted to go to the boatyard?

If Marcus could put himself in that car, if he could only hear what had been said instead of just reading it, he might find some nuance, some...

He slapped his forehead, shut down the file he was reading, and accessed the dispatch recordings. It took nearly ten minutes to find what he was looking for, and when he hit play, there was a moment of static before the voices boomed out.

First, Sherman, relaying the information.

Then, Hanson: *received*.

Then, Grange's question and Hanson's answer, the same question and answer Marcus had read so many times he'd probably see the words in his sleep. They were talking to each other rather than Angela Sherman, but the exchange was clear enough.

And not what he'd expected. There was something about it that jarred with the way they'd been looking at this all along.

He played it again.

"You want to bother with that?"

"Nah, leave it till morning shift."

And again.

It wasn't until he'd played it a third time that he had it.

Grange had asked the question, and Hanson had answered, and that had led them to believe that Hanson had been the one calling the shots. She was the more experienced officer, after all. She hadn't been much help when they'd been over it with her, whereas Grange had expressed concern about it, about the decision she'd made.

That was something, Marcus thought, that Grange had been keen to emphasise. The decision *Hanson* had made.

But the more he played it back, the less it sounded like that.

"You want to bother with that?"

"Nah, leave it till morning shift."

Grange's question didn't sound like a question, or at least, not an open one. It sounded more like a statement.

Like Grange was leaving it to Hanson to decide whether

to bother with the boatyard, but really, it would be ridiculous to.

Marcus played it again. And again. By the time he'd listened a dozen times, he was sure of it.

The transcript was only half the story, and reading it, instead of listening to what had actually been said, had led them down the wrong track from the start. There had been one person in that car who was in control, one person making the decisions.

And that person was Stephen Grange.

CHAPTER EIGHTY-NINE

Tom had warned Harriett about Greg, the new manager at the Bassenthwaite Manor Hotel, but she was still taken aback by the man's appearance, drifting into the reception area wearing a pair of garish pyjamas with a fake fur lining – at least, she assumed it was fake – that gave the impression of a boxer who'd got lost in the Lake District on his way to Las Vegas.

"Watkins, right?" said the man, his gaze sliding past Harriett to land on Tom, then sliding back to Harriett and resting, not on her face, but a little lower.

She stood and walked right up to him.

"I'm DC Harriett Barnes. I understand you're the manager here?"

"That's right." He grinned at her. "What can I do for you, Miss Barnes?"

She took a breath, aware that putting the man in his place wouldn't help them, but might make her feel a bit better.

"It's DC Barnes," she said, "and I'd be grateful if you'd look at my face while I'm talking to you."

Greg took a step back, shocked, and Tom gave a low chuckle.

"I'm sorry," said the manager.

"We need to talk to you about one of your employees," Tom told him, and a warm glow smoothed its way through Harriett's body as they followed the manager to his office.

Putting an arsehole in his place, she thought, was an underrated experience.

Inside the office, Harriett explained what they needed from Greg as he sat behind his desk, his deepening frown interrupted by the occasional yawn.

"Anton, you say?"

"That's right," Tom replied. "Anton Greengrass."

"I don't think we have an Anton Greengrass," said Greg.

Tom and Harriett exchanged a look.

"Thin face," Tom said. "Sandy hair. One of your cleaners. He said he'd seen the man we were interested in with a woman in his room, the morning after the event here."

"Ain't no crime, having a woman in your room," Greg observed. His eyes fell on Harriett's, and she stared back at him until he looked away. He leaned forward and tapped on his keyboard, then turned the screen around so they could see the results.

"No Anton Greengrass here," he said.

Tom picked up his phone, located the contact details he'd taken off the cleaner, and dialled. Harriett could hear it ringing, eight times, before it was answered, and a male voice demanded, "Who the fuck is this?"

"Is that Anton?" asked Tom.

"What? No. There's no fucking Anton here."

"I'm sorry," said Tom, but the inadvertent victim of his early morning wake-up call wasn't willing to let things end just like that.

"Do you know what time it is?" said the man.

"I really am sorry," insisted Tom.

"I'm calling the police," replied the man, and ended the call.

Harriett stood and left the room with a cursory 'thank you' to the manager. She walked in silence to the car, Tom beside her, and it wasn't until they were inside it with the doors closed that either of them spoke.

"If Anton Greengrass doesn't exist," said Tom, "we can assume the whole thing about Hanson and Bateman's a lie."

"Which means," Harriett pointed out, "that someone's setting Hanson up."

"Shit," said Tom.

"What?"

"I think you might owe Marcus an apology."

"Fine. He can have one. There's just one thing bothering me."

"What?" asked Tom.

"We agree someone planted this fake cleaner here to talk to you and throw suspicion on Niamh Hanson, right?"

"Right," agreed Tom.

"So," said Harriett, the words coming slowly, "how did they even know you'd be coming to the Bassenthwaite Manor Hotel?"

CHAPTER NINETY

It wasn't until he'd signed into the case file to update the rest of the team that Marcus spotted the update from Lynn.

It was nearly six in the morning. Late enough to call. And besides, there was the note she'd left, saying she'd be up for a while. Marcus wasn't sure whether six o'clock the following morning counted as 'a while', but he wasn't giving himself time to think about it.

The phone was answered after a couple of rings, and then Marcus heard the sound of things being moved about, things falling, and something that sounded like the tinkle of glass.

"Hello?" said Lynn.

"I've just read your update about the company. You sure about this, Lynn?"

"Company?"

He forced himself to breathe slowly and stay calm. It wasn't like there was someone's liberty at stake here, was it?

Oh. It was, as it happened. But getting impatient and cross with his colleagues wouldn't help Niamh Hanson.

"The consortium. The payment for the surveyor. You've—"

"Oh, yeah. That." Lynn was suddenly all business, and Marcus remembered that he'd been impressed with her, both in person and on-screen. "Insurance company."

"Havering Milton Ltd," he said.

"That's the one."

"The same company that paid Stephen Grange for his flood, right?"

"Nope," said Lynn. "I mean, that's what he said, but it can't be true. It's a captive insurer. Only covers incidents on building sites operated by Headland Stamp Construction."

"Who are they?"

"No idea. They're part of that consortium. I've put in a request for information on them."

Marcus realised he'd been pacing the room in the dark, and was in danger of bumping into things. He returned to his desk and sat down.

"So Grange is lying," he said.

"Right," agreed Lynn.

"And his so-called insurance payout is linked to the consortium that Alexander Godwin was competing against, just before he was murdered."

"Right," said Lynn, again.

"And," continued Marcus, his mind now on the little they knew of Godwin, "Grange somehow knew Godwin was from Liverpool."

"According to Rashid, yes."

"Which means he must have read about it in the post-mortem report. Before the team night out. And that's odd, right? I mean, if you're Stephen Grange, you're a local PC, yes, it's a local crime, but why would you read the PM?"

"It's odd, for sure," agreed Lynn. There was another noise, a crash, and she said, "Shit," then, "Sorry. Knocked over a bottle of Baileys."

"Why is there a bottle of—?" Marcus began, then decided he didn't want to know the answer. "Anyway," he said. "I think—"

"Shit," said Lynn, again.

"Knocked something else over?"

"No, not that. What you just said. He read the post-mortem report, right? That's the only way he could have known the victim was from Liverpool. It refers to the tattoo, and the likelihood that the spinal fusion procedure on Godwin's back took place in the hospital in Liverpool."

"Yes," agreed Marcus.

"And Grange was talking about this, about Godwin being from Liverpool, during the team drinks the night before you pulled them all in?"

"According to Rashid, yes," said Marcus, still not sure where Lynn was going with all this. He'd just decided to cut things short and ask her when she spoke again.

"Shit," she said.

"You keep saying that. What's the—?"

"The post-mortem report didn't contain that information."

Marcus pulled it up on his screen, scanned it, and shook his head.

"It does. I'm looking at it now."

"You're looking at the update. Check the date."

He checked the date. Thursday. Three days after the body had been found.

"Now see if you've got the original report."

He scanned the folder until he found it, then pulled it up and searched for one key word.

Liverpool.

The words 'no matches' appeared on the screen.

"Shit," he said.

"Indeed," agreed Lynn.

"So, Grange couldn't have read about the tattoo or the spinal plate before the team night out. He couldn't have even known about the tattoo unless..."

He fell silent, and Lynn completed the sentence.

"Unless he'd seen it before it was removed."

There was a moment's silence before she spoke again.

"Is it possible Rashid has his timings confused?"

"No," replied Marcus. "Because Rashid made his 'dead Scouser' comment next morning. If he heard it from Grange, he heard it the night before."

"Could Rashid be the one lying?" asked Lynn. "Maybe he's the one who saw it. In the flesh, so to speak."

"Oh," said Marcus. Rashid had managed to slip under the radar, what with the focus on Hanson, and now Grange.

But it had been Rashid who'd made the mysterious phone call that no one was willing to tell them about.

"Are you still there?" asked Lynn.

"Yes. Sorry." His phone buzzed, and he checked the display before speaking again. "Hang on," he said. "Harriett's trying to get through."

CHAPTER NINETY-ONE

"You're in the office?" asked Harriett. She sensed Tom glancing over beside her, and pointed a stern finger ahead.

Harriett didn't like it when he took his eyes off the road. Of the two of them, only one was a good enough driver for that, and it wasn't Tom.

"Yeah," said Marcus.

"I thought you'd be asleep."

"So why'd you call?" he asked, and she laughed.

"I thought you'd be interested in what I've found."

"Hang on," he said. "I'll patch Lynn in."

He was gone before she could ask if Lynn was awake yet. There was a beep, followed by a few clicks, then the sound of her voice.

"Hello?"

"Hello," said Harriett and Marcus at the same time. Marcus took the lead.

"Harriett has something to tell us. We've got news, too. You go first."

As succinctly as she could, Harriett outlined what they'd learned at the Bassenthwaite Manor Hotel.

"So Hanson *is* being set up," said Marcus. Harriett was listening closely for a note of smugness in his voice, but if there was one there, it was well-hidden.

"Yes," agreed Harriett. "But there's something else. They knew we were heading to Bassenthwaite Manor."

"Does this mean our systems are compromised?" said Marcus.

"Shit," said Lynn.

"Are you OK?" asked Harriett.

"Shit," said Lynn, again.

"She's fine," said Marcus. "This is how she announces she's got something to tell us."

Harriett waited, and after a moment, Lynn stopped swearing and started talking in sentences.

"It was Grange and Rashid," she said. "Well, one of them."

"What do you mean?" asked Harriett.

"When I was digging into the police functions. Trying to see where Bateman might have been, who he hung out with. Trying to find the Real Cops. I looked round, and they were standing behind me. It was when Rashid made his comment about me helping the rats."

"Was your screen visible?" asked Marcus.

"I didn't know they were there," replied Lynn, a touch of defensiveness in her voice. "But the point is, either of them could have seen it there. They knew about the investigation, or at least, some of it. There was enough on the screen for them to figure out what was going on."

"That's not all," said Marcus. "Lynn, tell them what

you've learned about the insurance company. And the post-mortem."

Harriett listened while Lynn outlined her findings, then tried to summarise it herself.

"So Grange lied about his insurance payout. The money actually came from the people who were bidding against Godwin."

"Exactly," said Marcus.

"And he knew Godwin was from Liverpool before anyone else did. Well, either he did, or Rashid did."

"Spot on," said Lynn.

"It's one of them," said Tom from beside her, finally breaking his silence.

Nobody spoke for nearly a minute.

"It's Grange," said Marcus, finally. "He kills Godwin, then he kills Bateman, then he gets Niamh Hanson drunk, drugs her, and plants the drugs, the phone, and the fibres."

"It's possible," conceded Harriett.

"But then," Marcus continued, "the only reason we know Grange was buying drinks for Hanson is because Rashid told us he was. Maybe it's Rashid who's been lying. We know he had Hanson's bank account details, so he could have put that two hundred and fifty quid in there to set her up. And there's the phone call, too."

"It's one of them," said Tom again, and again, there was a long silence, each of them turning it over in their heads. Someone had set up Hanson, and sent a message to Starling to lure him to the crime scene and cement the job.

A convenient former couple to hang a double murder on.

"Oh," said Marcus.

"What?" asked Harriett. She could hear the sound of fingers on a keyboard.

"What's this?" said Marcus.

"Marcus?" said Harriett, but there was no response. "Just sit tight. We'll be in shortly."

The sound had died. All of it, not just the fingers typing, but Lynn's breathing, and the gentle background hum of the machinery in the team room.

"Marcus?" said Harriett again, but it was no use.

The call was over.

CHAPTER NINETY-TWO

Harriett Barnes was still talking when Marcus ended the call, but that was OK.

He could apologise to her later. But only after she'd apologised first. Apologised, and admitted that he'd been right all along.

He hadn't meant to end the call like that, without at least explaining why. He was still getting used to the system. All he'd wanted to do was mute himself for a moment, because he'd started thinking out loud, and he knew how irritating that could be.

At least now he was alone, and he could talk to himself without fear of annoying anyone else.

"Bloody hell," he said.

This particular bout of thinking had been prompted by the arrival in his inbox of a report from Errol Winter at Rosebank.

Preliminary Analysis, it said in the subject header.

"Christ," muttered Marcus as he scanned through the results on his screen while waiting for them to print out.

Winter and his colleagues had worked intensely overnight, finding matches in the sort of timeframes that wouldn't have been possible if the garage where the car was being taken apart wasn't right next door to a world-class lab housing state-of-the-art equipment and some of the nation's brightest technicians.

The fact that these people achieved all they did and still had to work with Keisha Middleton only raised them further in Marcus's estimation.

"Oh," he mumbled, stopping on a line and rereading it twice to make sure he had it right.

He was going to be in all kinds of trouble. He'd known that last night when he ordered the work done and lied about his authorisation, and the three hours' sleep he'd had since then hadn't made him any happier about his chances.

He'd hoped they'd find something that would make that trouble worthwhile.

And they had.

There were matches for plenty of police officers, mostly prints, but also hair that could be analysed more quickly than a full DNA work-up. Of course there were matches for plenty of police officers. It was a police car. There were matches for Bateman, which was a little more surprising, given it was a patrol car and there was no record of him having been in it, as well as matches for the same blue fibres that had been found on Hanson's clothes.

Nothing conclusive there, though. Bateman could quite easily have grabbed a lift in the vehicle without it being noted down in official records.

The match that had Marcus muttering, though, wasn't for a police officer.

It was for Claire Saunders. The same Claire Saunders

whose call about noise outside her flat had been the reason Hanson and Grange hadn't stopped at the boatyard that night. The same Claire Saunders Marcus had visited, and spoken to, and believed entirely when she'd told him she knew nothing about any of it.

Her hair was all over the car, in the sort of quantities that were unlikely to be the result of transfer via someone else, but which indicated she'd actually been in the vehicle herself.

The fact that her prints were all over the car, too, just confirmed it.

"Bloody hell," said Marcus, again.

Claire Saunders knew something. Even if she didn't realise it, she knew something. Marcus jotted a note down, stood, pulled on his coat, and headed out of the team room just as the timer finally kicked in and the lights came on.

There was a big clock on the wall of the main entrance downstairs, and as he walked past it, he glanced up in time to see it swing past seven in the morning.

It was early, but he had a drive ahead of him.

CHAPTER NINETY-THREE

DENISE WAS on the way out of her house, but still blinking herself awake, when her phone rang.

She'd have shot it a look of disgust if she'd been able to, but her pills were in one hand, her blister pack in the other, and the phone in her bag. She dropped the blister pack on the hallway floor, threw the pills down her throat, and retrieved the phone.

"Yeah?" she croaked.

"Is that DS Denise Gaskill?"

"Yeah," she said again, then swallowed.

"This is Emily Saunders. I think you've been trying to reach me."

"Yeah," she replied, a third time. "Thanks for calling," she added, opening the front door and stepping outside. It was just a few minutes past seven, but she'd wanted to be in early, with the decision on Hanson's charge looming.

"What did you want to know, then?"

"Oh, right." She fumbled with the keys for a moment before she got the car door open and slipped in. Eileen was standing by her own front door, watching, with a friendly smile that told Denise her neighbour wanted a chat.

Eileen would have to wait.

"I wanted to ask about Claire," she said. "Your email, back in twenty twenty-three, I've only been able to see a redacted version, and I'm trying to work out what happened."

"Someone finally looking into it, then?"

"That's the thing," said Denise, as she started the engine. "I'm not entirely sure what I'm looking into."

Emily Saunders gave a short, bitter laugh. "She gave us a hard time, you know?"

"Claire did?"

"Yes. She was into all sorts. Drugs and prostitution, mostly. I was around as much as I could be, but I've got kids, and our parents... You don't want to know about all that. Anyway, she's always been a smart girl, whatever scrapes she gets herself into. She was getting out of it. Getting clean."

"That's what she told you?"

"That's what was happening," Emily Saunders insisted. "I was there three days a week. I could see things getting better every day. And then she got herself arrested."

"This was the caution for soliciting?"

There was a truck stopped ahead of Denise as she headed out of Aspatria onto the main road going east. Half on the road, half off, trying to change a tyre while the local excuse for rush hour eased past in a fury of blaring horns and two-fingered salutes.

"Right. It wasn't the first time she'd been arrested, and she admitted it, so that wasn't the problem. The problem was the cop."

Denise tapped her brake harder than she'd intended, and received her own share of those horns and salutes.

"Cop? What cop?"

"The one who arrested her, I think. I don't even know that for sure. And no, I don't know his name either. She just called him 'my officer' when she spoke about him, like it was funny."

"What was the problem?"

"Do I have to spell it out, DS Gaskill?"

The traffic had settled into its usual steady flow now, and Denise could give more of her attention to the conversation.

"She was seeing a lot of him, right?"

"All the time, it seemed. Either seeing him, or talking about him. I thought he was taking advantage of her. Grooming her."

"For what?"

"For what?" For the first time, Emily Saunders sounded angry. "My sister was a vulnerable young woman, with a background in prostitution, a caution for soliciting, the last dregs of a drug habit, and some unsavoury friends. And this cop, he... It was obvious what he was after. And no, before you ask, I don't know if he got it, but I'm thinking he probably did."

"Right. So you contacted the local police."

"I made a complaint, yes."

"And?"

"And nothing. We never heard a thing. I called a couple of times, and someone would say it's being looked into, but that was, well, it's got to be a couple of years now. And Claire seems to be over it all these days."

"Does she still see the police officer?"

"I don't know. If she does, she hasn't mentioned him to

me. I've just got to hope she's shaken that habit along with all the others. She's not in trouble, is she?"

Denise considered this for a moment. Emily Saunders deserved the truth, at least.

"I don't know," she said, eventually. "I don't think so. But I can't be sure. And she never mentioned his name?"

"Never."

She'd read all the updates before she'd left the house. Hanson was all but in the clear. So it had to be either Rashid or Grange, didn't it?

"Did you ever see him?"

"Briefly, once. And yes, I could understand what she saw in him. Gorgeous lad. Tall and muscly, with thick dark hair—"

"You've been very helpful," Denise told her, "and if we manage to find anything out that's relevant to your complaint, I'll let you know. Thanks."

She ended the call and dialled the number for Rashid.

"What time do you call this?" said the sergeant when he realised who he was talking to.

"Time to stop pissing about," she told him.

"What?" He sounded half asleep.

"What? Two cops are dead, so far, and your friend Niamh's in the frame. I'm starting to think she's being set up, but the fact that neither of you seems willing to tell us about the phone call between the two of you isn't helping her."

"This is all too complicated for me," said Rashid.

"Someone put money in her account. It's possible the same person drugged her and planted evidence in her house and on her clothes. Someone led us back to her relationship with Zack Starling. We—"

"You know about Starling?" Rashid asked.

"Yes."

"Oh."

There was a long silence, Denise navigating the outskirts of Carlisle as she waited for him to go on.

"Are you still there?" he said eventually.

"Yes."

"Starling," he said. "That's what the phone call was about."

"Explain."

"I'd found out about... You know all this, right?"

"We know Niamh Hanson had a relationship with a drug dealer named Zack Starling. Starling's been set up for the murder alongside Hanson. This phone call is the last piece of the jigsaw, Sergeant Rashid, so the sooner you put it in its place, the better for everyone."

"Shit," he said. "Right. Well, I didn't know about Starling. Not until that day. Then... I'd heard some things over the years, and then I heard some more things. I pieced it together. It's not important."

"Why did you call her?"

"Because she's part of my team," he said. "And that makes her my friend. We stick together."

"Explain," she said again.

"Look, Starling's a dealer. If one of my officers has a link with a dealer, I need to let people know, right? I can't just slip something like that under the carpet."

"Right."

"But I didn't want to land her in it."

"Yes," said Denise, who was starting to see where this was heading, and was filled with a growing sense of anger and frustration.

"So I called her. Told her I was going to report it, so she'd better get her own report in first. I didn't want her getting into too much trouble, see?"

She slowed as she passed the castle, and shook her head, scarcely able to believe what she was hearing.

"So you did this out of loyalty?"

"Yeah, I suppose so."

"Your colleague's being questioned in connection with multiple murders, and you didn't think you could tell us about her two-year-old relationship with a dealer?"

"It was up to her to tell you. Not me. And look, if you're going to tell me Stevie's behind this, I'm not—"

She ended the call without another word. The man was useless. Blinded by his own loyalty.

Mind you, Hanson wasn't much better. Denise could see now why she, too, had kept quiet about the call. Rashid tipping her off wasn't a good look for him. She'd been trying to protect him, just as he'd been trying to protect her.

There was a line between loyalty and stupidity, and Hanson and Rashid had gone so far beyond it, they'd need a fucking telescope to find it again.

And Stephen Grange had been sitting there in the centre of his web, laughing at them both. Laughing at all of them.

CHAPTER NINETY-FOUR

The lights in the team room were on, but there was no sign of Marcus.

"Where the hell is he?" asked Tom, as if Harriett would know.

She loved him dearly, but he did have a tendency to speak when speaking really wasn't necessary.

She ignored him and made for her desk. A notification had come through just as they'd parked, a message from her friend Paul at the Financial Crime Unit in Penrith. She opened the message, scanned it, and tried to work out whether it all fitted in.

It did.

Taking a leaf out of Tom's book, she decided to say it aloud, just to make sure.

"Winterburn," she said.

"What?" asked Tom.

"The Caymans company that put two hundred and fifty quid in Hanson's bank account the day Bateman was killed," she explained.

"What about it?" Tom asked.

"Guess who owns it," she said.

He shrugged. "How am I supposed to know?" he began, then grinned. "Unless it's Cumbria Estate Facilities Servicing Group."

She nodded. It was the right answer. It told them, as if they needed telling, that someone had been trying to set up Niamh Hanson.

But it still didn't tell them whether Rashid or Grange was the man behind it. It was possible Marcus had made some progress on that before he'd disappeared, but if he had, surely he'd have left a note?

She thought about the way he'd conducted himself since he'd started there. And the way she'd treated him, too. Like they were in a competition, and she wasn't prepared to lose. She could tell herself it was his fault more than it was hers until the cows came home, and she'd probably be right, but it didn't change the facts: Marcus had disappeared, he hadn't told her where he was going, and she wasn't likely to find out.

She sat in his empty chair and looked at his screen, and was surprised to find a Post-it note stuck to the side of it. No words, just an arrow, pointing to a small pile of papers beside his keyboard. She picked up the papers and began to read.

Her first thought was that Marcus Hosgood was in a lot of trouble. He'd played fast and loose when he'd ordered the hunt for Zack Starling, and he'd been warned, but now he'd done it again. Half a dozen lab techs had worked through the night on the word of DI Whaley, who, she was convinced, knew nothing about it.

She hoped the results had been worth it.

She read on, through lists of police officers she'd never

heard of, boilerplate text and caveats and explanations of the technology, alongside polite complaints about the timeframe.

"Bloody hell," she said when she reached the first reference to Claire Saunders, her hair, in the car, and she said it again when she reached the part about her prints.

"What?" asked Tom, but she ignored him and dialled Marcus's number.

It rang eight times, then went to voicemail. She cursed again, and her phone rang while it was still in her hand.

"You in yet?" asked DS Gaskill.

"Yup, Sarge," she replied. "And we've got news."

"You're not the only one. You first."

"Hanson's being set up," Harriett said. She started with what they'd learned from the Bassenthwaite Manor Hotel, and moved on to Grange's insurance payment and the timing of Rashid's comment about Godwin being from Liverpool.

"He couldn't have known about the tattoo, not before the team night out. Not unless he'd actually seen it."

"It's not looking good for Grange," said the sarge.

"It's not looking good for Rashid, either," Harriett replied. "Grange has to be in the box seat. But Rashid could have put that money in her account. And we only have his word for it that it was Grange who mentioned Liverpool. And there's the phone call."

"Rashid's in the clear," said the DS.

"Really?"

"The phone call was just him tipping her off that he'd found out about her relationship with Starling. Neither of the idiots wanted to get the other one into trouble, that's why they've been keeping it to themselves. But I think there's a link to Claire Saunders."

"Oh," said Harriett.

"Why, 'Oh'?"

Harriett explained what she'd found on Marcus's desk, as well as the fact that Marcus himself was nowhere to be found.

"Bloody idiot," said the DS. "I've spoken to Claire Saunders's sister. They think she was being groomed by her arresting officer. Way she described him, it has to be Grange. And now we know her prints and hair have turned up all over Grange's vehicle."

Harriett ran the search as she listened. She frowned at the response and ran it again, with the same result.

"Nothing here, Sarge," she said.

"What do you mean?"

"I mean, when you run a search to find out who arrested Claire Saunders, it comes up blank. It doesn't make sense."

"Oh, it makes perfect sense," the DS told her. "In the same way it makes perfect sense that the report Emily Saunders submitted, complaining about Grange, was so heavily redacted I couldn't make anything of it. Grange isn't working alone, Harriett. He couldn't have manipulated these records by himself."

"And now Marcus has disappeared," Harriett pointed out again.

"I'd like to hope he won't do anything stupid," said DS Gaskill. "But a few days' exposure to the man suggests he will. Sit tight. I'll be in shortly."

Sit tight. Harriett had used the same words, to Marcus, and he'd ignored her.

She could only hope it wouldn't cost him.

CHAPTER NINETY-FIVE

A GROUP OF YOUNG OFFICERS, newly qualified by the fresh-faced look of them, hovered nervously by the main desk. As Denise walked by, one of them detached himself from the others and approached her.

"Excuse me," he began.

"Sorry," she said. "Not the time."

She walked on, refusing to look back, hoping whoever they were waiting for would eventually show up.

In the team room, Tom Willis was on the phone in one of those never-ending cycles of dial, listen, and give up. Harriett was leaning over Marcus's screen.

"Sarge, you might want to see this," she said, without looking up.

Denise stood beside her, watching some grainy black-and-white footage of what looked like an alleyway behind a block of flats.

"What am I looking at?" she asked.

"The CCTV Marcus requested from Claire's flat. It's taken them five days, but they finally got back to him."

They weren't the only ones who'd decided to step up when the game was already over. There was a text on Denise's phone from Nikolas Costas, the man she'd been badgering to hand over Bateman's phone data. She could look at that later. This was in front of her now.

"See?" said Harriett, pointing at a series of blocks moving jerkily through the darkness.

Denise could see them. Figuring out what they were was something different.

"That's the night Godwin was killed," Harriett added. "And the thing you're looking at, that's a person. Watch now."

As Denise watched, the blocks resolved into a shape that could, at a stretch, be called human. It moved to a point between two lines, and stopped beside another series of blocks, these ones larger, squarish, and stationary.

"Those lines are the fences where the bins are kept," Harriett explained. "And those things—"

"Are the bins, yeah," said Denise.

The human shape approached one of the squarish shapes, and a moment later, the square was a rectangle. The same thing happened twice more before the human moved out from between the lines and into a blank, dark space. When it passed briefly through a patch of light, it was clearly recognisable from the photos Denise had seen.

"That's Claire Saunders," she said.

"Yup," agreed Harriett. "She knocks the bins over, and then a few minutes later, she makes the call. Keep watching."

Harriett tapped the screen, dragging a line to the right, and the footage cycled through a period of brightness back to dark.

"This is the following night, around the same time."

The same time, with the same thing happening: Claire Saunders knocking over her own bins, and those of her neighbours. If you were going to pretend there were foxes or cats or feral teenagers causing trouble around the back of your block, it made sense to do it more than once.

"OK," said Denise. "So now we know—"

"One more," said Harriett, and skipped forward another two nights. "This is the evening after we first interviewed Hanson, Grange and Rashid. They'd all been drinking the night before. Well, one of them wasn't. He was framing Starling and Hanson for the murder he'd just committed. Keep an eye on the light patch."

Denise did as Harriett asked, and was rewarded by the passage through the brighter area of not one but two human-shaped figures, heading over to topple the bins. On the way there, the faces were angled away, but on the way back, they were both as clear as if they'd been posing for a fashion shoot.

"That's Grange," said Denise.

"Right. He pops over and gives her a hand, keeping the illusion going."

"You managed to get hold of Marcus yet?" Denise asked, turning to Tom.

Tom shook his head, his phone still pressed to his ear.

Denise had just sat down to see what Costas had sent her when the text arrived, a simultaneous buzz on the three phones in the room. She reached for her own and read it.

Am sure Grange is our man. Am at Claire Saunders. She knows something. Will see what she tells me.

"Shit," said Denise, with similar responses coming from Harriett and Tom. "Any luck, Tom?"

Tom shook his head.

"Keep trying," she said. "Idiot doesn't realise how much danger he's in."

CHAPTER NINETY-SIX

THIS TIME ROUND, Marcus didn't spend time looking for somewhere to park, leaving his Citroen on the street by the same double yellow line he'd left it on six days earlier. The town was coming to life around him now. A man dragging a reluctant toddler along the pavement stopped and watched with brief interest as Marcus ran past him towards Claire's block, then resumed his slow progress. Two women chatting loudly as they marched in the opposite direction didn't seem to notice him at all.

Marcus couldn't understand why he'd noticed them, for that matter. He had a clear focus, a clear set of questions to ask, and yet everything around him seemed sharper and more vivid than normal. Maybe that was just the way the world was when things came to the crunch. He pushed the outer door open – it wasn't locked, hadn't been last time, either – and took the stairs two at a time.

He stood outside her door, hand poised, then pulled out his phone. It was bad enough that he'd faked the authorisation for a rush job on a forensic search, then raced out here by himself without telling anyone where he was going and ignoring all their calls.

Sending a text now wouldn't exactly make up for it, but it wouldn't hurt.

Am sure Grange is our man, he wrote. *Am at Claire Saunders. She knows something. Will see what she tells me.*

He tapped send, then knocked.

No answer.

He knocked again, then put his ear to the door and listened, but there were other noises around him now, and he turned to see a couple approaching the staircase, talking quietly as they watched him with undisguised suspicion.

He pointed his warrant card in their direction and knocked again, and this time he accompanied the knock with a shout: "Claire? Are you in there?"

When he put his ear to the door again, he thought he could hear someone. Movement. Maybe a voice, maybe not, and if it was a voice, it could just as easily be the radio as a person. But if she *was* in there and she wasn't answering...

If Marcus was right about the man, Grange wasn't the sort to leave loose ends hanging around. Liabilities got dealt with, the way Bateman had been dealt with, the way Illingworth would probably have been dealt with if he hadn't solved the problem himself.

He knocked one more time, shouted Claire's name one more time, and then he took a moment to examine the door, before taking one step back, planting his left foot firmly on the floor, and driving the heel of his right foot into a space an inch to the left of the lock.

He heard a crack and felt the door shiver, but not give. His foot didn't hurt too much, so he tried it twice more before he felt more significant movement.

On the fourth kick, the door swung open.

He paused for half a second, confirmed the narrow corridor was empty, and took two long steps through it to the kitchen and living area.

There was no one in there either. It was a mess, but not the sort of mess that said something bad had happened. More the sort of mess that said you'd had a good night, and you'd worry about the consequences in the morning. Empty bottles, unwashed glasses, plates with the detritus of an evening meal still glistening on the counter.

He stopped. Held his breath. He was sure he could hear voices.

And that wasn't a single glass stained red beside an empty bottle of Malbec. It was two.

He pushed open the bedroom door, and was greeted by the terrified face of Claire Saunders, staring at him from the bed.

Beside her, shirtless and sitting up as he pulled on a pair of jeans, was Stephen Grange.

CHAPTER NINETY-SEVEN

THE MESSAGES KEPT COMING as Carl drove, his phone buzzing every few seconds, the in-car system attempting to convert the text into speech and spewing a jumble of words at him in an American voice he still hadn't figured out how to change.

Most of it didn't make any sense. The bits that did make sense were enough to tell him that things had moved fast. Hanson – or 'Handsome' as the car insisted – was in the clear. Grange wasn't, and neither was someone the system kept referring to as 'Rushing', but was presumably Rashid.

It was progress, he supposed, but the speed of it had caught him off guard. The pounding inside his head didn't help, but the American accent just put the seal on it.

It still wasn't eight in the morning, and already Carl couldn't wait for the day to be over.

His phone was still buzzing as he parked and strode into the building and upstairs. He walked into the team room to find the sort of chaos he'd half-expected. Denise Gaskill was shouting. Harriett Barnes was shouting back. They weren't shouting at each other, as far as he could see, but the only other person in the room was Tom Willis, and they weren't shouting at him, either. He was looking between Denise and Harriett, at the screen, where Lynne Hedley was talking. Carl knew she was talking because he could see her lips moving, but he couldn't hear a word above the noises coming out of Denise and Harriett.

"What the fuck is going on here?" he bellowed, and the room fell quiet.

It was Denise who spoke first.

"Marcus is in trouble," she said, her voice low and calm now, and then he listened as she laid it all out: the tattoo, the payments, the discoveries about Claire Saunders. He interrupted once when she described the forensic search Marcus had ordered on Grange's vehicle.

"I didn't authorise that," he said.

Denise nodded. "He's over there now. At Claire's. We've been trying to reach him, but he's not answering his phone."

"And from what we've seen, Grange isn't the sort of person to come quietly. Let's hope he wasn't there. Have you called in backup?"

"Of course."

"Then what's all the shouting about?"

Denise looked at Harriett, frowning. Harriett frowned back.

"Not sure, boss," said Harriett, finally. "Things are just a little overheated at the moment."

"Let's try keeping the heat down, shall we?" he suggested, and collapsed into the chair by Marcus's desk.

CHAPTER NINETY-EIGHT

GRANGE FROWNED, as if trying to place him, then grinned.

"DC Hosgood, isn't it?" he said.

Marcus ignored him, addressing the woman on the bed. "Are you OK?"

She looked from him to Grange, then back again.

"I'm... Yes," she said. "I'm fine. What are you...? Why are you here?"

Marcus turned to Grange.

"Stephen Grange," he said.

"That's me," replied Grange, looking at his own bare feet and then down, by the bed.

"Look, we know, Stephen," he said.

Grange was rummaging on the floor, feeling around in a pile of clothes that looked like they'd been dropped there in a hurry.

"Hang on," said Claire Saunders. "I heard... Did you just break my door?"

"Sorry," said Marcus.

This wasn't going the way he'd expected it to go. He'd thought... He wasn't sure what he'd thought.

He'd thought Claire Saunders might be in danger. He'd pictured himself crashing through the door to rescue a damsel in distress.

Instead, he'd found two lovers in bed after a night of alcohol-fuelled, and what he could only assume was entirely consensual, lovemaking.

He blinked, and reminded himself why he was here. Claire Saunders wasn't in danger. But Grange was still a dangerous man.

"We know all about it, Stephen," he said, but it didn't sound right. Didn't sound firm enough.

"You know what?" asked Grange, pulling a t-shirt on, a questioning grin on his face when it emerged.

"What you've been doing," Marcus said. That didn't sound right either.

"Well, yeah," said Grange.

"Yeah?" echoed Marcus.

"I mean, it's pretty obvious when you come crashing into the bedroom and we're both in here without any clothes on. But what's that got to do with you... You gonna replace that door?" he asked, working a sock over one foot.

"We know what you've been doing," said Marcus again, and this time he went straight on, ignoring the small voice in his head that was telling him this should wait for the interview room. "We know you were involved when Godwin was killed. You must have come and gone, helped prepare the ground, then joined your shift so you could be here when the man was being murdered. We know you killed Bateman. We know about the Telegram group and the message you sent to

Starling, the dose you gave Hanson, all the stuff you planted in her house."

He felt himself growing in confidence as he spoke, spooling out each item, the whole thing more solid the more he said.

"You what?" said Grange, reaching down for a second sock that lay half-hidden under Claire's top, bulging at the toe.

"How long has all this been going on, Stephen?" he asked. He was looking away now, at the door, embarrassed to watch a man getting dressed, even more embarrassed to meet the eye of the woman whose door he'd just broken down.

"How long's what been going on?" replied Grange.

"Who's in the consortium?"

"You're not making sense, mate. You been drinking or something?"

Marcus caught a sudden movement out of the corner of his eye at the same moment that he realised what had been wrong with that second sock. There was something in it, something hard and long and solid.

As he turned toward Grange he met the full impact of that something, a sharp pain in his neck, so extraordinary in its severity that he felt briefly detached from it and from himself, and had a moment to wonder at it before he understood what had happened.

The last thing he saw, before everything went black, was the wide-eyed, terrified face of Claire Saunders, her mouth opening in a scream, but he was unconscious before he could hear a thing.

CHAPTER NINETY-NINE

THEY WERE TAKING it in turns, the three of them. One dialling Marcus, one listening to the updates from the patrol car as it drew closer, an ambulance following behind just in case, and one dialling the number they'd found for Claire Saunders.

Neither phone was being answered, and the updates from the patrol car were nothing more than the names of streets. The DI sat in Marcus's chair, watching them all wearily, as if he knew this would all come to nothing.

Marcus's phone was finally answered on Denise's round.

"Hello?" she said, switching it over to speaker so the others could hear.

"Hello?" said a voice she didn't know, a female voice, a break in it like someone trying to speak at the same moment a chicken bone got stuck in their throat. The others had got to their feet now, even the DI, all three of them standing by her desk and listening.

"Who's that?" said Denise.

"Is this the police?" asked the woman.

"We're trying to reach DC Marcus Hosgood," said Denise.

"He's... Is that the police?" said the woman again, and then she screamed.

Denise gave it a moment before speaking again.

"Is this Claire?" she asked.

She waited, as the scream gave way to what sounded like a sob.

"Yes," said the woman, finally.

"Is Marcus there?"

Another scream, and the tension Denise had been feeling for the last few minutes blossomed into full-blown fear.

"Can I speak to him?" she said, and had to wait another few seconds before Claire Saunders could respond.

"I think he's dead," said Claire, and Denise felt the world turn around her, and then stop, and watched as Harriett and Tom Willis and DI Whaley and the room itself seemed to recede, and with it the sound of Claire Saunders's voice, the breathing of her colleagues, the hum of the computers.

I think he's dead.

A second. Two, at most. And then it was back, the sound of Claire Saunders sobbing again and Tom Willis talking to the patrol car and the DI on the phone, too, updating the threat. Harriett was tapping on a keyboard, and the world was present, and Denise was in it.

"OK," she said. "The police are on their way. They'll be with you shortly, and there's an ambulance coming. Is Marcus in the room with you?"

"There's so much blood," said Claire.

"Is Marcus there?"

"Yes. He's... He's on the floor. I didn't know he was going to do this."

"Do what?" asked Denise. "What did he do?"

The question was greeted by another burst of sobbing. Denise waited.

"Is Marcus conscious?" she asked.

"No," replied Claire.

"Is he breathing?"

"I don't know."

"Do you think you can check? What's happened?"

Denise could hear movement on the other end of the line now.

"He stabbed him."

Denise felt herself falling, and reached out to grab the desk. She didn't remember standing in the first place.

"Who stabbed him?"

"Stevie stabbed Marcus. And now he's gone."

"Have you checked his breathing, Claire?" asked Denise. There was too much going on, but she had to stay calm. She dropped gently into her chair as she waited for the other woman to answer.

"I can't hear anything," she said.

"Do you think you can take his pulse, Claire? The easiest way is—"

"In the neck, I know, but I can't... There's so much blood."

"The ambulance will be with you shortly," she said, and Tom, who was on the other line with the patrol car, quietly explaining what was going on, nodded in agreement. "What happened? Where's Stephen Grange?"

"He ran. He didn't even say anything. He just..."

"Right." Denise thought she could hear the faint sound of sirens. She pulled a sheet of paper towards her and grabbed a pen. "Do you know where he was going? Any idea what car he—"

"He took my keys," said Claire. "Yellow Fiat 500."

You couldn't hide a yellow Fiat 500 in Cumbria. Not for long, anyway. She noted down the details and passed the sheet of paper to the DI. The noise of the sirens was louder now.

"Do you think you can take Marcus's pulse from his wrist?" Denise suggested.

"Yes," agreed Claire. "He... Stephen stabbed him in the neck. He came over last night, told me it was nothing, the police had it all wrong, it was just a misunderstanding, nothing to worry about. I didn't... I believed him. He... Oh, God."

Claire fell silent.

"What is it, Claire?"

"I can't feel a pulse. I think..."

"Are you sure you're feeling in the right place, Claire? You need to..."

"I take tourists out on the lake. I'm first-aid trained. I know what... Oh, God."

The sirens reached a peak and then cut out.

"They're almost with you, Claire," Denise said. "Just hold on. Try the pulse again."

She was looking around the room, as if one of the others might be able to do something or say something that would change it all, that would make it all wrong, just a misunderstanding, nothing to worry about.

Claire Saunders was sobbing again.

"Just hold on," Denise said again, even though she wasn't

sure why. And then there were more voices – a woman and a man – the sound of footsteps moving quickly across a room.

Questions. Instructions. Urgency and efficiency.

Denise put the phone down on the desk and closed her eyes.

CHAPTER ONE HUNDRED

It was a good thing, Carl thought, that he didn't keep a bottle of gin in his office drawer.

He'd known police who did that. Bottles of gin, whisky, rum. There'd been one DCI who'd toasted his own impending arrest on misconduct charges with a bottle of vintage Cristal he'd produced from his desk, along with a pair of champagne flutes. Carl hadn't joined him in the drink that time, for obvious, professional reasons, although part of him had always regretted the decision and wondered whether twelve-hundred-pound champagne tasted any better than the stuff he bought at the supermarket.

If that bottle had been in the office with him now, he'd have gone through it in ten minutes, and then moved on to whatever was next. A good thing, then, that what was left of the bottle of gin was still at home, in the sideboard.

Marcus Hosgood was dead.

There was a bang on the door, and he ignored it. He'd been ignoring it for fifteen minutes, and it was starting to become little more than background noise. Maybe he didn't need a drink after all. Maybe it was all just a state of mind.

Marcus Hosgood was dead, and Carl was sitting alone in his office, staring at a computer screen, and trying to ignore the chaos and noise inside his head and the banging on the door outside it.

There was another bang.

"You need to come out, Carl," said Denise. She'd been saying that, or variations on it, for ten of the fifteen minutes she'd been knocking. Maybe she was right. Maybe he did need to come out.

He just didn't think he could.

He stared at the screen and saw things on it that weren't really there. He saw Marcus Hosgood's face grinning back at him. He saw John Illingworth hanging from a rope and Isaac Bateman dead in his car. He hadn't seen any of these things in the flesh, and he knew they weren't there now, but they were, too.

He stared past those things, as Denise's voice sounded somewhere out there, at the email he'd written.

Recommendation, it said, in the subject field.

Marcus Hosgood was dead, and that meant many things. One of those things was that there was a vacancy in the team.

Too soon?

He scanned through what he'd written, checked DCI Branthwaite's name was in the 'To' box, and as he hit send, he heard a different sound. A foot falling on carpet. He tore his eyes from the screen and turned to see Denise walking into the room.

"You need to talk to the team, boss," she said.

He'd done that already, hadn't he? He'd waited until one of the paramedics came on the line and confirmed that

Marcus was, as Claire Saunders had repeatedly told them, dead. Then he'd stayed in the team room for another twenty minutes, listening to everyone else shouting and swearing, and tried to calm things down, and failed.

He had tried, hadn't he? He'd talked quietly to them, to Harriett and Denise and Tom Willis, amazed at the calm in his own voice when inside his head there was nothing but chaos and noise. He'd listened patiently as they blamed themselves, all three of them, and he'd told them it wasn't their fault, because it couldn't be their fault.

Not when it was his.

He was the one in charge. He was the one Marcus had been trying to impress.

After twenty minutes, the chaos and noise had started to drown out everything else, and he'd walked quickly away, announcing that he'd be in his office if there were any further developments.

"I've talked to the team," he told her.

"And it helped," she replied. "So do it again."

She was probably right. He shrugged and tried to explain why he couldn't talk to the team, not now, not with all that chaos and noise, but nothing seemed to come out of his mouth.

"You need to get a grip," she said.

"You can talk," he replied, and blinked, surprised to hear the words.

"What?" she asked.

"You. Anyone can see you've got enough problems of your own."

She took one unsteady step back, like he'd kicked her, and he could see the pain in her face, and that did it.

"I'm sorry," he said.

"Sir," she replied.

"I mean it. That was uncalled for. And you're right. I need to get a grip." He took a breath and gestured to the chair on the other side of the desk. Denise approached it warily, and sat down.

"I need to speak to the team. I need to get things going. I need to..."

She nodded. There was no need to complete the sentence. He'd have to speak to Marcus's parents. The DCI could do it, probably would do it, too, but the news had to come from him.

"What's the latest?" he asked.

"They've got Grange," she said. "He crashed after a short car chase across the border on the road to Dumfries."

"What was he doing there?"

"No idea. He had no phone on him, he'd dumped it before they got him. But they found a fake passport."

"Don't suppose he was badly injured?"

"Unfortunately not," she said. "They're bringing him in shortly. You want to do it?"

Did he?

He imagined himself sitting opposite the man who'd just stabbed Marcus Hosgood in the neck and left him to bleed to death. He pictured himself lunging for the man. Grabbing him around the neck and squeezing until the life drained from his eyes.

"Probably best if I don't," he said.

CHAPTER ONE HUNDRED ONE

"IF I TOLD you I was just following orders, I don't suppose you'd buy that and let me walk out of here?" said Grange.

"Whose orders?" asked DS Gaskill, but Grange just winked at her.

The DS was sitting opposite Grange. Harriett had taken the seat opposite Grange's lawyer, Carla Staines, a small, bespectacled woman who spoke so quietly Harriett could barely hear her and seemed almost as shocked by what had happened as the rest of them.

"Mr Grange," said Harriett.

"My client should be addressed by his rank," the lawyer pointed out. That was almost the first thing she'd said, and Harriett smiled at her before turning back to Grange.

"Mr Grange," she said again. "Are you going to tell us who you've been working for?"

"Cumbria Police," he replied.

"We have evidence that you murdered Isaac Bateman and Marcus Hosgood," said the DS, "and were complicit in the murder of Alexander Godwin. You weren't working for Cumbria Police when you did that, were you?"

For a moment, it looked like Grange was about to object, but then he simply sighed and nodded.

"OK," he said.

"OK?" echoed Harriett.

"OK. Yes. You want the lot? I'll give you the lot."

And over the next fifteen minutes, with minimal interruption, Stephen did precisely that.

He admitted to creating the Real Cops Telegram group, intending to exploit it for blackmail material. He admitted aiding in the kidnapping of Alexander Godwin and clearing the path for his murder. He admitted to killing Isaac Bateman because Bateman was about to blow the whistle, even if he didn't know who he was blowing the whistle on. He admitted framing Hanson and Starling.

"I'm sorry about your friend," he said. "If I'd known you'd get me anyway, I wouldn't have killed him."

That was the extent of his remorse.

"Why Godwin?" asked the DS.

"I'm sorry," said the lawyer, "but you'll have to be clearer than that."

"Your other crimes, I can see why you committed them. Sort of. But why exactly did the murder of a businessman from Liverpool have to be undisturbed?"

"The people I work for," replied Grange. "They owed someone a favour."

"And if I ask you who any of those people are, are you going to give me some names?"

"Nope."

"What were you doing in Scotland?" asked the DS. "Where were you heading?"

"Off to the Highlands," replied Grange.

"That's not really true, is it?" asked Harriett. She and Lynn had been working through the details with Paul from the Financial Crime Unit. "We found your passport, Stephen. The fake one, the one with your face on it, but someone else's name."

"Dave Wilson," added DS Gaskill. "Easy enough to forget."

"And," said Harriett, "it can't just be a coincidence that a ferry ticket was booked online in the name of Dave Wilson, from Cairnryan to Belfast, shortly after you fled Claire Saunders's apartment. Who booked the ticket for you, Stephen?"

Grange said nothing.

"What about Claire Saunders?" asked DS Gaskill.

"What about her?"

"Did she book your ticket? She was complicit in your crimes, after all. She lied about knocking over the bins, both at the time and subsequently when DC Hosgood interviewed her."

Harriett stumbled a little as she said his name, but other than that, she thought she'd managed the line well enough.

"She didn't know what was going on."

"We found a hammer in her flat," the DS said. "Plenty of human tissue on it. If we examine that hammer, are we going to identify it as the weapon used on Isaac Bateman?"

"Yes," confirmed Grange.

"And it was found in Claire Saunders's flat. Along with Bateman's phones. She's been arrested, and we're trying to work out what to charge her with. Just how involved was she in all this? How much did she know?"

Grange laughed, and Harriett ground her nails into her palm.

It was the only thing stopping her from punching him.

"Know? Claire? She doesn't know what bloody day it is. She was just... useful."

"Useful?" said Harriett, repeating the word as if she hadn't heard it before.

"Useful," said Grange, again. "Bloody good in the sack, too. Experienced." He winked at Harriett, and she pushed a little harder with her nails.

"Back to your employers," said the DS, no doubt sensing things were about to take a dangerous turn. "And no, I don't mean Cumbria Police. We've established that files dating back several years were removed or altered to aid you in your activities. Emily Saunders's complaint, for example. Claire Saunders's arrest record. Who did that?"

Grange turned to her and rolled his eyes.

"Look," he said. "I'm not giving you any names. All I'll say is that there are people who know things only a limited number of people are supposed to know."

He grinned at them.

"What sort of things?"

"Information," he said. "They have access. They can slip in, get what they want, and slip out again. Like a skeleton key."

Nothing in his expression had shifted as he spoke. The same grin, the same playful look in his eyes.

"Who are they?" said the DS, her voice suddenly louder and more forceful, but still there was no change.

"I've told you," he said. "You're not getting any names. You know that, I know that, so why don't we stop this charade and just get on with things?"

"You seem very relaxed for someone who's just admitted

to committing two murders and abetting a third," Harriett told him.

"I am. You've got me. The evidence is there. Claire saw me kill Hosgood. I'm going to prison."

"And aren't you worried?" asked the DS.

"What's the point in worrying?" he said. "Either I'll be well looked after, or I'll be taken out, hopefully as painlessly as possible. And there isn't a thing I can do about it."

"We could keep you safe," Harriett said, and he laughed again.

"I don't think even you believe that," he said.

And the worrying thing was, he was right.

CHAPTER ONE HUNDRED TWO

THE REMAINS of that bottle of gin hadn't been enough, in the end, so it was a good thing there was a convenience store across the road that could supply whatever he happened to want.

"You choose," he suggested, and the young woman behind the till examined him, his crumpled suit and bloodshot eyes, and picked out something suitably cheap. It didn't really matter. Carl had long since passed the point of being able to taste it.

He'd stayed sober long enough to visit Elias Hosgood in his little flat in Preston and witness the man's valiant efforts to keep the tears at bay. Elias Hosgood had made him sit down and meet Marcus's dog, an overactive springer spaniel named Lolly he'd agreed to look after for a few weeks while Marcus got used to his new job and put daycare arrangements in place.

"Don't know what's going to happen to the thing now," Elias told him. "I can't keep hold of her forever. Don't have the energy. And this place – she needs somewhere with a garden."

There'd been a moment when Carl had been so close to saying he'd take the dog that the words were almost in his throat. But he couldn't look after a dog. He could hardly look after himself. So he'd stayed silent and nodded, and then he'd listened quietly to the family history and learned the reason Marcus had joined the police, the reason he'd picked PSD in particular.

"It were different back then," Elias told him. He couldn't have been much more than sixty, but he moved with the slow cautiousness of a man a generation older. "When I figured out there were bent men on my team and tried to bring it up, it were me that got kicked out."

"You were fired?"

Elias shrugged, his brown eyes distant. "Not as such. Just told there wasn't a place for me if I didn't have my fellow officers' backs. I told Marcus not to join the force, but he wouldn't have it. Said he wanted to be part of the reason things like that couldn't happen any more. And look at him now."

That was the point at which Elias Hosgood's battle to keep from crying had been lost. Carl sat with him for an hour before succumbing to the man's entreaties to join him in a drink. Just one.

And then another.

Carl had left his car in Preston and made it back through a combination of train and taxi that seemed like some kind of miracle. He wasn't entirely sure where his car was, but he'd remember tomorrow, if he was sober enough to pick it up then.

He sat now in the small front living room, stared at the

detritus of the last two days, and thought of the old man he'd just visited. Marcus's mother had died two years earlier, but they'd been estranged for years before that, and Marcus hadn't seen much of his dad in nearly twenty years.

"We used to meet up at the service stations," Elias had told him. "Four times a year. Big Mac or a Double Whopper." He smiled. "Highlight of every season."

For a moment, the sadness of it all had him so choked up he could barely breathe. He put out one hand for the cat, but Yoda wasn't there any more, had gone with Zoe to Dorset, where she was no doubt terrorising anyone brave enough to risk purchasing fish and chips. The seagulls down there would prove stiffer competition than their cousins up here, though.

He picked up his phone and scrolled until he found her number, stabbed at the green button, then stabbed at the red one before it could start ringing.

No.

He couldn't keep doing this. Couldn't keep drinking or just wallowing in misery and then phoning Zoe and talking at her, or into her voicemail, until he fell asleep.

It had to end.

Instead, he staggered out of the front room to the kitchen, past the post piling up unopened on the little table by the front door. He stopped, turned, and retrieved it.

He wouldn't open any of it tonight. But bringing it into the kitchen was a start.

His eyes caught on a handwritten envelope. An unfamiliar hand. He opened it carefully, to find a circular from a local politician – the 'handwriting' had been printed, after all. But as he dropped it in disgust and opened the fridge to scavenge something to eat, his mind found itself stuck on the image of another piece of paper, also handwritten.

Where had he seen it?

He shook his head and focussed on making himself a cheese sandwich, and then he sat down and ate it. It wasn't until he'd finished it, decided he was still hungry, talked himself out of heading out for a kebab, and started making a second sandwich, that he remembered.

Two days ago, on DCI Branthwaite's desk. He'd looked away, and when he'd looked back again, something had been missing. At the time he hadn't known what, but now, oddly, he did. It was a sheet of paper, covered in writing in light blue ink, in a delicate, slanted hand, the text formatted into paragraphs and spaced out at the top like a letter.

Branthwaite had been reading a letter, and he'd hidden it from Carl.

Problem solved.

Douglas Branthwaite had his own life, and he was entitled to it. If he wanted to read his letters in private, that was fine.

He'd nearly finished the second sandwich when the knock came, and it startled him so much he knocked the glass of water he'd poured himself twenty minutes earlier and still not drunk onto the floor.

He swore, and began to clear it up, and the knock came again.

He ignored it.

He heard a clattering, the letterbox being pushed open, and then a voice.

"Carl, you need to let me in."

Jake Frimpton. What was Jake Frimpton doing here?

"Carl!" shouted Jake. "I know you're there."

Carl stayed where he was, on the kitchen floor with a towel in one hand and an empty glass in the other. He felt cold spreading through his leg and realised he'd knelt in the water.

"I'm worried about you, Carl," shouted Jake.

You and me both, thought Carl, but he didn't move. He stayed there for five more minutes while Jake alternated between shouting through the letterbox and phoning him, and he ignored the shouts and the phone calls, and eventually the journalist gave up.

Another lonely man in Whitehaven. He meant well, did Jake, but he wouldn't understand. Nobody would understand.

Carl stood finally, and reminded himself that wasn't entirely true.

There were people who'd understand. Not many.

But even one was enough.

CHAPTER ONE HUNDRED THREE

THERE WAS a woman in the middle of the room mangling *Heart of Glass* in a voice that was even worse than the Debbie Harry wig she was wearing, but after four vodka-and-oranges, Harriett found she could cope with it. That was the thing you learned when you spent enough time at the Miners' Yard. Everything could be wonderful if you were drunk enough.

Not four vodka-and-oranges, she thought. Five. Maybe more. The only times Tom had left her side had been to head to the bar and back again. She'd told him to stop being silly, that he was as much a part of the team as she was, and she didn't need him worrying about her when he could be worrying about himself, but it didn't seem to work.

And she didn't mean it, either.

Tom had been there. Tom had worked alongside Marcus Hosgood for the few days Marcus had been part of the team.

But Tom hadn't been the one who'd sparred with Marcus. Tom hadn't been the one who'd insulted him and put him down, who'd spurred him on to take the sort of risks that...

"Here you go," he said, placing another drink down in front of her. This one was purple rather than orange. She frowned at it.

"What is this?" she asked.

"Don't ask, don't tell," he replied, as if that meant anything.

She picked it up and knocked it back, and it was disgusting, but it was only disgusting for a second or two before it was gone, and she was feeling that warm glow spreading through her.

"My round," she said, and stood and headed for the bar before Tom could object.

While she was waiting to be served, the sound system started up again, a few notes picked out on a guitar followed by a chord Harriett thought she recognised, and she looked round to see Nina Kapoor standing there in her full Elvis regalia.

Nina spotted her, winked, and launched into *Are You Lonesome Tonight?* Harriett found herself swaying in time, losing herself in the music, so that the barman had to ask her three times what she was having.

"Vodka and orange," she said. "Two of them. And a lager."

"Which lager?" asked the barman.

She'd forgotten. "Don't care," she said. "And the vodka-and-oranges? Make it three."

She drank one at the bar and staggered back with the others clasped carefully around Tom's beer. By the time she got there, Nina had finished and joined them at the table with her boyfriend, the fireman who called himself Skip, but who had to have a different name, a real one.

"You got me a drink?" she said. "Cheers." She reached out and grabbed one of the vodka-and-oranges, and had taken her first sip before Harriett could object.

It was probably for the best. The room was starting to sway a little, and there was a man with white hair and a walking stick belting out an Iron Maiden track Harriett hadn't heard in years. There was a minor commotion by the door that she must have imagined, because the man who'd just staggered in, straight into a group of people, looked a lot like...

"Shit," she said, pushing herself up and nearly knocking over the drink-laden table.

She made her way towards the door, where the man in question was blinking in confusion, shrugging and apologising with the air of someone who wasn't sure what he was apologising for but thought it was probably best.

"I'll take it from here," she said, injecting more authority into her voice than she felt.

The man started at her voice, his eyes drifting slowly from the group towards her, his body working a few seconds behind his brain.

"Ah," he said. "Good. I was hoping to find you here."

"Let's get you sat down," she said.

"Let's get me a drink," he replied.

"Are you sure that's wise, boss?" she asked.

"Of course it's not wise," said DI Whaley. "But I'll need something if I'm going to get up there and do *Stand and Deliver*."

"If you're going to do what?" Harriett asked, not sure

whether the boss had really just said what she thought he'd said, or whether she'd imagined it.

"You heard me," he told her. "And besides, after a day like the one we've just had, wisdom can be overrated."

CHAPTER ONE HUNDRED FOUR

"Thanks for sending through the data," Denise said.

"Do you know what time it is?" replied Nikolas Costas. "And how did you get my home number, anyway?"

Denise ignored the man's questions.

"I thought you should know that they led us to the phones we were after. Looks like they were switched on and off again by the woman whose flat they were being hidden in."

"Right," said Costas.

"She didn't know whose they were. Certainly didn't know they'd belonged to a murder victim. But we got there in the end, didn't we?"

"We did," Costas agreed.

"Of course, by the time we got there, one of my colleagues had been stabbed in the neck and bled to death, but you can't win them all," she said, and ended the call.

She sat down on her sofa and tried to work out if making Nikolas Costas feel bad had made her feel any better. It had, she thought. Even if it only lasted a few minutes, it had been worth it.

She stood, went to the kitchen, looked in the fridge, and realised she couldn't be bothered to eat. She couldn't be bothered to drink, either, which was probably a good thing. Nothing mattered enough to justify the effort it would take to do it. Even the pain in her back and neck and shoulders seemed insignificant somehow, numbed by everything that had happened that day.

She'd only been home twenty minutes. She'd stayed late at Durranhill, talking to the DCI, sorting out the aftermath of events.

Events. That was one way of looking at it.

The DI had visited Marcus Hosgood's father. She'd tried to reach him after, but he hadn't answered his phone. She hoped he was getting drunk somewhere. She closed her eyes and tried to shut out the day, but her mind kept returning to Grange and that grin he'd given them.

"People who know things," he'd said.

"Like a skeleton key," he'd said.

That couldn't be a coincidence, could it? There was someone within Cumbria Police who had access to information and decision-making, someone who could steer the direction of an investigation in a way that suited the criminal more than it suited the police. Someone who'd been helping Myron Carter before he was put away. Someone who might still be helping the people who'd stepped into Carter's shoes.

Someone to whom they'd assigned the codename *Skeleton Key*.

There were so many options. There were people within the sprawling empire presided over by Assistant Chief

Constable 'Little Joe' Carghillie, people like his policy advisor, Becca Grey. There were questions over the Custody Suite at the Cumbria Police Hub, where Aaron worked. There were questions over the leaking of information about Aaron's mental state to Carter and his people.

Could this be the same person who'd manipulated records, removing any reference to Stephen Grange from the reports and complaints about Claire Saunders?

Denise only realised she'd been staring into the fridge for five minutes when it started beeping at her, warning her it had been open too long. As she pushed it shut, the doorbell rang.

The DI, she thought. Hopefully not so drunk he'd be sick on her floor, but maybe drunk enough that they could talk things through. The DI, or Eileen from next door, who'd no doubt spotted her late arrival and popped over just to make sure things were OK.

Denise opened the door, and there, her black hair shining in the orange light from the streetlamp across the road, stood Sinead Conway.

Denise took a step back.

"I wish you'd answer my calls," said Sinead.

Denise opened her mouth to say something in response, but the words wouldn't come. Sinead took a step towards her, and she felt herself tense, but she didn't know if her body was preparing her to fight or to flee.

"We used to be friends, Denise," said Sinead. She smiled then, that smile Denise had once thought so beautiful. "We used to be more than friends. I wish you'd speak to me."

"I don't want you here," Denise managed to say, but Sinead had taken another step, and was now just inches from being inside her house. She could feel her heart pounding and hear her own breath, loud in her ears, the blood and the air and everything that made her human and alive.

"But I come bearing gifts," Sinead said, and only then did Denise see what the other woman was holding in her right hand, holding up so it reflected the light.

A bottle of cheap Irish whiskey.

It was the same whiskey she'd helped herself to more than a week ago, the last time she'd mixed painkillers and alcohol, the last time she'd sat in her house tormenting herself over the identity of Skeleton Key.

The same whiskey Sinead Conway had introduced her to, all those years ago, the whiskey that had been their cheap, dirty drink of choice through cheap, dirty nights that felt like part of someone else's life.

"Come on, Denise," said Sinead. "For old time's sake."

Once again, Denise found herself unable to speak.

"I think we could really help each other out," Sinead said. "And I think you should listen to me."

"I'm not interested in anything you have to say," Denise told her, and Sinead shrugged.

"That's a shame," she said. "Because you and your colleagues, you're making life difficult for me and my friends."

That was as close to a confession of criminal activity as Denise had ever heard from her. She willed her heart to slow down, her breathing to quieten, so she could focus on what the other woman was saying.

"And I wouldn't want you to get caught in the crossfire," said Sinead.

Denise waited, but Sinead was now staring at her, a hopeful, expectant look in her eyes.

"I can look after myself," Denise said after a moment.

"Maybe you can," replied Sinead. "But you can't say the same for your friends, can you?"

Denise felt that like a physical blow.

"I'm sorry about your colleague," Sinead went on. "But it's a dangerous job, Denise. You need to be careful where you put your size nines. All of you."

"No," said Denise. "That's not—"

"And by the way," Sinead continued, ignoring Denise's attempt to interrupt her, "I'm not sure you *can* look after yourself."

Denise realised Sinead was looking past her, into the house, and down, and she turned to see the blister pack lying on the floor where she'd let it fall that morning.

"That's nothing to do with you," said Denise, but even that wasn't true, because wasn't Sinead a friend of Myron Carter, the man whose bomb had left her with the injuries and the pain?

Not just a friend. *A colleague.*

"Maybe not," agreed Sinead. "But it looks to me like you need all the help you can get just to stay on your feet. Imagine what would happen if your supply dried up."

She bent down and carefully placed the bottle on Denise's doorstep, and then she turned and walked away, Denise watching her progress to the green E-Type Jaguar she'd parked a little way down the street. She picked up the bottle, and closed the door, and stood there for a moment, wondering if there was something else she should have said or done, anything that might have made a difference, now, or earlier in the day, or on some previous day.

Any way that things might have turned out some other way from the way they had.

She took four steps away from the door, and then she turned to face it, and with a howl of despair and every ounce of strength she possessed, she hurled the full bottle of whiskey at the door and watched it shatter into a thousand pieces.

CHAPTER ONE HUNDRED FIVE

It was hardly surprising, after a day like the one she'd just been through, that Lynn couldn't sleep.

It was hardly surprising that she decided to call Gerry. He'd be in Berlin by now, after his most recent stop in Vienna. Just three more days in Germany, then Zurich, then home. The date was marked in the calendar in the kitchen.

"Hello?"

Gerry's voice was groggy. It was only ten, but he sounded like he'd been sleeping, or drinking, and it took him a moment to find the camera button, and then he hit it, and Lynn saw that he hadn't been sleeping at all.

He was in bed. She could see the lower half of his face, and the upper half of his chest. She could also see a foot-long length of blonde hair that definitely wasn't Gerry's, falling across that chest.

"Fuck," said Gerry, and immediately hit the button to switch the camera off, but it was too late.

Lynn stared at the black screen of her phone in silent shock.

"Fuck," said Gerry. "Lynn?"

Lynn tapped the red button to end the call, went downstairs, ignored the Baileys, and poured herself a large scotch. She drank it neat, fast, savouring the way it burned her throat as it went down, and wondered why she hadn't done this in the first place.

Why hadn't she just gone home and got drunk? That's what anyone else would have done. She'd have gone home and got drunk and never known that her husband was in bed with Maria Tattersall, whose blonde hair she'd just seen splayed across his chest.

Maria Tattersall, his boss. Maria Tattersall, the person he'd spent more time with than anyone else over the last year.

Was that how long this had been going on?

Lynn poured herself another scotch, and it wasn't until she'd finished it and poured herself a third that she realised she was still holding her phone, and it was buzzing.

Four missed calls from Gerry. And one, from hours ago, from a number she didn't recognise, unnoticed until now.

She tapped to call it back without considering the time, and it rang for nearly a minute before a man answered with a confused, "Hello?"

"Who is this?" she asked.

"Paul Gardner. Who's this?"

She frowned at her phone and took another sip from her glass.

Paul Gardner. The name sounded familiar.

"Seriously, who is this?" he said again, and Lynn realised she hadn't answered him the first time.

"Sorry. It's Lynn Hedley. DC Hedley."

"Oh, right. Harriett's friend. Yeah, I tried to get hold of you earlier."

Harriett's friend?

Lynn was still trying to figure out who Paul Gardner was while he went on.

"So, we were looking into that ticket, right?" he said.

"Ticket?"

"You know. Stephen Grange. Or Dave Wilson, as he called himself. Harriett asked us to figure out who'd bought it."

Paul Gardner. The Financial Crime Unit. Of course.

"Yes, that's right," Lynn said.

"I thought you'd want to know," Paul continued. "I couldn't get hold of Harriett, either."

Lynn found herself gripping the phone a little tighter.

"You know who bought the ticket?" she asked.

"Yeah," he said. "Well, not the actual person. But the overall buyer, yeah. It's a big corporate account."

"Go on," she said, although she was sure she knew what was coming.

"Conway Holdings."

Lynn was nodding, as if this explained everything. Paul Gardner was still talking.

"Like I say, we don't know specifically who bought the ticket. Could be any number of people. I'm putting together a report. Should be with you tomorrow."

"Thanks," she told him. "You're a star."

She could hear herself, hear the words slurring. *Shtar*. She thanked him again, and ended the call before she said something she shouldn't, and then, while she was in the frame of mind to do the sort of thing she shouldn't, she brought up another number.

Mike McKenzie didn't answer the phone, but not

answering the phone wasn't going to deter Lynn with the mood she was in.

"It's Lynn Hedley," she heard herself say, only the 'it's' was more like an *itshhh*, and even the 'Hedley' sounded wrong. "Listen, right, that drink idea you had. Me and you, and a drink."

She paused, and waited two, maybe three seconds before she remembered he wasn't actually there and she was just leaving a message.

"Anyway," she said. "I think it's a good idea. We should do it. Call me."

She was smiling when she ended the call.

Fuck Gerry. Maria Tattersall could have him. He was getting fat, anyway. Fat and boring. Lynn would move onto a younger, fitter model.

She looked at the bottle, an expensive scotch Gerry had bought years ago and neither of them had drunk, because neither of them really liked whisky, shook her head, and poured herself a Baileys instead.

She opened her emails as she sipped it, more out of habit than expectation, and was surprised to see a new message, sent just five minutes earlier.

The name in the 'From' column was DCI Douglas Branthwaite.

DCI Branthwaite was PSD, which meant there weren't so many rumours about him, the way there would have been if he'd been with any other department. People might have their opinions, but no one wanted to admit they'd come into contact with the man.

But there was one thing she'd heard.

Branthwaite was a blunt man, people said. He didn't do subtlety. If he thought something, he said it, and her limited interactions with him over the past few days hadn't done anything to suggest otherwise.

Neither did the email.

She read it six times, and had to force herself not to reply immediately. Instead, she poured herself another Baileys and took it to the living room, turned on the TV, and watched old episodes of *Friends* until she felt her eyelids drooping. She didn't bother moving after that, instead simply drifting off to sleep where she sat, and waking four hours later with a headache and a stiff neck.

The first thing she did was check her phone.

She hadn't imagined the email. She read it again, twice more, and decided she still wasn't in a fit state to reply, but that was fine. It was only five in the morning. DCI Branthwaite could wait.

She lay down on the sofa, wriggling into a more comfortable position, and opened the email again, and this time she fell asleep in the ten seconds it took to read it.

The subject of the email was *Job Offer*, and the text was brief and to the point.

DI Whaley and the team tell me you're a good cop, it read.

And if you are a good cop, you're wasting your time with Jasmine Woolley.

Come and work for PSD.

Thank you for reading *The Boatyard*. The story continues in *The Viewpoint*, which you can buy in ebook or paperback from book retailers or Amazon.

Happy reading!

Joel

THE VIEWPOINT

'A gripping continuation of the story begun by DI Zoe Finch.'
Rachel McLean

Months after the traumatic events of *The Boatyard*, the PSD team is beginning to settle down – on the surface, at least.

DI Carl Whaley's moved into a new flat, with paper-thin walls and miserable neighbours. DS Denise Gaskill seems comparatively untroubled, but that's only because no one knows about her painkiller addiction. DC Harriett Barnes has become obsessed with unlocking the identity of the so-called Skeleton Key. And the newest member of the team, DC Lynn Hedley, has ended her marriage and started a new job in the space of a few short weeks.

The last thing they need is a complicated new case. And the murder of a known criminal found shot to death in a beauty spot by the Kirkstone Pass looks like the sort of gangland killing that wouldn't normally involve PSD.

But when one of the investigating officers is attacked and crucial evidence goes missing, Carl and the team are dragged into the heart of the mystery.

Why was the dead man targeted? What secrets was he planning to spill? And is there a connection with a recent spate of vigilante attacks?

As the investigation takes the team in unexpected directions, sorting truth from lies becomes a matter of life and death. And with the shadow of recent events haunting their every move, can they unmask the killer before more people die?

The Viewpoint is the second book in the exciting new Whaley & Gaskill series, featuring Carl Whaley, Denise Gaskill and a host of colleagues from the bestselling 'Cumbria Crime' books.

READ THE CUMBRIA CRIME SERIES

The Harbour

The Mine

The Cairn

The Barn

The Lake

The Wood

The Port

The Marsh

Buy from book retailers.

ALSO BY JOEL HAMES

The Sam Williams Series – buy now in ebook, paperback and audiobook.

Dead North

No One Will Hear

The Cold Years

The Art of Staying Dead

Victims, a Sam Williams novella

Caged, a Sam Williams short

Printed and bound by CPI Group (UK) Ltd, Croydon, CR0 4YY

14/03/2026

02071362-0001